THE MAIDEN HEADS

Benny B. Peterson is a writer and editor based near Washington, DC. A contributing editor at *Washingtonian* magazine, they have also worked at *Foreign Policy*, *The New Republic*, and Street Sense, DC's street newspaper. They have written about culture, politics, gender, and LGBTQ+ issues for the *New York Times*, *Washington Post*, *Elle*, *Slate*, and *Atlantic*, among other places, and received an MFA in fiction from Bennington College.

THE MAIDEN HEADS

BENNY B. PETERSON

TEXT PUBLISHING MELBOURNE AUSTRALIA

The Text Publishing Company acknowledges the Traditional Owners of the country on which we work, the Wurundjeri people of the Kulin Nation, and pays respect to their Elders past and present.

textpublishing.com.au

The Text Publishing Company
Wurundjeri Country, Level 6, Royal Bank Chambers, 287 Collins Street,
Melbourne Victoria 3000 Australia

Published in Australia, New Zealand and the UK by The Text Publishing Company, 2026
Published in the US by Dutton, an imprint of Penguin Random House LLC, 2026

Cover design by Sophie Chu-O'Neil
Page design by Alison Cnockaert

Printed and bound in Australia by Griffin Press, a member of the Opus Group. The Opus Group is ISO/NZS 14001:2004 Environmental Management System certified.

ISBN: 9781923058866 (paperback)
ISBN: 9781923059733 (ebook)

A catalogue record for this book is available from the National Library of Australia.

EU Authorised Representative: Easy Access System Europe—Mustamäe tee 50, 10621 Tallinn, Estonia, gpsr.requests@easproject.com

FSC www.fsc.org MIX Paper | Supporting responsible forestry FSC® C018684

The paper this book is printed on is certified against the Forest Stewardship Council® Standards. Griffin Press holds chain of custody certification SCS-COC-001185. FSC® promotes environmentally responsible, socially beneficial and economically viable management of the world's forests.

To my family writ small, and my family writ large—trans and queer kids, and the people who support them.

THE MAIDENHEADS

PROLOGUE

WHEN I THINK of Mari, and I am always thinking of Mari, we're onstage. We're surrounded by darkness, we can barely see the upturned faces of the crowd. But we're in the light, and I can see her distinctly as she takes her spot behind the keyboard: black hair shaggy over huge black eyes, wide mouth curling upward, one haunch balanced on her stool. Our bodies are separated by several feet of space, at least you'd think so looking at us. But I know, she knows, we're one. She bends to pick up her drink and I feel it slide down my throat. I push back my hair and it's her fingers stroking my scalp. There's a bite mark above her T-shirt collar, my teeth preserved in her skin. I can feel the pressure of her touch aching in my breasts, my cunt. All of me has been shaped by her shape; we are cast and mold, mold and cast.

The strangers who paid to hear us perform have shushed. I breathe in slowly. Mari's fingers brush the keys as if they're brushing my lips. Then her eyes flick to mine, a silent command, and I release my voice.

PART ONE

1

A WEEK AFTER we broke up, Peter called to ask when he could drop off my record player, which I'd left at his house when I moved out. The record player was a vintage Sansui I'd owned for ten years, since my senior year of high school. I loved it, but it hadn't fit into the cab I'd squeezed everything else into. Besides, I was sure Peter would eventually bring it over. He'd want it gone—he was very angry at me—and it wasn't something you could mail, so he'd be forced to drive with it. "How about Friday after work?" I asked, and it took Peter a long disgruntled moment to admit that yes, that was a fine time for him as well.

Friday afternoon, I left work early. It was April, and walking home from the bus stop, I smelled spring and pictured myself cleaning up, sticking a flower in a vase, demonstrating to Peter some basic functionality. But once inside my new apartment, a hastily rented one-bedroom in an anonymous area of Baltimore's midtown, I remembered there was nothing to clean. I'd been living for the past two years in Peter's house in Charles Village, surrounded by all his inoffensively luxurious objects. I owned barely any furniture, and nothing decorative except a painting by my mom that had moved with me from closet to closet since college, and that went directly into the closet here. I'd bought a mattress but no frame, so it was on the floor. Everything else was still in cardboard boxes stacked in my bedroom, because I had nothing to unpack them into: no coat hangers or bureau for my clothes, no shelves for my books and records. For Peter, I pushed the boxes flush with the walls and swept the wood floors with the janitor's broom from the basement. I'd carried the stereo speakers on my lap in the cab, and I set those up now in adjacent corners of the bedroom. I showered, brushed my teeth, put on clean underwear.

To be clear, I didn't go into the evening intending to seduce Peter. I only thought that if we did have sex, it might help fix the feeling I'd had constantly since the breakup, that I was looking down at my body from a great distance and I was a grotesque Franken-freak cobbled from scraps. It was an old and bone-familiar sensation, but over the two and a half years with Peter, I'd effectively kept it at bay.

Peter called from downstairs just after six—he was always punctual, even when he didn't want to be. In a few minutes, I heard him shuffling down the hall in his stiff work shoes. Then he loomed in my entryway, dripping rain onto the bare wooden floor. Peter is very tall and always has an expression of mouth-half-open expectance, like someone's just yelled, *Go long!* His skin is the smoothest I've ever seen, like a child's, white and freckled. His dark red hair curls sideways across his forehead like Superman's.

The Sansui was balanced on his forearms, wrapped in a mostly dry quilt I recognized from our old bedroom. "Where should I put it?" he asked, eyes turned from mine.

"Bedroom," I said. Peter glanced from right to left, through the doors of two identically bare rooms. "To the left—yeah, in there, sorry about the . . ."

Peter carried the Sansui into the bedroom, unwrapped it, and placed it in the spot I'd cleared, lining its edges up with the wall. Then he backed rapidly out of the room and paused in the entryway again, clutching the quilt to his chest.

"Could I get you a drink?" I said. "Just a thank-you for bringing over the Sansui."

"I have to go soon," he said. "I have a thing later." I knew this couldn't be true; Peter very rarely had "things." He was leaning against the wall, long legs crossed.

"Oh, me too, me too," I assured him, "but just a quick—" and I leapt into the kitchen. "I ordered bookcases, they're coming soon," I called, clanking bottles. I'd absconded with our liquor cabinet, now in a cardboard box on my counter. "And plants. Thought I would get, like, a *lot* of plants."

"It'll look nice," he said. "You'll get good light. North-facing, right?"

I carried out two mugs of the fancy bourbon Peter's mother had bought us for Christmas the year before and gestured him into the living room, empty apart from three boxes. I'd asked the landlord to spackle the fist-shaped hole in the drywall, but he hadn't yet. Peter found another wall to lean against, placing the quilt, folded, at his feet.

"Cheers," I said. I leaned next to him, not so close that he'd step back.

"Cheers," Peter said. He sipped, made a face, sipped again.

We both looked out the window, down to the rain-sheened strip of road four stories below and the flashing red LOTTERY TICK sign in the store window opposite. I said, "You know, I care about you a lot."

"You've said that."

"I'd like to be friends."

"It's not up to you, is it?" he said. "Traditionally, it's the dumpee who makes that decision."

"Dumpee," I said. "That's funny."

Peter swished his mug like he was testing the legs on a glass of wine. "I care about you too, Jamie. That doesn't mean I want to be your friend."

"Of course. Sorry," I said. "I'm used to lesbian breakups, you know? You go camping right after, split custody of the cats."

"Noted," he said. He stood up off the wall in preparation to go.

But I wasn't ready to be left alone with the bare walls, the bottles of alcohol, my jumbled-up body: I knew where nights like this went, and it wasn't pretty. "You have a right to be mad at me," I said quickly.

"I'm not mad at you."

"Right—I mean, you've never even yelled at me. Peter, hey, what if you yelled at me?"

"Stop acting like a child," he said. His mug was empty, his voice warmer.

"I'm serious. Yell at me. Like, primal scream therapy."

"What would I yell? You don't love me. I can't be angry about that."

"Know what, you stay right there," I said. I grabbed his mug and went into the kitchen for more bourbon. Returning, I held it up to Peter hopefully. He wrinkled his thick eyebrows—mistrusting, cornered—and took it.

"Yell at me," I said, with new confidence. I could already feel my body twining itself back together, smoothed into shape by the pink along his cheekbones, the way he didn't inch back when I leaned closer. "Tell me I'm a bitch. What do you say to your friends about me?"

"I say, Jamie's on her own journey and needs to sort a few things out."

"Oh yeah, right."

"OK. I say, she's pretty immature and has a messed-up family situation, and I definitely dodged a bullet on the marriage question."

"You're *mad* at me," I said. "Just—let it out."

"I couldn't call you a bitch," he said, hesitant before the word. "I just can't do that."

"Fine. Call me whatever you want to call me."

He laughed and rumpled his hair. For a second, he was my old Peter, not this stiff stranger. "Fine," he said. "OK. You're a selfish cunt."

I laughed with pleased relief. "Fair."

"Well, to be honest, you really are a bitch as well."

"Do you want to hit me?" I said, keeping my voice steady.

"What the fuck, Jamie!"

"You know, if I tell you to hit me, it's not like 'hitting a woman' or whatever. You're not breaking the gentleman's code."

His eyes lifted from his drink to my lips. "I could hit you," he said. "If you wanted me to."

"I want you to."

"OK," he said. He had finished his second bourbon, and now he leaned down to place the mug on the ground between us. Then he squared his body to mine, craning forward as if to erase the height difference, and tapped me on the shoulder with three fingers.

"You can do it harder."

I could hear the catch in his breath. "I thought you weren't into this sort of thing because of Mari," he said.

"This has nothing to do with that," I said, batting away private images. "This is you and me."

"You and me," he said. "What does that even mean right now?"

But he was breathing heavily, and I could see his erection lifting the khaki cloth of his pants. I shifted to press it with my hip, and his body shuddered into mine. He followed me into the bedroom, where he sat on the mattress, bent knees shooting straight up, and untied his shoelaces.

I crouched by the Sansui and plugged it into the speakers—I'd missed that unshowy gray box with its red control lights, kind eyes in the dark. I dug out *XO* from a carton (I knew Peter had played Elliott Smith on lonely aimless drives in high school) and placed the record on the dustless black circle, set down the needle so it crackled into life. Then I took off all my clothes except for the green lace bra and underwear set I'd put on after work. Peter had bought it for me, and just wearing it made me feel less mismatched, like my body was a worker with a purpose and a uniform. I watched Peter recognize the bra, recognize the first few notes of "Sweet Adeline," recognize it was all for him. I closed my eyes against the weariness in his.

He fucked me carefully, keeping our bodies otherwise distant. Only once he leaned close and I smelled his deodorant and had to smush my face into the pillow. I knew I couldn't cry or none of this would work; I would spill into chaos again. So I took deep breaths, I matched his rhythm. Peter pushed me into a few different positions, and I tuned into his sadness, felt him thinking, *This is the last time I'll ever fuck her from behind.* Elliott Smith had been a terrible choice.

"I could hit you again," Peter whispered from behind my shoulder. "If that's what you want, I could do it."

"Do it," I said.

Peter slapped me tentatively at first, on my ass, legs, back, then a stinging slap on my left tit, clearing my sinuses like spicy food. I thought of Mari; of course I did: Mari ripping her nails along my thigh, Mari biting me until I bled. Mari biting her own knuckles to distract from the actual pain. Mari's face crumpling; Mari gray and horrified at me.

"Ow," I said with a gasping laugh.

"Oh, shit," Peter said. "Should I stop?"

"No, you're good, keep going." Another light slap, then several that burned. "Ow, actually ow, Peter," I said, accidentally loud into a silence between songs. My knees buckled, we both slipped so I was flat on my stomach, and he blanketed me. I wrapped my arms over my head like a hood, wanting to black out all thoughts of Peter, Mari, everything.

"Shit," he said, "I'm sorry, hold on, shit," and came inside me. Then he flopped out next to me and tried to peel my arms off my head. "Are you OK?"

I could hear the grudging tone—he didn't want to worry about my feelings—and I forced a smile and let my hands drop. "I'm good."

"You're really OK?" he said. "You don't want me to . . . ?" I shook my head. "If you say so," he said, and nuzzled into my neck. He was all loosened up now, his body boneless along mine. The warm pressure against my skin was enough so that I could breathe, so that, later on, I could sleep.

AFTER THAT, FOR the rest of April, Peter came over once or twice a week. Most times, we'd have a drink and fuck. He never stayed over; we never discussed anything beyond practicalities. I didn't risk putting on music after the *XO* debacle. We didn't use a condom. If I'd gone to the store for condoms, or if he'd brought them from home, it would've made the situation too real. I didn't take the bottles out of the cardboard box in the kitchen either, even after we drank through the nice Christmas bourbon and moved on to a dusty handle of rye. I didn't unpack my boxes, didn't buy plants or bookcases. Peter's quilt stayed folded on the floor in the living room.

I knew that fucking Peter was a bad idea, the act of a selfish cunt. He'd cried like a child when I broke up with him, head down on the table, hands twisted in his hair. He'd begged me to stay, told me he'd do anything I wanted, couples therapy, whatever. He was a kind person who deserved to be with another kind person, not someone who dumped him abruptly after two and a half years, then fucked him out of loneliness.

The first week in May, I woke up with a sickening ache along my spine and at the base of my stomach. I put on black underpants and stopped for tampons on the way to work. But my period didn't come. I wore black underpants the next day and the next day too. The ache didn't subside; my period didn't come.

As the week passed, I noticed a new exhaustion. I worked as an editor at the *Baltimore Bugle*, an alt-weekly newspaper with a downtown office building that had been built in a pre-elevator world. I'd gotten used to the four flights of stairs, but now I had to stop at each landing. Probably depression, I figured, or lack of exercise, or maybe I wasn't getting enough iron now that I wasn't cooking meat with Peter. On Thursday morning, I ran into my boss, Jeremy, in the lobby and we began the climb together. Halfway up, I had to pause. My legs were wobbly, hips sore. I bent and pretended to tie my bootlace.

"These boots take forever," I told Jeremy, nodding so he'd go ahead without me.

Jeremy, like most of my coworkers at the *Bugle*, was a white man in his thirties who wore New Balance sneakers and band T-shirts to work every day. It was 2012, and yet Jeremy had a stuck-in-the-'00s look with his thick black eyeglasses and permanent half inch of stubble, forever the Johns Hopkins lit mag editor making Wilco-heavy mixtapes for his crushes. He had hired me because his knowledge of obscure Maryland and DC cultural trivia included the Maidenheads, my old band with Mari, as well as *Jennifer's Not There*, the 2002 indie film we'd performed in right before our final implosion. "Jamie mother-*fucking* Cain," he'd said with some astonishment at my first interview. I'd known that a) I'd get the offer, and b) I'd probably regret taking it.

"I'll wait," Jeremy said on the stairs. He was telling me about a show he'd gone to that weekend, the scene was so lame now, Howard County punks, blah blah. "I never see you at shows," he went on. "Don't you ever go?"

I was drawing breath hard to propel myself up the last flights. "Guess I've aged out. You really don't have to wait."

"I'll stay, I'll stay," he said, smiling as if pleased that he'd seen through my polite refusal to the underlying desire for company.

When I finally closed my office door upstairs, I googled my symptoms: fatigue, nausea, back pain. The first conditions I saw were migraines, Addison's disease, meningitis—and pregnancy.

The *Bugle* occupied the whole fifth floor of our building, two long hallways lined with small offices and a conference room at the back. When I started as a copyeditor in 2007, I'd sat in a cubicle close enough to the bathrooms that I could smell my coworkers' poop. The offices were all occupied then: we had a real estate reporter, a crime reporter, two investigative reporters who'd been at the paper since the 1970s, two columnists, an entire food team, two culture critics, a culture reporter, and five editors. After the 2008 crash, we had a round of buyouts, then a round of layoffs. In 2010, a conglomerate out of Minneapolis (Western Media Properties, or as we called them, "womp womp") bought us and enforced even more buyouts. Two years later, it was just Jeremy, one of the columnists, a music critic, two reporters, the art director, and several shell-shocked interns. Plus me: with everyone else gone, I did two jobs for the price of one, copyediting the whole paper and overseeing the events calendar.

As a bonus, I had my own office, which had once belonged to an investigative reporter and still had his napping couch and his empty Jim Beam bottles in the file cabinet. That morning, I lay down on the couch and fell dead asleep for fifteen minutes. Waking with a jolt, I went next door to Jeremy's office and told him I was sick and had to leave early.

I bought a pregnancy test near my apartment. Once upstairs, I went straight to the bathroom and peed on the stick. Sitting on the toilet, holding the stick in my pee-wet hand, I watched the cross form, feeling a kind of surreal fatalism. Of course Peter and I were extraordinarily fertile together; of course I couldn't take a chance without consequence. I washed my hands very slowly, avoiding my eyes in the mirror. I took off my boots, lay flat on the bedroom mattress, and considered my situation.

I was twenty-eight, single, employed at a dying publication in a dying industry. I'd only ever loved one thing, making music with Mari, a mostly nonlucrative pursuit that, in any case, I'd torched for good ten years ago. I was careless with money, I had credit card debt, I was a selfish cunt. I drank too much. Babies scared me. Even after a half decade in Baltimore, I had very little community here. I'd made a few friends when I first moved from DC, other queer people, but they drifted away after I started dating Peter. Now Peter, who wasn't even my boyfriend anymore, was the only person I talked to regularly besides my mom.

I found the number for the Baltimore Planned Parenthood and entered it into my phone. Then I paused. I was a shoddy person, I knew that. But maybe I was being offered a way to rise above shoddiness. I had seen this happen in films, where the selfish career lady gets accidentally pregnant and ends the movie with a cute baby in a sack, a bearded husband, and a renewed appreciation for the important things in life, plus a new job as a florist or something. There was a baked-in morality to motherhood that felt in that moment very appealing.

Being with Peter, my first long-term relationship with a man, had made me feel like my body was for once doing something socially useful. I hadn't hated it. And pregnancy, motherhood: those were the most socially useful, legible functions my body could execute. This was both a disturbing thought (patriarchy!) and one that yawned open into a trembling desire.

I didn't have to decide yet, I told myself. Digging into one of the boxes, I found my eternal comfort album, *Supa Dupa Fly*, put it on the

Sansui, and turned the volume down very low so Missy Elliott's voice was just a rumble. I got into bed and let the sound glide me into a long nap.

I CALLED IN sick the next morning, a Friday. I felt very low—the kind of low where you go into the kitchen, forget why, and stand for several minutes staring at the fridge, trying to sort it out. Surrendering to the aimlessness, I stayed in bed and used Peter's password to stream Poison Ivy episodes from the old animated Batman series. I listened to safe music, music I didn't associate with either Peter or Mari, mostly '90s pop and hip-hop. I unfolded Peter's quilt and wore it around the house like a cape. I probed myself for symptoms and found just an edge of nausea when I didn't eat (so I ate constantly, mostly pita chips), a new laxness in my limbs anytime I made some effort (so I made no efforts). I nearly tricked myself into believing that the test must've been wrong, that I would wake up one of these mornings with my period after all.

On Sunday, I decided it was time to get my shit together: change my underpants, catch up on the work I'd left undone since Thursday. I ate leftover pad thai for breakfast, then propped myself up on the mattress with my laptop, toga'd in Peter's quilt. It was raining outside, making the bedroom feel close and cozy even without anything in it, and Janet Jackson purred through the Sansui's speakers. I felt cocooned, like I didn't have to make any choices at all, forever. I wiped pita chip crumbs onto my bare thigh and opened the *Bugle*'s editing software.

The calendar section ran smoothly without much labor on my part. All the Baltimore-area event spaces, galleries, venues, and theaters sent us their listings by Friday morning. An intern entered those listings into a spreadsheet, which we uploaded into our editing software and sent to the production team for layout. I was responsible for pulling out upcoming events that I thought deserved more notice, then proofreading the rest of the section. If I thought an event needed a full review, I'd email it to Jeremy, who would assign one of our culture critics to cover it for the following issue. For several others, I wrote very short previews within my section. That afternoon, I had to write three—a series of Spanish-language poetry readings at Red Emma's, a punk show at Ottobar, and a gallery opening. It was soothing work, challenging but not overly so, like assembling a jigsaw puzzle.

Once I'd finished, I began proofing the rest of the listings. This was calming too. I'd learned to titrate my attention so I could pass my eyes down a column and note all the misspellings and errors without absorbing any unnecessary information, like what the words actually said. I scanned the first and second pages, found a typo in a gallery listing, corrected it with satisfaction, and rewarded myself with a second bag of pita chips.

On the third page, we always included some DC events: new exhibits at the major museums, big-name concerts, plus a few random other things for balance, depending on what the interns had thought worthy of note. That week, the intern had included a Saturday concert at the 9:30 Club. I checked the listing for typos without otherwise reading it; then my eyes scanned down the next few rows before shooting back up.

The main act at the 9:30 was Sealbone, an indie band from Portland whose new album had just gotten a 10/10 review on *Pitchfork*. Opening for Sealbone was a DC band called Les Somnambules: Mari's new band.

It wasn't rare to see Les Somnambules in our listings. As far as I could tell from my occasional Google stalking, they had started playing together about two years ago and quickly attracted a following. Their sound was completely different from the scrappy art-punk songs Mari had written for the Maidenheads, but still familiar to me somehow: melodic, mournful indie folk about fairy-tale characters and mythological beasts, with an electronic edge from Mari's keyboards. In the past year or so, they'd opened for Rilo Kiley and put out their first EP—they were clearly on the verge of breaking out of local-band status into something bigger.

I'd never gone to a Les Somnambules show, but I always marked them out for a preview and usually a review. It felt good to do a tiny anonymous favor, or maybe what felt good was exercising this minor control over Mari's success. Or maybe it was that, a decade after our breakup, three years since I'd last seen her (an awkward, brief encounter at a Cat Power show), this was the only opportunity I had to write something she might read. "Les Somnambules, a beloved DC band," I had written last time, "sound like Kate Bush and Björk's musical love child. Named for a character in a Djuna Barnes novel, the group melds mystical lyrics with a lush, occasionally riotous sound. Songwriter and keyboardist Mari Dvali is the DC indie folk scene's answer to Bruce Springsteen." A love note in a language only Mari would understand.

I highlighted the listing in orange, my color code for "review," and tried to move on, but I kept glancing back. Mari was playing the 9:30—my favorite DC venue, a huge deal for local bands—while I was pregnant, alone, editing a spreadsheet with chip crumbs in my underpants. Mari was playing the 9:30, and I could barely listen to my records, couldn't hum in the shower let alone consider trying to sing, because all music except '90s Top 40 sounded like Mari—in fact, *my own voice* sounded like Mari—and it all broke my heart.

I lay back in the pillows and tugged the quilt up around me, let the laptop slide off my legs. I did not want to see Mari: my ex-girlfriend, ex-bandmate, first love, forever love. I wanted to stay in bed, potentially forever. I wanted to have a miscarriage so I wouldn't have to decide about the pregnancy, so nothing would be my fault, so no one could say I was selfish. I wanted comfort, numbness. I wanted shelter from my fuckups, and my breakup with Mari was the greatest fuckup of my life.

I knew it might not be helpful, in this moment, to go watch Mari perform with her new band. And yet cutting through the doubt was a deep visceral yearning to be where Mari was, to watch her play. Maybe, I thought, maybe, it would be an *unshoddy* move to go see Mari's show—a necessary step to achieve closure and move forward. Of course I couldn't make any big decisions when just reading something about Mari in a newspaper made me feel as wind-whipped and flailing as a car dealership tube puppet! In fact, going to the show was probably the correct thing to do, the adult choice. With some relieved self-abandonment, I called the 9:30 Club and got my name on the press list for the Sealbone show. Then I called my mother. "I'm coming to DC this weekend," I said. "Kind of a work thing. Would it be OK if I stayed with you Saturday night?"

"Oh—*this* weekend? *This* Saturday?"

"Is that not OK?"

"It's a strange time," she said. She paused, long enough to—I guessed—walk into the bathroom at work and kick the door shut. "Carla died on Thursday."

Carla was the wife of my mother's boss and boyfriend, Michael Callahan. My parents divorced when I was fourteen, and my mother moved to an apartment in DC's Adams Morgan neighborhood, her initial liberated glee crashing out when she ran through her savings and realized she would have trouble getting a job as a lifelong stay-at-home mom in her forties. During the glee phase, however, she took a class at the Corcoran Gallery, where she learned to paint vaginal flowers, including the one now in my closet, a large Georgia O'Keeffe–ish rose, halfway budded with a clitoral dot at the center. One day, my mother took a vaginal flower to Michael's Frames and Oddities around the corner from her apartment, struck up a conversation with the silver fox owner, and got herself hired as an assistant. Michael was about ten years older than my mother, married to a woman who didn't recognize him anymore: Carla, in a blissed-out, goofy state of early-onset Alzheimer's. Soon my mother was describing Michael as "saintly," and before long, they were going on secret dates, and soon after that, they were, hideously, in love.

"Well—is it still OK if I come home?" I asked her.

"Sure," she said. "I'll just tell Michael he can't come over the weekend after his wife dies."

"Michael can come over. I won't be weird."

"You said that at Christmas too."

Christmas was the last time I'd seen Michael. It had gone poorly. "This time for real, though."

"Jamie, you know I'd love to see you," she said. "But Saturday was the only night he could get away. His kids are at the Bethesda house right now, you know what that's like."

"I would just sleep there. I wouldn't even bother you."

"I need this night," she said. "Please, Jamie? After that, anytime you want you're welcome. OK?"

"OK," I said. She had put up with a lot from me over the years, and now I tried to be respectful when I could. Plus, I wasn't thrilled about the idea of encountering Michael in his raw guilt-ridden grief. "Fine."

After a moment's uncomfortable silence, she said, wistfully, "You'll stay with your dad, then?"

Years after telling my mother he was gay and divorcing her, my father went and married a woman, Sally Nyugen, who now lived with him in my childhood home, just over the DC-Maryland border in Silver Spring. Sally, who was only fourteen years older than me, was recently pregnant, something I'd found out through an Instagram post where she wore a quirked smile, a messy ponytail, and a sweatshirt that read "Pregnant AF." It hadn't occurred to me until that moment that if I kept the baby, it would be the same age as my new half-sibling.

"No," I said. "I can take the train back after the show lets out."

"Oh," my mother said. "Well—if you really *need* to stay with me . . ."

"The train is fine. Don't worry about it."

"OK," she said. "I'm sorry! I'm really sorry, I just—"

"It's really fine. Good luck with Michael."

"You're sure?"

"I'm sure. Seriously. I'll see you another time soon."

"OK," she said. "If you're sure. Anyway, how are you doing, sweetheart? How's work? How's Peter?"

"He's good, everything's good," I said. She adored Peter and believed we were on the fast track to matrimony; I wasn't planning to disillusion her until I had to. "I should go. Love you."

THE FOLLOWING SATURDAY, I stuck my laptop in a shoulder bag—pretending to myself that I might take notes on the show and make it a work trip after all—then rode the bus to Penn Station. I bought two jelly donuts and an iced coffee at Dunkin' Donuts and pushed through weekend crowds to the DC-bound Amtrak platform. On board, I found a seat, pulled up my sweatshirt hood, dug out my iPod, and leaned my head against the chilled window. I put on Stevie Wonder's *Talking Book*, a favorite of my dad's that I didn't associate with Mari or Peter or anything at all except Saturday morning freezer waffles, and it buoyed me all the way through to Union Station and on the Metro to U Street.

It was an embarrassing DC cliché to talk about how much U Street had changed since I'd lived in the city in the late '90s and early '00s, but it was also a truth with the power to startle me each time. Back then, it had been a fully Black neighborhood, DC's Harlem, with go-go bars, jazz clubs, and religious bookstores. Now, getting off the U Street Metro, I was in a crowd of early-evening white people: college kids, men in gingham shirts and khakis, young parents pushing strollers. With two hours to kill before the show, I walked in one direction along U Street and then abruptly turned, veering into a pack of teenagers who all yelled at me. I stared at a used furniture store's dusty window display: a collection of milky green glass egg-cups, a gilt-framed sad-clown painting. At every step, I was aware that Mari was nearby—that radio static of her proximity that I'd fled years ago.

I hadn't eaten since the donuts, and a couple of blocks from the 9:30, I found a café and ordered tea and a meat-lovers panini. Sitting at a table by the window, I pulled on my headphones and scrolled through my iPod to Kate Bush, *Hounds of Love*, an album I had at some point downloaded but hadn't listened to in—I knew with precision—ten years. I was going to see Mari soon, I told myself; it was time to stop avoiding certain albums, certain singers. I hit play.

2

"**YOUR DAD WANTS** to sleep with men," my mother said. It was 1998, fall of my freshman year of high school, and I was in the back seat of her Volvo humming along to Kate Bush on the car cassette player. My mom had let me pick music on the drive to my swim meet that day, a rare concession that I knew meant something bad was coming. Nothing could go wrong with Kate Bush singing, but if it did, you'd be wrapped in the witch's cloak of her voice, magically protected.

"He what now?" I said. I was fourteen, scowly and scraggle-haired, all knees and knuckles. Over my bathing suit, I had on my best shirt—a navy blue gas station uniform name-tagged "JIM," also the name I used on pinball leaderboards and bowling score sheets because it looked cooler than my initials.

"I've known for a long time," she went on, reaching up to fluff her bangs in the rearview mirror. My mom had a perm then; she was pretty in a '90s-mom way with shiny pink lipstick, FUPA-prone jeans, body shaped by the Atkins diet. "But when we got married, he seemed so eager, and we were so young! We didn't know anything."

"Dad's *gay*?"

"I didn't think we'd ever divorce, I didn't! But you understand, right?" she said.

I funneled all my listening energy into Kate Bush's voice. A girl at my Maryland high school had copied this tape for me—a cute sophomore who always wore a knocker-ball hair tie looped around one finger, like a ring with two globular rubies. She'd said, "I think you might get this," and it was still the best thing anyone had ever said to me. But I hadn't really understood the album until I played it on my headphones. Then I realized it was less music in the way I thought of it then (letters from performer to audience) and more a series of sonic dreams. Kate Bush was like the Big Friendly Giant with his trumpet, blowing iridescent, twisting fantasies directly into your ears.

"I've already found an apartment in DC, in Adams Morgan," my mother was saying. "Looks right out onto Rock Creek Park and the zoo. It'll be an adventure, right? Single ladies in the city?"

I ignored her harder. The cross-thatching cellos kicked in. I was racing with Bush into the forest; I could smell the pines, could smell the fox's raw blood.

"Frederick Douglass High, in Northwest DC, is supposed to be excellent. We wouldn't make you change schools midyear—don't worry about that. But you'll start tenth grade there next fall."

The hounds howling, my bare feet struggling through the lake. The fox's tiny heart beating against my palms.

"Jamie? I don't want you to be angry at Dad. It's not his fault. OK?"

"OK," I said mechanically.

She turned to give me an intense stare—"OK? Really? Are you sure?"—and then drove the Volvo up a curb and into a mailbox.

• • •

I TOLD THE story to my friends, keeping back the part about my dad being gay. This was partly because I was sure that if he *was* gay, he was probably about to get AIDS and die, and divorce was shameful enough without adding AIDS. But I also couldn't quite say the word "gay" aloud: it caught in my mouth, flapping around in there like a trapped bird.

All my Maryland friends were boys, suburban punks, fans of DC hardcore music, then in its nostalgia-soaked waning years of "Is punk dead?" articles in the *Washington City Paper*. They argued about wars in countries they couldn't find on a map, they were vegans with straight-edge *X*s Sharpied on their hands, they cried at Disney movies. I adored them unreservedly. That year, anytime we could convince our parents, we went to all-ages shows in Metro-accessible venues, city parks, church basements, and community rec centers. One of our friends had a cool older sister, and she drove us to the Wilson Center, Fort Reno Park, house shows in Mount Pleasant. The shows were ramshackle, cathartic: kids jumping up onstage (if there even was a stage, not just a taped-off area of floor), performers throwing themselves into the audience, sweat spraying everywhere, sweat dripping down the walls, afterward your body bruised and spent, ears echoing, heart somehow both dulled and elated.

The first riot grrrl zines had been published out of a Northwest DC group house, and there were plenty of all-girl punk bands in DC at the time. But most of the bands we saw were boys. Stuff happened at those shows, you knew it would, and you girded yourself going in: mystery hands snaking around my body, a hard cock pressed against my butt. "Just pushing through," the guy would say if I caught his eye. One of my friends once punched a guy who grabbed my boob, and I felt the weakness of my gratitude, plus a kick of lust that clogged like mucus in my throat. I didn't talk to him for days after.

Still, I didn't think about going to different shows, watching girls sing. I didn't think about girls very much at all, except in private, or when I watched Angelina Jolie movies or Michelle Pfeiffer's catsuit in *Batman Returns*. I somehow understood that I *wasn't* a girl in the way people talked about girls—"Girls" as in the Beastie Boys song; as in Jordan Catalano's shrug, "Just a girl," after he kissed Claire Danes in the boiler room in *My So-Called Life*. I had only a loose notion of why—a sense of a poor fit, a stone in the shoe, an abstract shame that kept me silent in conversations about boys, marriage, clothes. I was abnormal, that was clear. But I also knew abnormality was a kind of freedom. Perhaps if I was abnormal, the rules didn't apply to me. Perhaps I could wear what I wanted to wear, listen to what I wanted to, form my own opinions.

And so, at least in the privacy of my Maryland bedroom, I did. I listened to everything: my dad's old soul and rock records; hip-hop on 95.5 and Top 40 on Z104 ("From the capital of the planet, this is the Z!"); my mom's triangle-breasted folk singers, Joan Baez or Kate and Anna McGarrigle, which she played on her kitchen cassette player anytime my dad went out. I couldn't admit this to my friends, who all had absolutist opinions re: this band versus that, this album versus that, the early catalogue versus the late, the ethical pitfalls of signing to major labels, selling merchandise, charging more than $5 a ticket. For me, I just wanted to listen and listen, and occasionally, when my parents were out, sing along.

Not long after she crashed the Volvo, my mother moved into the Adams Morgan apartment. It was only twenty minutes' drive from my father's house, but it was in DC, just around the corner from the 18th Street strip of hookah bars, late-night pizza joints, and college-kid dives. My mother had a vision of being a fun divorcée, reliving some of the youth she wasted on my dad, and apparently she thought Adams Morgan was where you did that. Without her, the Maryland house became a fully different environment: different sounds and smells, a different static hum in my ears when I woke in the middle of the night. My dad never said anything to me about the divorce, just walked around with his head slumped, dandruff on his sweater vests because he stopped showering, shame draped around him like Pigpen's dirt cloud. We ate only baked potatoes and frozen waffles. I stopped going to shows, stopped calling my friends, skipped swim practice until they kicked me off the team, couldn't listen to any of my old tapes or CDs even after my parents guilt-bought me an expensive new stereo for Christmas.

Once they had a custody schedule in place, I began staying at my mom's during the week and my dad's on the weekend, and for tenth grade, I switched to her DC school district. Before it happened, this seemed like it would be the worst part of the divorce. But by the time fall came around, it felt fine. I'd already cut off my friends, I'd already been prepared to spend the year keeping my head down in the cafeteria. It seemed easier to do it in a new place.

Northwest DC was very different from the middle-class Maryland suburbs where I'd grown up. In DC, Republicans and the truly wealthy sent their kids to private schools. But Democrats with political futures, keeping the sheen on their populist credentials, sent their kids to my new school, Frederick Douglass High in Upper Northwest. My school educated the children of high-ranking State Department officials, senior Hill staffers, and Clinton White House advisors. On my first day, I recognized the group of kids who approximated my old friends: Fugazi and Bad Brains T-shirts, tight black jeans with chain wallets and Converse, girls in camouflage jackets and striped leggings under cutoffs. But they were better dressed, clothes bought new at Commander Salamander in Georgetown instead of thrifted from Value Village, and some of them went home in cars with official government license plates. I was runty, melancholic, sexually baffled, my scruffy blond hair green-tipped from junior lifeguarding at the Silver Spring YMCA. I had skater body—flat-chested, slope-backed, low-hipped—without skater grace. Every day, I wore the same pair of baggy frayed-hem corduroys under an assortment of thrift store T-shirts with permanent sweat stains. There was no hope for me, and I spent most of my free time that fall hiding in the library, in an isolated chair sheltered by the plant sciences shelves.

Douglass High had an athletic requirement three seasons a year. If you didn't get onto varsity, JV, or "recreational" teams, you were assigned to either "General Phys. Ed.," which meant jogging and lifting weights in the gym, or, if you were a girl, aerobics. That first fall, I washed out into aerobics. The class took place in one of the black-floored rehearsal spaces for the school's theater program, thirty girls sidestepping into each other as wedding-DJ music, "September" or "Celebration," played on a small stereo. The aerobics instructor, Ms. Spencer, was one of the school's two drama teachers, who were rumored to be fucking. All class, I stared at her tiny breasts and Barbie-flat leotard crotch as she cried out, "Sashay! Sashay! Now sliiiide, sliiiide, and grape. Vine."

One afternoon, a couple months into the school year, I arrived late, and Ms. Spencer waved me up to the empty front row and revved the tape player to "Stop! In the Name of Love." Then another girl appeared in the door, and Ms. Spencer gestured her to the front too. "Come onnnn up, Mari!" she said.

In those years of confused sublingual yearning, I mentally flagged girls who fit a certain difficult-to-name profile, and I had flagged this girl. I somehow knew her full name: Mariam Dvali. We rode the same school bus route home, winding east through Upper Northwest's mansions, French restaurants, and gourmet grocery stores, into what were then middle-class, ethnically diverse neighborhoods, Adams Morgan and Mount Pleasant. I'd overheard her speaking to the bus driver with an accent, so I thought she might be an exchange student. She dressed the way I imagined foreign people did (later I found out it was hand-me-downs from a cousin in Dallas): acid-washed jeans with thick stitching up each leg, off-brand crew sweatshirts. I had noticed her hair, which was shaggy-short and black. I had noticed her jaunty hitched-shoulder walk, lazy smile, watchful black eyes. She didn't change clothes for aerobics like the rest of us, just took off her Reeboks to reveal a pair of graying tube socks.

"OK, girls!" Ms. Spencer yelled, a distracting two feet from my face, and we launched into our "Stop" routine, a sideways crab-step with palms stuck out, uncertain traffic guards. I crab-stepped stiffly, preoccupied with what I might be revealing to the back rows: was there something stuck to my butt, had I unknowingly gotten my period and bled through my sweatpants, did I have a hunchback I'd never noticed before?

The "Stop" routine involved a number of spins, and on one spin, I went the wrong way and nearly collided with Mari. Our eyes met, Mari's eyes huge, and I blinked and reeled back—the eye contact a jolt, a slap. Her lips widened.

"You look funny," she whispered as she came around on the next spin. She sounded like Natasha from the Bullwinkle cartoons: *"eff-unny."*

"Why?"

"Scared. Like—" And catching my gaze again, she pursed her lips, slouched her back, and performed the crab slide on hesitant tiptoe, like she was walking a tightrope. With her black hair and eyes, she looked like a mime version of me.

"Fuck you," I snarled, and she laughed harder. Ms. Spencer growled at us between calling steps, and we were both quiet for the rest of class, but Mari's eyes kept flashing out at me.

After class, we all pulled dry clothes over our sweaty bodies and ran out. That day, Mari reached the school bus stop before me, wearing an enormous purple quilted coat with a sparse fur lining around the hood. When the bus pulled up, she followed me to my usual seat at the back, where I liked to prop my feet on the wheel well and stare moodily at my reflection in the window.

"It was your face," she said as the bus lurched off. In the unnatural-feeling early dusk of post–daylight savings time, the bus was a bright square sauna on wheels, smelling of gym class and rubber, cold windows misted with condensation. Although most of the other seats were full, the noise and palpable heat seemed to cloud out everyone but the two of us.

"What?"

"Like a frightened rabbit." Mari pulled the mime face again, then broke character with a laugh.

Instead of anger, this time I felt a hungry gratitude. Someone at school had noticed me, recognized my fear. And she didn't seem to be judging me. Mostly she seemed curious.

"I don't like being in the front row," I confessed. My heart beat rapidly, as if I were admitting some dark secret. "Everyone can see you—it's like being onstage."

"What's wrong with being onstage?" Mari asked.

"You're just—up there. People are staring at you. What if you mess up, what if you fall?"

"What then?" she said. As she spoke more, the accent seemed to lift—almost as if it were a defensive effect for strangers. "Everyone falls sometimes. You just get back up, yeah?"

I was sure that if I ever fell on a stage, or at the front of aerobics class, I would not get up but would crawl out the door and leave forever. When I didn't answer, Mari went on. "I fell off a house once," she said. "In the country, with my cousins. I got back up! But my foot was broken, so I fell again."

"That's insane," I said, impressed.

"My mother's a doctor," Mari said, with a small jerk of a shrug. "She fixed it. What are you listening to?"

I had put on my headphones automatically as soon as I sat down, but I hadn't turned on my Walkman yet. We were seated very close together, and somehow it didn't feel strange to lift off the headphones and place them over Mari's ears, nudging away her hair and some of the plasticky fake fur of her hood lining. Her eyebrows shot up, but she didn't move her head otherwise. When the headphones were in place, she patted them and smiled.

I was listening to the Shangri-Las, a compilation tape I'd stolen from my dad. The Shangri-Las were teenage girls who sang mostly about love that was volatile, antisocial, destructive; love like dynamite. It was one of the few albums I owned that didn't remind me of my old Maryland friends, and I'd been listening to it constantly. I loved "Leader of the Pack" and often sang it alone in my room, calling and responding to myself, but it felt too obvious, potentially cheesy. I skipped ahead to "Remember (Walking in the Sand)," and I could hear, from my headphones, through Mari's ears, "*Seems like the other day . . .* " Mary Weiss, the lead singer, in full Queens diva mode. "*Oh no*"—I died for those whispers, the controlled escalation, "*oh no NO NO NO NO.*" Ba-*dump.*

"I like her voice," Mari said after a minute.

"It's the Shangri-Las. You know—'Leader of the Pack'?"

She shook her head. "I don't know it."

I couldn't imagine anyone not knowing that song. "Where are you from?" I asked.

"Georgia. The country. But I live in Mount Pleasant, with my mother. Do you want to come over? I can play you something too."

I rode with her two stops past where I normally got off, into Mount Pleasant, a small residential neighborhood tucked under the armpit of Rock Creek Park. At the time, it was inhabited mostly by punks and refugees from the Salvadoran war packed into ramshackle, code-violating group houses. Mari's apartment was on Irving Street, about fifteen minutes' walk from my mother's building, on the second floor of a subdivided three-level house. We stomped up the back staircase, through the kitchen, and into the living room, which felt very dark and crowded, large plants in giant floor pots and wall hangings embroidered with tiny mirrors and a white baby grand piano. Asleep across the couch was a woman with Mari's face under bleached-blond hair, wearing blue hospital scrubs.

"That's Yevgenia," Mari whispered. "My mother. She works at night and sleeps all day. Sometimes she doesn't make it into bed when she gets home."

With a gentleness I hadn't seen in her before, she twitched a blanket out from under Yevgenia's feet and spread it across her body. Then she nodded me into her bedroom, where I sat on a twin bed under a poster of Bruce Springsteen. Mari shut the door and hit play on a pink plastic cassette player, whirring up the tape that was already loaded. It was a terrible punk band, jangly guitar and a seagull-voiced singer.

"That's me," Mari said proudly. "It's my band from Tbilisi. There were two of us, both girls, we called ourselves the Dollface Singers. It sounds better if you understand Georgian."

"I bet," I said. On the bus, I'd felt enthralled, but the song killed it. It was bad, this girl was weird, there was no reason for me to be here. "Well—I probably should go."

"Can I come over sometime and listen to music at your house?" she said, and her need was so blatant, her eyes so black, that I nodded despite myself.

The next day, and the next, Mari found a spot by me in aerobics, her cackle audible when I dropped a step or twirled left instead of right. It was annoying, and a little disturbing. I had noticed Mari immediately, aware of some unspeakable commonality. Now she appeared to be pursuing me—had she recognized something as well?

That couldn't be, I reassured myself. There was nothing in me Mari might recognize, nothing for anyone to notice. She was lonely and new to the country, and I'd been friendly to her; that was all.

On the bus going home those nights, Mari sat next to me and pushed back her hood, expectant. But I put on my headphones and scooted away across the vinyl seat. "What are you listening to?" she asked once, and I stared out the window, pretending I couldn't hear.

Finally, on the third night, she sat down and said, loudly, "Can I come see your house? I want to listen to your music."

It had been a long, lonely day. I'd woken up early to my mother crying in the next room, wild wails, as if she didn't care who heard. At lunch, a kid pushed past me and knocked over my tray, spilling refried beans and yogurt down my jeans. I scrubbed myself with wet paper towels until the towels rolled into worms, but a girl in English class had said, "Um, do you have jizz on your pants?" I didn't have the strength to deny Mari a third time.

We got off at my stop and walked to my mother's apartment, empty except for Millie, my mother's divorce cat, who licked our fingers for potential scraps and then stalked haughtily back to my mother's bed. My mother had just started working at Michael's frame shop then, and I knew she wouldn't be home for a while. I said, "Want to see my stereo?"

I hadn't wanted to move anything out of my Maryland bedroom: it was the only bedroom I'd ever had, and I couldn't bear it looking scooped out. So in my new bedroom at my mother's apartment, all I had was a futon, a desk, and the new stereo on the floor. The stereo was a blocky black skyscraper, the fanciest and most expensive thing I'd ever owned. It played AM/FM radio, cassettes, CDs, and MP3s. When you turned it on, it sang a robotic greeting and a light display began, flashing blue and purple zigzags that created the illusion of mountains rising and falling. I felt uncomfortable showing off to Mari after seeing her cramped apartment, so I didn't turn on the lights. But she was awed by the machine anyway. She knelt to run her fingers over it. "It's beautiful," she said. "Was it expensive?"

Startled into honesty, I said, "Yes. My parents bought it after the divorce. They felt bad for me."

"Why would they feel bad for you?"

"I mean—because divorce sucks? My mother moved, I had to start a new school."

"Single mother, single kid?" she said, and I nodded. Her face did something I couldn't read; then she said, "We were so happy when my dad left. He's a drunk."

"Is that why you left Georgia?"

"No," she said. She smiled vaguely and caressed my stereo again, like it was a musical instrument she hoped to learn. "Will you play me something?"

Most of my old Maryland friends, if asked to play a single self-identifying record, would've selected a Fugazi album. The band was the core of DC hardcore, its lead singer, Ian MacKaye, a godlike figure to us but with a friendly avuncular habit of popping up at fledging bands' shows and sitting for long interviews with high school journalists. On a whim, though, I slotted in my old Kate Bush tape and fast-forwarded to the second song: "Hounds of Love." Mari sat on the edge of the futon and leaned forward with elbows on knees, glaring into the stereo like she was trying to see the tiny musicians playing deep inside the box. The song starts with a sample from an old movie, a man yelling, "It's in the trees! It's coming!" while drums hit arrhythmically like gunshots, so it's a moment before you realize you're hearing music.

"Oh," Mari said in surprise, but Kate Bush was already singing, "*When I was a child . . .* "

I looked over and saw that Mari was clenching a fist around her other fingers. "Do you know Kate Bush?" I asked her.

"No. I really, really like it."

I'd thought I'd tell her about Bush's other albums or maybe about the girl in Maryland with the knocker-ball hair-tie ring, or maybe, possibly, about the time my mom crashed the Volvo. But she was listening so hard it felt wrong to interrupt. I kept quiet and stared at her squarish knuckles, the white line around her lips, the jagged red vein that ran down from one nostril. When the song was over, she said, "Can we listen to the whole album?"

So we did. It felt weird just to sit and listen, I'd never done that before, and at first, I kept finding reasons to pace around the room or go into the kitchen. But Mari stayed in her spot, staring at the stereo, and eventually I settled down next to her, and then I felt this hum of peace, so close to her, so quiet. After the tape ended, she wanted to go back to the first song, and then we listened to other things at random. I'd spent most of my lifeguarding money last year, and babysitting money from the summer before, on tapes and CDs—others I'd copied from friends, or burned-and-returned from Tower Records. My collection was solid, even if I'd barely played it in months, and I felt proud of that, pleased to show it off. I hadn't talked to anyone about music in a very long time. I had missed it desperately, it turned out.

And Mari was such a good listener. She had no preconceptions, no rules around purity or who was allowed to listen to what. "What about this?" she kept saying, pulling out different albums: Sleater-Kinney, the Breeders, Rancid, Minor Threat, L7, NOFX, Fugazi finally, the ska-core tapes an old friend had pressed on me, the Mariah Carey and Whitney Houston albums I loved but hid when certain snobby friends came over, random punk EPs and compilations I'd bought at shows, a mix from the kid who'd designated himself my boyfriend in eighth grade . . . We spent hours listening to music that first night, until my mom came in looking half dead in her wrinkled work pants. I walked Mari downstairs and stood on the stoop with her, freezing in my T-shirt.

"That was fun," she said. She had on her giant purple coat, and it made her look out of scale, like a doll in people clothes. Her wide cheeks were bright from the cold. I didn't want her to leave, didn't want to go upstairs to where my mother was almost definitely eating a pot of no-fat yogurt and staring at the wall.

"If there's anything else you want to listen to," I said, "you could always come back."

"I want to listen to everything," she said.

"Well—come back then." We stood there a moment grinning, and then she darted down the steps and into the dark.

Pretty soon, Mari and I were leaving aerobics together and riding the bus to my mother's apartment every day. When we got upstairs, we'd brew tea, dump in sugar and milk, pour Doritos into cereal bowls—Mari did this once, and it felt so classy I kept it up—and take our snacks to my bedroom. We'd pick out an album, or more usually Mari would. I'd do homework at my desk while she lay across the futon listening, sometimes stroking Millie, sometimes reading—never a schoolbook, though, she was indifferent to school.

Nearly always she would lie on her left side facing the stereo, her arms bent under her cheek making a second pillow on my pillow. Glancing up from my desk chair, I'd see her high-arched bare feet, one cupping the other, the slope of her thigh in jeans, the sliver of soft hip where her T-shirt always hiked up. If she sat to reach for her mug, her hair would be smashed to one side, her left cheek creased pink. Her hair was coarse and shiny, like a horse's cropped mane, her hands very wide. Occasionally she would stand up and stretch both arms over her head, then rock side to side on the balls of her feet. "Ufff," she would say, a syllable that sounded foreign to me.

She wasn't hot in the way I was used to thinking about people being hot. Her front teeth were crooked and yellow; blackheads pocked her nose. She liked to clean her nails on paper edges, so I would find black deposits at the corners of my homework pages. But

I watched her obsessively, I thought only about touching her. In aerobics now, I watched her precise buoyant movements—she was actually good at aerobics, after years of Soviet gymnastics instruction—and imagined us dancing together, something I'd never thought of doing with anyone. Her hand on my neck, mine on her back, my hips bumping hers, her sturdy thigh slipping between mine.

One night, we were listening to a Björk album, and absentmindedly, focused on algebra homework, I started singing along to "It's Oh So Quiet."

"You have a really good voice," Mari said, sounding both impressed and concerned, like someone assessing an incoming tornado.

I knew I had a good voice; people had been telling me that since I was a kid. I'd been the lead in every school musical from third through sixth grade, even though I had a squirmy, giggly stage presence and felt like a dumpy weirdo in the school's assortment of nylon costume dresses. I could hit all the high notes in "I Will Always Love You" without cracking or going hoarse. But I hadn't sung around Mari yet; had felt shy about it, perhaps in the way I felt shy telling her that I felt a certain way about certain girls.

"Sing that again, but like it's you singing it, not Björk," Mari said. She reached to hit stop on the stereo, then rolled over to watch me. It would never have occurred to me to say no: I turned my chair toward her, locking into the complex magnetism between our bodies. Then I sang, eyes on my hands. The song veers back and forth between elfin whispers and a brash big band refrain—self-conscious, I didn't go full throttle on the refrain, just kept it airy and soft: "*You fall in love, zing boom . . .* "

"It's beautiful," Mari said softly when I was done. "You're a soprano but a strong one. Like the Shangri-Las singer."

I could feel my shoulders tighten. "Soprano" felt so official, such an identity. "Kind of girly, though, isn't it?"

"Boys can be sopranos," Mari said, watching me.

"Oh, like the boys with no balls?"

"Like beautiful boys," she said, "beautiful, tough, sad boys," and the words seemed to slice open a deep hungry river along the whole front of my body. I stared at her, terrified I might start crying.

"We could," she went on, in the same very cautious, gentle tones, "play together sometime. I play piano."

This was an understatement, I learned later. In fact, Mari had attended the Tbilisi Conservatory, placed in international piano competitions as a child. But it was good I didn't know, because otherwise I would've been too intimidated to try. Shrugging to regain composure, I said, "OK, I guess," and the next time we hung out, it was at her apartment to fiddle with some songs on Yevgenia's white piano, occasionally glancing at each other with shy pleasure. The same absence of intimidation also helped a week later when I kissed her for the first time, a decision that felt like a nondecision, like getting pushed out of a plane. I grabbed her in the elevator, our teeth clashed; then we jumped apart once the doors opened onto my mother's elderly neighbor, shar-pei on the leash.

If I had known more about Mari, I might never have risked any of it. But I didn't, and so I did, thank God.

3

AROUND EIGHT, I bought a bag of Doritos at the coffee shop and ate it walking to the 9:30 Club. The corner of 9th and V was already lined with people waiting for tickets, smoking cigarettes, faces lit up by their phones. At the box office window, I said, "Jamie Cain, I'm with the *Baltimore Bugle*." I had figured Mari wouldn't read the press list, but I was still thinking there might be a flash of recognition, an asterisk next to my name, *Mari says come backstage*. But the kid just crossed me off and nodded me in.

I'd been too young to earn old-timer cred by seeing shows in the original 9:30 on F Street, but I'd been to many shows in the V Street location, mostly with Mari. Together we saw Sleater-Kinney, PJ Harvey, Sonic Youth. We made out in the girls' bathroom, tried our fake IDs at the bar. When a friend of a friend's band opened for Juliana Hatfield, we coaxed our way backstage and jealously devoured the 9:30's signature backstage cupcakes, black frosting with the clock-numbers logo in white. I imagined Mari backstage with those cupcakes right now, and wondered if she remembered too. She used to get so nervous before shows: did she still hide in the corner playing solitaire, did she still refuse all food except gummy bears?

The houselights were on in the concert hall, but the room was filling. People clumped around the stage and the two ground-floor bars, while others flowed into the balconies above. Music played loudly from fridge-sized speakers suspended above each side of the stage, thrumming my eardrums. This had once been my favorite moment of a show: audience electric and hospitable, whatever drugs they'd done in the cab or bar bathroom kicking in, final moments of makeup and clothes looking right before it all went to sweaty hell. Now I just felt an introvert prickliness, all nerves raw. A drink would've blunted it, but it felt wrong to drink pregnant, even if I didn't know whether I wanted to stay that way. I found a spot on the back wall and licked Doritos dust off my fingers. Up onstage, I could see the space that Mari would soon occupy, the keyboard and standing mic awaiting her. I zipped up my sweatshirt and tugged down the hood to feel its calming pressure on my scalp.

The room slowly stuffed with people. My last 9:30 show had been before the smoking ban—now I was immersed in the raw tang of body and breath. The music seemed to be playing inside my skull, like it was trying to punch its way out. Just as I reminded myself I could still leave, the lights dropped and the music went down. The crowd stirred with common purpose. A vacuum seemed to have opened, sucking all focus to the front. I felt it too, the anxiety in my body shifting to anticipation.

People walked onstage, shadows in the dark, and found their spots. A girl next to me with dyed-pink hair screamed directly into my ear. Then four stage lights shot on, spotlighting four musicians: The drummer, pale and freckly, with bushy tan-colored hair, gangly knees bent high like a spider's. A long-legged blond guitar player with a flame-shaped dark-wood Gibson. The violinist, low-key goth in Docs and a plaid skirt. And at the keyboard in front, Mari, glaring directly at me, or at least at the audience.

I'd forgotten what Mari looked like onstage: a bristly thick witch, focused and ferocious. Her short hair was unkempt as always, her wide smile Jagger surly, her black eyes huge and hungry. Everything about her was purposeful, from her wrists cocked over the keyboard to the sideways jut of her hip. She had on black jeans, black boots, and a loose black T-shirt with a red bandana knotted around one bicep—she always wore it at shows in honor of Springsteen, whom she adored with all the unironic passion of a Soviet-raised soft butch. Same old tattoo on her left wrist, a faded outline drawing of two hands cradling a sleeping fox cub. I had the same one on my right wrist; we'd gotten them together on her eighteenth birthday in nerdy teenage homage to the Kate Bush lyric. I pressed mine now, as if I could somehow signal from one to the other.

Her eyes moved across the crowd, across me. I knew she wouldn't notice me from the stage, but I held back against the wall anyway. "9:30 Club, we love you!" she yelled, and everyone cheered again. The drummer smacked his sticks, the guitarist tore into a riff, and then Mari was singing and everything else went quiet.

I'd always felt like my high-pitched, feminine voice jarred weirdly with my slouchy tomboyish ways. But Mari's voice—low, resonant, scratch-edged—was exactly her. She was a growler, like if Tom Waits were a twentysomething dyke with a very faint Georgian accent. She didn't think of herself as a singer, rarely wrote lead vocals for herself. But when she did sing, people paid attention.

Usually when she played keys, she balanced halfway on her stool. But she stood to sing, and I could see the rooted strength of her thighs in the tight jeans, her shoulders falling back to urge out the sound. That body, its power and deliberation: I'd interacted with it in all possible ways, and I couldn't watch it now, performing for strangers on a stage seemingly miles away from me, without feeling socked in the gut.

As the song went on, I tried to pull myself back into neutral journalistic observation. The song was their biggest single, "Firebird," a track I'd downloaded from Bandcamp earlier that week. Like all the Les Somnambules songs I'd heard, it had a folk-infused sound, bolstered by Mari's shimmery keys, and a melancholic twinge. The lyrics appeared to be about a girl turning into a firebird and evading her pursuers, which was pretty typical as well. I'd often tried to decipher Mari's lyrics, searching for hidden message like the ones I embedded in my previews. But if Mari's songs were about me, you'd never know it: she loved fantastical narratives that seemed untethered to anything in our world.

The song ended, and I watched Mari breathe in the cheers, barely smiling, scratching the back of her neck. I could sense her suppressed exultation. "You liked that one, huh," she finally said, tossing her audience the chin nod she would've once tossed me.

Mari and the violinist traded lead vocals on the next few songs, the contrast between their voices similar to ours, but without the clash in tone: the violinist's voice was sweeter than mine, and it wove Mari's occasional harshness into a gentler texture. On keys, when she wasn't singing, Mari bopped around like an exuberant church organist, hair bouncing in her face. Between songs, she kept up an easy patter, teasing the drummer, the only male onstage: "We forgot to feed Andrew before the show, that's why he's so cranky tonight." Both the violinist, smiley and self-contained, and the guitarist, a punk girl with full-sleeve tattoos on both arms, watched Mari for their cues, never the drummer. But the guitarist seemed more disconnected, standing a few steps away from the group. At one point, she dropped a bar, earning a death stare from Mari.

When they'd been playing for about forty minutes, Mari paused for a sip of beer and said, "This is our last song tonight. Everyone ready for Sealbone?" We cheered and she went on, "Yeah! But before we go, we're going to play an old song. A song from another life." Then, with a deepening sense of unreality, I watched Mari close her eyes and speak the opening lines of "Forgotten"—*my* opening lines. "*I combed my hair,*" she growled. "*I bought silk stockings bought a hairpin bought a purse.*"

"Forgotten" was the last song I'd expected to hear that night. It was the best song Mari ever wrote for the Maidenheads, the song we'd performed in *Jennifer's Not There*. We recorded a version for the soundtrack, and although we were broken up by the time it came out, it got some minor play on indie music stations and college radio. If we'd stayed together, it would've been our first single, the cornerstone of our first album.

"Forgotten" was about a girl at Douglass High, Emily Steinhart, who killed herself with an overdose of aspirin because the boy she liked hadn't asked her to prom. The song began with a short spoken-word section, modeled after a Shangri-Las song we both loved, "I Can Never Go Home Anymore." Then I sang Emily's story from her perspective, while Mari sang a third-person chorus over percussive keyboards ("*Emmy, Emmy, forget it / He's not worth it, forget it*"). The song grew more chaotic as it went on, until at the end Mari was just banging keys as I screamed, "*I'm not gonna be, I'm not gonna be forgotten!*" Before that, she'd written songs that could be sung by anyone, but "Forgotten" was written specifically for me, for the disturbing collision between my girl-group yippiness and the bleak subject matter.

Hearing the Les Somnambules version felt like seeing your own face in the mirror without totally recognizing it. I'd told Emily's story in my little-girl Maidenheads voice, like I was uttering her most uncertain, desperate thoughts. But in Mari's rougher intonation, over the bulking force of the instruments, you could hear Emily's cruel hate—the rage directed not at her boyfriend, even, but at her own body. The effect was fresh and a little scary. Mari had shredded our old song, then quilted the shreds into a fully new creation—darker than the Maidenheads version, spikier and more punk-inflected than most Les Somnambules songs, somewhere in between and completely brilliant.

The song reached its climax, Mari screamed out a final "*Forgotten!*" and then they stopped abruptly. I felt the crowd all around me release, like they'd been holding their breath. That release had once been for us, this had all once been for us, and the unreality took savage hold. If I wasn't singing on "Forgotten," if I wasn't onstage next to Mari—who was I, where was I?

With the set over and the houselights up, people streamed out, shoved past me on the way to the bathroom, crowded around the bars. I paused irresolute against the wall, knowing I had to leave but not ready to go. Then, in the crowd pushing past me, I saw a familiar turquoise-braided head: Nora Jackson, the *Baltimore Bugle*'s music critic. Nora was just three years out of the University of Maryland, but with an archivist's knowledge of Baltimore and DC music. We were the only two female employees of the *Bugle*—she was also the only Black person on staff—and Jeremy was always putting our names together in sentences, like "Nora and Jamie may disagree, but I think we need to put the Santorum profile on the cover." That enforced grouping had put a damper on our work friendship. I felt it would be pleasing to Jeremy, somehow, if the only two female staffers began eating lunch together every day, and for various reasons I didn't like to please Jeremy when I didn't have to. But with Jeremy not present, I was just happy to see her. I called her name, waved her over.

Nora was taller than me, slender and quiet. At work, she kept her head down in jeans and sweaters, so I was surprised to see her dressed up for the concert in a sequined miniskirt and high platform sneakers, mermaid-blue braids hanging down her back. As she crossed the room toward me, she gave her skirt a shy tug.

"I thought I might see you here," she said, leaning in for a cheek kiss. "They sounded great, huh? Mari must be excited?"

Nora knew about the Maidenheads, but nothing about me and Mari personally, as far as I could tell. I said, "I'm sure she is, yeah."

"I'm headed backstage to get a quote for my story—you coming?"

I hadn't planned to try to see Mari. But "Forgotten" had me jumbled up. I was sure Mari couldn't sing that song without thinking of me, even if she'd excised my part musically. And if she was thinking of me—what did that mean? I could say hi quickly, I thought, still get out with plenty of time to catch the last train back to Baltimore. "Sure," I said. "If you don't mind me tagging along."

A security guard to the right of the stage shot a flashlight beam onto Nora's backstage pass, then waved us up the black-and-white-striped stairs to the warren of opening-act greenrooms tucked above the balcony level. In high school, Mari and I had snuck into the headliners' room on the opposite side, with its ceiling fresco and six bunk beds for touring acts in need of a nap. The rooms on this side were much smaller, just enough space for a couch and a mirrored dressing table. Nora led me to the third level, under the eaves of the concert hall, past a storage area stocked with cleaning supplies and bulk toilet paper, to an open door with a sign clipped to it: LES SOMNAMBULES.

A startling number of people occupied the bathroom-sized room, spilling into the hallway. I saw the rest of Mari's band, plus a few other faces I didn't recognize, everyone flushed and laughing. Mostly, though, I saw Mari. She was two feet away from me, lying across the black fake-leather couch with her socked feet propped on someone's back, head cushioned on her upflung arm, sweat-soaked hair tumbling around her face. She'd taken off her T-shirt—I could imagine her ripping it off in the wings like a victorious soccer player—and just wore a black sports bra and jeans. I could see the lick of hair in her armpit, new tattoos on her arms and torso: a bird with flame-orange wings flowing up her left bicep, traditional-style roses and a dagger at her right forearm, a long block of text running up her ribs. A beer can balanced on her stomach—she always asked for beer in a can after shows, as an ice pack. In a moment, I knew, she would press the can to her wrists and cheeks before returning it to her belly.

I hung back in the hallway—I had no idea if I was welcome or not. But then Mari turned and saw me. She swung her legs around to sit and nearly toppled the beer, grabbing for it as it fizzed out onto her knees.

"*Jamie Cain*," she said, laughing, flicking foam off her fingers. She pushed past a few bodies to hug me. Her arms were slippery with sweat; she smelled sweet and sour, the spilled beer soaked from her jeans into mine. I put my hand on her bare back, touching the sweat puddled at the base of her spine. The guitar player, I noticed, had turned from her conversation to watch.

"Guys, this is Jamie *Cain*," Mari said. She introduced me to her band: Andrew, the drummer, balanced on the edge of the dressing table jogging a knee; Fikre, "but please call me Freddie," the violinist, crunched in the corner with her arms around a smaller person in a black Les Somnabules T-shirt; and Amanda, guitar player, still giving me a searching look. "And this is Sal Evans, obviously," Mari went on, gesturing around the room, "and John from the 9:30 and Freddie's partner, Dani." Everyone did half waves, then returned to their conversations. Nora sidled over to talk with John from the 9:30, and Mari pulled me onto the sticky couch between her and Sal Evans, who'd been reviewing music at the *Washington Post* since I was a kid and was now an old man in a soft cashmere sweater and silk scarf.

"Jamie Cain," he said. "Not from the Maidenheads?"

"The very one," said Mari. She smiled—her front teeth were

straight now; she must've gotten them fixed at some point—and pressed the beer can to her cheek. "Surprised you'd know about us, we weren't exactly *Post* material."

"I watched your horrible movie," he said. "The *Post* made me. But I refused to review it. Low-hanging fruit."

Mari made a face at me. "It wasn't *that* bad," she said. "Was it?"

"Believe me," said Sal, laughing authoritatively, "it was," and then he went back to the story he'd clearly been telling before I showed up, about the time a certain famous musician, coked up beyond sense, put a gun to his head in this very room. "You can still see his boot scuff on the wall over there," he said, pointing to a dark spot next to the mirror. I listened politely—I would've paid good money, a decade ago, to meet Sal Evans. But my brain was scrambled by Mari's body, so close I could feel the heat of the show still inside her. I said "Mm-hm" a lot and tried not to stare too obviously.

Mariam Dvali, my Mari. I hadn't seen her in three years, hadn't been this close in ten, and she was older, her hair coarser, her eyes more tired. But in most ways, she was the same, a body I knew in such intimate detail I could've sculpted it blind: soft belly drooped over the tight waist of her jeans, small low-slung breasts, sloping nose and doll eyes and mad wide smile. As she listened to Sal, she balanced forward with her elbows on her knees, beer can cooling the fox tattoo on her wrist. Without thinking, I reached over and lifted her arm to uncover it. She kept smiling, but her forearm muscles hardened under my fingers. "Too hot," she said, and pulled back to replace the can.

Sal completed his anecdote, declared, "Kids, don't do drugs," and then moseyed out without a goodbye. Mari and I glanced at each other and laughed, and then she said, "So what did you think of the show?"

"It was all right. Not bad."

She waited a beat, then: "Shut up."

"It was awesome, obviously. You guys killed it."

"Thanks," said Amanda. She had been leaning against the wall to Mari's other side this whole time but had barely spoken. She was very tall and skinny, her ropy long arms tanned like a farmworker's under the tattoos, hair in a dirty-blond topknot over shaved sides.

She was gazing at me like someone who'd already formed an opinion, and I automatically went deferent. "I like how you're doing 'Forgotten,'" I said. "Sounds like a totally different song."

"That's sort of the point," Amanda said.

"It's a test run for September," Mari said, shoving Amanda's shoulder with her own. "You got that email, right?"

"What email?" I said.

"From the Silver Spring AFI theater—I thought an address of yours was on it. About the *Jennifer* screening? No? Shoot—well, they're screening *Jennifer* in the fall for a festival with a bunch of other locally filmed movies. The AFI events guy emailed to see if we'd perform 'Forgotten' at the screening. I thought that's why you came tonight."

I'd thought she seemed surprisingly unsurprised to see me. I had taken it to mean that she was always on the lookout for me, therefore never startled by my presence. That's how I would've felt seeing her walk down my street in Baltimore: that my constant vigilance had finally done its job and conjured her up.

"Anyway," she went on, "I told them you and I weren't performing together anymore, but that my new band could do 'Forgotten.' We just started practicing it, so I'm glad it sounded good to you."

"It did, yeah," I said. It was deeply painful to imagine Mari performing this new version of "Forgotten" at a *Jennifer* screening. I'd been wrong to think she couldn't play it without thinking of me. In fact, it was the opposite. She was able to play it because she wasn't thinking of me at all.

"I really thought you'd gotten the email," Mari said, shaking her head. "I thought you didn't reply because you weren't interested. I'm sorry—I hope this isn't weird."

"It's fine," I said. I was working to be rational. "It's your song, you wrote it."

"Sure, but—argh. I feel bad. If I'd known you didn't get the email, I would've reached out."

"It *is* a very different song now," Amanda said. She spoke slowly, staring at me through narrowed gray eyes, volumes of thought seeming to compress into each word. "I'm not even sure people would recognize it from the old version."

Mari gave me an anguished look which I suspected was partly performance: she didn't tend to experience guilt as much as to enact it as a strategy. But as always, her guilt face was so charming I couldn't help but respond. "It's really OK," I said. "It sounds amazing the way you guys do it."

"Well, listen, we're having a party back at my house after we load out—do you want to come? We can talk it over, catch up a bit."

"We can't have a party! Andrew didn't buy beer," Amanda said.

"Of course we can! Andrew can buy it on the way," Mari said, and they began bickering gently over logistics: could Freddie and Dani drive people back if Andrew took the gear and stopped at the beer store on Georgia Ave, was the house too messy, did someone need to go buy toilet paper, etc. After a few minutes, Mari turned to me. Her humid hair flopped around her temples; her cheeks were pink and damp from the frosted beer can.

"It seems we are having a party, just a bad one with no beer or toilet paper," she said with a snort. "But you should come anyway, OK?"

"You're selling it so well," I said. The last Amtrak to Baltimore left DC around midnight, in two hours; it wasn't impossible.

She laughed. "Jamie, Jamie, come?" and made a little praying gesture.

I knew better, I always knew better with Mari. "Of course," I said anyway, "of course I'll come."

4

TRYING NOT TO worry about the time or probe too deeply into my motivations, I took a cab to Mari's house in Petworth and arrived before anyone else. I hadn't been to Mari's house since right after she bought it, using her cut of the *Jennifer* money. She and Yevgenia hosted a housewarming party, and I'd somehow wound up on the invitation email, although we had broken up on extremely bad terms a few months prior. I went, hoping it might be a gesture of friendship. But Mari had ignored me, then vanished upstairs for nearly the whole night while I tried to make conversation with mutual friends who didn't know about the breakup. It had been weird at the time—we were both eighteen, I had just started college—to know someone my age who owned property. I'd explored Mari's house alone, not sure whether to be jealous or sorry for her: walls recently stripped of wallpaper but still unpainted, stained and chipped linoleum floors, rotting pool table in the basement.

Petworth was then a middle-class Black neighborhood on the east-of-the-park edge of Northwest DC. Now the neighborhood looked unaffordable: houses shiny with new paint, expensive-looking strollers padlocked to porch railings, huge gleaming cars parked trustingly in the street. Mari's house halfway down the block was the only scruffy one, its small front yard bound by rusted chicken wire and grown over with ivy. At some point since 2002, Mari had put a couch on the porch, an obvious trash-day scavenge with ripped seersucker covering, and a metal table with a shell ashtray that overflowed with butts. Sitting on the couch to wait, I felt cramping at the base of my spine, weariness in my hips, and told myself I wouldn't stay long.

An old Honda Civic pulled up and everyone tumbled out yelling at each other: Freddie, her partner Dani, Mari, Amanda, and a couple other people who'd been at the show. Nora emerged from someone else's car, in operator mode now, talking to four people at once as she stepped through the stubbly yard in her impossibly high platforms. Mari, cooled down and sparking with post-show elation, unlocked the gated front door. I was the last one in, and she held the door for me. "Hey, stranger," she whispered. "Just give me a minute and then we can talk."

Inside, it was dark, and Mari ran around switching on lights. Amanda went straight into the kitchen, where I could hear her washing dishes. Freddie and Dani sat whispering on the living room couch, arms around each other's shoulders, until Amanda stuck her head in and said, "It would be really helpful if someone would run to the Giant for toilet paper," and they jumped into service.

The house was laid out like most of Petworth's mid-century row houses: long and narrow, with a living room in the front, small dining room by the stairwell, and kitchen overlooking the alleyway in back. The walls were painted the same shade of warm yellow Yevgenia had painted the kitchen of their old apartment in Mount Pleasant. Above an elephantine leather sectional in the living room, someone had nailed up bookshelves that were still filled with

Yevgenia's books: novels in Russian and Georgian, medical textbooks, leather photo albums. Her white baby grand stood in the corner, under a gilt-framed ikon of the Virgin Mary.

When I'd run into Mari at the Cat Power show in 2009, she'd told me Yevgenia had recently died of breast cancer. I'd been drunk, my ex-girlfriend Carrie was there being terrible, and I'd stammered a few things before Mari walked away. But that night, after Carrie passed out, I cried for a long time—I had loved Yevgenia. In Tbilisi, she had been a gynecologist at a prestigious hospital. After she published an article arguing that government corruption had become a public health issue, a beefy tracksuited man took up permanent residence in a doorway across from their building, and she and Mari fled the country. Here, she'd retrained as a nurse and gotten hired in the maternity wing at Sibley Hospital. Yevgenia only wore white when she wasn't in her scrubs. She had bouffant blond hair and Mari's wide black eyes, only Yevgenia's were always thickly shadowed by sparkly blue paint. Every Friday night as long as I'd known her, she would put on a swishy white dress and sing Georgian love songs to Mari's accompaniment on the white piano. There were photos of her everywhere in the house, including, at the base of the stairs, a blown-up image of her and Mari that I remembered from the old apartment: Mari a tiny gremlin in a pink snowsuit, Yevgenia in a white snowsuit with sequins along the seams, their matching grins manic with joy.

Beyond these Yevgenia relics, it was clearly a Mari space: cluttered and unattended, like she only passed through to sleep. I recognized some of her framed show posters, including some we'd been at together, and her records on a shelf in the corner. I looked in vain for one of the Maidenheads posters we'd printed for our ill-fated 2002 tour—mine were in a box in Baltimore. On the couch lay an orange cat, uninterested in my extended hand. I climbed the carpeted steps to the bathroom, where I peed and then rummaged through Mari's cluttered cabinet: hair gel, tampons, an age-curved postcard with a picture of the Seattle Space Needle, message on the back in Georgian script.

When I came down, there were more people in the living room and kitchen, and more people filtering in every few minutes. Some of them I'd met after the show or vaguely recognized from the old days, but most were strangers. Unmistakably queer strangers, though: punk trans girls in skirts and boots, suave butches in short-sleeved button-downs, rockabilly femmes with red lipstick and undercuts. Anxiety streaked up my spine, seized my shoulders. It had been so long since I'd been in a group of queer people, maybe a handful of times since I started dating Peter, and then always as an outsider, or at least I'd felt like an outsider. But here, no one knew me as Peter's girlfriend—in fact, if anyone knew me, it was as Mari's ex—and after a moment's panic, I readjusted. My shoulders dropped, my joints loosened, softened by an old warmth. I hadn't realized how differently I'd been walking, standing, all these years living as a straight girl.

Nora waved from across the room, and under the eyes of someone who didn't know I was queer, I stiffened up, waved politely back, and escaped into the kitchen, where Amanda was spreading handfuls of grated cheese across a baking tray filled with chips. Without turning around, she said, "Can you grab jalapeños and vegan sausage crumble from the fridge?" I opened Mari's fridge—takeout containers, beer, many varieties of hot sauce—and found a jar of jalapeños and a Ziploc of something I thought might be vegan sausage crumble. Then I stood by Amanda at the stove and sprinkled sausage over her nachos, hyperaware of her agile bony fingers.

"Get into the corners," she told me, inspecting my work with a cool gray stare. "And a few extra jalapeños, Mari loves those."

"Where is Mari, anyway?" I hadn't seen her since we'd come in.

"Probably upstairs, taking a break. She'll be down once she feels ready."

"She still hides at parties?"

Amanda went to the sink to wash her hands. I could hear her take a deep breath. "She's under no obligation to stop," she said. "At least not until she wants to. And certainly not because it makes you uncomfortable."

"No, I just—is she doing OK?"

"She's doing great, actually. A lot better now."

"How long have you two been together?"

"We're not together anymore," Amanda said. Lifting dripping hands from the sink, she looked around in vain for a towel, then, with a disdainful exhale, dabbed them dry on her jeans. "If you're done with the sausage and jalapeños, stick it in the oven and set the timer for five minutes. The extra chips you can put out on the dining room table, in bowls, and there's salsa in the fridge as well. I gotta check on something, I'll be back soon." She bustled out of the kitchen.

I didn't want to consider the lift in my spirits, hearing Amanda and Mari weren't together. I put the chips and salsa out on the dining room table, then stuck Amanda's nachos into the oven, set the timer, and leaned against the counter. Alone and functionless, I wasn't sure what to do next, and it was a relief when Freddie and Dani came in, Dani balancing a twenty-four-pack of toilet paper on one hip.

"Jamie! This feels like meeting a celebrity, we've heard so much about you," Freddie said. She poured herself a glass from the tap, nodded at Dani to set the toilet paper down on the counter. Freddie was tall, slender, and Black, with a shaved head; Dani was small, round, and white, with a shaved head. "And of course I've listened to you all's 'Forgotten' a thousand times."

"You do it better," I said. "Mari's voice . . ."

"It's awesome, isn't it? But there's something special about your version and I don't think we'll ever hit it." So even if Mari had rewritten our old song, people still loved it; it comforted me to know that.

"Freddie was scared to meet you," Dani told me. "In the car over, she was all, 'I hope she doesn't hate us . . . '"

"No way!" I said, involuntarily grinning. "I was so intimidated meeting you guys."

"It's just," Freddie said, "we wouldn't be here if it weren't for you. You started this."

"It was all Mari."

"I know that's not true. That's not what Mari says, anyway."

I wanted more than anything to know how Mari described me or my contributions to her career, but it felt shaming to ask. I said instead, "Anyway, the show tonight was amazing. You must feel great."

"Nahh, I fucked up a bunch," Freddie said. "Mari's going to kill me."

"She's *not*," said Dani. "You were perfect."

"Dani's a babe," Freddie said with a staged eye roll. "But they know literally nothing about music."

"I know you're my favorite musician," said Dani.

"Me and the Beebs? Thanks."

"Justin Bieber is our most talented lesbian artist," Dani said to me, smirking. The joke was cheesy, but it was a queer joke, an invitation to laugh from the inside. I laughed probably a little too loud.

"Where is Mari, anyway?" Freddie said.

"Amanda said she was upstairs taking a break," I said.

"Oh, right." Freddie looked worried. "I hope it's not a long one. Last time . . ."

"She OK, generally?" I asked.

"No, she's good, it's just parties. You know. She always wants to have them, she's such an extrovert, but sometimes she can't handle it. We're just going to restock the downstairs bathroom and then sit on the porch, if you want to join us? We don't love parties either."

"That sounds great," I said, relieved to have a plan. But as I followed Freddie and Dani through the living room, I saw Mari, paused at the top of the stairs.

She had changed into a clean white T-shirt and combed her hair, still slick with sweat. Even from across the room, I could see a tiny twitch at the corner of her eye. Amanda, who had been loading beers into an ice-lined cooler, seemed to notice something too. She ran up the stairs, tucked an arm around Mari's back, and steered her downstairs and into the kitchen.

"I'm going to catch Mari," I said to Freddie, who smiled and let Dani pull her away through the crowd.

As I came into the kitchen, the oven timer blared. Amanda lifted the tray from the oven and forked a bunch onto a plate. Waving a hand to cool it down, she set the nachos in front of Mari, who was sitting at the kitchen counter.

"Eat this, babe," she said. She hadn't seen me yet, and her voice was softer. "You'll feel better."

But Mari looked up and said, "Hey."

Amanda snapped around. "It's not a great time."

"No, it's OK, it's OK," Mari said to both of us. "Want nachos?"

I didn't want to interrupt, but I was hungry beyond words. I sat down next to Mari at the counter and let Amanda serve me a plate. "Is it vegan cheese?" I said, picking up a chip. "I've never seen it melt like this."

"Well, to be honest," said Amanda, who was very clearly suppressing irritation at my presence, "I added a bit of real cheese, for melting purposes. Sorry. I should've said something."

"I don't care," I said. "I'm not vegan."

"Freddie and Dani are, but they don't mind. No one else cares at all. I still feel bad."

"You'd feel bad even if it were vegan," Mari said fondly. "You'd find a way. Plastic packaging, or the fact that you bought it at Whole Foods."

"Don't tell her I go to Whole Foods! Anyway, it's actually cheaper there."

"The fuck it is," Mari said, taking a huge bite.

I could see the complexity in Amanda's frown, concern and frustration. She glanced between us, clapped her hands on her thighs, and said, "Right. Well, I should check on Andrew, make sure he hasn't gotten lost. Mari, you need anything else?"

"I'm good." We watched her leave the room; then Mari said, "Want to go out back?"

We both served ourselves more nachos, then walked through the kitchen door onto Mari's small back patio: a concrete-floored area separated from the alley and neighbors by a wooden fence, with a few dead plants in plastic pots and three rickety iron chairs around a low table. It was a warm night, even for May, and I looked up to see a gray-violet starless sky intersected by fire escapes and the branches of a tree in a neighbor's back patio. People were laughing across the alley. I could hear sirens, car radios, the patter of a baseball game on TV somewhere. I hadn't been alone with Mari since August 2002, and I kept getting distracted by small discoveries: a new scar at the corner of her lip, the way she cupped her plate in a single broad hand, fingers splayed underneath. We scraped our chairs closer to the table, and I set my plate down dangerously close to another overwhelmed ashtray, this one a giant glass bowl that read "Charlotte Bobcats" on the side.

"That's gross, sorry," Mari said, and placed it on the ground by her foot. "I quit smoking years ago, but I keep, you know. Unquitting."

"I don't mind," I said.

"Sorry Amanda's being so intense. We've been broken up for years, but—lesbians. You still dating that Carrie person? The one who took off her shirt at Cat Power?"

I'd been dreading this: coming out. "Actually, I was living with a guy. Peter. For a couple years. We just broke up."

"Oh." Mari grabbed wildly for the beer she'd not gotten. "Hold on," she said, pushing back her chair. I waited alone, breathing through my nose, until she returned, two opened bottles in one hand. "Cheers, anyway," she said, clinking them together and passing one to me. "So boyfriend, breakup—what else is new?"

"Well, I'm pregnant," I said. I had not intended to say this. It was just the most honest answer to her question, and I wasn't used to being dishonest with Mari.

She sputtered on her beer. "Oh!" she said. "Oh, wow. OK."

"Sorry. I just found out, I guess I'm still a little weird about it."

"So—Peter? Or someone else? Am I allowed to ask that?"

"Peter."

"Is that why you broke up?"

"He doesn't know," I said. "Actually, you're the first person I've told."

Mari gave a little snort. "Wow, you're a bit of a mess, aren't you."

"I know. I'm sorry."

"Don't be." She was looking down her long nose at me, eyes unreflective.

I had so much I wanted to tell Mari, ten years of one-sided conversations wound up inside me. But I could tell she didn't want that, was perhaps dreading it. After a few silent moments, she stretched out a leg to ease the cigarette packet from her front jeans pocket. Tapping one out, she lit it with a match and leaned back in her chair. I'd always thought she looked extra Soviet when she smoked, cigarette between thumb and first finger. She leaned forward and knocked ash onto her empty nacho plate.

"So what are you going to do about the pregnancy?" she asked. "And should I not be smoking?"

"No, you're good. I don't know what I'm going to do."

"You're not drinking, though," she said, nodding at my untouched beer.

"I guess not."

Without a pause, she stubbed out the barely touched cigarette. "You're doing a good job, Jamie," she said. "You'd be a great mom, if you wanted to."

I laughed, but she appeared to be serious. "I mean it," she said, nodding at me. "You're a kind person."

I could feel tears pressing my eyes. "Thanks for saying that." I knew it wasn't true; that couldn't be what she thought. I remembered the final time we'd spoken honestly with each other, Mari's cold damning rage. No—she was just being polite. "How are *you*, anyway?" I asked.

"Fucking terrific. That show felt incredible. Sal fucking Evans!"

"Sal *fucking* Evans," I agreed.

"And Nora liked it too, right? But you guys always like us. What was that, 'DC indie's answer to Bruce Springsteen'?"

I felt soft all over. She'd read my previews.

Amanda came out then—checking on Mari—and a few other people followed, and a joint went around and the patio fugged up cozily. I sat for a while, mostly listening, and then it started feeling late and I got up to leave. Mari noticed and stood too. "You leaving? I'll walk you out." Amanda waved, but her eyes stayed cold. I could feel her watching as I went up the stairs into the house.

Freddie and Dani were holding hands on the front porch couch, and I said goodbye, then Mari and I walked down the front steps to the sidewalk, where we paused.

"Thanks for coming to the show," she said. "It was good to see you."

Face-to-face like this, alone in the dark, her politeness was suddenly too much to bear. "Mari, I really missed you," I said. It felt wrong as soon as it came out, but when I looked up, Mari was smiling.

"I missed you too," she said. "Know what, this is probably crazy, but we're practicing Tuesday night. Pretty close to your dad's. Any chance you'd still be around, want to drop in for one night?"

"That wouldn't be weird?"

"It's as weird as you make it," she said, with the exact two-shoulder jerk she'd always made shrugging as a kid. "I don't feel weird."

"OK," I said. "I'll be there." She gave me her number, and with a thrumming joy, I created a new contact for Mari Dvali—neither of us had owned a phone in 2002. Then she put her arms around me for a hug. Her hair was soft against my face, her ear cold on my cheek. She smelled like cigarettes and beer and herself.

"Well," she said, all business after she pulled away, "I'll see you Tuesday then."

"Yeah," I said. I had to cough to clear my throat. "OK. Bye."

I HAD MISSED the last Baltimore train by hours, and the next one wasn't until six a.m. I had my shoulder bag with my laptop but nothing else, no change of clothes, no toothbrush. Beyond finding an unoccupied bench in Union Station, there was only one option, one place where I still had a key: my mother's apartment. I'd have to see Michael, and worse, my mom would be hurt; she didn't assert boundaries a lot, so it seemed extra obnoxious to stomp on one. But I would've stomped on just about anything to get that time with Mari, that invitation. I hailed a cab on Upshur Street and gave my mother's address in Adams Morgan.

The driver was a South Asian kid about my age with ironic soft dice hanging from his mirror and an '80s dance-hits mix on the stereo. I hummed along to "Take On Me," but when "I Wanna Dance With Somebody" came on, I started crying. I didn't feel sad, just overwhelmed, and like my hiccupy sobs were relieving some pressure that had been there so long I'd forgotten to notice. I was crying loud enough that the driver finally said, "Uh—want me to skip this one?"

I swallowed. "No, no. I love this song."

"My mom watched the whole funeral. This song makes her cry too."

"It is the loneliest song," I said. "The part at the end where she's begging someone to dance over and over—*Don't you wanna dance . . .*"

"You're right, oh my god! It's like she can't get *anyone* to dance with her. Let alone someone who loves her!"

"Exactly!" I was excited now, and pretty sure my driver was gay.

"My question, though, is who wouldn't want to dance with Whitney Houston? Like seriously!"

"Right," I said. "But I think it's not so much that people don't want to dance with her, I think it's more that she can't *let* them dance with her. Like she's so depressed she can't conceive of a world in which people would want to dance with her, so she dances alone."

"Whoa," the driver said.

I knew I sounded high, but I couldn't stop. "'Greatest Love of All,' same thing. It's depression self-talk. Like, no one's ever going to love me except me, she even says loving yourself is 'easy,' which is insane obviously."

The driver was looking at me in a new way, like someone liable to puke on his upholstery. I shifted back against the seat and tried to look extra sober so as not to worry him, although I was feeling ill from the movement of the car and all the non-food-like foods I'd eaten that day. It was funny to remember all the times I'd effectively passed as sober while very much unsober; apparently this was harder with actual sobriety.

Then I thought about Mari noticing I wasn't drinking, stubbing out her cigarette to protect my unwanted pregnancy. She had always noticed things in me before I saw them myself. And if that's what she was seeing, someone taking action to nurture a life, maybe that was who I actually was, or could be. Maybe I *was* a kind person. Maybe I *would* be a good mother.

The cab left me outside my mother's building, and I paused on the front steps to dig out my keys. A straight couple walked by, arms linked and stumbling: it was two a.m. in Adams Morgan, everyone was stumbling. Right as they passed me, the man said heatedly, "Jennifer, you just weren't there! You weren't, I don't care what you say, you weren't!" I laughed in surprise at his words, loud enough that he gave me a hostile stare over his shoulder. This world was one of chance and mystery, I thought, and felt buoyed by a strange new peace.

5

IN JANUARY 2002, halfway through my senior year of high school, the Black Cat put on a local-bands showcase to raise money for a queer-friendly homeless shelter, and a musician friend helped get the Maidenheads on the list. We had been playing together at that point for two years, performing at some of the small venues I'd known since middle school. But the Black Cat was a huge step up—we'd seen Velocity Girl, the Mekons, and Tanya Donelly on the upstairs stage—and Mari and I decided we needed new clothes. The weekend before the show, we drove my dad's car to the good vintage store in Wheaton, and I stopped Mari on the sidewalk outside. Two 1950s prom dresses hung in the window, one ginger pink and one lime green, not exactly matching but close, with capped sleeves, satin bodices, wide skirts with tulle ruffles.

We asked the store clerk to unhook the dresses, then we bundled them up and brought them into the changing room, a back corner with a faded floral curtain pulled across, smelling of dead-person sweaters. We giggled and poked each other as we tossed away our sweatshirts and shimmied the dresses down over our bras and jeans. Both of us looked violently off in dresses, like boys forced into drag for laughs in a movie—other people didn't always seem to notice, but it was our great shared joy that we both saw it. We laughed at our own reflections in the mirror, my long gawky limbs sticking out of the green ruffles, Mari's sallow gloomy face above the pink. "You look like Clea DuVall," I said—we'd just watched *But I'm a Cheerleader.*

"You look like the frog prince," she said. "We could cut the skirts." She stuck out her leg, testing range of motion. "And the sleeves."

The dresses were $15 each. I paid—I got allowance now from both of my parents, doubling what I'd got before the divorce. Back at my dad's house, we experimented with scissors and my mom's abandoned sewing machine until we had two very short garments with slashed hems and low necklines: anti-dress dresses, dresses that made it visible just how absurd it was for us to be wearing dresses at all. The day of the Black Cat show, we got ready at my mom's apartment, pulled our winter coats down over our bare legs, and walked the mile over, switching off who carried Mari's new birthday Casio. In the backstage area, the Black Cat's manager gave us a look and laughed. "Y'all're *cute*."

Onstage, I felt self-conscious in my ripped-up dress: could everyone see my underpants? We were a weird band, nothing like the mostly male trios who dominated the scene: two very young kids with no instruments except Mari's keyboard and a sound that veered between creepy-cute melodies and ragged yelling, punk only by exclusion of all other categories. People sometimes looked at us funny when we walked out, like they were waiting for the actual musicians.

But we opened with "Forgotten," and once I got out the first words, everything was all right. People were laughing, dancing. Mari was sweaty and gleeful, hopping up and down behind the Casio. I did a pageant-queen twirl at the end of the song, and everyone cheered. The audience was predominately queer, a few older DC dykes but mostly suburban queer kids in flannels and black nail polish—my people! They knew some of the lyrics to our songs already and shouted along to others as if they did. We ended on a cover of "Leader of the Pack," and everyone howled: "*I met him at the candy store!*" At the end, riotous with possibility, I leaned across the Casio and kissed Mari, messy on the mouth. Everyone howled even louder.

A week after the concert, Mari got a phone call at her house, the contact number listed on the handmade cards we'd stuck out on the Black Cat merch table. Someone named Debbie said she was a DC-based producer on a low-budget detective movie. She'd seen and loved our Black Cat show, she said the dresses were "Lynchian," and she was looking for musicians to play in a bar scene. The film was called *Jennifer's Not There*, and it was a murder mystery about a dead stewardess named Jennifer, filmed in and around DC. It had mostly gone through production, but Debbie was still searching for a local band to feature in one scene. "I think the Maidenheads might be that band," she said. So that weekend, my mother drove us to Georgetown, prom dresses in a trash bag in the trunk, to play "Forgotten" in Debbie's disappointingly shabby office.

When we finished, she nodded, looking pleased. In the scene (she said "your scene," and we tried not to scream), the detective investigating Jennifer's murder enters a bar, where he spots the killer for the first time without knowing it. It was meant to have a gritty, noirish feel, but with a punk rock twist. Debbie wanted us to perform "Forgotten" in the background, wearing our dresses, and she wanted to include the song on the movie soundtrack, which she was planning to release with a small label. She told us she would messenger over our contracts right away.

In the car going home, my mother was skeptical. "She's just going to sign you on the spot like that? She must really need someone. And did you see how small the office was? I'm not sure we can trust her. Why can't she find older musicians, musicians who are more established? It feels fishy to me."

Mari and I sat in silence in the back seat, still in our dresses, holding hands below where she could see. I never shared Mari's calm assurance that we would succeed—very few people match Mari's self-confidence. But I did know that the sometimes jagged, sometimes gentle friction between Mari's songs and my voice made something extraordinary. In the car that day, Mari's hand pulsing in mine, I radiated with hope and love and ambition.

I didn't realize until I saw the contract that Debbie was planning to pay Mari a lot more than she was paying me. Mari was making $10,000 off *Jennifer*, while I would make $2,000. My father had insisted I call a lawyer friend of his to check on the terms, and the lawyer explained this was normal, that Mari had written the song and so her rights to it were worth more. My immediate thought was: it wasn't just the song that made Debbie call us, it was the dresses, and I'd spotted and bought the dresses. Shouldn't it be more equal?

Within a day, however, I pulled out of the sulk. I was being ridiculous, I told myself. This wasn't about money. Debbie said movie soundtracks were how everyone was getting discovered these days—I couldn't mess it up out of jealousy. I called Mari and told her I was excited for her, and I signed the contract. A couple weeks later, we drove out to a studio in Northern Virginia to record "Forgotten" for the soundtrack, backed by a drummer and a guitarist. Then we spent a day filming in a Rockville loft apartment decked out like a dingy bar interior, lip-synching to our own voices before an audience of extras and two actual actors. Finally, we settled down for what felt like an impossible wait for the movie and soundtrack release that fall.

$2,000 was less than what Mari was making, but even minus taxes, it was still the most money I'd ever had. When the check cleared into the bank account my mother had set up to receive it, I thought hard about what to do. Should I save it? Should I buy a million CDs, all the clothes, expensive meals? Mari had put hers into savings—she wanted to buy a house for Yevgenia. I felt that because my amount was smaller, though, it didn't matter as much what I did with it. So that spring, in the school computer lab, I used my new debit card to put down a massive eBay bid on the most gorgeous vintage Sansui record player—I'd been researching models for months. Then I ordered two plane tickets to Rome for me and my mother, printed them out, and put them under her coffee mug for her to find the next morning.

My mother was so sad in those years. She was working for Michael but hadn't started dating him yet. Her friends were all married and didn't invite her to things, and she spent every night alone unless I was there. If I took her to Italy, I reasoned, I wouldn't have to feel bad about abandoning her when I moved out for college.

When she lifted her mug in the morning, she burst into tears, and I felt like I'd done the right thing. But Mari thought it was crazy. "You already spent the entire check? What the fuck, James! We could've gone somewhere after the tour," she said on the phone that night.

"We still could."

"Only if I paid for you," she said. "Your money's all gone."

"Well, it's not like I had as much as you do," I said, and she grumbled some reply.

I went to Rome with my mother in June, right after graduation. It was a disaster. All I'd known to do was buy the plane tickets—I hadn't thought about booking hotels or planning day trips or anything like that, and my mother had to do it all and got annoyed. We ended up staying in a crappy hotel in a bad neighborhood, far from the tourist stuff. It rained all week, and there wasn't much to do except ride endless city buses, occasionally glimpsing famous-looking buildings down rickety alleyways, or trail each other at a distance through museums like a divorcing couple. By the time we came back, we were not speaking. I left almost immediately to go on tour with Mari and a DC hardcore band called the Shrillers, and my mother seemed relieved to say goodbye.

Mari and I and the Shrillers had planned the tour ourselves, a circuit of college towns down and then up the East Coast. We'd booked all the shows, borrowed a van, found places to stay with friends, and photocopied a million posters at Kinko's. All spring, we'd been excited about it, but already on the first leg—DC to Charlottesville—it became clear that something was very wrong with Mari. She threw my Taco Bell burrito out the van window because she said Taco Bell had cockroach eggs in it. She told the Shrillers that it was embarrassing to play with them—they were amateurs and we were a real band. She wore the same jeans and black hoodie every day, and they became dirty in a way I hadn't known clothes could be—stiff with food spills and her own sweat, filmy to the touch. She sat in the back seat of the van in her stinky jeans and hoodie with her headphones on, staring out the window, and only talked when necessary.

The shows themselves went well. We performed for a couple hundred people in Chapel Hill, a skinhead-heavy but enthusiastic crowd upstairs at the Middle East in Cambridge, a wild house party in Burlington where I dropped acid for the first time. But nothing seemed to shake Mari out of her mood. One night in New Haven, toward the end of the tour, someone gave the Shrillers coke, and we cut lines with my new debit card in a bar bathroom—except Mari, who gave me a disgusted look and slouched off to drink beer alone in the van.

"Is she always like this?" asked one of the Shrillers. There were three Shrillers, two female and one male, and they dressed similarly, in cutoff shorts and white men's undershirts. All three had dark brown hair with straight-across bangs. It wasn't a gimmick, one had told me: "We spend a *lot* of time together."

"This is pretty bad, even for her," I said.

That night, we slept in the common room of someone's cousin's Yale dorm, Mari and I sharing the futon and the Shrillers in sleeping bags on the floor. The mattress sagged me into Mari, her back sunk against my belly. She smelled like dirty hair and her peculiar sour-fruit sweat. We hadn't had sex since before I'd left for Italy, and I was stir-crazy inside my own skin. When I heard the Shrillers snoring, I stroked her shoulder, just once, a question. Without turning her head, she grabbed my hand and flung it away.

"Jesus Christ, Mari," I said. In my pajama pants and T-shirt, I crossed the room and went outside into the quad, where I stood and dug my toes into the expensively lush grass, wishing I'd brought cigarettes. It was a warm night, and the buildings looked like monasteries, with their arched entryways and engraved stone angels; the people rushing by, looking serious and collegiate, were like medieval scholars.

One of the biggest fights Mari and I ever had, earlier that year, was over plans for the fall. I was going to American University, where I got a tuition break because my dad taught there. Mari had signed up for a few classes at UDC, but she didn't want to go to college—her plan was to work and focus on the band. I told her that was a bad idea; she should get her degree. She accused me of making the compromise choice, the choice that would restrict practice time and make it harder to tour right when things were about to blow up for us. Looking at the campus that night, all the students doing important student-y things, I felt like I'd made the right decision. I believed in us, but it seemed prudent to have a backup plan.

We got back to DC in early August. The Shrillers dropped me off at my house before returning the van, and I ran upstairs and swam deep under the futon blankets—so clean, so soft, so exclusively mine—and stayed there for twenty-four hours. Earlier in the summer, I'd worked at a coffee shop on 18th Street, and over the next weeks, I took at least one shift a day, coming home caffeine-crashed and back-sore, not at all interested in seeing Mari or talking to her. We were supposed to practice, there had been talk of performing at a DC opening night event for *Jennifer* in October, but neither of us made the effort to set it up.

One Saturday a few weeks before classes were supposed to start, I was sacked out on the couch after a morning shift when the buzzer rang downstairs—"Package for Cain?" My mother, bustling in a way I knew was commentary on my idleness, went down to get it. She came back into the apartment holding a Mylar rainbow balloon on a stick.

"It's from Debbie," she said, her voice catching so she had to cough. She handed me the note, which she had already opened: "To the little lesbian movie that could—coming to a screen near you in just two months!—and to the lesbian musicians making it sing. Thanks for all you and Mari did for Jennifer."

It was news to me that *Jennifer* was a lesbian movie. We hadn't read the script or watched any of it except for our one scene in the bar. And I certainly hadn't realized Debbie knew Mari and I were lesbians, if indeed that word applied to us—we never used words; none of the words made sense. Was it that obvious, did that mean that everyone knew? I couldn't figure out how Debbie would've guessed—until later, when I remembered our onstage kiss at the Black Cat, that moment when every dream seemed to rest in our hands.

My mother said, "What lesbian musicians does she mean? Were there other musicians in the movie?"

"I have no idea what she's talking about," I said.

"*Jennifer* is a lesbian movie? Debbie didn't tell me that when we met in person. Did you know it was a lesbian movie?"

"Nope."

"It really sounds like she's talking about you and Mari," said my mother.

I could very easily picture my mother, if she found out about me and Mari, calling Yevgenia: "They sleep over at your place all the time, I just thought you should know!" Mari had told me she would never come out to Yevgenia, who was an affable but observant Georgian Orthodox. They were all they had, Mari said. She would never risk that.

Panicked, I said, "I barely know Debbie, I've met her like twice, how would she know that about me?"

"I don't know, you tell me—that's obviously the impression she got. She sent you a rainbow balloon! Why would she send a rainbow balloon if she thinks you aren't a lesbian?"

"I mean—why would anyone ever send *anyone* a rainbow balloon?"

But my mother saw something, and her expression gentled. "You don't have to lie to me," she said. "I wouldn't be mad."

I felt a helpless release. "I can't talk about it," I said.

"OK. OK. Hey," she added, "would you want to talk to your father about it?"

"Ah—no."

"He's doing so well, though," she said. "He has a boyfriend, Ted something. A doctor, I think."

My father had never mentioned a boyfriend to me, had not actually come out to me. "I don't think I'm supposed to know that," I said. "None of this is any of your business, OK? Why are you always so nosy?"

"I'm not *nosy*," she said, "just everyone in this family keeps secrets, so sometimes, yes, I have to ask questions."

"It's not just asking questions. You're telling me things I don't want to know, you're messing with my life and Mari's life."

"I'm not messing with anything!"

"Just because you're lonely," I said, standing, heat high in my face, "doesn't mean you can fuck with other people. Leave us alone!" My mother looked petrified, and I ran out of the apartment and downstairs. Rattled, desperate for solace, I walked the fifteen minutes through Mount Pleasant to Mari's building.

SO MANY TIMES afterward, I traced back from what happened at Mari's apartment that afternoon, as if reversing the story in my head could reverse the actual events. If only Debbie hadn't sent the balloon, if only I hadn't said those things to my mom, if only I'd gone for a walk in Rock Creek Park instead of meandering over to Mari's. If only I hadn't, if only I hadn't, if only I hadn't. But what happened happened, and then Mari broke up with me, and that was the end of the Maidenheads, the end of me as I knew myself then.

Over time, I thought about it so often and with such anguish that my brain seemed to construct a protective seal. When I approached the memory of our breakup, I would find myself softly but insistently bounced away. And yet somehow I was never not thinking about it, never not hating myself for what I'd done.

In the days and weeks after we broke up, the August weather turned cruelly hot. My mother took me shopping for extra-long dorm room sheets and sandals to wear in the communal shower. I worked double shifts at the coffee shop and went for long runs at night, trying to bludgeon myself into non-thought, non-feeling. I didn't call Mari, didn't go to her house, avoided her street, eventually avoided her entire neighborhood. Every day I woke up crying, as if I'd been crying through my dreams.

The weekend before classes started, my father took me out to dinner at a nice restaurant near the AU campus where he got a faculty discount. He was wearing what I thought of as his professor drag, tan leather vest over a flannel shirt and corduroy trousers. He ordered two glasses of wine "for me," he said, and winked at the server, then passed one across the table. I didn't want it, but I felt obliged and drank it, quickly because we weren't talking very much.

After our food came out, my dad stroked his beard and said, "That's a very nice dress." It was a dress I despised, a denim smock with large colorful buttons in places where buttons didn't belong. "You look like a girl from the '70s."

I was already tipsy, my lips coated and my head reeling. "Well, I'm not a girl from the '70s," I said. "I'm not even really a girl at all." I didn't know where it came from or what I meant. I just hated the way he was looking at me, I hated feeling observed and categorized.

"Oh," he said, sounding surprised, displeased.

"Dad, are you gay?" I asked abruptly.

He glanced at my empty wineglass, and I felt a coursing shame. He stroked his beard again and began a long disquisition on what departments to avoid as I picked a major.

I moved onto campus and started classes, everything feeling pointless and junior in comparison with what I imagined myself doing in an alternate universe where Mari and I were recording, performing, touring. In October, *Jennifer's Not There* premiered at a few theaters in DC. The *Washington City Paper* review was headlined, "Take a Seat, Fellas: This Jennifer's Not for You," and began, "Usually when a film begins with a beautiful stewardess lying dead on a bed, we know where things are headed. *Jennifer's Not There* takes viewers in some strange directions, while—not to give too much away—likely alienating the usual masculine audience for most thrillers." The review in the *Washington Blade*, one of DC's gay newspapers, was even harsher, describing the film's "retro gay-panic schlock," including a "messy stew of negative tropes, from the violent death of bisexual-coded Jennifer to the evil masculine lesbian who kills her." The *City Paper* article didn't mention us, but the *Blade* story did: "In a divey bar scene, the directors feature a just-below-the-radar punk duo from DC trussed out in, of all things, ripped-up prom dresses. It's a transparent—and exploitative, given the young age of the performers—attempt to garner credibility with the LGBT community that has, as a whole, rejected the film." With the soundtrack out, "Forgotten" got some play on college radio, including the AU station, WVAU—and that was even without us promoting it, going on tour, recording the EP! If we'd done that, what might've happened? It was impossible to know, and I was making every effort not to think about it: drinking too much at college parties, fucking random women and occasionally, with some private surprise, men.

I wouldn't have seen the movie at all except that my mother begged me, and I was feeling guilty about a long list of things having to do with her. One hungover Saturday, we went to a matinee at the cinema on E Street. Even in my bleary state I could tell it was a terrible film, with flat dialogue and wooden stereotypes: Jennifer, the slutty and duplicitous bi femme; her motorcycle-driving, tattooed butch killer. But none of that mattered to me. It was a train wreck in a distant country; I was numb.

About halfway through the movie, the detective entered a smoky bar and the camera panned back, revealing Mari and me onstage in our prom dresses. My mom grabbed my arm and whistled at the screen. "You look *so beautiful*," she said. She was trying so hard in those days, she had read books on supporting your gay teen, and I would hear recycled words and phrases, plus an insistence on my physical beauty, *just as you are*. But when I looked at myself onscreen, I saw that I was hideous. My hair stuck out in odd ways, catching the light—I'd refused a comb beforehand. My body looked patched together, disproportionate, like something collaged from cutout magazine pictures: legs dangling long, shoulders protruding like bony wings, the sliced-up dress wrapped around me like an unraveling towel. Only my face was recognizable—that old pale flat featureless face—but with my mouth open to sing, it looked like I was screaming.

The me onstage seemed aware of its own monstrousness. My eyes kept shifting to the camera, and I scrunched the hem of the dress over and over. The director had told me to stop fiddling, but I hadn't been able to. He'd given us matching electric guitars, very large to make us look even smaller and younger. I didn't know how to play guitar, and you could tell, but Mari held hers expertly. She looked perfect, of course. On her stockier, more muscled form, the dress did what we'd hoped: sang its own song about bodies and clothes and what happened when they didn't fit. With her eyes shut, blue light smoothing her face and streaking her hair, she was a fury, an angel, a beautiful boy.

After a minute, the shot changed. The detective crossed the room, the song subsided, and Mari was gone.

6

WHEN I SNUCK into my mother's fourth-floor apartment after Mari's party, the kitchen and living room were lit only by the orangish streetlights that glowed in through her gauzy old-lady half-curtains. But I had walked this path in the dark so often I knew every bump in the carpet, every cabinet corner grabbing out for my shoulder bag. I tiptoed through the living room and down the hall to my old bedroom, where I closed the door and switched on the light.

I found paper in my old desk and tore off a note—"Sorry, missed my train, needed to stay, sorry, Jamie"—which I placed just outside her door. I had delayed peeing for too long, and now I had to use the bathroom we shared, right across the hall. I didn't flush, to avoid waking them. Back in my room, my futon was folded up, but I was expert at sliding it open slowly so the mechanism wouldn't squeak. I found a blanket and pillow in the closet and curled up to sleep in my underpants.

In the morning, I woke to my mother's bedroom door creaking open, then her voice calling back into her room, "I think Jamie is here?" Someone went into the bathroom, flushed immediately, flushed again a few minutes later. Then the coffee machine, fridge door opening, voices in the kitchen, and finally the apartment door closing and a vacuous silence.

Relieved of the need to get up and be apologetic, I lay in bed, absorbing the familiarity of my room, which my mother had barely changed since I was in high school: My old boxy stereo on the bureau, looking like an antique now, its lights dim and dusty. The desk, which still had in its top drawer a snapped hair tie twisted with a few black strands. The futon where Mari and I would lie for hours, playing our favorite albums over and over until the songs broke into structures and drew their patterns inside our head. Where we'd fucked hundreds of times, trying to keep quiet late at night, her hand hard on my mouth.

As well as two of my mother's old flower paintings, I noticed new framed pictures on the walls: a boat, a New England–looking fall landscape. Michael let her take home the art people paid to frame, then never picked up. Their store mostly served inhabitants of the new Adams Morgan condos who wanted expensive-looking frames for their cheap mass-produced art, the kind of art people bought to hang in boardrooms and hotel lobbies. I had said that out loud once or twice, including to Michael's face at Christmas, when he walked out without another word.

I pulled on my jeans and went into the living room. "Out for a walk, back soon," read my mother's note on the table, and I could sense her unhappiness in the jagged script. I made tea, watched squirrels play in the branches outside the living room windows, heard the donkey-like bray out my bedroom window that I'd been told years ago was the DC zoo's solitary adult male tiger, a lonely long-distance call issued to any potential tiger buddies passing through the greater metro area. I checked out the books on my mother's bedside table, a biography of Eleanor Roosevelt and a detective novel set in Regency England. I shuffled through her closet, the sweaters folded over hangers, winter clothes separated by a cedar block, three of her father's oxford shirts she'd never been able to throw away.

Smelling her lavender lotion under the cedar, I felt tender toward my mother, toward our time together in this apartment. It hadn't been easy, but we had been a team. If I kept the baby, we'd be a team as well: we'd share half-awake conversations over breakfast, watch movies together, take late-night walks when neither of us could sleep. We would never be alone—*I* would never be alone. *Single mom, single kid*, I thought, remembering what Mari had said once. And although "mom" felt alien as a term for myself, I could still hear the respect in her words.

I hadn't eaten since the nachos at Mari's house, and as I stood facing my mother's closet, I felt sick, like someone was pulling a string up the back of my throat. I coughed and then retched. I went into the bathroom, where I sat for a long time on the toilet seat, hand pressed to my mouth, before I retched again and spat a clot of vomit into the sink.

"Jamie?" my mother called. I hadn't heard them come in. "Jamie, are you OK?"

"I'm fine!"

"Can I get you some water?" In a minute, her hand ventured around the door holding a glass. I drank it, but it made me feel worse, sloshy. I came slowly out of the bathroom and, hand on the wall, traced my way to the living room couch, where I lay down and kicked the crocheted blanket over my feet.

My mother and Michael stood over me, fresh-faced from their walk. Unlike my father and me, my mother is very tall, built like the Connecticut prep school field hockey forward she once was. But there's hesitancy in her movements, as if she's not quite sure she deserves to occupy the space she physically takes up. She wears her dark hair short, a practical cut she hasn't changed in decades. Her clothes too are functional: once a year, she picks out four button-down shirts in neutral tones, three pairs of black slacks, and a new pair of thick-soled walking shoes. She has a pretty, shy face—she's in her late fifties but looks younger—and you can be surprised sometimes by the exuberance of her laugh.

Michael, by contrast, is not a hesitant presence: taller than my mom, broad-chested and handsome, with short white hair and bright blue eyes. Looming above me, he said to my mother, "Eileen, it's just what you were worried about."

"Oh, Michael. Hi, Jamie," she said.

"Hi. Could I have some crackers?" I asked.

"We need to talk," Michael said to me.

"Or some toast, or . . ." I said.

"I'll make toast," said my mother, and disappeared into the kitchen.

Michael sat down hard in my mother's balding velvet armchair, capsizing a stack of embroidered cushions. "So," he said, "wild night last night?"

Talking felt risky—like opening my mouth might spill everything out again. I pressed two fingers against my dry lips and spoke through them. "I just went to a show. I'd meant to go back to Baltimore, but I missed the last train and didn't have anywhere else to stay. But I wasn't drinking."

"So you're just sick today for no reason at all?" He leaned forward, setting elbows on his huge square knees.

"Michael!" my mother called from the kitchen.

"Eileen, I'm trying to make sure she's OK," he yelled back, then turned to me. "Seriously, what happened?"

"I really, really want some toast," I said.

"Butter?" called my mother. "Jam?"

"Because you can tell us," Michael said. "We're not angry. Just concerned."

"Plain," I called to the kitchen.

"Like Michael said," she said, coming out with the toast on a plate, "we were worried. Are you sure you're OK?"

"Seriously, Jamie. Are you drinking again?" Michael said. After college, it had become impossible to conceal how much I was falling apart. I'd spent the whole four years trying to convince myself that I was OK with a life that didn't include Mari or singing. I majored in psychology—my father pleased but startled every time he saw me in the department hallways—told my teachers I was planning to get a social work degree. But once I graduated, that future started to look absurd. I didn't like people—how could I be a social worker? I applied to and got fired from a string of menial jobs, drank too much, ran up credit card debt, bounced between different awful girlfriends, told everyone who'd listen that music stopped being good after the '90s anyway, everything overproduced, corporate radio, etc., etc.

Eventually, having squandered all other bolt-holes, I moved back into my room in my mother's apartment. She cared for me ferociously: booked therapy appointments, forced me out on healthful walks, bought me self-help books that I lost or left out in the park to get rained on. My father didn't call the entire year, saying later that he "didn't want to be an added source of stress." Michael clomped in to fill the space, well-meaning but repulsive, offering to read my résumé and give me "interviewing tips." I got so sick of all three of them that I took the first job I could find in Baltimore, just to escape.

"I'm really not drinking," I told Michael. It seemed funny, and I laughed, woozily. "Look, OK, I'm pregnant. I just found out."

"You what?" said my mother. She was standing by Michael's chair and now put her hand on his shoulder.

"Peter and I broke up about a month ago, but we were still having sex, and yeah, it seems that now I am pregnant."

"You and Peter broke up a *month* ago?"

"Irreconcilable differences," I said. "Mutual. Amicable." I couldn't stop laughing; they were staring at me in horror.

"Are you still living with him?" she said.

"I moved out. I didn't know how to tell you."

"You've been living somewhere new this entire time and you didn't tell me? You're pregnant and you *broke up with Peter*?" Now she let go of Michael and sat down on the couch next to me, hands limp in her lap.

"I'm sorry," I said. "Is there more toast?" Somehow my plate was already empty.

"I'll make it," said my mother, and she stood up, paused on her feet for a moment, then went into the kitchen. I could hear her shock like the distant aliveness of an electronic device.

Michael ran a hand through his hair. "You know," he said, "Eileen hasn't had an easy month."

"I know."

"She doesn't ask for a lot, your mother. She doesn't deserve—"

"*I know*, Michael. Sorry for your loss, by the way."

He blinked and smoothed the wrinkled knees of his khakis. "Thanks," he said. "It's been awful, actually. So what are you going to do?"

"For right now, I'm going to stay in DC a few more days."

"With the pregnancy, I mean," he said.

"You're staying in DC?" my mother said. She came out with the second piece of toast. "Why? Did you lose your job?"

"I didn't *lose my job*! No, Mari invited me to band practice on Tuesday. And—I'm thinking about keeping the pregnancy." It was the first time I'd said it aloud, and it felt startlingly true.

My mother and Michael glanced at each other. In my mother's eyes, I saw apology—she was embarrassed, she was trying to reassure him that I wouldn't always be like this.

"I won't stay here, obviously," I said right away.

"You saw *Mari*?" my mother asked.

"It was her band performing."

"I wish you'd told me you were seeing Mari," she said. "I wish you'd told me any of this! You don't have to hide everything from me."

"I'm telling you now," I said.

"After the fact. Like always."

"It seemed like it wasn't the best time," I said, and my mother sighed.

"I'm sorry," she said. "I shouldn't have told you not to come."

"It's really OK, I get it," I said. Michael had, in his version of discretion, taken out his phone and begun scrolling.

"But you're pregnant. You're *pregnant*," my mother repeated, as if teaching herself the fact. "You should stay."

"No, I know it's not a great time. I'll be OK."

"Where will you go?"

"Thought I'd pop over and see Dad and Sally, actually. Meet the new sibling in utero." I knew I couldn't return to Baltimore or I'd lose my nerve before Tuesday. I wasn't in touch with any of my old DC friends; plus, they were all friends with Mari too, and I didn't want her to find out I was staying for her. I didn't want to see my dad, especially didn't want to see Sally, but it was the only real option.

"Oh!" said my mother. "Well, of course you should do that, if you want to."

"Only for a couple of days."

"No, of course. Of course." But she looked hurt. I retreated shamefacedly to my room, toast slice in hand, to dress, pack, and fold the futon back up. Once I was done, the room felt several sizes larger. I could imagine my mother coming in later and letting out a grateful sigh. Picturing this, I felt more energetic, steeled for a daunting step. I hadn't seen my father since Christmas, for our semiannual coffee date: standard questions and answers, his covert watch-checks, $100 in new twenties handed over at the end, my regular payment for not making other, more baffling demands.

Out in the living room, Michael had his arm around my mother as she pressed her fingers into the corners of her eyes. "Jamie, are you absolutely sure it's a good idea to see Mari right now?" she asked.

"I should go," I said. "I'll text you from Dad's, OK?" I bent down for a kiss, and she sighed and accepted it, then leaned back into Michael's meaty shoulder.

ON A BENCH in the park across from my mom's building, I dialed the only number I still knew from memory, the landline at my childhood home in Maryland. My father picked up, as always sounding like he'd forgotten he had a child. "Jamie?"

"Hey, I'm in DC and I'd like to see you guys. Actually, I also need a place to stay for a couple of nights. I'm pregnant? So."

Long pause. "Where are you?"

"I'm at Mom's, but I'm about to leave."

"I'll be at the station in half an hour," he said, and hung up.

It started to drizzle as I walked across the bridge over Rock Creek to the Woodley Park Metro stop. By the time my Red Line train went aboveground after Union Station, it was pouring. Water sluiced down the windows like a drive-through car wash. Wind rocked the train, and I hugged my bag close. Outside the Silver Spring Metro station, I jumped over a chute of water in the gutter to find my father's Subaru in the spot where he'd always waited to pick me up for our weekends in high school. When I got in, AC frigid on my wet skin, my father lifted his arms for a hug, then, realizing it wouldn't work in the narrow space of the front seat, swiveled away to watch for cars coming up on his left side. He was wearing the old fisherman sweater he always wore on weekends, and with his beard and balding head, he looked like a skinnier Ernest Hemingway—or "professor bear," as Mari used to call him.

In college, when it became clear my father wasn't planning to open up, my mother had told me what she knew. The ambitious eldest son from a large family of Scotch-Swedish immigrant-farmers, my father entered the Foreign Service in 1978, straight out of SUNY New Paltz. A few months into his first posting in Malaysia, word got back to his supervisors that he had visited a local gay bar. Homosexuality was deemed a security risk then—at best, you were shifty and un-American; at worst, vulnerable to blackmail. The consul general didn't fire my father, but revoked his security clearance, and he quit rather than face a lifetime in low-level visa-stamp positions, telling his family he hadn't liked living overseas.

The following year, he met my mother, an earnest New England girl looking for something real, and within two years, they were married. By then, he was a PhD student in psychology at AU, where my mother was getting a master's degree in education (never used). He didn't tell her about his Foreign Service experience until after I was born, and then he described it to her as youthful experimentation. She didn't question it until I was fourteen and out of the blue—at least to her—he sat her down on the back deck and told her he needed to date men.

After the divorce, he did date men, but then he married Sally, something my mother took as a personal insult. It had been a source of comfort that my father hadn't just rejected her but all women, and I thought she'd even enjoyed having a gay ex-husband—there was some cachet to it in those *Will & Grace*, *Sex and the City* years. Once he and Sally were together, I felt angry on my mother's behalf as well as my own. He'd misled us in one direction, and now potentially his correction had been false as well. But there was no way of knowing for sure because he never told us anything.

"Your mother called," my father now said in the car, watching the road. "She said to say she loves you."

I was silent, and he pulled into traffic for the short drive into east Silver Spring. When I was a kid here, this had been a largely Ethiopian neighborhood, with signs in Amharic above coffee shops and restaurants. But the year I moved out for college, the Discovery building was built in downtown Silver Spring. Now the area was unrecognizably bustling, with hipster cafés and a fancy gym next to the old laundromat. My father turned off Georgia Avenue onto our street, and I leaned back and shut my eyes. I'd believed as a child that I could identify our street with my eyes closed, by the rhythm of tire bumps, the pattern of light drumming through the trees onto my eyelids.

"Are you OK?" he said. "Feeling sick?"

"No—no, I'm fine," I said, and straightened up.

"Sally was sick all through the first trimester," he said, speaking fast as he pulled up in front of the house. He wasn't used to such tight proximity with me. "Did I tell you it's a boy? She has all kinds of ideas for names. Lingonberry, I believe, is the most recent."

I didn't say anything. We opened our doors into the pouring rain, and he gestured me up onto the porch. At the door, he paused. "You can stay as long as you need to, you know."

"OK," I said, and watched his smile soften as he reached for the doorknob.

My parents had moved from AU grad student housing to our Silver Spring bungalow right before I was born. But I had not been over since Sally moved in, and it was now a completely different interior. Sally had painted the living room pink and created a gallery wall of framed vintage postcards and photos above her new blue velvet couch—this I recognized from her Instagram feed, a frequent selfie backdrop. She had hired contractors to take down the dividing wall between the living room and the small dining room and kitchen, making it all one open airy space looking out through sliding glass doors to the deck and backyard.

Sally herself sat at the dining room table with her bare feet up on a chair and her belly cramped between her thighs and the table edge, reading a magazine. A long black braid hung over one shoulder, her face wasn't made up, and she wore yoga pants and the "Pregnant AF" sweatshirt, one sleeve now streaked with what looked like hummus. Sally's parents were Vietnamese immigrants, and she'd grown up in Falls Church. Since meeting my dad on a dating website several years ago, she'd launched an Etsy store selling handmade, hand-painted ceramic plates ("SalPlates"). The plates were thick cream stoneware painted with cute animals: querulous llamas or perky penguins in bowties. Sally also painted animals on canvas, and I'd noticed a few already in the house: a walrus wearing a barrister's wig just inside the front door, a shark in surfer gear behind the couch, a pair of bride-and-groom otters above the dining room table. Her Instagram presence was elaborate: Valencia-filtered timer selfies of Sally wheel-throwing a plate, tendrils of hair falling into her face; Sally in overalls painting the last whisker on a feisty cat; Sally in a cute sundress sitting in the garden eating sliced tomatoes off a dolphin plate (I had hate-read her page more deeply than I'd ever admit).

Over the weeks since the pregnancy announcement, I'd noticed Sally's body was less prominent in selfies, and when she pushed back the chair to stand, I was surprised by how large her belly was, pendulous on her slight frame. My father rushed over, unrecognizably eager and nervous, to help her up. With an arm around her waist, he kissed the top of her head, then turned back to me with a struck grin.

I moved toward Sally slowly in hopes of evading a hug (her hands had touched my father's penis). We stood just apart in the dining room, squared off like two pregnant chess pawns. Sally smiled and said, "Congratulations, Jamie."

"Oh! Thanks?" I said, surprised to be treated like an ordinary pregnant person.

"Sorry," Sally said, very nervous, "was I not supposed to know?" She shot my dad a helpless look; he placed a hand on the small of her back.

"No, it's fine. It's just, no one has congratulated me about it."

"OK," she said. "How are you feeling? I had the worst time during the first trimester."

"I'm OK," I said. "Tired, but OK."

"Oh gosh, it's awful. I was throwing up all the time. Would a sandwich help? Your dad makes a mean turkey sandwich."

I had never seen my father prepare food that wasn't either a baked potato, a frozen waffle, or mac and cheese from a box. "I'm good," I said. "Maybe I could just lie down somewhere?"

"Well, I'd show you to your room, but you don't need me to do that." My old room was right off the dining room, four feet from where I currently stood. "We want to use it for the nursery, but it's available for another"—and Sally pretended to check an invisible watch on her wrist, then glanced back up with an embarrassed laugh, as if to say she knew exactly how cheesy this action was and yet found herself compelled to do it by the awkwardness of this encounter—"fifteen weeks, give or take."

I dashed gratefully for my room and shut the door behind me. You still had to lift the handle to nudge it over the threshold, but otherwise, it was as fully transformed as the living room. A white wooden crib stood in the corner where my old desk had been, and next to it a white wooden changing table with a changing-pad top printed with butterflies. The walls, once pink floral wallpaper stabbed by a thousand poster pins, had been stripped and painted a smooth butter yellow. Someone, presumably Sally, had painted elephants parading around the top edge of the wall, each holding the last one's tail in its trunk, party hats propped on their sloping foreheads. On the rug sat an inflated air mattress, made up neatly with a duvet, two towels folded at the foot. I felt disoriented and also a layered jealousy: Sally was so obviously going to be a great mom. I couldn't imagine myself ever creating a room like this.

At the window, I tugged up the rattan blinds to see the backyard, where new vegetable plots—Sally's, I'd seen them in her photos—were shielded by mesh tents, everything rain-slicked and neon green. The catalpa tree at the bottom of the yard still had the hollow I'd used as a catacomb for cicada husks, but it looked much higher than I remembered it being. When I opened the closet to stow my bag, I found a strip of my old pink wallpaper on the back wall, nearly hidden by winter coats. Up on a shelf was a long plastic box, and I pulled it down. It held all the tapes I'd left behind when I packed for college, a mixture of albums I'd outgrown and albums I couldn't listen to because the Mari association was too intense: the *Bodyguard* soundtrack next to my dad's old Shangri-Las compilation and the Sleater-Kinney tape I'd worn out from listening to "One More Hour" on repeat after Mari and I broke up.

From the dining room, I heard Sally say, "Was that weird, I was trying not to be weird," and my father's voice, low and comforting, not a voice I recognized from his parenting repertoire, "Sweetie, you did your best, don't worry about her." I put the tape box back and pressed my hand against the pink wallpaper strip, stippled and cool to the touch.

7

THAT NIGHT, I emailed Jeremy to ask if I could work remotely for a few days, family situation, and because Jeremy prided himself on being a family-friendly type of boss, he said yes, provided I came in for the weekly all-staff meeting on Wednesday morning. So Monday and Tuesday, I worked on my laptop at the kitchen counter, looking out through the sliding glass doors into the backyard. In the afternoons, a mother deer and two fawns leapt over a low spot in the fence and picked their way through the tall grass to Sally's vegetable garden, where the mesh covering provided an ineffective defense system. The deer were everywhere now, my father told me later, climate change or something; two neighborhood kids had gotten Lyme disease from deer ticks. "You should shoo them away," he said, but I felt like I was the intruder, not the deer family, and I left them alone.

The house was quiet during the day. My father worked at an AU psych lab where he led studies on facial emotional recognition (a specialization my mom often cackled over, bitterly). Sally spent mornings at her studio in Northeast DC, then returned in the afternoon to process online orders at her desk in the renovated basement. If we passed near the bathroom or in the kitchen, she smiled shyly, but didn't initiate conversation. We ate dinner together at the dining room table, me at my childhood spot in the middle between Sally at the foot and my father at the head. She cooked tiny healthy meals, heavy on the quinoa, served on plates she hadn't been able to sell, including a full set of six painted with a boy porcupine offering a girl porcupine a valentine and a box of chocolates.

"He has a boner," she told me at dinner one night, pointing out a quill located between the boy porcupine's legs. "One of the commenters said something and I couldn't unsee it." My father giggled, a sound I had never heard before.

I didn't mention to my dad or Sally that I was practicing with Mari, just told them I had plans on Tuesday night. Mari texted me the details: they practiced in the basement of a house in Takoma Park, the Maryland suburb adjacent to Silver Spring, a ten-minute bus ride from my dad's. "Amanda can't make it, night shift at the hospital," she added, and the fact that she mentioned it sped my pulse.

Before I could leave, I had to proofread the whole paper, already laid out in preparation for going to the printer that night. Usually this took all day and much of the evening, but I was working faster out of the office. At 8:02, I entered my final changes, then emailed Jeremy to say I was signing off.

"We miss you!" he wrote. "See you tomorrow for the meeting?" I rode the bus to the Takoma Metro station and got briefly lost looking for the house. Around 8:30, I rang the bell at a dilapidated scalloped-shingle Victorian on a quiet street, a rusty kid's bike turned over in a yard scrabbly with dandelions and wild strawberry vine. The door opened on a burly bald man about ten years older than me wearing a Dischord Records T-shirt and sweatpants. "You're Jamie? Everyone's downstairs," he said, and shuffled off into a green-lit kitchen. I heard music, loud and jangly, through a door across from the entryway. I opened the door, stepped into the sound.

Basement practice areas have a common look and smell, and I felt like I was meeting an old friend as I jogged down carpeted stairs and into the large, overpacked space. To reach the practice area, I had to walk by shelves and piles of family detritus: dented plastic sleds, Halloween decorations spilling out of a bin, storage bags of clothes and winter coats, a broken hobby horse, dusty golf clubs. Toward the back of the basement, where Mari, Andrew, and Freddie were set up, someone had stapled soundproof padding to the walls and the ceiling, overlaid with posters from '80s and '90s hardcore shows: Fugazi and Marginal Man at d.c. space, Rites of Spring at Food for Thought. A cardboard cutout of Ronald Reagan loomed over Mari's shoulder, cock and balls scrawled on his cheek in Sharpie. I found a metal folding chair stacked in the corner near a suspended punching bag and pulled it over to listen.

They were halfway through a song I recognized from Saturday, one of the slower and trickier songs, with a shifting rhythm. Mari was singing, but quietly: she didn't push her voice when she didn't need to. She had on black jeans and a black sweater, sleeves pushed up. Her short hair was wet and combed neatly back. I'd always known Mari to be confident, but when we were kids, she'd had a wild bravado that occasionally crash-landed into depressive self-doubt. Tonight she looked calm, like all the whiplash feelings had finally coalesced into a solid hard form.

The song required very fast, repetitive bowing from Freddie, creating sort of a high-pitched drone. She would get the pattern, then lose it and curse into her chin rest. Andrew wasn't helping, his beats loping a touch too slow. Mari tried to sing through it, force them along, but they kept dropping off. Finally, she said, "Andrew, my dude, you're the problem, can I just—?"

"Be my guest," he said, standing with an irritated smile. Mari sat on his stool, uncaring, and played the part for him, perky drummer boy with her back straight, elbows out.

"Try it again," she said. He shook out his shoulders like a wet dog and sat back down. They settled into the song after a couple of bumps and got all the way through.

"That's it, you got it that time," Mari said. Turning, she saw me, and blinked with what I thought was surprise. But her voice was steady when she said, "Glad you could make it." Freddie waved, and Andrew said, "Howdy," and lifted a drumstick in salute.

"Want a glass of water or anything?" Mari said. "The kitchen upstairs is OK to use, if you don't mind running into Earl—you may have seen him upstairs, it's his house."

"I'm good," I said. I didn't want to leave, not even for a minute. "What are you guys working on tonight?"

"We're hacking our way through a few songs. Mind if we just keep going?" And they started playing again, first another go-round on the song Andrew was struggling with, then a few others I recognized from the show. Mari bossed Freddie and Andrew through their parts, causing some minor stress. Freddie smiled extra hard a couple times; Andrew snapped back once, "I *did* fucking practice this, Mari!" But for the most part, they took it well, and I could see how long they'd all been playing together, the accumulated ease. After they tried starting one song seven times without getting the entrances right, Mari lay on the floor and yelled, "IT'S NEVER GOING TO WORK." Freddie poked her with a toe, Andrew said, "Oops, we broke Mari," and they all laughed.

Around nine, they took a break. Andrew and Mari went upstairs for a cigarette, and Freddie placed her violin and bow carefully on the weight bench, then collapsed in a folding chair next to me. Freddie's shaved brown head was shiny with sweat, and she had a delicate gold septum piercing I hadn't noticed before. She wore pink cutoff shorts and a black T-shirt sliced along the hem and collar. Tattooed vines ran up and down her strong, angular arms, purple and pink flowers blooming in the hollow of one elbow, along the back of the other bicep, above both wrists. As she scrunched down in the chair to rest her head sideways on its back, I saw the gray callus on her neck where the violin rubbed.

"I was up all night," she said, eyes closed, "and not for fun reasons. Liya, my four-year-old, keeps waking up with nightmares."

"What kind of nightmares?"

"She won't tell us. She just wakes up screaming but then is too frightened to say what's going on," said Freddie. She had an even, precise way of talking, as if she were reading from a page. "Dani thinks it's this wallpaper that Liya's dad put up at his place. Row upon row of grinning clowns."

"Oh no!"

"Oh yes. He's a nice guy, but sometimes . . ."

"What's it like having a kid on your own?" I asked. I'd never met a parent my age before; I brimmed with questions.

"Well, Dani and I live together," Freddie said. "But in terms of not living with my ex-husband, it's actually the best. I got married really young, before I really knew I was gay. Like I knew, but I didn't *know* know. I married an Ethiopian guy, someone I grew up going to church with in Rockville. But Liya was the only part of the marriage that felt right. We got divorced a few months after she was born. And then I met Dani—through Mari, of course."

"Really? How?"

Freddie laughed. "I'd known Mari for years from punk shows, starting back when I was at UMD. We always gravitated toward each other because we both came from immigrant families, although I was born here and Mari wasn't. After the divorce, I was home with Liya a lot more, and Mari started coming over and making dinner, helping out. She was in a rough place too; Yevgenia had died the year before, and then she and Amanda had this spectacularly messy breakup. So we started playing together. We'd put Liya down, turn on the fan really loud in her room, and then play in the living room. One night, Mari brought over Dani—they worked for the same dog-walking company at one point—and that was kind of it."

"I thought Mari hated babies," I said. Mari's cousin had had a baby while we were in high school, and once, Mari's mom forced her to babysit. Mari returned looking traumatized. "It shat on my hand," she told me.

"Oh yes," Freddie said. She snorted. "For sure, she was only tolerating Liya because she wanted to write songs with a violin part. If I'd done jazz saxophone in high school, like my dad wanted me to, I never would've seen Mari again. Same with Amanda—once Mari decided she should be our guitarist, it was like, *what* devastating breakup?"

"Is it hard balancing a kid with the band?" I asked, pushing down all the questions I had about Amanda and Mari.

"Oh no, don't ask *that*," said Freddie, smiling. "The ultimate chick-in-a-band question."

"Well—I'm actually pregnant, so I was wondering."

"No way!" she said. She sat up, looked at me head-on for the first time. I could sense warmth and curiosity streaming out as if I'd unlocked some private sea gate. "How far along?"

"Not far. I think maybe five weeks?"

"How are you feeling?"

"Fine, I guess. Tired a lot."

"First trimester is *tough*. But you'll survive. It gets easier, until it gets hard again. Ginger tea really helped my nausea. To answer your question, it's hard, but it's doable. I work full-time for USAID and travel a lot, so my life is already crazy. I couldn't do it without Dani and my ex and my parents, who've been remarkably chill about the whole thing."

"My ex isn't really in the picture," I said. "And my parents don't live near me, and probably wouldn't be helpful if they did."

"You'll be OK," she said, with great authority. "People have babies in all kinds of situations. You adjust, the baby adjusts. And—I know I'm not supposed to say this—but babies are the fucking best."

It felt like she was anointing me, and I ached to hear more. Somehow I had forgotten that mothers could be queer. "Did your back really hurt during the first trimester?" I asked. "Because mine is just . . ." I was about to say more when I heard Andrew's boots clomping down the stairs.

He and Mari walked in, smelling of smoke and summer heat. Freddie placed a gentle hand on my shoulder—"Acupuncture. But we'll talk more, OK?"—then urged herself up from the folding chair and went to get her violin and bow.

"A little kid crossed the street to yell at us for smoking," Mari said as she sat back down on her stool behind the keyboard. "Said we were contributing to global warming."

"What did you say?" I asked.

"Um, 'Sorry'? What was I supposed to say?"

"Kids are scary now," Andrew said. "They know we fucked up their lives and they're *pissed*."

"They should be pissed," Freddie said, smiling into her violin as she tuned up.

"I told her Obama would fix climate change and everything would be OK," Mari said. "Maybe she'll believe it. Hey, Jamie—we need to run through 'Forgotten' tonight, any chance you'd want to sing lead?"

Mari's tone was casual, but when I glanced over, I saw a subtle pull at her eyelid, her old twitch. I could feel a shift in the silence from Andrew and Freddie, both head down, making unnecessary adjustments to their instruments.

"I haven't sung in a really long time," I said. "I'm not sure I even can."

"Is that true? Or do you just not want to?" Again, her tone was extremely casual.

"Of course I *want* to," I said, and then, after a brief pause, "I'll try. I mean if no one minds."

Mari's smile came slow and smug. She turned to Freddie and Andrew. "Freddie, you do your usual part on the chorus, and I'll do Amanda's. Jamie's voice is a lot higher and brighter than mine, so for contrast, go kind of dark."

Andrew said, "You guys did it faster, right?"

"Yeah. Just let her set the tempo at the beginning. Come on up, Jamie."

I went to stand beside Mari's keyboard, Andrew and Freddie out of sight behind me. I pulled the mic stand closer and tried to unscrew the arm to adjust it, but on the uneven carpet, it wobbled and tipped. Mari leaned over and fixed it for me, laughing. I could tell she was enjoying my discomfort.

The concrete basement walls seemed to tighten around me. Mari was punishing me, I thought, reminding me I never would've had the chops to make it, even if we'd tried.

"You good?" Mari said.

"Yeah, just—" I said. I coughed, stuck my hands in my pockets, and bent shyly toward the mic. I'd sung "Forgotten" hundreds, probably thousands, of times. But I felt as uncertain as if I were leaning in for a first kiss. When I opened my mouth, I was unsure whether I'd be able to make a sound.

The day I got the rainbow balloon from Debbie, after the fight with my mother, I ran directly to Mari's apartment in Mount Pleasant. It wasn't a conscious decision, just need-propelled instinct. I thought she probably wouldn't be home. But when I climbed the back steps and yelled up to the kitchen window—the front-door buzzer was always broken—Mari yelled back, "It's open!"

I didn't want to see her anymore, didn't feel equipped, but now it was too late. I walked upstairs and into her kitchen: a rectangular room at the back of the building, which Yevgenia had painted yellow and decorated with philodendrons in baskets, onions from hooks, ropes of garlic and herbs. It always smelled wonderful, except on summer trash days when the dumpster in the alley below turned fetid. Above the wooden table floated a rainbow balloon like mine. Below it sat Mari, drinking Diet Coke from a can.

"You got the balloon too," I said. My voice sounded funny in my ears. "Did Yevgenia see it? Debbie outed us. And then my mom told me my dad has a boyfriend? Who is, of course, named *Ted*, what a fucking cliché, he probably has a single earring and a mustache."

"It'll be fine. What does it matter who your dad dates, anyway?"

I had expected a much more intense reaction, and this startled me out of my own thoughts. Sitting down across from Mari at the table, I leaned forward, hands in my pockets, to observe her. She was looking even worse than she had on tour. She hadn't cut her hair all year, and it was as long as I'd ever seen it, oily-dull and uncombed, a black gnarl rubber-banded on top of her head. Her skin was yellow with olive stripes under each eye. She didn't look back at me, just huddled deeper inside the black hoodie.

"What is going on with you?" I asked, frightened of her answer.

"Nothing."

"Stop it. Fucking tell me."

"It's not a big deal," she said. Then she began to cry. It was the first time I'd ever seen Mari cry, and I didn't realize she *was* crying at first because she didn't make any sounds, just shut her eyes hard, then lifted a hand to her face and bit a knuckle, the skin whitening around her teeth.

"Fuck, Mari," I said. I came around the table and knelt on the floor beside her, got my arms around her back, pressed my body as close to hers as the chair arms would allow. "What happened?"

She pulled me up and made me sit in the chair next to her. I felt her looking at me, appraising my reaction.

"You can't be weird about it, OK?" she said. Then she told me, drawing circles on the tabletop with a finger. While I was in Rome, Mari had, on a bored whim, gone alone to a senior class party—a fancy house in Upper Northwest, a rich kid with K Street lobbyist parents. None of the kids she knew from shows or her classes were there. With no one to talk to, she drank too much and went upstairs with a boy.

"Uh—why?" I asked, and Mari looked at me sharply.

"I wanted to make out with him," she said, like it should've been obvious. "You were away and I thought, maybe it's my only chance to kiss a boy, why not?"

He hadn't wanted to kiss, though. He'd pinned her on the bed and forced down her jeans, dragged down her underpants. Mari yelled and fought, but she was really drunk; it was the nightmare of running with sand legs. And no one came, although she'd seen people milling in the hallway outside. The new Strokes album was playing downstairs. Someone turned up the volume.

Afterward, the boy had been solicitous, gentle. He brought her a glass of water, Kleenex. He said, "I really enjoyed that. Thank you." Mari had been so frozen that she said, "You're welcome"—the words choked in the retelling. She left the party and walked home, all the way from Friendship Heights, hours in the dark. Then she had waited a month, through our whole tour, terrified she might be pregnant, convinced Yevgenia—a gynecologist—would intuit it somehow if she brought a pregnancy test into the apartment. She was only telling me now, she said, because it didn't matter anymore. She had gotten her period.

"So everything's fine," she said, voice flat. She swallowed the last of her Coke, then chucked the can across the kitchen into the sink, where it rattled around the drain.

I was remembering a time we'd gone to smoke cigarettes in Rock Creek Park and an animal emerged from the woods, a sharp-spined gray beast roaming its nose back and forth across the dirt. I'd thought it was a dog, and I'd laughed, "Hey cutie, hey lost dog." But Mari stepped in front of me, tucking me behind her. I could feel her bristling, daring the coyote to attack, until it trotted back into the trees. I'd watched Mari stare down skinheads at shows, drunk guys who called us dykes or yelled, "Make out! Make out!" And yet a boy—a *boy*!—had given her eyes this capsized look, left her chewing her knuckles like she was trying to gnaw out the bone.

"Who was he?" I asked. "Do I know him?"

"Um," she said, clearly displeased by the question, and said his name, Josh something. And I did know him; I'd had Spanish class with him. He existed on the outskirts of the popular-kid group. He wore T-shirts with Abercrombie and Express logos; his sweaters all had a single horizontal stripe across the chest. He'd done an in-class presentation on Machu Picchu, wearing a peaked hat with earflaps he told us his cousin had bought on a trip to Peru.

"We have to do something," I said. "Go to the police, tell people at school."

"James, I said 'You're welcome.' I can't go to the police. Anyway, it was ages ago now."

"We can't let him get away with this!"

She didn't reply, just let me nestle into her and stroked my hair with absent, dry hands. When I looked up, I could see her eyelid shivering, and I flattened it with my palm. "I'll kill him," I whispered. "I'll slash his tires, I'll take a shit on his porch. I'll call his parents and tell them he's a rapist."

"That's so stupid, what's the point?" she said. "Anyway, 'rapist,' I don't know. I went upstairs, right? I wanted to kiss him."

"Mari, no!" If she chose to go upstairs, tried to kiss him—did that mean she'd cheated on me, or wanted to? And I felt a grinding doubt: What if boys were what Mari really wanted? What if I were a disappointing half measure—boyish, not a real boy? "None of this is your fault. You're the victim here."

"Oh Jesus Christ, Jamie, I'm not a *victim*, OK? I knew I shouldn't have told you."

I couldn't respond, ambushed by the sick nameless dread that had stalked me all summer, the sense I wasn't enough to hold Mari, that I was losing her. And I couldn't lose Mari. If I ever lost Mari, I'd be lost forever myself. Fingers trembling, I stroked her cheek, and then I kissed the edge of her closed mouth. She opened her lips slightly, and I tasted her warm, stale breath. Finally, she kissed me back, our first real kiss since before I'd left for Rome. I felt an explosive relief that propelled me closer—now I was on her lap on the chair, one foot propped on the fridge behind her. Now I was pulling the rubber band out of her hair, looping it around my wrist, finger-combing her clumped curls, relief bursting out in laughter. *I can still have her, she's still mine, I'm still OK.*

"Why are you laughing?" she whispered.

"I just love you," I said.

"That doesn't change anything."

"I know," I said, but I wasn't sure what she meant. My hands climbed up under her shirt, brushing her nipples—Mari never wore bras. She pushed me back and I felt the terror again. But she took my hand, and we went into her bedroom. We lay down face-to-face on her twin bed as we'd done a thousand times before. My eyes crossed to focus, and her two eyes overlapped into one enormous eye, her eyebrows forming one long black ridge.

I stroked her shoulders, lifted her shirt. Mari lay still as I kissed down the blade of her hip. "He couldn't get the buttons," she'd said about Josh, and I knew she only had one pair of button-fly jeans; his hands had fumbled with the same buttons I now rapidly undid. My hands and mouth on her skin were frantic, desperate to stamp out his touch with mine, make him illegible. I kissed her everywhere I could imagine Josh's hands going, licked her skin. I bared her thighs; I placed my palm lightly over her cunt, gentle where he'd been rough.

I still felt Josh's ghostly trace, though, a boy-shaped space of cold air. He had been here, in a sense he was *still* here, and the more I thought about it, the more my hands pulsed hot. His hands where my hands were—the echo too tight, too close. I wanted to tear him out of her, out of us. I ventured one finger inside Mari, and she made a sound—I thought it was a good sound, a sound of pleasure, encouragement. But I could feel Josh's repulsive cock there as well, its movements twinned with mine, and again my rage throbbed. I twisted my fingers deep inside her, like I could claw him out. I did it again, and again, and again.

I've gone through these memories so many times, and I always stop right at that moment: my gasping need, my fury. But time didn't stop there. Instead, in the next moment, Mari leapt away from me on the bed. "Stop," she was saying. "Please, Jamie, please stop."

Her words echoed. It was possible, I realized—my ears seemed to be ringing—that she had already said them several times.

"Shit, Mari," I said, with immediate engulfing horror. "I'm so sorry."

"That wasn't what I wanted," she said stiffly. Her face was stark white.

I tried to put my arm around her, but she flinched up her shoulder—not to shove me off, but to shield herself. I whipped away my hands and crushed them between my knees.

Mari pulled up her underwear and buttoned her jeans, tugged her shirt down over her breasts. When she turned her face back to me, it had shed all vulnerability. "I didn't even want to *kiss* you," she said.

"I just did it to make you feel better because you were acting so weird. And then you *fuck me*?"

"I'm so, so sorry!" I said. And if there had been an opportunity, right then, to disappear myself permanently, I would've jumped at it. "I really didn't mean—"

"It's OK," she said. "It doesn't matter, I don't care. But you need to leave right now."

"Mari, no—please."

She found her stuffed bear under the pillow, plucked at its fur. "Go away, Jamie," she said, not looking at me.

After a long pause in which my body emptied of air, I forced myself to stand up from the bed, walk out of the room and down the back stairs. I sobbed openly the entire stumbling walk home, not even trying to cover my face, pressing my hands into my chest like I was pulling together torn skin. My mother was waiting in the living room under the rainbow balloon. "Jamie?" she said uncertainly when she saw me, but I pushed past her into my room and didn't come out again.

The phone rang around ten the next morning. I was still in bed. My mom brought in the portable handset and gave me an inscrutable look, then closed the door softly behind her. "I just talked to Debbie," Mari said. She sounded unnaturally calm. "They want us to perform at the DC release party, and it's soon, in a few weeks. Could you come over and practice this afternoon?"

I began crying the moment I heard her voice. "Are we broken up?" I said. "As a couple?"

Mari's laugh was quick and sardonic. "Clearly, yes," she said. "But hey, it's not your fault. It's my fault for trusting you with something you obviously can't understand. I knew you were protected, your childhood was very different from mine. I shouldn't have told you. But I did, and you really fucked up, and so yes. We are broken up as a couple."

"I'm so, so sorry, Mari." Rubbing my eyes with my hands, I realized I was still wearing Mari's hair band on my wrist, her black hairs tangled around it.

"I don't care," she said evenly. "That part is over now. You don't need to apologize, we are never going to talk about it ever again. But we still need to play together. Debbie said the Donnas' manager is going to be there."

"Just play together even though we're not actually together?"

"Do we have another option?" she said. "Get the fuck over yourself and come practice."

"I don't think I can," I said. It felt like a statement of fact. A voice isn't the same as a guitar or keyboard—it's inside a human body. And my body felt broken. I was still on the futon, where I'd been since the afternoon before. I had stolen a bottle of red wine from my mother's cabinet and drank it under my blankets, then threw up in my trash can around three a.m. and fell back asleep without brushing my teeth.

I knew it was deeply shameful to miss a practice right after what I'd done. And it was the last thing I wanted. All I wanted in life, all I had ever wanted, was to play music with Mari. I wanted to meet the Donnas' manager and get famous and go on a European tour and hang out with all our favorite bands backstage. I wanted music journalists to write, "Cain's echoing voice elevates the Maidenheads beyond their fringe art-punk roots," or one of the many other lines I'd imagined for them. I wanted us to be onstage forever, just spend our lives moving from one stage to another with occasional breaks to fuck in hotel rooms. But even my speaking voice was a croak, and I had a shriveled feeling in my throat, like something had already atrophied.

"You can't come to practice?" Mari said.

I tugged on her rubber band, snapped it against my skin. "I can't sing. My voice isn't working."

"So not today but tomorrow? We don't have a ton of time, but we could wait a day."

"I don't know, Mari—I can try, but I don't know."

"Wait," she said, "wait. You're saying you might not practice with me at all. Ever again."

"I really don't know," I said. And the fact that she could—that she would've been able to perform normally through her hard shell of mistrust and anger—that hurt too. I yanked again at the rubber band, so hard my wrist turned white.

"Let me get this straight, James, because I'm confused," she said. She spoke calmly, but her words held a killing rage. "We're a month away from the soundtrack release date. We should be planning another tour, writing new songs, recording an EP. And—instead you want to quit? Because, what, you feel *bad* for trying to fuck me when I didn't want you to? This isn't high school orchestra. This is our job, this is our *life*. You can't let the way you feel on one day derail that."

"Maybe if we could talk about what happened? You could tell me how you feel, you could yell at me? I know you're angry, you're right to be! I feel horrible, I feel like I—"

"I'm not interested in your feelings," Mari said firmly. "This is better anyway. We're more stable in the long term as friends. Like Sleater-Kinney."

"I just don't think I can," I said. For a second, I felt relief. I loved Mari, but she was so hard to be with: mercurial, secretive, mean. All year, even before this last crisis, I'd felt cramped by her. Maybe it was time to break free, start fresh that fall, be a normal college student. Be anything besides a Maidenhead. "I wish I could. I'm so sorry."

"This is so fucking stupid," she said. "I don't even know what to tell Debbie, like what, we can't perform at your show because Jamie's having some crisis over *my rape*. But OK then. You absolute fucking idiot." And she hung up. I'd broken the rubber band at some point, and now I put it into the top drawer of my desk, as carefully as if I were interring a corpse.

AS THE DAYS passed, the blip of relief I'd felt on the phone evaporated, leaving me in a permanent bog of shame and self-hatred. It was clear I was hideous, a monster, a rapist—I was *Josh*. I started avoiding my own face in the mirror, too terrified of seeing Josh look back: dead eyes under his dumb fucking Peruvian hat.

Meanwhile, Mari was right: this was the best, probably the only, chance I'd ever have at being a successful musician. It was catastrophically stupid to throw that away. What was wrong with me? A day might come, I hoped, when I'd realize my voice was fine after all. I'd be able to call Mari, apologize, start practicing again in time for the *Jennifer* opening. But every time I tried to sing, my voice stalled. I forced it, trying to sing along to my favorite bands or hum tunelessly or sing nursery rhymes. I was capable of making noises, but nothing remotely musical. Eventually, miserable but dully relieved, I stopped trying. I wouldn't again for ten years.

In Earl's basement, I felt the burn of Mari's presence, always and forever the only audience that mattered. If I failed now, I knew I'd never try again. I took a shallow breath, and then I got out the first line of our song: "*I combed my hair.*"

Right away, it took: a match scratched in the dark, a ball rolling downhill. The shape of my mouth transformed, altering the timbre of my voice. I heard my Maidenheads voice, that eerie unpolished Betty-Boop-in-rehab sound I hadn't heard since 2002. "*Bought silk stockings bought a hairpin bought a purse. Waited all night, but you didn't come, didn't come, didn't come.*" Then Andrew kicked in hard, and Mari slammed down her fingers, and we were in flight.

Almost immediately, we crashed out. Freddie missed her entrance, I got confused and tried to sing her line for her, and we stopped, laughing.

"Not bad," Mari said. I couldn't read her face. Then, "Again?"

This time, we didn't stop. With just Mari and me, the song had been a ramshackle pony cart, and now it was a four-horse chariot: nimble, urgent, its rhythm steady and fierce. Freddie and Mari sang the chorus: "*Emmy, Emmy, forget it / He's not worth it, forget it,*" and I sang right back at them, "*I'm not gonna be forgotten!*" I remembered the song's mocking edge, the harsh mismatch between the two vocal parts, arguing instead of harmonizing. I remembered how it had felt to roar out the words with Mari on that hell-bound tour with the Shrillers, all the love and pain and fear crackling between us like tangled electrical wires.

After we finished, Andrew added an extra drum flourish and everyone laughed—it was like after a good orgasm, that shy giddiness. I looked back over my shoulder to see Freddie's relief, Andrew's grudging pleasure. My body vibrated wildly, everything pulsing, alive. Mari pushed the damp hair out of her eyes, laughed again.

"Freddie," she said, "could we try it with just me on backup?" We did it again and again, Mari's voice alone on the chorus forcing me to push back even harder and louder, like we were each wielding half the song as a weapon against the other. Mari looked astounding to me: pert on her stool like the child prodigy she'd always been, fingers racing across the keyboard while her sharp-boned wrists stayed perfectly flat and still. But more astounding was the sensation of slicing my voice through a song, driving it, allowing it to sweep me away. I'd fully believed I would never feel that again—that I didn't deserve to feel it.

Finally, we started yet another time, and I couldn't get through. My throat was scraped clear; my lungs ached like I'd been summiting mountains. I hadn't yelled like that in a decade.

"Take a break," Mari said, generously, like I'd passed some test. They moved on to another song, and I sat back down on my folding chair, sipping tea from Freddie's thermos, froth-brained.

By about 10:30, everyone was too tired to make sense. Freddie mixed up two different songs and got the giggles; a drumstick flew out of Andrew's hand and hit cardboard Reagan in the stomach. I wanted to stay forever, but I had already fallen asleep twice in the chair. They packed their instruments, and we trudged up the stairs in a line like exhaustedly docile schoolchildren. Freddie's car was parked out front—"Dani's waiting up, got to go"—and Andrew slouched off to the Takoma Metro. I walked Mari to the corner where she'd locked her bike and watched as she unslung its heavy chain lock.

"What did you think?" she said.

"I mean," I said, and stopped, overwhelmed.

Mari took out a cigarette pack from her shoulder bag, lit one, then swatted her exhale, swirling the smoke in opposite directions. "It's better with Amanda there," she said finally. "But yeah, 'Forgotten' sounded pretty rad tonight."

"I really couldn't sing," I said. "Back then. I kept trying, for years, and my voice would choke up. I wasn't lying to you about why I had to quit."

"I believe you," she said, like it wasn't a big deal. "Maybe I didn't at the time, but yeah, I believe you."

A knot in my chest seemed to loosen, and I said in a rush, "Mari, I'm so sorry for what I did to you."

I'd pictured this moment so many times, and mostly I'd imagined Mari's rage, her voice going cold the way it had on the phone ten years ago. Instead she laughed. "Oh, Jamie," she said. "Still so dramatic. Listen, you didn't do anything wrong. Sure, it was messed up in the moment. But I handled things badly, I pushed you away."

"No," I said, "no, it wasn't your fault. You were really struggling and I failed you."

"OK," she said, a verbal shrug. She narrowed her eyes for an exhale. "Have it your way, if you want to feel bad. *I* don't care, though. I cared about getting raped, obviously. I cared about losing the band. But I'm not holding some deep grudge or whatever you've clearly been thinking. None of that was really about you, you know?"

I let my body absorb what felt like a blow. She was right, of course. On a second breath, I could feel Mari's harshness scrubbing away all my confusion and hurt. I'd had no right to dwell on it. It was her hurt, her confusion, and I'd stolen it and held it close for years.

"OK," I said. "OK."

"Not to be a dick about it!" she went on quickly. "Just, you shouldn't feel bad. I'm not angry."

"Maybe a little?"

She laughed. "Maybe a little. But really not that much! Mostly it's just good to see you."

I pressed my hands against the soreness in my hips. "You too," I said. "Tonight was fun."

Mari paused to snap away her cigarette butt and shove the helmet down over her hair. As she buckled the chin strap, she looked up, her grin a sudden burst. "You could come to another practice or two, if you wanted," she said. "Try 'Forgotten' again, maybe a couple other songs. Usually we meet Tuesday and Thursday nights and Saturday morning—this week people can't do Thursday, so next practice would be Saturday. And after that, Tuesday and Thursday. If you wanted to, I mean."

I couldn't recall ever wanting anything more. "Would everyone else be OK with me coming?"

Her hand wave was brutally dismissive. "Don't worry about that, I'll work it out. Would you be able to make it, though? Aren't you heading back to Baltimore?"

Yes of course, yes I was. But surely I could spend some time here first, feel this feeling a little longer? I was only a few weeks into the pregnancy—I had almost nine whole months to get ready.

"Actually," I said, "I thought I'd stay at my dad's for a week or so. So I could come to a practice or two, yeah. Just as a temporary thing, while I'm here."

"Well, that makes it easy," Mari said. "I'll text you once I can talk to everyone." She threw a leg over her bike and sailed off under the streetlights. I walked all the way home, too excited to wait for the bus, my whole body still reverberating.

Halfway down my father's street, a deer leapt out of someone's front yard and began walking toward me on the sidewalk, placing her long elegant feet as carefully as a drunk girl in high heels. I paused, then kept walking toward her. Closer, I could see the streetlights shining off her bulbous black eyes, a patch of bare skin on one flank. She was so unafraid that I got nervous, and finally, when we were just a few feet apart, I stepped off the sidewalk into the street and let her pass, then turned to watch her strut away.

When I got into the house, I took out my phone to find a text from Mari: Polled the group, you're welcome to join on Saturday if you still wanna. See you soon?

PART TWO

8

I MET PETER in November 2009, at one of Jeremy's cursed parties. Jeremy and his wife, a former Baltimore Symphony Orchestra cellist who now stayed at home and cared for their three children, owned an enormous house in Roland Park (wealthy parents). They threw parties often, and it was an unspoken rule that *Bugle* staff were required to go. Bad things happened at Jeremy's parties. It was at a Jeremy party that two interns had sex in a hall closet, requiring me to fire both and spend the rest of the summer doing their work as well as my own. It was at a Jeremy party that Bear Gomez, the *Bugle*'s legendary columnist, pinned me against a wall and tried to kiss me, and when I pushed him off said, "Oh, sorry, I thought you were the coatrack."

After that, I'd stopped wearing anything even remotely revealing to Jeremy's parties, although it was clear that wasn't a deterrent. I also avoided alcohol, because you never knew when you'd be called upon as a designated driver for some sodden and embittered male journalist. At this particular party, I leaned against the marble kitchen counter in jeans and a turtleneck sweater, sipping my tonic with lime and watching the clock.

"Having fun, Jamie?" Jeremy's wife called as she breezed through the kitchen, her dress a collection of tiered scarlet frills, like an exotic lizard.

I called back, "Definitely, yeah," and toasted her departing shape.

"You sound very sure," said a voice, and I turned to my right to see a tall red-haired person, stooping slightly to meet my gaze. He was clean-shaven and looked like a high school English teacher, in a tweedy jacket and denim shirt. He was vividly handsome, but it had an accidental quality; you felt his body cringe away from the handsomeness, as if embarrassed by it.

Flustered somehow, I swiveled to face him, propping myself sideways on the counter with an elbow. "I work for Jeremy at the *Bugle*," I said, "so I'm essentially hired help. Gotta stick it out until ten, then I'll go."

"What happens at ten?"

"Just calculating the vector of drunkenness among Jeremy's writer friends," I said. I seemed to be flirting, something I couldn't remember doing with a man before—my college hookups had required very little conversation. "Ten is late enough that no one notices me leaving, but not so late they start needing rides home."

"Are there a lot of writers here?" he said, glancing over his shoulder as if I'd alerted him to a cockroach problem.

"Most of Jeremy's friends are out-of-work journalists. He invites them to parties so they won't feel bad when he doesn't publish them. But later in the evening, they start pitching him ideas for stories. It's very awkward."

"I see why you'd want to escape," he said. "You could pretend that I'm a drunken journalist and you need to drive me home, if you'd like."

"That's very chivalrous, but I hope you don't actually need a ride home—I don't even have a car, I'd have to borrow Jeremy's."

"Of course not. We'll walk out together and go our separate ways. Shall I lurch for verisimilitude?"

I nodded, and he took my arm and lurched out through the living room to the front door, tripping over oriental rugs while I said, "Steady there, sailor—steady!" Jeremy laughed when he saw us. Once he realized I was actually leaving, he called my name, but I was far enough gone that I could pretend I hadn't heard.

We started giggling once we were outside, on Jeremy's neat front lawn with its iron lampposts shaped like pagodas. I'd left behind my jacket, and it was biting cold. My new friend offered to lurch back in for it, but I told him no, that would destroy the ruse. "I don't think it's much of a ruse," he said, very seriously.

"Well, sure," I said. "Your technique leaves much to be desired. Who are you, anyway?" Another unfamiliar thing about men—that edge of physical fear.

"I'm Peter Stevens," he said. "I work for *Street Beats*. My boss told me to come tonight because, I think, he's hoping Jeremy will say nice things about us in the *Bugle*." So not a journalist but a do-gooder—*Street Beats* was the Baltimore street paper, written and sold by the unhoused. It fit with Peter's English-teacher demeanor. I could imagine him shuffling into a room full of homeless poets and writing some mild prompt on the blackboard: "Today let's all write about birds."

"He probably won't," I said. "Jeremy thinks that saying nice things about people is bad journalism."

"He may be right," he said. "Oh well. I'm glad I came anyway," and he gave me the sweetest, most vulnerable smile. I cajoled him back to my apartment that night, and a week later, when Jeremy asked what was happening with that nice fellow Peter, I said, "Well, I suppose he's my *boyfriend* now."

I had not had a boyfriend since the self-appointed one in middle school. But Peter actually reminded me of the boys I'd been friends with then. He had grown up in Northern Virginia, going to all the same DC shows I'd gone to. Like me, he'd later self-exiled to Baltimore: a place far enough from home that he could pretend he'd escaped, close enough to suggest that, perhaps, he never really would. Alienated from his mother and stepfather, who were both Republicans, he continued to accept their money—including for the down payment on his Charles Village Victorian—which he rationalized by thinking of it as a necessary subsidy to his low-paying job at the street newspaper. His social life was quiet, mostly spent with his two tenant-housemates, earnest sweet people who baked vegan carrot cake for each other's birthdays and hosted crafting and board game nights.

I felt safe with Peter in a way I hadn't with the radio station bros and would-be poets I'd slept with in college. But I also felt some fascination around our relationship, or around me in it. Who was this new Jamie who was telling a man her secrets, getting dressed up to see a man after work? She was me but also not me. She wore better clothes and more expensive underwear, noticing Peter's reaction to certain bras. She let her hair grow, brushed it regularly. She held herself differently because he stared at her tits when she sat straight, and she actually liked that; she liked the (embarrassed, compelled) way Peter stared at her tits, the way she felt like an object, the way her power—though substantial!—was passive, not active. This Jamie felt different—not even a femme but a *girl*. I'd never experienced that before. If anything, I'd defined myself in antagonism to girlhood: the chink in my armor, the bloody pad stuck to my jeans leg. I'd never imagined that girlness, let alone girlness in the context of straight boyness, could be pleasurable, could turn me on.

And Peter was just so nice. I'd learned from rom-coms and women's magazines and other annals of heterosexuality that boyfriends didn't care about your day, didn't want to hear about your feelings. But Peter was the opposite. He was hungry to learn about me, even the weird shit. He was the first person I talked to honestly about the breakup with Mari. I told him that remembering what I'd done to her still made me want to hurt myself in sharp nullifying ways. He hugged me and said he understood; we'd all done bad things, but that didn't make us bad people.

Within a few months, I moved into his place, our lives intertwining to the exclusion of outsiders. Most of my Baltimore friends then were queer people I'd made out with at some point. They were also all heavy drinkers, so pulling back felt less a betrayal of my sexual identity and more a healthy, adult choice. I stopped going to shows as well—too much risk of seeing someone I'd known as old Jamie. The few times I did run into friends, I didn't mention Peter, just said I was taking a break from going out, really focused on work, you know how it is.

One Sunday morning when Peter and I had been together for about a year, I was sitting on his West Elm couch doing the crossword puzzle in his copy of the *Times* when I got a call from my mom. "Your father's dating someone new. A *woman*," she said, and started to cry.

"Oh?" I said. I'd just figured out the answer to a clue ("they might atone"), but hadn't written it down; it was immediately lost forever.

"They met online. She's barely older than you. She's moving into the Silver Spring house, she's some sort of artsy person on the Internet."

"She's already moving in?"

"It sounds like they've been together for a while. He just hadn't told me. Did he tell you?"

It was always embarrassing to admit how little I knew about him. "He hasn't mentioned it," I said.

"Of course," she said. "Typical Kenneth. Anyway, apparently he's not gay anymore. Or he's back in the closet."

I hesitated. "Couldn't he be bisexual?"

"Jamie," she said, her voice rising, "your father is *gay*. I've known him my whole adult life. That man is *not* bisexual."

When she ended the conversation, I fell back on the couch, feeling extremely upset, far more than I'd realized I was on the phone. Peter walked in from the kitchen and saw my face. "You OK?" he said. "Want to take a walk?"

We went out for a walk, and I told him what had happened. It was a chilly day and Peter had on a striped sweater. He looked like a rugby player, but with a gently perturbed expression. "Do you think you might be upset she dismissed the idea that your father could be bisexual?" he said after I'd finished the story.

"That's not what this is about," I said, annoyed. "It's about the weirdness of how they share information. I'm constantly finding out stuff about my dad filtered through my mom's crazy lens. I never know what's real."

"But that must've been strange to hear while you're sorting out your own identity. She was pretty harsh."

"I'm not sorting out my identity, ew, Peter."

Peter wrapped a woolen arm around me and said, "Jamie—you're closeted at work."

"I'm not closeted! It's not my fault Jeremy makes assumptions."

"But you could've told him at any point. And you said you never brought Carrie to work parties."

"If you ever met Carrie, you'd understand that in a nanosecond."

"You know," he said, "Derek's sister, who just came out as gay, she goes to this support group. They do a bunch of different ones, I think there's a bisexual one."

"Why on earth would I go to a bisexual support group? Do you know what kinds of people go to those things?"

"I'd guess, bisexual people?"

"Like—annoying people. Girls who kissed their best friend once and are having a crisis."

"You don't know that, you've never been," he said. "Maybe you'd make some new friends."

I realized I was walking very quickly and slowed down to match his pace. "I don't need friends! I have friends."

"Do you? You never see them."

He was right. I'd never had such a steady, domestic relationship, and I was scared to screw it up by introducing my old friends, my old self. And it was true I hadn't told any of them about Peter. I knew what they said about queer girls who fucked men, the eye rolls, *Oh, she says she's* bisexual *now . . .*

Peter shook his head. "You know I don't need you to be straight. I just think you'd be happier if you were able to embrace that side of you."

"My dude, I've embraced it plenty. *Plenty.*"

But Peter got the information from Derek's sister and texted it to me. I wasn't intending to go, it felt humiliating to admit I might need bisexual support, but I couldn't stop looking at the number. Finally, I called and found out the bi group had a meeting that Monday night. "I'm going to this ridiculous thing, are you happy?" I said to Peter, and he kissed me.

On Monday, I put on my most emphatically gay clothes, boots and a flannel and a beanie pushed over my bangs, to demonstrate to the bisexuals that I was a *real* queer, and I walked to the community center in Hampden where the group met. The room looked like an AA meeting—folding chairs, cracked linoleum floor, people drinking coffee out of paper cups. But they were older than I'd expected. Out of a group of seven, including the moderator, only two were about my age, both white girls dressed exactly like me and looking as nervous as I felt. Shamed to be twinning with the most awkward people in the room, I slouched into a folding chair as far away from them as possible.

The moderator was a woman probably in her forties with long scraggly braids and a Joy Division T-shirt. When we were all circled on our chairs, she introduced herself as Amber. "I'm so excited to be here tonight," she said, sweeping us with a bright stare. "I just love being around the bis."

We began with introductions. Of the older people, one was a trans woman named Betty who had just, after decades of loving men, found herself in love with a woman for the first time. Then there was Gordon, in a civil union with a man but bisexual and polyamorous and a nudist who belonged to the Radical Faeries—he appeared to have no stress around his own identities, just enjoyed hanging out. Sitting next to Gordon was a man named Perry who had been married to a woman his whole life but recently come out as pansexual. He cried as he talked about his wife's conflicted reaction, and Gordon petted his shoulder. I found myself gripping my thigh very hard, thinking of my dad.

After Perry was a guy probably in his thirties I'd assumed was a gay man, a slight guy in a beanie and Members Only jacket. He sat with one ankle propped on the other thigh, jeans leg hiking up over a narrow, furry shin. "I'm River," he said, in a reedier voice than I'd expected. "I'm a trans guy, might be nonbinary, not really sure about these new words sometimes," drawing a friendly laugh from the older members of the group. "My longtime partner's transitioning too now, and I'm having some feelings about it and needed to talk to someone."

I'd met very few trans men up until that point. My queer friends had all been women, mostly femmes with a few friendly butches hanging around on the outskirts of the group. I didn't know anyone who considered themselves "nonbinary": this was a word that in 2010 I had only heard once or twice and still associated with kids at liberal arts colleges. River was hot, for sure; he reminded me a little of Mari, in fact, that messy black hair. But that didn't feel like the whole reason I couldn't stop watching him. The two girls in their twenties who introduced themselves after that, and whose names I instantly forgot, were objectively hotter, but they didn't draw me the way River did.

"And you?" Amber asked. I realized everyone was looking at me, including River, who smiled with benign confusion when he met my stare.

"Yeah, hi, I'm Jamie. Not really sure why I'm here, don't know if I'm bisexual or what, just here to learn I guess?" I said, instructing myself to look anywhere but across the room.

With introductions done, Amber invited us to share. There was talk of bi invisibility in straight spaces, biphobia in queer spaces, did you know bi people have the highest rate of mental illness out of all queer people, what is bi culture, etc. The two girls talked about their boyfriends, who were scheming for threesomes. I wondered if I should have similar worries about Peter. It seemed unlikely, but maybe I was willfully ignoring the signs? Perry talked for a long time about how much he loved his wife and their children and how hard it was to have to choose. I imagined my father opening up like this to a crowd of strangers and nearly cried myself.

At one point, one of the girls (I couldn't stop thinking of them as "girls" even though they were my age) said something about "the difficulty of having a fluid sexuality in a nonfluid social context," and Betty replied, "Oh, please."

Amber said, "Would you like to elaborate?"

"Difficult! You're fine," Betty said. She shook her head.

Amber appeared to fumble for a moment, wordlessly. "We'd love to get your perspective, Betty," she said finally, "while always remembering that not everyone has the same background and set of experiences."

"Yes, of course," said the younger woman, with a big fake smile. "It's always good to hear from our elders."

Amber's eyes went glassy and panicked. Betty looked for a moment truly pained, then shrugged and smiled into the corner of the room.

River, who had been watching closely, now spoke. "Betty," he said, "what were you going to say?"

She tossed him a *you sure?* eyebrow raise, and he nodded vigorously. "Okay," she said, one hand tugging on the other hand's rings. "It's just such a different world now. When I was coming up, you couldn't go outside without someone messing with you. So I hear people say, 'Oh, it's so hard, oh *fluidity*,' and I'm thinking: That's not hard. Getting punched in the face is hard."

River's nod was grave now. Betty went on. "I don't mean to dismiss you. I just think you need to think before you speak, that's all."

The younger girl let out a nervous giggle and looked at her friend, who was staring at her feet. Amber said, "Right, yes. Well—maybe let's all share moments when we felt our bisexual identities were under attack?" and Betty rolled her eyes at River, who rolled his back.

Watching River, I could feel something stirring. It was a hunger, a lack; it felt almost like sexual desire, but it originated along my chest instead of between my legs. Also, unlike sexual desire, it didn't arrive along with clear instructions on how to resolve it. Yes, I did want to bite River's beautiful skin; I did want to muss up his thick, slightly oily hair. But it didn't seem like doing that would fully satiate me. It seemed like I might need to go further somehow.

After Gordon and the girl who'd been otherwise quiet shared moments of feeling under attack, I said, "River, what feelings were you having about your partner?"

"Well," he said, flashing me another mildly baffled smile, "I've never been attracted to masculine people before. But my partner, who's been a cis femme lesbian as long as I've known them, is now talking about transitioning and I'm actually into it? So I'm wondering if I'm bisexual."

"So your partner's nonbinary?" Gordon asked. "Maybe you're attracted to nonbinary people?"

"I don't really know," said River. "I don't feel like I understand how any of this works."

Gordon started talking about polyamory, and how you could feel different types of love simultaneously, and no one relationship could satisfy all your needs anyway. River nodded and pushed his denim shirtsleeves up over strong, tattooed forearms. His legs were crossed in front of him, black hair fell in his eyes. I felt the hunger again, and recalled feeling it another time: when Mari told me years ago that "beautiful, tough, sad boys" could be sopranos, and my body had seemed to split apart. Perry asked Gordon if the polyamorous community was welcoming to older people entering it for the first time, and Gordon made a catlike sound of satisfaction and leaned back in his folding chair, hands clasped behind his head, before beginning a long and detailed response. River scratched his fingers through his hair and glanced at me covertly, not with interest but with clear discomfort, an awareness that I'd been watching him. And an out-of-nowhere shame took me down so savagely that I mumbled something about having to go to the bathroom and instead left the church building and hurried home.

Peter wasn't at the house; he had a fundraising event for work. The housemates were out as well. I was relieved to be alone. I knew I'd behaved badly by walking out, and I'd have to invent a story about it when Peter asked. I had no words to explain how hungry and fragmented and lost River had made me feel. I didn't understand it myself.

After I brushed my teeth in our bathroom, I took off my clothes and tried to see myself in the mirror. Naked, without even the protective costume of my new fancy underwear, my body was what it always was: a cipher, an impossibility, something that seemed to fracture the closer I looked. But that wasn't anything strange or worthy of specialized language; that was just me. Probably lots of people felt that way. I kept staring at myself, not sure what I seemed to need to see, until finally, huffing out a deep breath, I pulled on baggy pajama pants and an old T-shirt and got into bed.

That night, I dreamed that I was River, that my hands were his hands, my lips his lips. But instead of sitting cross-legged and saying thoughtful things in a church basement, I was outside at night, stalking one of the girls from the support group. In the dream, I trailed her home, upstairs into her room, then pushed her down on the bed and raped her brutally, tearing at her fragile hair and skin with heavy clawlike hands.

When I woke up the next morning, I realized the dream had closely echoed the opening scene in *Jennifer's Not There*: the blond stewardess returns home from a dance club pursued by an unknown mystery man, seen only from behind as he mutilates her on the bed. Later, you watch the same scene from Jennifer's perspective and realize that the killer was a butch lesbian, a twist that would live on in queer studies infamy.

I felt sour and sick and cruel, revisiting the dream, and the feeling lodged at the pit of my stomach for a long time. Peter and I went on vacations and fought about chores and had good sex, bad sex, in-front-of-the-TV sex. I wore cute underwear, I stuck out my tits, I let him pay for stuff. New Jamie became just the person I was every day, a performance wedged so deep within me that my skin reformed around it.

Meanwhile, a famous gay filmmaker listed *Jennifer* as one of her "seminal lesbian films," and a queer website ran an article about it, describing its "problematic qualities" but also calling it an "early '00s classic, a worthy successor to *Bound* for its campy portrayal of butch-femme dynamics," and once, in a bar with Peter, I heard "Forgotten" playing and froze up so bad I had to go home. Mari began performing with Les Somnambules, and I wrote secret-message previews for her in the *Bugle*, carried on long arguments with her in my head, tried and failed to sing in the shower. I worked hard in every way to be a good girlfriend for Peter, the girlfriend I knew he deserved. But I never fully lost the sour cruel feeling I'd had waking up from the dream.

Two years after I moved in, Peter said at breakfast, "So have you ever thought about getting married?" The sour feeling erupted in a nauseous wave, and without giving myself time to think, I broke up with him. In the aftermath, I felt both unleashed and flattened by terror—what was I now, what was left without New Jamie?—and I left the Sansui behind so Peter would have to come put me back to rights.

The morning after I practiced with Les Somnambules for the first time, I woke up early in a baby-blue Juicy sweatsuit I'd borrowed from Sally. I hadn't brought a change of clothes with me to DC, so I was washing my one outfit overnight. I put on my still-damp jeans and T-shirt for the *Bugle* story meeting. On the MARC train to Baltimore, I texted Peter: Could we get lunch today? Need to talk about something. Then I raced to the *Bugle* offices, arriving not quite on time for the weekly all-staff meeting, takeout coffee sloshing across my fingers as I rushed into the conference room where everyone was already seated. Jeremy nodded toward the chair he always saved for me, to his left at the top of the long meeting table—a placement that had nothing to do with seniority and everything to do with gender, an attempt to balance the almost total lack of women. I sat down in my token chair and sucked my burnt hand.

Ideas meetings always started with everyone announcing what they were working on, escalating boasts thick with anxious bravado.

That morning, from the crime reporter: "I've been at the courthouse all week with the St. Patrick's Day kids. Think I can get the girl to talk."

From one of the interns: "We're slammed on the Bartlett race. Total shit show."

From Bear, the columnist, the senior-most employee and longest-term survivor at the paper, a galumphing bray-voiced presence in baggy suit and rubbed-shiny wingtips, his skin reddened and patchy from years of simultaneous substance abuses: "Jeremy, as you know, I'm gobsmacked by the Obama campaign's many half-truths. We can't just let him off the hook because of, you know. Battling to formulate coherent thoughts, but I'll send you something late tonight."

Next it was Nora's turn. "Just writing up my notes from the Sealbone show. Les Somnambules rocked, by the way." She nodded at me. "I saw you chatting with Mari after—Maidenheads reunion?"

"Oh, ha, no," I said, voice still threadbare from last night's practice. "No—that would never happen."

After the meeting, Jeremy ushered me into his office. "You seem tired today," he said. "Everything OK?"

Jeremy had taken the corner office when he got promoted to editor-in-chief several years back, but still hadn't decorated it much apart from two framed photos of his kids and wife on the desk. I thought probably he wasn't able to get comfortable, living in constant anticipation of losing his job. The previous editor had lasted a year, and his decorations still hung on Jeremy's walls like the specter of unwarranted optimism: maps of Baltimore and Maryland; a framed Orioles ticket signed by someone in gold pen; the front page of the *Bugle*'s thousandth issue from 1977, back when the paper had a staff of fifty and a budget for travel, extravagant lunches, and loosening up sources in Federal Hill bars.

"Actually," I said, keeping my eyes on one of the photos, the previous editor with his arm around David Simon, "I'm still dealing with this family thing in DC. Sorry to ask this, but would it be OK if I kept working remotely, just for a bit, until I can sort it out?"

Jeremy gave me only the faintest of skeptical looks before agreeing to let me work from DC for the next few weeks so long as I came to Wednesday meetings. And then it was on to the second hard conversation of the day.

Since talking with Freddie, I'd found it easier to imagine my life as a mother. The baby would have translucent pink sea-creature hands; it would sleep in my lap like a cat. It would say absurd, sweet things as it learned to talk. I'd complain about it the way Freddie did with Liya: with exhaustion but not a whiff of malice. Later on, maybe we'd be friends, the way my mother and I had been at times, and when I died, it would say, "She was so *beautiful*," at my funeral. I almost definitely wouldn't be a good mother, not like Sally or Freddie, but at least I'd be something—I'd *have* something—whereas currently I had nothing.

Meanwhile, though, I'd looked up the cost of full-time childcare in Baltimore and smacked a hand across my mouth. There was no way I could afford it if I stayed at the *Bugle*, even if Jeremy, against all odds, gave me a raise. I didn't think my parents could help financially, even if I felt comfortable asking. Peter, however, had rich parents, which was one reason I'd texted him that day.

When I reached the food-by-weight restaurant where we always met for lunch, Peter was at a table outside, having obtained a large quantity of General Tso's chicken. His hair was combed flat, and he had on a short-sleeved collared shirt in which he looked fresh, as if he'd just come from swimming in the ocean. I waved and went inside for my carton of kale Caesar (dark leafy greens, those were good during pregnancy, right?). When I came back out and sat down, he said, "How's your mother? Everything OK with Michael?"

"Unfortunately so," I said. "I ended up staying with my dad for the weekend. Actually, I think I'm going to stay there a bit longer. Maybe a week or two." Then, because I felt like he needed to know what sort of conversation this would be, I went on, "I'm pregnant."

Peter had just bitten into a chicken globule and received this barrage in silence. After he swallowed, he said, "Pregnant?"

"You know. With a baby. Sorry."

"No—I just . . ."

I had watched this scene so many times in movies, I knew exactly what to say. "And yes, it's definitely yours."

"OK," he said. He leaned back in his chair and closed his eyes, looking like my mother when I'd told her—worn out from years of enduring me. "So do you need money? Or what?"

"You think I'm just telling you because I need money?" I said, trying not to sound too theatrically shocked.

"I figured you wouldn't be telling me if you didn't need something."

"I could be telling you because it's your baby too and you should know."

He peered at me in horror. "*Baby?* You're not actually thinking about keeping the pregnancy, are you? You're the last person in the world I can imagine—"

"Peter!"

"Sorry," he said. "But still—right? You're not keeping it?"

"Actually, yes," I said. "I might keep it."

Concern widened across his face. "OK," he said. "OK."

"I think I'd be a good mother, actually," I said, even though I wasn't sure, just because he'd been so rude.

"OK," he said again, the way you'd say it to a crazy person brandishing a knife.

I couldn't, in that moment, kill him. So I smothered the rage and asked about work, his upcoming kayak trip with one of the housemates. He answered my questions abstractedly, and I could feel him watching me, trying to figure out if this was all a sick joke. I stayed calm, tried to telegraph sanity. When the conversation ended and I stood to leave, we sidled awkwardly into a hug, keeping space between our torsos. "Keep me posted?" Peter said, sounding panicked.

Walking away, I felt jangled up, craving escape. I had brought my shoulder bag with me from work, and so instead of returning to the office, I rode the bus to my apartment. There, I threw away a bunch of black bananas and rotting takeout from the fridge, packed my roller suitcase with clothes and my toiletries, and took the bus to the station, where I boarded the MARC train to DC. I got to my father's house around four to find Sally lying across the living room couch, a plate of crackers balanced on her belly, her long shiny braid hanging almost to the floor.

When she heard me, she sat up abruptly, brushing crumbs off her chest. "I'm working," she said, "I'm busy, I'm just taking a minute." She had on maternity yoga pants, the stained sweatshirt, slip-on house shoes printed with koalas: the clothes of someone not expecting to see another adult anytime soon. I heard a female voice croon over bashing pianos, and I realized that it was coming from the nice new Bose I'd never seen either of them use.

"Is that Fiona Apple?" I said. "I love this album." A favorite of Mari's, in fact.

"It is. Me too." Then she noticed the suitcase and her eyebrows rose.

"So," I said immediately, "how would it be if I stayed just a little longer?"

Sally bit into a cracker, exploding crumbs. "Well—it's your room," she said, wiping cracker bits self-consciously off her breasts.

"It's not," I said. I wanted to stay, but it wouldn't work if Sally resented me. "I was going to say, I'm glad you took down that awful wallpaper. The room looks so much better."

She smiled, gratified. "It's yours until the baby comes, anyway," she said. "Are you feeling OK? You look a little pale."

I'd stood all the way home on the crowded MARC and then the crowded Metro, and I felt more pregnant than I ever had: creaky, nauseated, echoing with anxiety and irritation after the talk with Peter. "I'm fine. Tired, maybe."

"Oh no! Can I get you something?"

"I might just lie down for a minute . . ."

Sally shepherded me into the bedroom, where she reinflated the saggy air mattress, huffing over the foot pump even though I told her not to. Then she rushed to the kitchen for more crackers and a tangerine seltzer. "I have magazines," she said, hopefully, once I was in bed.

As she waved her copy of *People*, I realized that the past fifteen minutes was the longest we'd ever been alone together. Sally had married my father a year before, in Hawaii, a justice of the peace thing in matching flowy white shirts and leis. I found out after the fact through a giant group email with all the addresses in the cc field, including mine and my mother's. I'd felt excluded and hurt and thought the shirts were gross; I still thought of Sally as my father's beard. I hadn't gone to the Silver Spring house in years, had never suggested he bring Sally along to one of our coffee dates. Now, with Sally standing breathlessly over me, I realized how rejected she must've felt.

"Sure," I said. "I love *People*."

Sally smiled and placed it on the bed next to me. "Can I ask you something personal? You don't have to answer if you don't want to," she said. She settled into the fancy-looking rocking chair with its cloth cover and silent hinges, let her slippers drop to the floor, and stretched out her bare feet: they were surprisingly rough, unmanicured, with a very high arch and twisting toes.

"OK," I said.

"How are you feeling about the baby these days? I know the pregnancy was—unexpected."

The question didn't feel invasive coming from Sally. It felt more like we were both members of an embattled minority and could say things that outsiders couldn't. "I'm feeling good about it, actually," I said. "I know it might be hard, but I think I'd be a good mother. And I think I'd like having a kid."

"I bet you'd be a great mother," she said. "What's making it feel hard?"

"Well—I don't have a partner or any money. And then also, if I had a baby, it might be hard to do other things. Like be in a band, for instance."

"People have babies and stay in bands."

"It's more complicated, though. You can't tour. Harder to stay out late for shows."

"Babysitters exist." She smiled, but I was annoyed: all of these things were so easy for Sally. My dad had tenure; their mortgage was long paid off.

"You need money for babysitters," I said.

"Jobs exist."

"Sure, but jobs that pay money also make it hard to be in a band. You can't quit for two months to tour if you have a normal job."

"I feel like sometimes," Sally said, "women are very black-and-white about these decisions. Like, art versus baby. And it makes sense you'd have those fears. But I'm still making art. It's complicated, you're right, but it's possible. You'd work it out."

For an animal-themed pottery career supported by your husband, maybe that's true, I thought. But it didn't matter, anyway, since I wouldn't be in a band—I wasn't joining Les Somnambules. The dilemma wasn't art versus baby. There was no dilemma at all. "I think I would too," I said, and added mentally, *And fuck you, Peter.*

"No one really knows what kind of a mother they'll be until they actually have a baby," Sally said. Her chair-rocking pace had visibly accelerated. "I'm doing all this work to prepare, but maybe I'll be a horrible mother."

I was shocked she could even entertain this thought. "Oh, wow, no, you're going to be the best mother ever! You painted those amazing elephants," I said, gesturing up at the parade ringing the ceiling. "I could never do anything like that, my kid's going to be, like, sleeping in a box."

"You like it?" she said.

"I love it."

"Sure," she said, smile vanishing, "but I could be a really controlling mother. Plus, kids form their attachment styles by two, so I could be a negligent mother for the first two years and then great for all the years after that and it *wouldn't matter.* And my family's Asian, so what if I'm a Tiger Mom without even intending to be. *And* I'm forty-two, geriatric pregnancy, so the kid could have all kinds of problems; plus, I'm probably going to die before he's even married, and obviously Kenneth will be dead then too, and I'm too old to give him a sibling, besides you, of course. Not to mention, you know, climate change."

"Wow," I said, stunned by all the varieties of anxiety it hadn't even occurred to me to have.

Sally inhaled deliberately. "Anyway," she said, "it's nice talking to you about this. You can talk to me anytime, you know, if you want to. About babies or whatever."

"Thanks!"

"Of course. Also, I should say, you're welcome to stay with us as long as you need to. I'm sorry if I've been strange about it. This"—she hesitated—"*stepmother* thing is confusing."

"You're fine," I said. "I know Dad isn't always the most helpful when it comes to complicated relationship stuff either."

"Ah yes, Kenneth," she said. "Communication—not his forte."

"He has other strengths," I said. This was something my mother used to say when I complained about him. But it sounded so condescending that I'd appropriated it as an insult: if my father forgot yet again to pick me up after soccer practice, "He has other strengths"; if he fed me baked potatoes all weekend and I came back constipated, "He has other strengths."

Sally's nostrils flared. "I'm told he's excellent at folding towels," she said, and she made a face I'd never seen before, an obvious imitation of my father's anxious mouth twist. It looked so much like him, and it was such a shock to see Sally mimicking him so cleverly, that I snorted with laughter, and she flipped her braid back over her shoulder with a pleased smile.

9

SATURDAY MORNING, I showered, then stood naked in front of the foggy bathroom mirror, pressing my hands into my stomach and hips. I still couldn't see any change. If anything, I looked skinnier, more like my gawky swaybacked kid-self—not a body that seemed equipped to nurture another. I closed my eyes to imagine myself with wide hips, drooping breasts, basketball belly like Sally's. It was an unsettling, Franken-feeling image, but in some ways comforting: a body doing its assigned job.

On the way to practice at Earl's, I stopped at Starbucks for a large coffee and a spinach pastry. Earl's son opened the door—maybe seven years old, buzzed blond hair, skull and crossbones drawn in purple marker on his forearm, opaque blue stare. I pointed to the basement, laughed nervously, then fled downstairs to find Mari and Amanda on stools, drinking coffee from mugs.

"That smells awful," Amanda said as I unwrapped my oily pastry. She was wearing cutoffs and black Keds, her hair pulled tightly up over the shaved sides. Amanda was a pediatric nurse at Georgetown University Hospital, someone had told me, and now I saw that irritable competence every time she made a small movement: lifting a mug with her fingers touching just the handle, while Mari warmed both hands around the cup.

"It tastes better than it smells," I said, although it didn't.

"What's the plan for today, Mari?" Amanda asked. "Tackle the new song?"

Mari glanced at me. "Maybe," she said.

"Did you look at my lyrics?" Amanda never sat quite still, constantly making small adjustments to her clothing, her hair. Just then she was tugging at a loose piece of hair at the back of her head, trying to tuck it into the topknot above the shaved area. It kept slipping out and hitting her neck and then she'd retuck it and it would fall out again.

"I did," Mari said. "Yes."

"And?"

"I already wrote lyrics for this song."

"But they're—you know."

"Obscure. Weird," Mari said, impatiently. She dug out an unopened cigarette pack from her jeans pocket and began tapping it down.

"Well, yeah, and if we're performing at the *Jennifer* screening this fall, I think we need to consider our responsibilities as a politically informed band."

"'Politically informed band'? Is that what we are now? *Jennifer* has nothing to do—"

"It *does*, though, Mari. People are going to be talking about it."

"I don't feel any need to apologize for that movie," Mari said, smacking the cigarettes from palm to palm. "Anyway, *Jennifer* is 'seminal' now, don't you read? The queers reclaimed it."

"They shouldn't! That ending set butches back by a decade in terms of their cultural significance. It was like *Basic Instinct*, the end of *The Crying Game*, only for masc lesbians."

"The butches are fine," Mari said. "Seminal or no, very few people ever saw that movie, and half of them were butches themselves. I don't think we have to worry about it, and I certainly don't think we need to change what we do because of it."

"Would it kill you to have just one song that isn't about, like, dragons?" Amanda finally tugged the hair out of her bun and shook her head to smooth it out. Her hair was thin and moved stiffly along with the movement of her head. I couldn't help imagining Mari, in the old days, smoothing it behind her ears. "There's a lot going on right now, Mari. We don't have to write directly about Trayvon or Occupy or any of those things, but I think people want to know what we stand for."

"Isn't it obvious what we stand for? We're a queer band. We don't also have to be like, 'Support gay rights!'"

I laughed, but Amanda did not. "Why not?" she asked. "If it's important to our audience, if it's part of connecting with the people who matter to us."

"I don't write for meaning, you know that, Amanda. The words are just rhythm."

"That's bullshit, Mari. Your songs have meaning, you just like being mysterious about it. But that's elitist, it's not inclusive. It's like playing with your back turned."

Mari flung the cigarette pack across the room, where it smacked against a plastic sled. "If you want to play some dumb literal shit, you can join a different kind of band. You know who I am, you know what I do."

"You're not the only person in this band, Mari," Amanda said, her voice gritty with an old anger.

"Sure, but I write the songs." They both seemed to take a breath after this. "Listen, Amanda," Mari went on in a kinder voice, "we are never going to unfuck the world with our song lyrics. The world is far too fucked! All we can do is make beautiful, weird music and be our gay-ass selves onstage. Be the rock stars we needed when we were kids. There's nothing we can say out loud that means more than that."

At the end of this little speech, Mari glanced at me with uncharacteristic shyness, the exact way she used to after playing me a new song on Yevgenia's piano: once again, she was performing for me. I didn't quite want to indulge it; I was familiar with the argument they were carrying out and had often taken Amanda's side against Mari back in high school. But I softened nonetheless.

"You're being lazy," Amanda said. She shook her head. "You don't want to engage. But it's so privileged, it's so . . ."

"*Privileged*, hah! Listen, where I grew up," Mari said, standing to fetch her cigarettes, "politics are very different. I don't have this glamorization of—"

"Oh god," I interrupted, and I felt so lighthearted, like I could say anything now. "Next it'll be the Tbilisi blackouts, punk flourishing under the surveillance state, the crucible of revolution . . ."

"Don't get her started on the Kalashnikov story," Amanda said, turning to me with a smile. It seemed like she appreciated the distraction, appreciated a chance not to be at odds with Mari.

"The soldiers in the café? Oh lord, no," I said.

Mari made a mock-hurt pout as she slunk back to her chair. Amanda and I both laughed, and I could tell Amanda thought the pout was for her, the joke was between the two of them. But I knew, and I felt Mari knowing, that it wasn't.

Just then the house's front door banged open, and Freddie and Andrew came down the stairs together, talking loudly about a local band they wanted to hate but accidentally loved. Freddie wore a yellow dress over boots and very bright red lipstick, radiant and sweet; Andrew looked hungover, stubbly in sweatpants and an undershirt.

After hugs from Freddie and chin nods from Andrew, everyone started unpacking instruments from cases or the locked cabinet on the basement's back wall. Amanda tuned up, and Freddie rosined her bow, releasing a cloud of sparkly pine-scented rosin dust. Mari flipped through her notebook until everyone was ready, then said, "I'd like to try the new song with Jamie singing lead. Just as an experiment, see how it sounds." She hadn't mentioned this song to me, nor had we discussed me singing lead on anything but "Forgotten."

"And with your lyrics. Just checking," Amanda said.

"Yes, Amanda, my lyrics." Mari gestured me over and showed me her notebook. In her childhood room, Mari had piles of song notebooks, filled out in her spiky, distinctive handwriting—I still put crosses through my sevens because she had. Now I scanned the lightly penciled lyrics, surprised to recognize a few lines.

"Is this 'Tiny Animals'?" I asked.

Mari flushed along her cheekbones. "A version of it, yes."

Mari had been working on "Tiny Animals" just before we broke up—she sang it for me one afternoon in the back of the tour van. It was a quieter, more melodic song than we usually performed, and Mari told me she'd written parts for guitar and drums. At the time I'd laughed—neither of us played guitar or drums, what was she thinking? It hadn't sounded like a Maidenheads song at all. But it did sound like a Les Somnambules song, I realized now—as if Mari had been, even then, looking to a post-Maidenheads future.

The lyrics were written from the perspective of a child playing with toy animals that come alive and attack her: *We were playing on the bedroom floor / Now you're fierce, slam the door / Tiny animals, I don't want to fight you / Tiny animals, I don't want to bite you.* There's a note of absurdity, but also surreal terror, and a creepily sexual refrain: *Push me down, I don't care / Pull me in, I'm nowhere.* The final words of the song were ambiguous—had the child defeated the tiny animals, or become one? *Tiny beast tiny teeth tiny nose / Tiny heart tiny claws tiny toes / Tiny animals, I didn't want to fight you.*

"Why didn't you tell me you'd decided on lyrics?" Amanda asked Mari. "I wouldn't have written mine."

"I haven't totally decided," Mari said, almost too quietly for me to hear. "I just wanted to hear these lyrics with Jamie's voice."

I stood by the mic, back stiffened with pleasure and nerves, and read through the song again, trying to swallow it whole so I could deliver it up exactly the way Mari wanted. They ran through it twice with Mari singing in her rough, low voice, watching me to make sure I took it all in. Then she said, "Want to try?"

I breathed in but stopped; singing in front of Amanda felt very high-stakes. "Can I practice alone first?"

Mari nodded, and led me upstairs into Earl's ground-floor bathroom, passing the little boy in the living room, where he was watching cartoons and scrawling marker across his other arm. The bathroom was small and pink, with browning pink tiles and a fluffy pink toilet seat cover, on which Mari now sat. I hadn't expected her to stay—I'd meant "alone" as in away from her as well. I balanced on the edge of the dirty pink bathtub and our knees brushed; I could smell her unwashed hair and morning cigarette.

"Ready?" she said, and I drew in my breath as she tapped out a bar on the edge of the sink.

We sang it twice together with me reading the lyrics from her notebook, balanced on my knees. My voice sounded awful, off-key and muddled, all flaws amplified in the tight echoing space.

"Try on your own now," Mari said. Her face was close to mine, I felt the disturbance of her hot breath on my forearm, and I inhaled hard again. But my lungs constricted, and I couldn't start.

I couldn't look Mari in the face, feeling the failure, the fear. In a careful voice, she said, "I'm going to hold your hand, OK?" She took my hand and held it between both of hers. In high school, she would do that sometimes to slow my pulse, steady my breath. Now it had the opposite effect, at least for a needle-jumping moment, until I felt the warmth spread from her hands into mine and ease through my bloodstream. "You can do this," she said.

I began the song again on my own, singing directly to Mari—like I was telling her a story, lulling her to sleep. The sound reverberated against the walls; we were enclosed by its waves. Underwater, undersound. The animals were monstrous, scary-beautiful. Their fur muffled my lips; their claws scraped my skin. By the end, I could feel the child's power. She had conquered the animals and become one herself, corrupt and triumphant.

After I finished, Mari and I looked at each other silently. I felt her eyes and mine widen, taking in the full person opposite. Then she dropped my hand and shifted away on the toilet seat.

"If I hadn't come back," I asked, not ready to exit the moment, "would you be practicing this with Amanda's lyrics?"

"I don't know," she said. "Maybe. I'd've figured it out. But I'm glad you came. Let's try it with everyone, OK?" I followed Mari downstairs, and Amanda cut off a sentence midway through; Freddie avoided my gaze with a complicit half smile.

The first few times, we couldn't get through—Amanda and Freddie both struggled with their parts, giving me cover for my own mistakes. Finally, on the fourth try, we made it to the end, and I could tell everyone was surprised by how good it sounded. Mari's whole body turned spastic with excitement, one knee jumping so hard it whapped the underside of her keyboard. "It's good, right?" she said to me.

"I just—did you even think about trying my lyrics?" Amanda said.

"Do you like these lyrics?" Mari said. She nodded at Amanda, supplying the correct answer.

"They're a little twee, but fine," Amanda said. But she continued to look pained for the rest of practice, and when we finished, she packed her guitar and walked upstairs ahead of everyone else. Mari followed her out. Freddie said to Andrew, "Not great, that," and Andrew shrugged without looking at me.

At home that afternoon, I lay on my air mattress in the future child's room, hands resting on my stomach. My throat was raw, my back and hips ached, but I felt like pure energy, all force and no mass. I felt myself levitate up to the ceiling, breasts and toes scraping the glow-in-the-dark stars and comets and ringed planets that I'd stuck up there when I was eleven and that had endured Sally's renovation. I lay flat against the ceiling, alive and ferocious and free, until Sally knocked to ask if I wanted lunch, and I called back, "OK, sure, thanks!" and crashed down onto the air mattress, where I reassembled myself into a human adult so I could go eat a sandwich.

WHEN I RETURNED to practice on Tuesday, we sang "Tiny Animals" and "Forgotten," and Mari pulled me in for backing vocals on a few other songs. I could hear how much I brought to each song, could see it in the reactions of the other band members, in Mari's growing confidence: my voice was strong, and I meshed well with the rest of the group. At Thursday's practice, Mari wanted me singing on nearly all the songs, and at the end of the night, she turned to me and said, "See you Saturday?"

The rest of the band audibly shifted behind me. Les Somnambules were rehearsing the set list for a show in late June, about a month away, opening for Lucia Brahe at the Atrium, a large new venue in Southeast DC. Lucia Brahe was a singer-songwriter from New York City who was getting compared to Sinéad O'Connor and Tori Amos, a dreamy, tortured artist who wrote songs about drugs, sex, and death. Mari had gotten a sense from conversations with Brahe's manager that if the show went well, Les Somnambules could be invited to join her Europe tour next year, maybe get signed to the same record label. Tickets were already sold out, and the *Washington City Paper* had called Mari, wanting to interview her for a short feature about Les Somnambules—the first time they'd gotten that treatment. Ordinarily, Mari would've been full-tilt preparing for the show. Instead she was fiddling with different arrangements based on my voice, just weeks before they'd need to perform without me. I couldn't figure out why she'd do it, and although everyone had been kind, I could tell the rest of the band was getting antsy about my continued presence.

But I wasn't ready to leave either. Mari's Les Somnambules songs were much more complicated than her Maidenheads songs, and it was both an intellectual and artistic challenge to learn my parts. I loved the new sound and what it revealed about Mari's growth as a musician over the past decade. I loved feeling pushed as a musician myself, after so long not considering myself a musician at all. I loved the unexpected transformation of my voice on Les Somnambules songs: not my Maidenheads voice at all but smokier, sweeter, still eerie but without the old chirpiness.

More than anything, I loved singing with Mari, loved her bossiness and charm and absolute commitment. I loved hearing my voice shatter her songs like a fist through glass, I loved the way our eyes reflexively met in the first breath after a song ended.

"Sure, I can be there on Saturday," I told Mari.

They still had a month, I told myself on the bus ride home; that was plenty of time to rehearse the set list as they'd perform it. I wasn't a member of Les Somnambules. I was just singing along for a few practices, a final gift to myself before the realities of parenting set in. It was only temporary, I told myself, as well as my mom, who balked when I mentioned on the phone that week that I was practicing with Mari: "Are you sure?"

Of course I was sure. When it was over, I'd return to Baltimore, to my sad apartment and sad job and, eventually, to a baby who would make all that sadness more tolerable. I'd order my days around feedings and naps and tummy time, I'd stay in on weekends, I'd make small talk with other moms on the playground. Maybe I'd find a community of cool queer moms like Freddie, and we'd support each other, swap babysitting nights, push our strollers to coffee shops and nurse our babies under blankets. I wouldn't miss singing at all, not with so much else to occupy my time.

Although I knew having a baby would be difficult, it didn't feel impossible. I had paid June rent on my Baltimore apartment. I'd pack up my suitcase and move back, negotiate maternity leave or a raise with Jeremy, potentially find a new job: it would be good for me to leave the *Bugle* anyway. My mom would help; she loved babies and wouldn't miss a chance to demonstrate her superior childcare skills. Regardless of Peter's feelings about the pregnancy, he wasn't the type to abandon an actual baby. He would almost definitely stick around to judge my child-rearing, maybe take the kid on weekends sometimes. His parents might help pay for piano lessons, college down the road.

In a fit of eager practicality, I found a daycare near my house that was cheaper than the others, run out of someone's basement; I made an appointment with an obstetrician near the *Bugle* offices. I read up on cribs and strollers, and one day, I ordered a stuffed bear printed with black and white geometrical shapes, since I'd heard that was good for newborns, and had it shipped to my Baltimore apartment.

I didn't spend a lot of time with my father and Sally that week, but I heard them in the house: Sally sighing over a plate design that hadn't come out right, my father complaining about a grad student who kept submitting forms too late, Sally teasing him when he got too serious. They were tender and cuddly, bursting with shared delight over the future child; I stayed in my room to avoid them. On Friday afternoon, Sally had an appointment with her obstetrician and my dad left work early to drive her (had he ever left work early for me?). Around four, I heard the front door open and close and then a sob. I hurried in to see Sally crying on the living room couch, my father's arm around her shoulders. "It just hurts," she said into his neck. "It really, really hurts."

I felt obtrusive, but it was too late to leave—my father had already seen me. "Do you want some water?" I asked.

"Maybe an aspirin?" he said. "Her wrists are bad today, and the doctor said it probably won't get better until she has the baby." Sally's hands and wrists had become painful and stiff, a symptom that for reasons I couldn't understand was related to pregnancy. One afternoon, with a pained laugh, she showed me an aborted plate design: a custom job for a kid's birthday—"You're Our Hero, Henry!"—next to a skunk in a mask and superhero cape. But the lettering straggled, all her colors ran outside the lines, the skunk looked like a striped raisin. She had tried rubbing her wrists with arnica cream, she had tried tart cherry juice and chamomile tea, turmeric and ginger, hot pads and ice packs, but nothing was working.

My father was stroking Sally's hair back from her face, unsticking it from her teary eyes with one finger. The aspirin was in the downstairs bathroom, but I paused a moment to watch. I had never seen my father tend to anyone before. He whispered to Sally like he was soothing a spooked horse: "It's going to be OK, shhh, baby, it's going to be OK."

Then he glanced up at me and his face shifted into anxiety. "I'm going," I said, "I'll get water too." He nodded and turned away, back to Sally.

I got the aspirin, went to the kitchen for the water, brought it all back, and set it down on the table next to the velvet couch. My dad was still clasped around Sally, and this time, he didn't even look up. I slunk back to my room, where I sat in the baby's rocking chair and soothed myself by humming through one of the songs Mari had set me to learn for Saturday's practice.

• • •

MARI DIDN'T MENTION the Lucia Brahe show on Saturday, nor at the following Tuesday's practice. I could sense everyone's silent consternation when we ran through "Forgotten" and "Tiny Animals" with me on lead, and I felt uneasy myself, like I was there on expired credentials. As we were packing up to leave on Tuesday night, Mari said, "I don't have work tomorrow, do you guys want to go out for karaoke?"

Amanda and Andrew looked at each other. "I have a shift in the morning," Amanda said. Andrew was reluctant too—he had a new girlfriend, it was intense.

But Freddie convinced them. "We never do anything together except practice," she said. "It'll be good for morale."

"OK if I tag along?" I asked. Mari nodded like it was obvious, but Amanda was twisting her fingers in her topknot, and even Freddie just smiled vaguely at the wall.

We stuck Liya's car seat in the trunk of Freddie's Civic and she drove us to Adams Morgan, Mari in the front seat making unpopular radio decisions while Amanda, Andrew, and I were squashed silently in back. Three blocks from 18th Street, I guided Freddie to the secret parking spot behind my mom's building. As we walked past, I glanced up to her fourth-floor strip of windows: all dark.

On 18th Street, we passed the sketchy sushi place with black-painted windows, the used bookstore where I used to surreptitiously flip through 1970s sci-fi novels looking for sex scenes, all the bars that had replaced old bars I'd known and loved (RIP Asylum, Toledo Lounge!). The basement karaoke bar was one of the survivors, a place Mari and I had gone in high school. She pulled us downstairs and found the owner, a Korean man named Jeff. He greeted her with a cheek kiss, then swept us into one of the rooms and brought out dumplings, popcorn, and beer, plus two giant laminated song binders.

Freddie went first with "Jolene," which in her sweet voice sounded like a polite series of requests. Amanda and Andrew did a theater-kid rendition of "I've Had the Time of My Life" from *Dirty Dancing*. When it was Mari's turn, she stepped up to the touch screen and clicked directly to "Dancing in the Dark" without consulting the binder. As the first chords rang out, she cocked her hip and tossed her head to the side, holding the mic at her shoulder between first finger and thumb, the way she held cigarettes. "*I get up in the evening*," she muttered, pumped her fist on the next line, then did a stage kick. Amanda rolled her eyes—I suspected she'd seen Mari do Springsteen karaoke at least as often as I had—and Andrew went upstairs to call his girlfriend. Ignoring them, Mari belted out the song at full volume, voice at its raspy limit ("*Wanna change my clothes my hair my FACE*"). Afterward, she flopped onto the bench and tugged up the collar of her T-shirt to swab her forehead.

"You going to do anything besides Bruce this time, Mar?" Amanda said, eye roll still audible.

"Now that you said that, nope," Mari said.

Her bravado sounded wobbly. I knew how vulnerable Mari felt after singing, maybe the only time she let herself feel that way. "Mari, I'd do 'Leader of the Pack' with you," I said.

As the Maidenheads, we'd closed all our shows with a Shangri-Las cover. Nearly all their big songs worked well as punk covers—they weren't really bubblegum at all, more a mix between spoken-word performance art and primal scream therapy, filtered through Mary Weiss's mad yodeling heart-wild voice, her working-class babysitter realness. I didn't think Freddie, Andrew, and Amanda would know that, and I was sure they wouldn't know about the time on the high school bus when I'd tucked my headphones over Mari's ears so she could hear "Remember (Walking in the Sand)" without distraction.

Mari pulled her knees up to her chest. "Sure, yeah. If that's how you want to use your turn."

"Don't do it if you don't want to."

"No," she said, standing with a sigh. "Let's fuckin' do it."

The karaoke track started, and we swung into parts we knew very well. Mari had always done the bitchy girl chorus, so the song starts with her talking, something she'd always done with gravely force. That night, though, she started off mechanically, just delivering the lines as if reading from a menu. My first line, *"I met him at the candy store!,"* always felt to me like the bleakest cry in the world, carrying so many crashed-out dreams. But balanced against Mari's blankness, my voice came out overbright and brittle.

"Ugh, stop," I said, interrupting myself. "It sounds terrible. I'll do something else on my own."

Mari glared at me. The music was still playing, tinny without the vocals. I could feel Amanda and Freddie watching us. "You're the one who wanted to."

"I don't care," I said. I couldn't explain how miserable it felt to hear us fucking up that song. I just didn't want to hear it anymore.

"So we're just going to stand here until the song's over and not sing?" Mari shook her head and said, "Such a prima donna." Then she picked up the line and began singing my part, an octave higher than her usual range, adding a girlish singsong. Mari was imitating my Maidenheads voice, and doing a pretty good job at it. I laughed, and she guffawed and kept going.

At the end, for the dirgelike repetitive part Mari usually would've sung, I began singing—but in her voice, deeper than my throat could really bear. By now, we were giggling so hard we struggled to finish.

"Does anyone want to do 'I'll Stand by You' with me?" Amanda said after our track quieted. "I can't get the high notes."

"I'll do it," Freddie said, and together they belted out an operatic version, eyes squinched shut, arms flung out. Mari settled back on the bench with her beer propped on her stomach. "That was good," she said to me. "We sound good together."

"We always sound good together," I said.

"Not when you have tantrums," she said. I looked over, but she didn't look back, drawing circles in the condensation on her beer can.

"I don't have tantrums anymore," I said, feeling defensive.

"You just kind of did."

"Not real-life tantrums. Just karaoke tantrums."

"Karaoke tantrums are the worst kind," she said, smiling at her beer.

I HADN'T TEXTED my father to tell him I was going out after practice, and when Freddie dropped me off around midnight, he was in the living room watching a movie, Sally asleep across the couch with her legs in his lap.

"Oh," I said when I saw them. "You weren't waiting up for me, were you?"

"We were worried," my father said, rubbing his eyes. "You weren't picking up your phone."

"We just went out after practice," I said. "It's not even that late."

Sally had woken up by now and put her hand on his arm. "I told you not to worry," she said. "She's a grown-up, she doesn't have a curfew."

"You weren't around when she was younger," my father said to Sally. "There's history here."

"History, yeah?" I said. "What history do you mean?" I was feeling amped up after karaoke, the new softness I'd felt from Mari after our song. She'd kissed me good night on the cheek, the first time she'd done that; she'd said, "See you Thursday?"

"Drinking. Running around with Mari."

"So you give a shit about me now, is that right?" The words shot out so fast they startled even me. My father stirred on the couch, glanced at Sally in fear. A tuft of his dark brown hair stuck up diagonally over the bald spot, like the needle of a sundial.

"What are you talking about?" he said. "Of course I give a shit about you."

I thought of his glance at my wineglass after I told him I wasn't sure I was a girl; I thought about the years after college when he hadn't called. "Don't pretend," I said. "You've never actually been worried about me drinking or running around with Mari. When all of that stuff *was* happening, you didn't call me once. I was just alone with Mom and fucking *Michael* the whole time."

"And was that so awful?" he said. Sally put her hand on his thigh and tapped out a reassuring beat. "Mom is better at that stuff than I am. She always knows what to say."

"You didn't even try, though," I said.

"Ken, listen to her," Sally said, stroking his shoulder. "She's asking for an apology."

The combination of her words and her gesture—had I ever felt entitled to casually touch my father, had he ever accepted my touch without something that felt like a shiver?—somehow made me frantic. "I'm not!" I yelled. "I don't need an apology! I just need you not to be a dick about my *history* when you were barely part of it!"

My father stood up and swiped down his pants. I could see him trying to summon dignity, but his hair was still rumpled and his face very flushed. "It's late," he said stiffly. "We're likely to say things we'll regret." Sally followed him upstairs, glancing back at me with a sad smile. I went into my room and kicked the air mattress and wished I could drink and thought about Mari singing Bruce, how beautiful she'd been.

10

WHEN I WALKED up to Earl's house on Thursday night, Mari was outside, leaned up against his chain-link fence smoking a cigarette. In black jean shorts and a tank top cut off above her soft belly, she looked like an overgrown behind-the-gym kid. She hadn't gotten a haircut in a while, and black curls sprouted behind her ears, approaching mullet territory. My fingers itched to smooth them back.

"Don't go in yet," she said when I was close. "I need to talk to you about something." She hitched up a belt loop with her thumb, glanced around. "OK, I know I should've done this sooner, I was nervous. I really want you to sing in the Lucia Brahe show."

I'd worked hard not to envision this as a possibility, but that didn't mean I hadn't been desperately dreaming of it. "Of course I will," I said.

Mari went on talking as if she'd prepared a whole argument and had to deliver it to be sure: "I know this is last minute, and you probably can't stay at your dad's much longer. We could look for practice space somewhere in between DC and Baltimore, or do longer practices less often, or—"

"It's no problem at all," I said. "I can stay with my dad." Although my father had been gruff with me since our fight, I knew I could stay there. Jeremy hadn't said a word about me continuing to work remotely, which I'd decided to assume meant he was OK with it. And spending a few more weeks in DC didn't affect the pregnancy. I had months and months before I needed to start planning for that.

"Oh, shit," Mari said. A wild grin spread across her face. "Really?"

I was grinning now too. "Of course. Did you think I'd say no?"

"Sweet," she said, "Sweet! I thought we could tell the *City Paper* reporter, drum up some interest. They owe us after that crap story they wrote about *Jennifer*." This was the first reference she'd independently made to any event from the summer of 2002. I adored how she said "us," and the idea that the two of us, together, made a newsworthy item.

"So have you already talked to everyone else about this? What did they say?" I asked.

"Let me handle it," she said. She tossed away the cigarette butt and tucked her hair back behind her ears, then huffed a deep breath. "Don't worry, it's going to be great."

We walked in together, the last to arrive. Andrew and Amanda were chatting on the weight bench; Freddie was playing scales in the corner. Mari let everyone take their time to assemble, tune instruments, complain about the stink in Earl's basement, which had flooded yet again that week. Earl had inherited the house from his parents several years ago and lived here alone, with week-on, week-off custody of his kid. He'd set up the basement practice area for his own hardcore band back in the '90s. Now he worked for the postal service and didn't play music, but he let a few local bands use his basement for very cheap—everyone from us to a high school jazz trio—because he said it kept him "connected with the scene."

Earl did nothing to keep up the house. I'd once checked the expiration date on a jar of olives in the pantry: January 1998. One of the many improvements he had not made, although Mari had asked numerous times, was to install a sump pump in the basement or build French drains outside or do literally anything to prevent the constant flooding that occurred in most DC-area basements during the weeks of regular, heavy rain in the summer and fall. We stored everything off the ground, but the stink was ineradicable, and Freddie especially was concerned about the effects of breathing moldy air. "You know what it does to your lungs," she said that night, but it was a conversation we'd had so many times that no one responded. There weren't many affordable practice spaces in DC, and all of them had problems like this, if not much worse.

"Before we get started, just one thing," Mari said. "You all know I'm doing the *City Paper* interview this weekend. I want to mention in the interview that Jamie's singing at the Lucia Brahe show."

There was a long silence. Then Amanda said, "Hold up—Jamie's singing at the Lucia Brahe show?"

Freddie put her violin down, pulled her knitting out of her violin case, and began clicking needles. Andrew lifted his Nationals cap to scratch his curly hair, then tugged it down hard.

"Well, yeah. We've been practicing with her, the songs sound great, the show's in just a couple weeks. I sort of thought it was a given."

"Mari! There aren't supposed to be *givens*, we make decisions together. And you haven't consulted us at all. No offense, Jamie." Amanda nodded in my direction without looking at me.

"None taken," I said. "Mari—I thought you'd already talked to them about it?"

"Wait," Amanda said, "you've talked to *her* about it but not us?"

"I talked to her literally a minute ago," Mari said, sullen, hands in pockets.

"Not to mention, if Jamie's singing at the Brahe show, that changes the *City Paper* story," Amanda went on. "Suddenly it's all Maidenheads reunion tour, they'll write about *Jennifer.* I thought we agreed we wanted to get away from that."

"I don't see how it matters. Having Jamie sing is good, right? Being covered by the *City Paper* is good, right?"

Amanda slapped her fingers across the Gibson, emitting an aggressive G chord. Everyone jumped; Andrew touched his hi-hat as if to prevent it from vibrating. "So what about the *Jennifer* screening, then?" she said. "Is Jamie singing for that too?"

"I don't think so, right, James? Just this concert, then you're back to Baltimore?"

Mari hadn't called me James since high school. "Right, yeah," I said.

"Can we talk upstairs?" Amanda said to Mari, ignoring me.

As soon as they were gone, I said to Andrew and Freddie, "I'm sorry. She only just asked me, I assumed she'd already talked to you." It was true I had assumed this, but I also wasn't surprised to be wrong. Mari would always choose the easiest route to get what she wanted, would always ask forgiveness (if that) and not permission. She would've waited to tell Amanda on purpose, knowing that the closer we got to the show, the harder it would be for Amanda to do anything about it. I felt sorry for Amanda, but mostly I felt a shy glee: Mari was scheming on my behalf.

"It's not your fault," Freddie said. But she was watching Andrew.

"It's not your fault," he said after a moment.

"And it's still temporary, anyway," I said. "Just for the show, then I'm moving back to Baltimore to get ready for the baby."

Andrew stretched out his long legs, wiped an invisible speck off a drumhead. "It's not us you have to convince," he said. "Amanda's not in a great place about you coming back."

"I've noticed," I said. "What's going on there?"

"Mari cheated on Amanda," Andrew said. "Like a lot. That's why they broke up. So it's weird for Amanda to be around someone Mari used to fuck." He paused. "Sorry, obviously you're more than that, it's just . . ."

"No, no," I said, but I was shaken. "I mean, it's accurate."

"Andrew—cool it. Amanda and Mari will be fine," Freddie said; then she turned to me, her eyebrows anxiously pursed. "You can't worry about that history, OK? Mari can be selfish sometimes, we all know that, but *you* shouldn't worry—you're not doing anything wrong."

Andrew shook his head, seeming ready to say more, but just then Amanda and Mari came back down, Mari gripping Amanda's hand. Mari said, "OK, guys, this was my fault and I'm sorry. Can I try this again, get it right this time?" Without waiting for a response—Amanda stared down at her Keds—she went on: "I think Jamie adds a lot to the band and I'd like her to sing as a special guest at the Brahe show. After that, she'll go back to Baltimore. But this is a big decision, so we need to make it together. What do you all think?"

Freddie and Andrew were both watching Amanda. Mari turned to her as well. "Amanda?" she said. She tugged on Amanda's limp hand.

"It's fine," Amanda said. She looked up and gave me a tight, quick smile. "Sure. Welcome to the band, Jamie."

Mari did her phone interview with the *City Paper* reporter that weekend. Afterward, she texted the group—I think it went OK???—and no one replied. The story went up online the following Monday. It focused primarily on the Lucia Brahe show and the new songs, but still included a paragraph on Mari and me: "Longtime DC music fans will be pleased to note that singer Jamie Cain's recently announced presence at the show marks a reunion: Cain and Dvali's first band, experimental punk duo the Maidenheads, was a local favorite back in the early '00s, when the two were still students at Frederick Douglass High School. The Maidenheads had a moment of notoriety after appearing in a 2002 film, *Jennifer's Not There*, that was panned at the time for its stereotypical LGBTQ characters but has since become an underground classic." They included a photo of Mari, Freddie, Andrew, and Amanda from the 9:30 Club show, plus an old photo of Mari and me, a still from *Jennifer* showing us onstage in the prom dresses, so blurry and small I couldn't make out our individual faces.

An hour after the story posted, Mari texted it to the band group chat. Once again, no one replied. I wrote directly back to Mari: Looks great! Everyone happy? But she didn't respond. At practice on Tuesday, we were all quiet, but I felt like I could hear everyone's cranky thoughts, particularly Amanda, who showed up disheveled and late. We played through the set list for the Brahe show, sounding mechanical and dull, then everyone left in separate directions without speaking.

THE NEXT MORNING, I took the MARC to Baltimore for the Wednesday all-staff meeting. Jeremy intercepted me after: "Could I talk to you a minute?" I followed him down the hallway into his office.

"I saw the *City Paper* story," he said after he shut the door behind us. The print copy was on his desk, open to our photos. "Are you playing with Les Somnambules now? Is that why you've been working from DC?"

"I've been practicing with them, yeah," I said. "That's not why I'm in DC, though."

"The family thing?"

"I'm pregnant," I said. I hadn't planned to tell him, but I knew female-body stuff flummoxed Jeremy. If I wanted to keep working from DC, it felt like a necessary sacrifice. "Not far along. But I've had a lot of morning sickness, and I wanted to be near my parents. And yeah, while I'm there, I'm practicing with Mari, and I'm singing in this show. But just on a couple of songs, and just for this one show. I'm not joining the band."

Jeremy's eyes darted to my belly; my ab muscles reflexively tightened. Then he leaned back in his seat, resting one sneakered foot across his opposite knee. "Well, first of all, congrats," he said, and rubbed a finger across his eyebrows. "And from a fan perspective, I'm excited to hear that you're playing with Les Soms. Wish I could get to that show. But from the perspective of being your boss: you *are* coming back to the office eventually, right? Because you can't be remote forever."

"Yeah, no, that's what I'm saying. I'll be back in a couple weeks."

"You know, you could always commute here from DC—lots of people do that."

I had thought about it. From my dad's house, the commute was about an hour and a half door-to-door, sometimes longer depending on train and Metro schedules. I would need to leave around seven every morning and would get home at 6:30; on Tuesday nights, with issue close, I might not be able to get back at all. There was also the option of staying in Baltimore but commuting to practice in DC three times a week: leaving directly after work on Tuesdays and Thursdays, getting back close to midnight, and spending most of Saturday away from home. It was all doable, just not as a single parent.

"No, I'm coming back to Baltimore to have the baby," I said.

Jeremy swung his foot to the ground and smacked his hands on his knees. "Then I'll look forward to having you in the office soon. In terms of maternity leave—we haven't had any new mothers working here since I've had this job, so I'm not sure what it is. I think official WMP leave might be two paid weeks; plus, there's always unpaid FMLA time if you wanted to look into that?"

"Oh, wow," I said. "OK." Sally had told me she was planning to take six months off work. "It's crazy that our country expects anyone to go back to work sooner than that," she'd said. "Your body takes so long to recover." But with my dad's salary, she could afford six months.

Jeremy looked at me, and I could sense him trying to gauge how much resistance I would put up. "At least we *have* a leave policy," he said, spinning sideways on his chair to fiddle with some proofs on the desk. "For now. WMP is always pushing us to cut back. Being a manager sucks—really, it's the worst—but sometimes I have to make hard decisions. You understand, right?"

"I think so?"

"Great. Let me know what you decide," he said. His smile was firm and dismissive. I walked out in a daze: Had he just threatened to take away my leave entirely? Had he threatened to fire me?

After work, I walked over to the obstetrician's office for my appointment. "Yep, definitely pregnant," the doctor said, looking at my urine test results. She used her paper calendar wheel to calculate my due date—early January, a Capricorn—and prescribed me a prenatal vitamin. "Congratulations," she said, and it felt different from when Sally had said it. This time it felt like a declaration of identity, like being called by a new name. The baby was real, it was growing inside of me, and unless I took action (and immediate action: I was already at nine weeks), it would continue to grow until it was a person.

Up until that moment, I'd been thinking about the baby abstractly, a theoretical force acting on my life. But I walked out of the doctor's office horror-stricken: there was an actual human in there. I stopped just outside the doors of the medical center and pressed blindly at my belly, took several deep breaths. A woman walked out the doors behind me pushing a stroller, and I stared at her real fucking baby, wrapped in a blanket printed with SpongeBob SquarePants. That baby had once been an idea in the woman's head, but now it was crying and pooping and on its way to growing up and becoming an adult who had sex and did hurtful things to people and then, at some point, would die.

Babies needed food and a place to sleep. Babies needed soft fleecy blankets printed with SpongeBob. Babies needed a parent with a job that paid enough money to buy those things. They needed a parent capable of providing steady unflagging care—not just on good days but on every day, forever. It had felt bracing and inspiring to imagine myself becoming that parent. But if I did, I couldn't be much else, at least not for a while. I was fooling myself, I saw, standing in the sun with my hands clamped around my belly, to think I could be that parent without returning to Baltimore immediately, even before the Lucia Brahe show. For one, I needed to find a new job with an actual maternity leave policy right away, before I started showing. I'd been telling myself I had ages to mess around in DC with Mari, but in fact, I had no time at all.

Peter texted that night. Saw the City Paper article, he wrote. You and Mari performing together?

Just this one time, I wrote back. Since when did Peter read the *Washington City Paper*? He must have a news alert set up for my name, this was gratifying to learn.

When are you coming back? he replied.

After the show. So about two weeks

After the first trimester then

Have you been calculating the date of my last period, Peter?

No, I just wondered

I felt hot, shaky. *What business is it of his? What right does he have to ask?* His three dots flashed on and off for a long time; then, It's really OK if you want to get an abortion, he wrote. I don't think anyone would judge you. If you're worried about that.

I was so tired. I'd been laying my pregnant body on a poorly inflated air mattress every night for weeks now, and parts of me hurt I'd never known could hurt. I had decisions to make that I knew might hurt even worse. I wanted to do everything and be everything: I wanted to be a rock star and I wanted not to be shoddy and I wanted to be wherever Mari was and I wanted to be a person you'd see on the street and think, *She seems like someone who has her life together.* I wanted a child, and I wanted to be a child. But in every direction, the secret shame that had dogged me all my life, the essential bad fit, doomed me now. I would always be wrong, always come up short. I wrote a long and ferocious reply to Peter (none of your business . . . condescending prick . . . I always knew you'd . . . MY body), then deleted it and wrote just, What the fuck

Seriously. It's OK

I know it's OK, don't need
your fucking permission

That's obviously not what I
meant and you know it

Fuck off seriously. Don't text
me again. Actually peter it's
not even yours I fucked some
other guy fuck off forever

Three dots on and off. Then nothing, until the nothingness hurt my brain, and I turned off the phone to extinguish it.

THE FOLLOWING NIGHT'S practice, a Thursday, marked nine days to go before the Lucia Brahe show. When I got to Earl's house a little after eight, the door to the pink bathroom was closed. Downstairs, Freddie and Andrew sat on adjacent folding chairs, looking grim.

"What's going on?" I asked.

"Mari and Amanda are talking upstairs," Freddie said. She was knitting a purple scarf, its long tail coiled around her lap. "They said to wait."

Andrew drummed on the edge of his chair, bounced his knees, then sprang up. "Fuck this, I'm getting a cigarette," he announced on his way out.

"Have you talked to either of them recently?" I asked Freddie, taking his chair.

She made a Marge Simpson "hrrm" and glared at her neat row of stitches. "I did talk to Amanda earlier and she was pretty upset about the *City Paper* story. Just that, you know, automatically when you're in the story, it becomes a story about you and Mari, not about the band."

"I get why Amanda would be sensitive about that," I said. "But I don't completely understand why she's holding on to it still. They broke up years ago, right?"

Freddie sighed. "They're so trauma-bonded, though. They started dating right before Yevgenia died, and Amanda's a total caretaker, classic Taurus. But Mari started spiraling out: drinking too much, fucking around. Amanda couldn't take it and she left. I think they never really separated, though, know what I mean? Mari still leans on Amanda for so much, and Amanda feels this compulsion to care for her, even though she resents it. It's not a good dynamic, either for them or, obviously, for the band. Andrew and I used to joke, like, uh-oh, Mommy and Mama are fighting again."

I didn't like thinking about Mari leaning on someone else, Mari close to someone else. "Poor Andrew," I said, to change the subject.

Freddie sighed. "Yeah. He's the only one who wasn't our friend before the band, we found him on Craigslist. So he's not used to all the lesbian chaos. We were both nervous when you came on—like, damn, we just figured out how to be in a band with two exes, now we have to deal with *three?*"

"Three Exes would be a great name for a queercore band," I said.

Freddie's laugh came sharp and loud. Then she said more soberly, "Well, we'll see—right?"

"See what?"

"See what happens with Amanda and Mari. And you and Mari. Because, I have to say, that doesn't seem quite resolved either."

I'd been telling myself that it *was* resolved—that despite all the little sparks of connection I thought I'd felt, we were focused on the band, not each other. "It's as resolved as it'll ever be," I said, with a casual shrug. "Hey, I'm going to get some water upstairs. You want anything?"

Freddie gave me a slow look, then shook her head. I bolted upstairs and into the kitchen, poured myself a glass from the tap, leaned against the counter to drink it.

The pink bathroom was across the hall from the kitchen, and I could hear Mari's and Amanda's echoing voices. I wasn't really trying to listen, but just then Amanda said very clearly, "You're fucking her, it's obvious, stop lying about it."

"I wouldn't do that," Mari said, quieter.

"You wouldn't lie, or you wouldn't fuck her?"

"Either. That's in the past. This is different: Jamie's just staying for this one show, then she's going back to Baltimore to have the baby."

"I don't know—I get a feeling she wants to stay longer."

I held my breath. After a pause, Mari said in a weary voice, "I'm just going to say it one more time—that would be a *good thing.* Jamie's voice is fucking insane. There's so much we can do with that."

Warmth ran through my body. "Maybe," Amanda conceded. "I'm not sure it's worth it."

"It's worth it. Trust me."

"Mari—she destroyed you last time. Destroyed you *and* the band. Don't you see how easily that could happen again?"

"It wouldn't happen again—I won't let it," Mari said. She sounded very sure: I could picture her tossing her hair to the side in a rough headshake.

"You don't control everything."

"But I know Jamie. Trust me."

Amanda clicked her tongue and said, "I can't stick around to watch you do this to yourself, not to mention the rest of us. If Jamie stays after Lucia Brahe, I'm out."

"Fine. Then I can find a guitarist who can actually get through 'Tiny Animals,'" Mari said, voice thick with anger and pain.

I heard the sharpness in Amanda's reply, but I couldn't make out the words. Just then the front door opened and Andrew came in. He heard the voices from the bathroom and his eyes went wide. "What's happening?" he whispered.

"I don't know. They seem pretty upset."

"We should go downstairs before they come out," he said, and I followed his narrow tense shoulders down the basement steps.

When she saw Andrew's face, Freddie put down her needles. "What's wrong?"

"They're fighting in the bathroom. Did you hear anything, Jamie?"

"Not really," I said. In fact, I had heard too much, but the thought blacking out all others was: *Mari wants me to stay.*

"If Amanda quits before the show, we're fucked," Andrew said.

"She wouldn't do that," Freddie said.

"You don't know that. *Mari* doesn't know that. Fuck!" he said. "Fucking Mari!" He was standing right next to the Reagan cutout, and he started kicking it wildly, like a kid kicking out into space, until the cardboard buckled and Reagan collapsed. Andrew picked it up and threw it on the ground and stomped on it, and then he did it again. "Fuck!" he yelled again, and a few more times.

"OK," Freddie said, "you've taken down the Gipper. You good now?"

"Fuck," Andrew said again, more calmly, and he shook out his shoulders and tugged at his shirt collar, getting everything back to rights. "Just *fuck*, though, seriously, Freddie. Aren't you mad at her?"

"I'm so fucking mad at her," she said, in her quiet precise way. "But what choice do we have?"

"We could quit," he said. They were ignoring me, and I stayed very still in my folding chair to allow them space. I could only really think about Mari anyway: *Mari wants me to stay.*

"Andrew, don't be stupid," Freddie said. She smoothed down one forearm, then the other, like she was smoothing out the tattooed vines. "This is a good band. And the Lucia Brahe show is a huge deal. If it goes well, if we get signed, get on the European tour, I could think about going part-time at work. It's the worst moment to leave, although obviously I'll support Amanda if that's what she needs to do."

"You're right," Andrew said. He propped Reagan back up against the wall, then re-propped it when the cutout toppled over its own knees. "Fuck. Why do you have to be so damn smart all the time?"

"Just next to you, buddy," she said.

"Ah, shut up," he said, and they laughed, but cut it off when the basement door opened and two sets of footsteps started down. Mari came first, wearing the black sweatshirt she always wore to work. Her hair was damp at the roots, like she hadn't had a chance to shower after her shift. Amanda dragged behind. She had on cutoff sweatpants and Adidas shower sandals and a worn-thin black T-shirt, bedraggled hair sticking in all directions. When she saw us, her mouth fell at the corners. Freddie rushed over and the two of them stood embracing while Mari, Andrew, and I hung back awkwardly. I could hear Freddie whisper, "Are you OK?" and Amanda shook her head hard.

Mari gave her bangs a futile finger-raking and said, "Hi, so, this is uncomfortable, but obviously there's been some words between Amanda and me. She has generously decided she'll practice with us tonight and through the Brahe show, and afterward, we'll figure things out. Anyone got something to say?"

Amanda leaned into Freddie's shoulder and Freddie whispered something I couldn't hear. Andrew rapped a drumstick on his knee.

"I know everyone's stressed right now," Mari said. She said it with an eyes-wide cheer that reminded me of her voice describing the rape, brightness plastered over dread. I was watching her differently now, more tenderly: she wanted me to stay. "But let's get through this fucking show and then we can feel our feelings, OK?" No one said anything.

"So—set list? Start with 'Forgotten'?" Mari said.

We garbled our way through, crashing and burning on every song. Every single mistake we'd ever made, we made now all at once and then some. Amanda left even before we'd gotten to the end, just said, "OK then," halfway through a song, packed her guitar, and walked out.

"See you Saturday?" Mari called up the stairs as the front door slammed shut.

Freddie put down her violin and said, "Mari."

"We just have to make it through next week," Mari said. "I promise, I'll fix everything after that."

Freddie's shrug was expressive. Andrew said, "Mari, don't bullshit us. You're not going to fix this."

"It's OK, Andrew. It'll be OK. Let's go, I'll drive you home," Freddie said. She packed her violin, then guided him up the stairs without looking back at Mari.

Once the door to the basement stairs closed behind them, it became very quiet, just the hum of the water heater and TV voices upstairs. Mari slammed her fingers down on the keyboard and then played a fast jazzy riff with one hand, something I didn't recognize, fingers tickling it out as if acting freely from the rest of her slumped body. I forgot sometimes how talented she was, head and shoulders beyond the rest of us.

"You're doing your best," I said.

Her eyes went hard. "Get the fuck out, Jamie," she said, with another key slam. "*My best*, what is that bullshit." I could tell that she was seeing us next week in front of the enormous Atrium crowd, sounding as atrocious as we had in practice, getting booed off the stage, reviewers embarrassed by how bad we were, the end of all possibilities for signing with a label, recording an album, performing ever again. And Mari would never be Mari if she couldn't perform.

But she'd known that adding me to the concert lineup would upset Amanda, and she'd taken the risk anyway because of how badly she wanted me there. I felt a lurking joy, and I couldn't help but reach across the keyboard and put a hand on her shoulder.

"I meant it, though," I said, my voice coming out ragged. "It's going to be OK."

"No, it's not," she said. She pulled away from me and raked through her hair again so the sweaty front pieces spiked up. "It's going to be like last time. We're so fucking close! But it's happening again, Amanda's going to leave and I'm going to have to start from scratch."

"It's not going to be like last time," I said.

"It's my fault. I keep making the same mistakes."

"It's me, though, isn't it? If I hadn't come back, Amanda wouldn't be upset."

"Don't make this about you, it's really not about you," Mari said, sounding tired.

"I know it's not," I said. "I know."

"I failed with Amanda, on so many levels. This was going to happen eventually. It just sucks it's happening right now." She turned to pack up her keyboard. "I'm glad you came back," she said over her shoulder. "Even if you're annoying sometimes."

I felt warm again, remembering what she'd said to Amanda about my voice. "I'm glad I came back too."

"Well, so that's settled, and we don't have to worry about Amanda, unless she torpedoes the show and we're fucked forever."

From her jagged resigned laugh, I could tell she thought the conversation was over. But I knew I needed to ask one question before I could go home. "Mari," I said, "what would happen if I stayed in DC after the show?"

"What do you mean?" she said, still turned away from me.

"I mean just theoretically," I said. I felt the pulse along my neck, my wrists. "If I didn't go back to Baltimore. If I didn't have the baby."

She started around, black eyes fierce. "Is that what you want?"

"I don't know," I said. "But just—if that happened, if I were here, would you want me in the band?"

"It wouldn't be easy," she said slowly. "Amanda would probably leave. Freddie and Andrew, who knows. I'd have to work on them."

"Would you want me to stay anyway, even if that were the risk?"

"James," she said, tossing her bag over her shoulder in preparation to go, "I think you know that I would always want you to stay, whatever the risk. The songs I write—they're for you to sing. No one else. But it's not up to me, you know?" And she ran away, sneakers pounding up Earl's basement stairs.

11

WHEN I GOT home that night, I stopped in the kitchen to pour myself a glass of water from the filter pitcher, cold shooting through my chest as I swallowed it down. Sensing movement on the back deck, I looked out the sliding doors to see my father's bald spot shining under the light, encircled in smoke. Since I could remember, on nights he couldn't sleep, my father would sit on the deck smoking the joints he sourced from a former lab assistant and kept in an old Altoids tin in his desk. I didn't want to talk to him, just wanted to lie in my room holding my shaky sore body and play back Mari's words to Amanda a thousand times. But my father turned and saw me, then beckoned me out, so I slid open the doors and went to sit in the Adirondack chair next to his. The backyard was very dark beyond the reach of the deck lights, but I could see a few fireflies. From the neighbor's yard came the soft trickle of the vaguely Asian rock fountain they'd installed years back, in which a rat had recently drowned.

"You're up late," I said to my dad.

"Couldn't sleep. How was practice?"

"It was fine," I said. "How's Sally?" She had been in the upstairs bath when I left, trying out a new sore-muscle soak her parents had sent.

"Not great," he said. "She's worried about work if her wrists don't get better. I told her we're OK financially, but she doesn't like to hear that. She's always earned her own way, it frightens her to be dependent."

I'd noticed that day that Sally hadn't posted anything new on Instagram in weeks, just a photo of a magnolia tree in bloom with the caption "Summer's here y'all!" I said, "That's hard."

"I know you think the plates are silly," he said. When my father was high, his voice got squeaky and querulous—I'd always found it charming, a cute counterpoint to his usual seriousness. "But Sally is really good at them, and she's a great businesswoman. She earns way more than when she was a paralegal."

I hadn't realized Sally made money from the plates; I'd assumed they were an elaborate hobby financed by my father. "I never said they were silly," I said.

"You thought it, though. I could tell."

"They're maybe a little silly? I don't know. I think I was just nervous about Sally, maybe the plates were an excuse. I like the plates, actually."

"Nervous because she's your stepmother?" he said. "I can understand that."

He was in his fisherman's sweater. It had holes in the elbows and the hem was unraveled and it smelled like wet sheep. I could anticipate exactly the way it would scratch my cheek if we were to hug, if he were to put his arm around me the way he had Sally after her doctor's appointment. But my father wasn't going to hug me; he never did. "That, and also—I mean, Dad, I always thought you were gay."

He winced, the harsh porch light twisting his mouth. "Gay?"

"That's what Mom told me."

"Oh," he said. "That's interesting. Eileen does sometimes draw her own conclusions."

"So you're not gay?"

"Would you mind just telling me what she told you, first?"

"She said you wanted to date men," I said, carefully. "That you broke up because that was what you wanted. And when I was in high school, she told me you had a boyfriend."

"She told you that?"

"I guess she thought, maybe, it'd be good for me to know I had another queer family member. If that's what you are." I had never used the word "queer" to describe myself to him either, and my heart flapped loose and loud.

My father said, "Well, I'm certainly your family member. At least that's been my understanding."

"*Dad*."

The joint was halfway finished, and he carefully ground the tip against the wide wooden arm of his chair so the hot coal dislodged and smoldered out. He twisted the paper neatly to seal the remaining inch of joint and tucked it into his Altoids tin, then, pulling his sweater cuff up over his thumb, scrubbed away the black ash stain on the chair arm. "After you got so upset the other night, Sally told me I have to do better," he said finally. "I'm trying. I know I'm not the best at this stuff. So, queer—OK, if that's what you want. I don't really like labels."

"Is that why you never talked to me about it, because you don't like *labels*?"

"I wasn't sure you'd understand," he said. "What I am is a little confusing to people. So I don't always say it."

"How is it confusing?" I wasn't angry, just overcome. I had been waiting for this conversation for so long.

"Well—I'm not gay. I like men and women."

"But if you like women—what happened with Mom?"

He sighed. "We don't have to talk about it, you don't need to . . ."

I tried to sound gentle. I couldn't scare him off now. "Dad, I really want to know."

"OK," he said, settling more easily into his chair. The Altoids tin rested in the palm of his left hand, and he ran his thumb along its edge, back and forth. "You know, it was a very different time. I had tried dating men early on and it ended in disaster."

"The Foreign Service thing?"

"Mom told you that too?" he said, and I nodded. "Well, yes, the Foreign Service. After that—I suppose I believed that my superiors had been right to send me home."

"Oh, Dad."

"Well, perhaps they were!" he said. "I'd certainly broken the rules of the posting. In any case, I didn't think about dating men, at least not much at first. But over time, it started to feel like something I needed to explore. I felt I might cheat on your mom if I didn't tell her, and she didn't deserve that. But when I told her, she asked for a divorce."

My mother had always heavily implied that my father initiated the divorce. I had to admit, remembering my father's cloud of shame after she left, that his version made more sense. "So then what happened with the boyfriend—the one you had while I was in high school? Did you love him?"

"Sure, I loved him—Ted." His voice softened on the name, and then he went on quickly, "But we wouldn't have ended up together, even if he'd stayed in DC."

"Did you want to?"

"End up together? I suppose. He took a job in Texas and left, and that was that."

"Why didn't you tell me?" I was trying to remember my father while I was in high school, and I barely could. I'd spent weekends in Maryland, but most of the time, I was scheming to leave: meet up with Mari, go to a show, drive to thrift stores. I slept over at Mari's all the time. If I didn't have plans, I'd cook dinner, and then my dad would go to bed early while I watched TV. He asked awkward questions about school; I told lies. I'd seen no clues of him living a life apart from that.

"It just didn't seem important," he said.

"How was that not important? It's a huge fact about you."

"Is it?" he said. "I never felt like it was."

"But what about Sally, then? Why did you want to be with a woman?"

"Not just 'a woman'—Sally. I didn't choose her because she's a woman. I chose her because she made me happy, because I love her."

"So you're what, bisexual? Pansexual?" I was remembering Perry from the support group, the care with which he'd pronounced the word "pansexual," as if it were a fancy French dessert he'd just allowed himself to taste for the first time.

"Sure, if you like," my father said. "Does the word really matter?"

"It matters if it helps you understand what you want. If it helps other people understand."

He took his glasses off and massaged his closed eyes. "You told me once," he said, "you told me you didn't think you were a girl. I probably didn't react well. But it made me wonder. Are there words you need to understand what *you* want?"

I was conscious mostly of irritation, that he'd brought up something so tangential and random when I was trying to coax him into opening up. "*No*," I said, and it came out to my surprise in a baffled howl. "No, this is not about that at all! This is not about me, it's about you."

"Sure," he said. "OK." Then, more meekly, "Well, for me, I tried using all those words and no one understood what I meant. So I gave up. But that doesn't mean I gave up on understanding what I want. And I still think I deserve to be happy, even if what I want doesn't make sense to other people."

The word "deserve" pinged in a funny way in my head. I had never believed I deserved any of the things I wanted. I didn't deserve to sing after what I'd done to Mari. I didn't deserve any of my privileges, my freedoms, because of how secretly corrupt I knew myself to be. I didn't deserve to end the pregnancy, didn't deserve to stay in DC playing with Mari, didn't deserve to give my body what it wanted, didn't deserve even to learn what that was.

"I'm sorry," my father went on. "Are you angry at me?"

A crest was rising inside me, and I didn't know how to suppress it, not be swept away. "No. I think I'm sad."

"I'm so sorry," he said. "I know I made so many mistakes when you were younger, Sally's always telling me—"

"I really fucked up with Mari, back in high school," I said, interrupting him. "She still doesn't trust me. But I want to play music with her so bad. It's completely crazy."

"That's not crazy," he said, smiling.

"Stupid then. No one succeeds as a musician. And last time Mari and I played together, it fucked me up for a decade. There's no way this ends well."

"That's true about everything, though. Right? It's all going to end badly."

This jolted me into laughter. "Dad, that's very depressing."

"Does it have to be? The fact that my child with Sally is going to die one day doesn't mean I won't love that child. You will die someday—but I love you now."

"But I don't *want* the band to die," I said, hearing my own sulkiness. "And I don't want—I don't want Mari to die. I just want everything to be real forever."

"I know," he said. His smile was very sad. "I want you to be real forever too."

My hand was on my belly, and I forced it aside. I didn't want him to see me cry. "OK, Dad," I said, doing a fake teenager voice to cover up. "OK. Thanks for the talk."

"OK," he said. "Are you OK, or—?"

I could tell he wanted more; I could see how hard he was trying. But I wasn't ready to risk fully lowering my guard. "I'm OK," I said. "It's late, though. Should go to bed."

He nodded, stuffed the Altoids tin into his pocket, then stood. He paused under the deck light, peering at me—I saw yearning in his eyes, fear. Then he slid open the door and went inside, and I sat alone on the deck and cried hard for a long time. When I finished, I was very cold. The sky was black and starless; the air smelled like wet grass and rotting catalpa blossoms. I went into my bedroom and got under the blankets and shivered in the dark, kept awake by the erratic beating of my own heart.

I'd thought I had to have the baby, that the baby was what I needed, what I deserved. I'd gotten pregnant through sheer negligence—solely because I hadn't asked Peter to wear a condom for our bleak breakup sex. If I had an abortion, it wouldn't be because the fetus had a fatal malformation or because I was a teenager without a functional support network, but because I wanted to sing with Mari more than I wanted to have a baby. Did I deserve to make that choice? I didn't know, I didn't know anything. But as I fell asleep, I could still hear Mari saying, *For you—no one else.*

In the morning, I called the DC Planned Parenthood clinic and made an appointment for Monday at ten a.m.

I TOLD PETER first. I felt I owed him that, although it was galling, like an admission that he'd been right about me.

I'm having an abortion on Monday, I texted him. I'm sorry about what I said, it obviously wasn't true, but I still don't want to talk to you right now.

OK, he texted back, and that was it.

Then I called Mari. "I decided to get an abortion," I said. "I'm doing it Monday."

I had looked forward to telling Mari; I'd thought she'd be thrilled. I'd pictured a conversation about our future together, all the paths I'd cleared for us with this decision. But her voice was frightened. "Oh, wow," she said. "Why?"

"I mean—because I don't want to have a baby?"

"Of course, but why Monday?"

"I'm almost at the end of my first trimester. They said to come in right away."

"Sure, but isn't there any chance you could just wait a week, do it after the Brahe show?"

"Um—no?"

"OK," she said, very slowly, measuring disaster. "Jamie, I'm glad you're doing this and it's clearly the right decision. But maybe just don't tell anyone yet?"

"That I'm having an abortion? You don't think they might notice if I'm sick or have to miss practice?"

"You can't miss practice this week," she said, now truly panicked. "Listen, are you sure? I know they can do a lot with later-term abortions now, right? There's no immediate rush."

"Ugh, Mari," I said, and I hung up on her. She texted, I'm sorry I'm sorry I'm sorry, but we can't tell anyone before the show. OK? and I wrote back, Fine.

I didn't feel ready to tell either of my parents, especially not after Mari's reaction. But I had to tell Sally because I was hoping she'd drive me. I found her lying on the basement couch, her wrists in thick plastic braces crossed over her belly.

"I decided to get an abortion," I said. "I'm going on Monday. Is there any chance you could drive me? Also, could you tell my dad so I don't have to?"

Half asleep, she opened her eyes in confusion. "Of course," she said. "How are you feeling about it?"

No one else had asked this, and I wasn't sure at first how to answer. "Relieved but also sad, maybe?"

"That makes sense," she said. "Do you need a hug?" I shrugged, uncertain, and she stood and stuck her belly against mine and stretched her arms forward to grasp my shoulders. It felt like we were leaving space for the holy spirit at a middle school dance, but instead it was Sally's future child pressing me, supporting me.

Saturday's practice was more functional, and I thought Mari and Amanda both seemed in better spirits by the end. Maybe Amanda wouldn't actually leave if I decided to stay; maybe we would go on playing together, Three Exes, forever? I didn't really want that, I knew now. I wanted Mari to myself. I didn't want Amanda around, with all their knotty history and codependence; I wanted to be the Maidenheads again, just newer and better. I spent the rest of the weekend lolling around, reading Sally's magazines, watching fawns eat Sally's vegetables. I finally called my mother on Sunday night and told her about the abortion, then got off the phone before she could offer any opinions.

On Monday morning, when I came into the kitchen after showering, Sally set out a plate of scrambled eggs and toast and a cup of tea on the kitchen table. I ate reading an old L.L.Bean catalogue from the junk mail pile, feeling shaky and ill. Around nine, Sally packed a tote bag with a water bottle, oranges, and bananas, plus the candied ginger chews she knew I liked. Then she turned to me, keys in hand. "Ready?" Her smile was unsteady; she had on the stained "Pregnant AF" sweatshirt. I thought perhaps it had been a mistake to ask a pregnant woman to come along for my abortion, but now it was too late.

When Sally turned on the car, a Jewel album began playing. "Oh my god," I said. "You still listen to this?"

The only way I know how to make friends is to be mean to people, and hope that eventually they feel comfortable being mean back (hence: no friends). Sally turned to me, uncertain, and I froze—I'd gone too far, as usual. But she laughed. "I can put on something else."

"No, no, it's cool, I like pretending I'm in a *Felicity* episode."

"You should be so lucky! *Felicity* was great."

"I never actually watched it," I said. "Were you a fan?"

"Well," Sally said, "my parents let me watch whatever I wanted because they thought it would help me learn to be American. Then, during my first marriage, I watched a lot of TV to avoid my ex-husband, which means I've watched all of *Felicity* as well as most other late-'90s, early-'00s WB shows."

"What happened to your ex-husband?" I asked.

"I think he lives in Arizona now," she said.

We were quiet as Sally wove in and out of traffic, playing chicken with the lights. "If you time it right at night," she said, accelerating through an intersection, "you can make it all the way down 16th without hitting a single red."

"I'm sorry I made fun of *Felicity*," I said.

She laughed. "You should be sorry."

The Planned Parenthood on 16th Street was very visible, not how I'd imagined abortion clinics to be: blue awnings and a large sign out front, alongside all the grand churches and Masonic temples and embassy buildings. I'd pictured a crowd of antiabortion protesters, signs with photos of dismembered fetuses. But when we parked and walked up, there were only two protesters, clean-cut and very young, no signs. The boy wore a Catholic University T-shirt, the girl was in jeans and a floral-print blouse. Their eyes shot to Sally's belly. "We pray for you," they said simultaneously, and I could feel her cringe. I took her arm and pulled her away.

"They think I'm going for an extremely late-term abortion, I'll probably end up on one of those crazy websites," she said, once we'd pushed through the heavy doors.

"Who cares what they think?" I said, and she gave me a hard look.

The front lobby was fitted out with a bulletproof glass box, inside which sat a receptionist at a small desk with a square gray computer—she reminded me of the gorillas in the DC zoo, who sit inside a similar glass container, except she was playing Candy Crush on her phone. I signed in, pressed my ID to the glass, and she tapped a button that opened doors into the waiting room, where we sat on plastic chairs and watched *Judge Judy* on a TV attached to the ceiling.

"Are you OK on this chair?" I said to Sally when we'd been there for half an hour. We were alone in the small waiting room; there was a nurse station at one end, people in scrubs shuffling in and out, but no other patients.

"I'm fine," she said, stone-faced. She took out one of the bananas and ate it, then a ginger chew. I'd assumed she was packing them for me, but of course they were for her.

"You don't have to stay. I could take a cab home."

"Of course I'm staying."

"Are you upset because I was mean about *Felicity*?"

"I'm not upset with you," she said. "The protesters threw me off. My parents used to do that sometimes. They're very Catholic."

"Oh!" I said.

"To be clear, my politics are very different from theirs. But it brought back some bad memories."

"Are you still close with them?"

"Well, less so after they told me I'd done a good job marrying an older man who could support my 'stupid plates,'" she said, doing finger quotes on the final words.

I was shamed into silence: my initial reaction had been the same.

We watched as Judge Judy told a man he needed to move his things out of his ex-girlfriend's garage. The girlfriend tapped her long nails on the lectern, vindicated; the man hung his head. We waited for another fifteen minutes, until a nurse called my name. As I walked out, I looked back at Sally, slumped over her belly, looking very tired.

The nurse was probably in her forties, with short hair, a nose stud, and cats printed all over her scrubs. "Hey, we're both Libras!" she exclaimed when she saw my chart, and the bell in my head went, *Gay*. While she stood respectfully behind a curtain, I changed into a smock that opened in front. The nurse took a pinprick blood test from my middle finger, smearing it onto two round spots on a small piece of paper. Then she started a video on a handheld DVD player. The video showed several women in doctors' offices, preparing for their medical abortions. They all said things like, "I've heard I will have significant cramping, as well as nausea, diarrhea, and possibly a low fever. Is this true?" The doctors said, "It is true that a small proportion of women will experience these side effects. But you will be fine." At the end, all the women said that the experience had not been as bad as they had feared, and their friends brought them tea in bed.

After the video, I lay back and balanced my heels on the stirrups so the nurse could administer a sonogram using a vaginal wand. "You can look at the picture if you want to," she told me, bent over a glowing screen in the corner. "It doesn't look like much, though—just an egg yolk."

I shook my head.

"How are you feeling about the procedure?" the nurse said. "Do you have any questions?"

I paused. Did I? Too many, but none she could answer. "I'm good," I said. "No questions."

"OK," she said. "The doctor will come in soon with the pill." And she went out.

For the first ten minutes, I thought the doctor would come imminently, and then I realized it would be a longer wait. I lay down on the table in my gown, thighs sticking to the vinyl, and stared at the asbestos ceiling tiles. Someone in another room was crying, the sound amplified through the vent. I studied the signs on the walls in Spanish, English, and Amharic. I read all the pamphlets I'd been given, then read them again.

Now would be the moment to change my mind, and I searched myself for regrets. I wouldn't have a baby now, maybe not ever. I wouldn't be a mother. I could start drinking again.

At that thought, I felt the first shard of serious doubt. Through all these weeks living with the fetus, I hadn't had a single drink. There had been a part of me honoring the life inside me—treating it as a *life*, not just a patch of cells. I'd given it agency, tried to anticipate its needs.

I did a final pro/con summing up. Pros of baby: Caretaker when old, build a new family to shield me from the old one. Demonstrate selflessness, possibly actually become selfless. A life that makes sense to outsiders, maybe even to me. Ineffable things like "beauty," "joy," "purpose."

Cons of baby: Expensive. Would need to return to Baltimore and start a job search while visibly pregnant. Would have to figure out how to parent, then endure Peter and my mom's judgments on my parenting for the next eighteen-plus years. Everyone assuming I'm straight, strangers calling me "Mom." The risk that instead of banishing the Franken-feeling, motherhood might actually make it worse.

Never again the alchemy of my voice and Mari's words, her song spreading my lungs, her song screaming out of my mouth. Never again that glance in the first breath of silence. We might say we'd keep going, we might schedule a few practices somewhere between DC and Baltimore, but it wouldn't be enough. The space we needed to be ambitious, take risks, make the music we were capable of making—that was incompatible with babies.

Finally, the door opened, and the doctor and nurse came in together. I sat up so rapidly I became dizzy. The doctor was a sharp-featured older woman with a long gray braid down her back. She turned away from me to wash her hands at the sink in the corner and said, "How're we doing today?"

I started to cry. She dried her hands, sat down on the stool, and nodded at the nurse to leave the room. "What's going on?" she said when we were alone.

"I need to have the abortion, but I'm scared."

"Scared of what?"

"Scared I'll regret it. Maybe I'm being selfish."

"Do you need more time to think? You're ten weeks along. If you came back in a couple of days, we could still do the medical abortion, although it gets less effective as time passes. Or you could wait a little longer, but then we'd have to do a surgical procedure."

I had thought she'd try to reason with me, talk me into it. But her tone was very practical and calm, and it calmed me down too. A small clear space opened in my head, and out of that space I said, "I'm good, actually. I can do it today."

"Are you sure? You don't need to if you're not ready." She looked me hard in the face. "You're free to make this choice in whatever way you need."

No one had ever said that to me before. Nearly every choice I'd made in life had been a compromise with someone else's needs, or if not, I'd labeled it as selfish. None of it had felt free. I sat up straighter on the table. I said, "I'm ready."

One little paper cup held the pill, another the water. I placed the pill in my mouth and took a sip of the water and swallowed. I felt a heavy thickness in my throat, and I swallowed that down too.

The doctor went through the instructions again and made sure I had all my pamphlets. She gave me my second pill, to take within forty-eight hours, in an orange plastic vial. I got dressed and went to find Sally.

She was still in the waiting room, in the exact same chair. She stood up slowly, and I could tell from her face that I wasn't looking right.

"What happened with the Italian restaurant guy?" I said—that had been the *Judge Judy* segment playing when I left.

"She made him pay damages to the father for the broken equipment," Sally said. "Are you OK?"

"I think so," I said. I still felt shivery; the cold had rooted in my body during the time sitting on the table in my gown.

We stopped at a CVS on the way home. I drifted through the aisles amassing a random pile in my basket: a cup of instant ramen, a lime-green eyeliner pen to replace a beloved one I'd left at Peter's house, a half-price bag of foil-wrapped chocolate Easter eggs, a few magazines, and, finally, maxi pads and Tylenol. Back at my dad's house, I poured boiling water into the ramen cup and stuck down the paper lid. Looking at my darkened reflection in the microwave door, I tugged my eye flat, then steadied my hand on my cheek and drew a long green stripe across the stretched-out lid. With the eyeliner on both eyes, I still looked pale and thin-faced, but ferocious.

"That looks nice," Sally said as she came in, and I was grateful she hadn't pointed out the weirdness of applying eyeliner to give myself an abortion. "When do you take the second pill?"

"Anytime within the next forty-eight hours, they said. I'm going to take it now so I'm OK for practice tomorrow."

"You're really going to practice tomorrow?"

"Of course," I said. "The show's Saturday, Mari would kill me."

I watched Sally think about saying something, then decide not to. "Can I get you anything else?" she said instead, and after I declined, she retreated to the basement to work.

Once I finished the cup of instant ramen and drank the dregs—grainy with undissolved broth mix and freeze-dried carrot crumbs—I felt better, ready. I poured a glass of water, swallowed the second pill and a Tylenol, and went into the bathroom to install one of the enormous, thigh-chafing maxi pads I'd bought at CVS. Back in the living room, I answered a few work emails on the couch, then started a movie on my laptop. Every fifteen minutes or so, Sally made an unobtrusive visit to the kitchen, and I could tell she was checking on me.

About an hour in, I started to feel tightness in my lower abdomen, like someone had gathered everything up in one hand and twisted. Sally was in the kitchen eating nuts out of a paper bag, saw my face, and came in.

"I'm having pretty bad cramps," I said. This was an understatement now: my belly and my back echoed with pain.

"I'll get a hot pad," Sally said. She came back with an old electrical one wrapped in blue felt, plugged it into the wall, and handed it to me. I unpeeled the cover and pressed the sticky hot plastic directly against my skin, but it still didn't seem to penetrate deep enough.

"How about you get in bed?" she said. But instead of leading me into my room, she took me upstairs, to her room with my dad. I hadn't been up here since Sally moved in, and I spent a confused second registering all the changes—bed in corner now, surprisingly fussy floral duvet cover, white curtains over the two triangular windows—before Sally helped me climb into bed.

Normally I would've been grossed out to lie in the spot where my father made love to his much younger new wife. But in that moment, I was just grateful not to be on the air mattress. The thick duvet weighed on me comfortingly. I played Missy Elliott on my headphones and lay there soaking in the pain, until it dulled and became a steady condition of my body instead of something sharply inflicted on me. I could handle this, I realized. It hurt, but I was OK.

I thought about yolks, yokes, jokes. "Yust a yoke," my father would say, imitating his Swedish mother. Yellow of the yolk, cracked across toast. My father liked his yolks hard, my mother runny. My mother had taught me how to catch one: crack the egg in half, plop the yolk from half shell to half shell until the white globbed out. I'd always wanted to lift the shell to my mouth and swallow: a shivery ball of sun. Would it go down warm? Would it light you from inside?

I listened to all of *Supa Dupa Fly* and half of *Under Construction*, always kept at the edge of awake by the twisting in my belly. Then I got up to use the bathroom. The giant maxi pad was soaked black. I looked into the toilet after I'd peed: red clouds swirled the water, dime-sized clots sank to the bottom. In the mirror, I saw the green eyeliner smudged across my eyelids and it gave me a hopeful lift—the look of a future in which I was ruthless and free.

12

WAKING UP THE next morning, I surveyed my body. My feet felt normal, my legs, my hips, my arms, my hands. My gut was sore, but the fist gripping my insides had slackened. My heart seemed to float and twist like sand on the wind. I felt elated, reborn.

Sally fed me toast and shooed me upstairs to her room, where I climbed under the floral duvet and went through the motions of working on my laptop. It was a busy Tuesday. The week's issue was going to the printer, so there were forty pages to proofread and a barrage of last-minute changes from writers and editors to type into the publishing software. But none of it seemed to matter: who really cared if we orphaned a syllable at the top of one page, or if we used an em dash where an en dash should go? I raced through and wrote Jeremy around four: "Looks good to me!" Then I wriggled deeper under the blanket, put on my headphones, and listened to the Kate Bush song "The Big Sky" on repeat, something yawning open inside me.

I hadn't talked to Mari since the abortion, hadn't wanted to. There was a purity to my feelings, and I was hesitant to complicate matters. But before dinner, I called and she picked up right away. "I've been worried about you," she said. "Did you bleed a ton?"

"So much blood," I said. "Like—so much."

"Ewwww," she said. "What do you think about practice tonight, can you—"

"Of course," I said. She laughed, and I could hear the delight. I felt it too: I was free now, and the only thing I wanted from that freedom was to sing with Mari.

That evening, I pulled on sweatpants and a T-shirt and drove my dad's car to practice. Walking down the stairs to Earl's basement, where everyone was already waiting for me, I felt like I was coming home. Mari looked up from her keyboard. "She's baaaaaa-ack," she said, and slapped out a horror-movie "dun-dun-*dunnnnnn*" with her left hand. Her grin lit mine like a torch.

AT PRACTICE ON Thursday, we played through the set list one final time, then packed the gear into Andrew's van for Saturday. Everything sounded fine, we weren't actively screwing up, but I could tell Mari was not pleased. I hung around after in hopes of talking, but she left immediately.

Then it was two days of pacing around my father's house, unable to focus or sit still for more than a few minutes. Before the abortion, I'd felt trapped by time, tied down like a girl on a railroad track. Pregnancy time, maiden to mother to crone—time both ladder and chute, riding you up toward death. But I'd fought loose, and now time was a circle, a cyclone, a billowing space.

Saturday's load-in at the Atrium was at four, sound check at six, doors at eight, we went on at nine, Lucia Brahe at ten. I slept late that morning, told my father and Sally I was resting my voice and couldn't talk, and hid in my room watching all the *Mummy* movies on my laptop. Around three, I packed my shoulder bag with the outfit I'd prepared for later—I knew I'd be flop-sweating all day—and rode the Metro to the Atrium, which was in Southeast DC near Nationals Park.

The Atrium was only a year old, all shiny and clean, in a new building that also housed a CrossFit gym and a bar that sold $18 hamburgers. It was the first time I'd been in Southeast DC since high school, when Mari and I convinced Yevgenia to drive us to a warehouse rave on a block of abandoned industrial buildings. The neighborhood was totally different now, comprised mostly of the anodyne tan concrete eight-story apartment blocks that had spread across DC over recent years like a skin disease. Banners wrapped around each building's first floor showing computer-generated images of its inhabitants, stiff-limbed humanoids barbecuing on roof decks or walking their robotic dogs.

Everyone was waiting in the small staff parking lot behind the Atrium, where Lucia Brahe was taking twice as long as allotted for load-in. Mari had gotten a haircut at some point since Thursday: the back was buzzed, the front jagged over her face. Raw as a freshly shorn sheep, she kept nudging the front bit out of her eyes. Andrew and Amanda were smoking at the edge of the parking lot. Freddie and Dani, who'd dyed their buzz cuts neon for the show—Freddie blue, Dani yellow—stood a few steps off, talking in low voices.

Finally, the manager nodded us in. The Atrium's main hall was cavernous, with high ceilings, black-painted floors, and several tiers of balconies, seating over three thousand people—at least four times more than anywhere else I'd performed. In a pent-up, nervous rush, we scurried around unloading and setting up. We were mostly using the Atrium's backline gear and drum kit, so setup wasn't complicated. But it took Andrew a while to get comfortable on the new kit, and Amanda, who seemed abstracted and sad, kept roaming off at inconvenient times.

Once we'd set up, we went backstage to wait for sound check. Our backstage room was pristine: no graffiti on the walls, no stains in the carpeting, just three armchairs and an IKEA couch and a few framed photos from past shows. The venue promoter had set up a table with sandwiches and cookies and Diet Coke cans for Mari, who took one into the corner and flipped out a solitaire game on the floor. Freddie and Dani folded T-shirts for the merch table, then went outside to call Liya's babysitter, while Amanda vanished again. Andrew lay across the couch reading a Philip K. Dick novel and tapping his foot erratically; Mari was bent over her cards. I stared at my phone, all its functions feeling unbearable.

At sound check, everyone was robotic and disengaged, and I could tell Mari was nervous. The Atrium staff ordered us Thai food for dinner, but no one was able to eat, and we continued to sit in silence, feeling the oppression of the gathering crowd in the concert hall.

"Andrew, shield your eyes," Mari said around seven, and we changed into our concert outfits. Freddie wore her clothes from the 9:30 Club show, a black denim skirt with a Siouxsie Sioux T-shirt and black Docs. Amanda put on a Carrie Brownstein–ish vintage collared dress, also over Docs; she looked gawky and sweet, and it made me uncomfortable. I didn't want to feel tenderness for her just then. Andrew did not change out of his black jeans and white undershirt. "Welcome to the gun show, ladies," he said, popping a bicep, and we all threw things at him.

Mari also put on her 9:30 Club show outfit: black jeans, black T-shirt, boots, a red bandana around her right arm—I heard her whisper something in Georgian as she tugged it tight, a prayer maybe. Then she looked over. "What about you, James?" she said.

I dug it out of my shoulder bag: a bundle of green satin and tulle. The week before, I'd found my Maidenheads prom dress in my dad's basement, stuffed into a box of things Sally had moved out of my old bedroom in preparation for the future child. It wasn't close to fitting: I'd been fifteen pounds lighter in 2002. But my mom's sewing machine was still in the basement, and I'd stitched it into a sort of cowboy vest with a strip of tulle cutting diagonally across the front. Up close it was a mess, but from a distance it looked amazing. As Mari watched, I took off my jeans and T-shirt and pulled on black jeans and a black sports bra, then shrugged on the vest.

"That's not . . ." she said, uncommonly tentative.

"It is," I said. I'd finishing tying my bootlaces, and I stood for Mari to see, arms out to the sides, feeling myself blush. I wasn't sure how she'd receive the vest; plus, she'd just seen me half naked for the first time in a decade.

Mari was sitting on one of the chairs, crossed legs stretched in front. I saw her shoulders rise and her nostrils flare in a long, slow breath. "It's perfect," she said quietly.

"Oh, Jamie," Freddie said, from across the room, "you look incredible! Where'd you get that vest?"

"Thrift store," I said, my eyes not leaving Mari's. "I've had it for ages." It was Mari who finally coughed and turned away.

In our final moments backstage, we all performed our last rites. I drew on my green eyeliner, hands shaking so hard they flapped against my cheekbones. Andrew tied and untied his bootlaces exactly three times. Freddie and Dani disappeared into the bathroom together, then came back looking pink. Amanda dry-swallowed several pills from a small bottle. Mari whispered something to her, and Amanda shook her head; I could see her lips saying, "No, no no." It was the first time I'd seen them interact all day.

There was a knock and it was time. We followed the Atrium's promoter down the hall and into the wings. "Group hug?" Mari said, but no one moved in except Freddie for one quick, suppressed second.

"Or—high fives?" Finally, with Mari in front, we were walking out onstage.

The lights were still down and I couldn't see the audience or really anything. I crossed to my spot at the front, close to Mari at her keyboard, wishing as always that I had an instrument to hide behind. The crowd was already cheering before the lights went up, and then, once we were irradiated by the hot orange light, they got very loud. I felt like lasers were shooting through me, like my hair was standing on end. The vest was too tight at the shoulders, and my stomach felt very bare under the sports bra. Mari gave everyone a long second to hit their spots, settle their bodies. Then she nodded, I grasped the mic and whispered, *"I combed my hair,"* and the room erupted in a scream.

"Bought silk stockings bought a hairpin bought a purse. Waited all night, but you didn't come, didn't come, didn't come," I chanted, and—like a miracle—I heard voices chanting along with me. I hadn't expected that; I'd prepared myself for apathy, a crowd impatient for Lucia Brahe. But when I looked out, I saw faces gleaming with sweat and love: girls jumping up and down, one right in front wearing what appeared to be—no, that wasn't possible, but it was, it was real—a homemade version of my green Maidenheads prom dress.

I risked a glance at Mari, and not losing a beat, she shook her head in amazed disbelief. My smile shaped the sound of my voice on the next line: *"Gonna end it all, gonna fuck it all!"* And they were screaming along—the girl in my prom dress was *screaming the words* like they poured straight from her soul. Who the hell were these people? Where had they come from?

Mari stammered out the first line of her chorus, and I flooded with anxious tenderness: it was so rare for her to mess up. But she gathered herself and her words sharpened to a fierce edge. *"Emmy, Emmy, forget it . . . "* And then we were dancing, our bodies trading the rhythm as our voices traded the words. I'd always felt the rage and destructiveness of this song, but onstage that night, I remembered how close to joy rage could feel. Every time I yelled out, *"I'm not gonna be forgotten!"* and the crowd, the girl in the Maidenheads prom dress, yelled it with me, I felt like I'd grown four sizes larger, like we'd all expanded together. When we finished, my eyes went to Mari and she was right there looking back, hair slicked with sweat, rakish smile. "OK?" she said, face turned from the mic.

"OK!" I said. With her eyes on mine, I forgot Freddie, Andrew, Amanda, my family in the audience, the girl in the prom dress. Mari and I were the only people in the room, the only people in the world. We had made something beautiful together, just kids fucking around on Yevgenia's white piano, and a decade later, people still loved it.

Although I was singing lead on about half of the set list, Mari would always be the talker. After "Forgotten," she yelled, "This is Les Somnambules! And we're lucky to have a special guest singing with us tonight, Jamie Cain." She waved a hand toward me, and I performed an unplanned bow, feeling absurd.

The next song was "Firebird," which Mari had told me was about Yevgenia—because of course her songs had meanings, whatever she said. It was a slower, folkier one, and Mari sang lead, rasping out the story, while I sang harmony on the chorus. I was able to watch her, so close I could see the tendons in her hands flicker as she played, and I remembered the surreality I'd felt watching from the back of the 9:30 Club. Because right next to Mari was where I belonged, the only place I'd ever belonged, and I felt that now with heart-stopping certainty.

"Firebird," she sang on the chorus, *"firebird, why have you flown away?"* When she finished, her shining eyes found mine.

Our set list was nine songs—the Atrium had told us to keep it under forty minutes. For each one, performance felt like a magical reveal. I was again and again astonished by meanings I'd never noticed in the lyrics, melodies that ripped my heart even as I sang them for the hundredth time. When I locked eyes with Mari, I felt awe. How the hell did she write songs like this, songs that made you want to transform into pure music so you could live in them forever?

The final song was "Tiny Animals." We'd always struggled with it in practice. The chord changes at the beginning were difficult even for Mari, and Amanda had simply given up on one section, forcing Mari to rewrite it. Freddie's part was supposed to be mournful, klezmery, but she played it with her usual cheeriness until Mari finally snapped: "It's meant to make us *cry*, you sound like you're in high school orchestra." Andrew was never able to hold back, plodding all over the song's delicate skipping undercurrent.

That night, it all worked. Amanda and Freddie mostly hit their notes and the eerie tone, and Andrew contained himself. But the song was really about my voice, I realized as I muscled it out into the Atrium's ceiling: "*Tiny animals, I don't want to bite you.*" My post-Maidenheads voice, specifically—this dark witchy, breathy sound that Mari knew about before I did, that Mari somehow had in her ears as she wrote the song ten years ago. The audience hushed to hear the lyrics, and I knew it sounded scary, fucked up. I closed my eyes as I sang, shutting myself inside with the child: with *Mari*, eighteen-year-old Mari, alone with her notebooks after the rape. This was how she told her story, I realized as I sang it aloud. She'd struggled to talk about it; she'd barely been able to say "rape." But she wrote this cryptic and brutal SOS of a song—and then buried it in a notebook for ten years, until I came home to sing it.

The song ended and we were wrapped in cheers. I found Mari's eyes and knew mine were blurred. She leaned across the keyboard, grabbed my vest to yank me close, and kissed me—something both startling and so deeply familiar I could only laugh. The cheers escalated, Mari pulled back, laughing as well, and then the lights went down.

Amanda, Andrew, and Freddie faded into the wings, but Mari reached for my hand with her limp sweaty one. I pulled her into me, and we stood embracing, sweaty together—still onstage, but in the dark. I felt the sob in her chest. My sob beat against hers.

"I love you, Mari," I said.

"You too, James," she whispered. We separated, giddy, and I followed Mari backstage through a line of people who slapped us on the back and applauded. In our little room again, I felt floaty and chilled, my ears blared, I was a ghost in my own body.

Mari took a beer can from the mini-fridge and pressed it to one wrist, then the other, then threw herself down on the couch. "That was incredible, guys," she said, then cough-laughed because her voice sounded weird and said it again. No one replied. I hadn't seen Amanda pack up, but she was already gone. Freddie was shawled in a crocheted blanket, feet tucked up on her chair. Andrew removed his boots and socks and sat down with one foot propped on his opposite knee, scraping at his toe.

"Everyone OK?" Mari said after a moment.

"Blood blister," Andrew said.

"Just tired," Freddie said, not looking at us.

"Andrew, you want Vaseline or a Band-Aid? I brought a bunch," said Mari. I could see through her chattiness to the post-performance loneliness, the need to relive it together—*did you feel that too, was that real?* I wished I could sit close against her sticky skin, help her ease back into her bones. I didn't know what the kiss had meant, if it was just the high of the performance or something else, but either way, I felt a new fizz between us. I couldn't stop watching her as she sprawled across the couch, whacking her own thigh with one of Andrew's sticks.

"I'm good," said Andrew. Then a long uneasy silence, until the Atrium promoter burst into say how good we were, so awesome, the crowd loved us, and Mari sighed in relief. Dani came in to kiss Freddie and say how many T-shirts they'd sold; Andrew's on-and-off girlfriend sulked in the corner over some fight. Mari's beer lost its frost on her wrists, so she drank it and started cooling herself with a new one. I was starving and I ate my veggie pad thai from the mini-fridge, then Amanda's as well. I wanted a drink so badly, and who cared anyway, I wasn't pregnant now, so I took Mari's second beer, warmed by her neck. Across the room, I saw Freddie's eyes follow the can to my mouth, but I didn't mind. The luxuriance of not being onstage anymore—that I'd been onstage, done a good job, and didn't need to go back right away—soaked deep into my body, erasing all other concerns.

I'd run into Lucia Brahe backstage, all pupils and ripped cuticles, so it was no surprise when she went on late. Everyone else left to watch from the wings, Freddie's blanket trailing behind her. Mari stayed on her couch. "We were good tonight," she said quietly, once we were alone. "But we should do 'Forgotten' faster. Andrew should kick in harder at the beginning."

We worked through each song like that, analyzing how it went, discussing what to do differently next time—talking, I realized, as if we both understood there would be more shows to come. I was expecting her to say something about the kiss, but she didn't mention it. After a while, we heard the swell of human noise out in the concert hall—Lucia Brahe had finished her set. Freddie and Andrew returned along with Dani and Andrew's girlfriend. Sal Evans stopped by in a kelly green velvet suit, along with several other people I somewhat knew. Mari said hello to everyone, soaked up compliments on our behalf, nodded regally from her couch. I felt at risk of overflowing, and I zipped up a sweatshirt over my vest and tugged down the hood to create a more secure vessel.

My father and Sally came in. He moved cautiously through the crowd, seeming confused by the noise and energy; on his arm, Sally looked very tired. I patted the chair next to me, and she made for it gratefully.

"Jamie, my goodness," my father said, standing above Sally with a hand on her shoulder. He had never seen me perform before, something I'd always resented, although, to be fair, I'd never invited him. "Your voice—it's really amazing."

Sally said, "I loved that last song. Creepy."

"Did you know," my father said, "that in a crowd of people listening to music, each person processes it individually depending on the individual shape of their brain? The musician plays the music, but the listener also plays it, in a sense, filtered through his or her own neural patterns. There's no one true version of any song, simply the interaction between the brain of the musician and the brain of the listener."

This was my father doing his best, I understood, and I gave him a hug. Sally was massaging the skin between her right thumb and forefinger. "Thank you so much for coming," I said. "But don't feel like you have to stay, OK?"

"We're on our way out," Sally said.

But just then the door opened and it was my mother. Behind her, looking everywhere but at me, hugging a jacket to his chest, was Peter. My mother spotted us, fired a big insincere smile at my father and Sally, and rushed over, Peter following slowly. "Jamie, you were absolutely wonderful," she said, with the WASP-ish vivacity that was always an anxiety tell. "Hello, Kenneth. Hi, Sally."

Peter was silent, staring down at the carpet. I was trying to sort out what he was doing here: Had my mother brought him? Was he stalking me now?

"Eileen, how are you?" my father said.

"I'm very well," she said. "How are you feeling, Sally?"

"Pretty lousy, actually. Can't wait to get this damn baby out." Sally laughed too loudly.

"The final trimester is so hard," said my mother, brows arching into her forehead wrinkles with the effort to show sympathy.

"Sally's such a trooper, though!" my father said. He reached down to pat Sally's thigh. "She's doing great."

"Not like me," my mother said with a spacey social laugh. "Sally, by this time with Jamie, I was flat on my back. I'd have never gone to a concert! It used to drive Kenneth crazy."

"No, no, of course not," he said, trying to catch Sally's eye, but she was gazing blankly at her hands.

Into their awkward silence, Peter said, "How are you, Jamie?"

"I'm great," I said, tensing a smile. "So this is my dad. And Sally. This is Peter."

"Oh," said Peter. "I've heard so much about you."

"You as well," my father said. Everyone seemed bewildered by the etiquette for this conversation—my ex-boyfriend, ex-impregnator, meeting my father and stepmother for the first time. The men shook hands; Sally and Peter exchanged a hip-level half wave. After a too-long pause, Peter said, "It looks like there's a refreshments table—can I get you all anything?"

"We bought T-shirts from that friendly person in the lobby," said my mother. "I looked for onesies for the new baby, but no such luck."

"Sally would probably like some crackers," my father told Peter.

"I'm not hungry," she said. "I really just want to go home."

"I don't see crackers, but it looks like they might have Oreos?" Peter said, and he set off for the refreshments table, clearly pleased to have a mission.

"Take her *home*, Kenneth!" my mother cried. "A pregnant woman wants to go home, you'd better take her home!" My father and Sally exchanged looks. Sally made some quiet noises, my father compressed his mouth in what for him was a very warm smile, and they left.

"Why are you being so weird?" I said to my mom when we were alone.

"I'm being friendly," my mother said. "Was that not friendly?"

"No—it was weird. Sally seemed uncomfortable."

"That's an unkind thing to say, Jamie. Kenneth and I are on good terms, and I've always wanted to know Sally better. I've been thinking maybe I could be helpful with the baby, go over every now and then and give her a break."

"I'm sure that would not be awkward at all," I said.

"You're very hard on me sometimes," my mother said. "Anyway, why did Mari kiss you? I hope you're not dating again?"

"No—definitely not."

The relief on her face was clear. Annoyed, I said, "What were you thinking, bringing Peter?"

"I didn't *bring* him," she said. "We ran into each other in the lobby, and he traded tickets to sit next to me. I don't know what he's doing here, he must be very lonely. You should talk to him!"

She gestured to Peter with her eyebrows: he was alone by the refreshments table holding a plate stacked with four Oreos. Craning his head around for Sally, he looked like a motherless giraffe.

I went over to rescue him. "They left," I said, "but I will eat those."

"Really great assortment of . . . refreshments," he said, staring hard at the table so as not to look me in the eye.

His discomfort made me feel gallant, like I could afford to be generous. "Peter, hey, I'm sorry. The thing I said—it's not true, and I should never have said it."

"That was fucked up, yeah." He shifted on his long legs, hands deep in his pockets. "But it's OK. I know I wasn't the best either."

I saw a razor nick on the underside of Peter's chin, and it reminded me what it felt like to kiss him right after he'd shaved. "That's

OK," I said. "You were trying, it was a weird situation. And I'm glad you came tonight."

"I never got to see you perform," he said. "I just wanted to see."

"What did you think?"

"I thought—it looked right," he said, hunching up his shoulders like I'd struck him. "It looks like you belong there. You and Mari."

"We're not together, that kiss was just part of the show," I said quickly. But we had both already turned toward Mari, and at that exact moment, midway through an artificial laugh at something someone had said, she looked straight at me and her face went dead serious.

Peter turned away. "Parking's going to run out," he said. I watched his polite stops and starts through the crowd: "Oh, excuse me, sorry, *sorry.*" He passed my mother, and they performed an awkward sideways half-hug.

After he'd left, I went over and put an arm around her shoulder. "I'm not with Mari, but I'm also not getting back together with Peter," I told her. "Just so you know. How are you planning to get home?"

"I thought I would call a cab," she said, nervously. She never took cabs because she never went anywhere, so I found a taxi company number and called it for her. When the yellow checkered station wagon pulled up outside the Atrium, I loaded her in, and she grinned up at me from her seat. "You were wonderful tonight," she said. "I was so proud I cried."

As I stood watching the cab drive away, I heard a tentative voice—"Jamie?" It was Nora, pushing out through the front doors. She was wearing a red fake-fur jacket and another very short skirt; she looked pretty and fancy, not like a journalist at all. "Hi! I thought it was you. That show was incredible."

"Yeah, I heard Lucia Brahe was awesome."

"She was, she always is, but you and Mari—that was pretty special," Nora said, a journalist again with her nerdy sincerity. "Makes me wish I'd gotten to see the Maidenheads back in the day. Off the record, just because I want to know—would you ever perform as the Maidenheads again?"

I was warm from Nora's words, from Mari's kiss, from the whole night. "Off the record," I said, "Mari and I will always be the Maidenheads." Then I turned and saw Mari a couple feet away, smoking a cigarette under the awning outside the Atrium's ticket window. Without saying anything, she ground the butt under her boot and went inside.

13

IT TOOK PEOPLE ages to clear out, and then we had to load Andrew's van. He and his sullen girlfriend drove off, and Dani and Freddie hugged us and left too. Mari and I hung on: Mari chatting with the Atrium staff, me lurking by her shoulder eating Oreos, neither of us ready to end the night. Eventually they politely suggested we leave so they could clean up, and Mari and I stood on the sidewalk outside so she could smoke a final cigarette before we called our respective cabs to go home. After she finished, though, neither of us took out our phones.

We were alone in the street, too late even for cars to be going by. A very soft mist was falling, so fine I could barely see it, only feel the freshness on my skin. I was exhausted but clearheaded, alert to the movement of Mari's thigh, inches from mine, as she skimmed her boot toe across a puddle.

"That wasn't such a bad show, huh?" she said. She had asked some version of this question about fifteen times.

"It was the best show of your life," I said. "You know that."

“I saw you talking to Nora,” she said. “What do you think she’s going to write about us?”

“Something good. She said she really liked it.”

“What exactly did she say?”

“I don’t know! Nice things. You don’t have to worry.”

Mari cocked her head to the side. Under the streetlight, her hair sparkled with mist. “Sometimes I think a show’s good, but other people don’t.”

“That must be extremely confusing for you.”

“It is! Don’t be rude,” she said. She slapped the puddle with her foot. “I heard you say something to Nora about us always being the Maidenheads. What did you mean by that?”

I laughed, self-conscious. “I don’t know,” I said. “It felt like that onstage. Maybe it was just me.”

“No, no,” she said. “I know what you mean. I felt it too.”

The silence between us grew heavy, and I could feel some wild declaration expanding inside me. What came out was “Mari, I want to stay in DC, I want to stay in the band.”

Mari stared down the street a moment, then turned the same chilly long-distance stare back on me. “Don’t say that if you don’t mean it.”

“I mean it,” I said, and it felt solemn.

“Because if you’re in this, you need to be in it for real. I can’t handle another 2002. I can deal with Amanda and the rest of the band, I’ll take it on, but I need to know you’re not going to leave again. Understand?”

“I’m not going to leave,” I said. “I’m in it for real.”

The tension around her eyes relaxed. For a moment, she looked so much like her high school self I felt like we’d slipped out of time. “Well, OK then,” she said, her voice softer. “OK!”

“OK!” We both laughed nervously, the dogs that caught the car. Mari’s gaze dropped to my mouth, and before I knew what was happening, for the second time that night, she bent forward and kissed me.

I was so shocked I didn't kiss her back, just made a closed-lips noise. Mari laughed, totally calm, and said, "So no?"

"Mari, what the fuck!"

"It's fine! Really. Pretend I didn't do it." She stuck her hands in her pockets, leaned away from me in preparation to go.

"I'm just confused. I mean—onstage, I thought that was part of the show."

"Well," she said, "it was. But now it's not. You don't want to?"

"No—no, it's just, Mari, I thought *you* didn't want to."

"Why would you ever think that?" she said.

A balloon of air rose in my chest. "Well, I heard you in Earl's bathroom with Amanda—you told her it was all in the past."

Mari stepped back to light another cigarette with a match, the flare illuminating her sharp chin. I watched her inhale, exhale, inhale again. "Listen, I didn't mean it," she said at last. "What I said to Amanda. I just couldn't let her quit before the show. It's not in the past."

"What do you mean when you say that? What's not in the past"

She glared at me under squinched eyebrows like I was forcing her to admit something painful. "You and me," she said. "We're not in the past."

I had believed all along that we were watching different versions of the same film: that in Mari's version, we were carrying on a long-term musical comradeship, any complications stuffed safely back in 2002, like the tapes at the back of my Maryland closet. But if her version was closer to mine, in which that part of us hadn't been extinguished ten years ago but instead simmered beneath everything we did, all the music and our arguments and the performance we'd just delivered—it was fundamentally disorienting, like discovering I was wrong about gravity. "I thought you hated me," I said, feeling a kind of vertigo.

"I could never hate you, dummy. But even if I did, I'd still want you."

It altered the shape of my heart to know that Mari didn't hate me. "I want you too," I said, and saw her blink, the hitch in her stance—she hadn't been sure.

Still keeping space between our bodies, but with growing confidence, she went on. "I know we have a lot to sort out with the band. But if you're staying, if we're playing together—it feels kind of inevitable, yeah? Being onstage with you, watching you sing—I don't think I know how to not want you in that situation."

"Just when I sing? Not any other time?"

"You know what I mean."

"Yeah," I said, and I did. "But when we broke up, you said it'd be better to be only bandmates. More stable. Is that what you really thought?"

"Did I say that? I must've been trying to hurt you." She took a step closer and reached out to swipe something off the front of my sweatshirt. "I don't actually think we're capable of being only bandmates. And I wouldn't want to be. I like it when we're more, I think we work well like that. Don't you?"

I felt unmoored, the way I had right after the abortion—untethered to time or consequence. "Yeah," I said, electrified by her nearness, eyes locked on her lips, "Yeah, I really do."

Her hand was on my cheek now, her breath on my face. "So this is OK?"

I didn't care in that moment whether it was OK or not—I'd lost the ability to think in those terms. I leaned forward and our lips met. Immediately my body sliced into hers, my hand on her lower back urging her close, and she stumbled away—I helped her rebalance, pulled her back in. I could feel her laughter rather than hear it; her lips were cold and soft. To hold Mari again after all the years spent rebelling unreasoningly against her absence, erecting walls against her, protecting myself from memories of her scent, feel, taste—it was devastating. My mouth went unsteady, I was crying.

Mari jumped back. "Whoa," she said. "You good?"

"So good!" I said, laughing, teary.

She put her arm around my neck, hugged me like a sister, laughed as I sheepishly wiped my nose. "I have no idea what we're doing here," she said against my ear, "but I feel like we should get off this sidewalk and go back to my house. Yeah?"

OUR CAB DRIVER was shiny-bald and avuncular, with a little Ethiopian flag and a lattice-woven gold cross hanging from his key chain. "What were you girls doing tonight?" he asked, looking in the mirror to where we were sitting on opposite sides of the back seat, the way we used to sit in my mom's car, fingers loosely and radiantly joined in the center, out of sight. "Big night on the town?"

"Yup," Mari said. She had no patience for dumb questions from men.

But I thought about his wife and kids at home, didn't want to be rude. "We're in a band," I said. "We played a show tonight."

"Oh!" he said. "A girl group, eh? I used to play drums in a band, we were pretty good." He beat a paradiddle on the steering wheel. "What's the name of your band? Would I have heard of you?"

"No," Mari said.

"The Maidenheads," I said at the same time.

"The Maidenheads, hm. Where does that name come from?"

I started our old lie: "It's a feminist reappropriation of—" but Mari cut me off, her fingers gripping mine.

"It was because at the time neither of us had ever fucked men, only each other, and we had some stupid teenage joke about keeping our maidenheads. Turns out it wasn't medically accurate, most girls lose their hymens well before puberty, and anyway, penetration is penetration, but it sounded cool, so we kept it," she said.

"Oh!" the driver said. He didn't say anything else until he dropped us off on Mari's street—I tried to imagine his thoughts, discomfort or horror or some secret impenetrable sadness. By the time he dropped us off, he was collected enough to yell, "Good night, girls!" out the open window as we crossed Mari's small yard to her house.

When the motion-sensor porch light flashed on Mari's face, I saw the tightness of her lips. Inside, she led me around her mother's long sofa, where the orange cat reigned supreme. "That's Beavis," she said as we climbed the carpeted stairs. "You're not allergic, are you?"

A twinge of disappointment—she should've remembered I wasn't allergic; she'd known my mother's cat. I would've remembered that about her. Upstairs, we passed one closed door and opened another into Mari's room: low bookcase under the window, desk hidden under books and papers, mattress on the floor with a denim-covered duvet, unmade and littered with laundry. Her old Springsteen poster over the bed, and over her desk, our tour flyer: our teenage faces photocopied in black and white, MAIDENHEADS WORLD TOUR '02 in cutout magazine letters.

"I didn't think you'd kept it," I said.

"Well, I did," she said, grouchy now. She crouched to unlace her boots, stacked them by the door, tugged off her sweatshirt. Confronting the messy bed, she uttered a Yevgenia-ish snort before scooping up laundry.

"Are you OK?" I asked. "Was it the driver?"

"I don't do great in situations like that," she said. She sat on the mattress, still holding a dirty T-shirt in one hand. "Like—talking-to-men-in-enclosed-spaces type situations."

I sat down next to her, just close enough to touch. "That makes sense," I said. "What can I do to help?"

"I want you to talk." She leaned into my shoulder. "Tell me something about you I don't know."

"OK," I said. The weight of our shared history felt abruptly paralyzing. But she had initiated this, I could trust that she wanted it, and I summoned a hearty voice and went on: "I got a good one. So in college, I was hooking up with this girl, her name I think was Irina? Elena? Anyway, she was Russian, and I liked her because her voice sounded like yours."

Now I paused to let her say, "Wow, please never say that my voice sounds *Russian*, but OK, whatever, go on."

"So Irina or Elena was very into outdoor sex, and one night, she wanted to sneak into the AU quad and have sex under a bush."

"Bad idea."

"Right? We did, though, because we were drunk. And guess what happened."

"Someone caught you and you got in trouble."

"No. What happened was, I got bit by a snake."

"*No.*"

"Yes! I'm on top of her, I'm wearing cutoffs, and I feel this intense shooting pain just above my knee. I look down and I see—no joke, Mari—a huge snake with its jaw clamped to my leg."

"This story is *made up*! DC doesn't have snakes."

"Tell that to the rat snake who caused permanent nerve damage to my left thigh."

She nudged my shoulder with hers, reached sideways to tousle my hair. "You were a bit of a slut then, weren't you," she said.

"Oh, I was a huge slut in college," I said, laughing. "Mostly not under bushes, though."

"Mostly," she said. "Were you fucking men then too, or was Peter your first?"

"No, I fucked a few men," I said; then, thinking back to how I'd felt seeing Peter after the show, "I like fucking men. Some men, at least. Are you bothered by that?"

"No, no," Mari said. "For sure, I find it confusing that anyone would elect to fuck men. But, you know, everyone's got their thing."

I reminded myself of her history, what it meant when she said "elect." "How about you?" I asked. "What was that time like for you?"

"Equally slutty, less bisexual," she said. "Hey, want to lie down?"

We fell back onto the unmade bed together, and I put my arms around her, stroked her hair, the soft shags in front and rough stubble in back. Mari had unusually small ears, I'd forgotten that, snail shells with almost no lobe. I'd forgotten how her face looked at tight proximity, the clear angelic beauty of her gold-shot black irises. I touched her cheekbones, the tip of her chin, as delicate as peaks of frothed egg.

"You're criminally beautiful, like it shouldn't be allowed how beautiful you are," I whispered.

"You're all right."

I bit her nose. We kissed, sticky dry-lip middle-of-the-night kisses. "You OK?" I asked. "Can I . . ."

"Yeah," she said, closing her eyes. "Yeah."

Everything still felt jerky and unreal. But as I sat up cross-legged and began undressing Mari, a calming sense of ritual descended over me, a desire to do everything slowly and with utmost diligence. She was still wearing her black T-shirt from the show, and I tugged it up over her head, then smoothed her breasts, her body lifting against my touch. I spidered my hand under her back to raise her hips so I could slide her shorts and underpants down her legs. I took my clothes off too, to keep her company, and then I sat back on my haunches to look at her.

Ten years without seeing or touching Mari's body, ten years in which it had just gone on apart from me: eating, sleeping, breathing, fucking. Her body had been a separate object in our relationship, a creature I'd loved as fiercely as I'd loved Mari. I'd missed it madly, chemically. I ran my fingers from her clavicles into her damp unshaven armpits, across her freckled breasts and down the sides of her rib cage to her soft friendly belly, drawing out a giggle—Mari was ticklish, you had to be careful. I found the fox tattoo on her wrist and placed mine next to it. I kissed her little fox, and without thinking, I lifted my wrist and kissed my own.

We had known nothing in high school. We knew other queer people, but we were our only friends—a closed circle, no one else to talk to about the other. We'd had no culture of queer sex, no understanding of concepts like "top" and "bottom," just our own feral instincts and brutal desire. Over those years of teenage fucking, we'd roughed each other up a million ways. Mari once sprained a finger fucking me, I'd ripped out chunks of her hair, we were always covered in bruises and bite marks and limping with swollen cunts. Now, though, I wanted to be tender and strong for her. I wanted to make her feel safe.

The new tattoo running down her ribs on the left—several lines in Georgian script. Her curved hips, the slope above her pussy. Her pubic hair, prickly and thick. I could feel how wet she was, I could smell it, she urged herself against my hand. But I shifted away, traced down her thighs, found the raised freckle I remembered on her right knee. Her high-arched dancer's feet, cracked yellow soles, bony toes.

When I glanced up from Mari's feet, I saw she was watching me from the pillow, chin folded into her chest. "You checking me for lice?"

"Yep," I said, "found one," and I pretended to pinch a bug off her raised arch. She laughed and kicked me.

"Get *on* with it," she said. "You're driving me crazy."

Her cheeks again, her thin wide lips, smiling against my fingertips. Her thick black eyebrows, the lightning-shaped vein under her nostril. Her triangular chin, the softness underneath. I slicked her armpit hair with my tongue, tasting her bitter, chalky deodorant. My leg was between her thighs, and I raised it to hear her groan. She bit my earlobe; I felt her hunger. But what if I touched her, what if I fucked her, and it didn't work—what if I hurt her somehow? My breath left me. Her teeth needled my ear.

I kissed her neck and crawled back down her body. Dubiously, I stroked along the base of her stomach, my fingers fumbling, remembering last time.

"This OK?" I whispered to the underside of her chin. "Are you OK? You sure?"

"James, yes, please, yes," her voice desperate.

I mustered my courage, dug my hands up under her ass, and lifted her hips to my face like I was drinking from a bowl. I ran my tongue all over, investigative little swipes, and then I settled into it and licked her pussy again and again, until my tongue root ached and she was soaked everywhere and she clutched the back of my head and my fears all vanished. I sucked her clit and fucked her with my fingers, driving up into the warm sloppy roughness, and I kept going until my knees got tired and I sprawled out on my belly and elbows, legs sticking off the bed, and I still kept going, chin dripping, forearms aching. I felt hot with success now, my own body arching against her leg, her shin pressing up into my clit, and I still kept going as I felt her muscles tighten around my hand, and then, finally, I looked up to see her stomach clench and she growled and shoved my face into her crotch with both hands. Mari always sounded hungry and furious when she came, like an animal devouring another animal. When she was finished and I could breathe again, I wiped my mouth on her thigh and tried to conceal the smugness, you're always such an asshole right after you make someone come.

"Fuck," she said, one arm stretched loose across her mouth. "Yeah."

"Yeah?" My fingers were still resting along her vulva and I could sense an unreleased tension, so I traced up and down, feather-light. Her back jerked like I'd pulled a string. In a minute, she shuddered again, more quietly, and finally, she shifted my hand away. I crawled back up and snuggled into her neck, shaky, triumphant, golden. We lay together like that, not speaking, and I could feel our bodies merge like two drops of mercury.

Once Mari's breathing slowed, I started running my fingers across her body again, friendly touches now, getting reacquainted: the new scar on her lip, the firebird on her arm, the Georgian letters running up her ribs. "What does this say?" I whispered.

"It's the lyrics to a lullaby my mother used to sing." She ducked her chin to look down at the tattoo. "Untranslatable, like most Georgian folk songs—something about violets and a nightingale and wine and a poplar tree."

"Sing it for me," I whispered.

Turning onto her stomach, Mari propped herself up on her elbows and sang it into the dark bedroom. The song was mournful, lilting—more a lament than a lullaby. Her voice was tentative, still hoarse from the concert.

"I had it printed on the funeral programs," she said when she was done, looking down at her pillow. "The next day, I went out and got the tattoo."

"I'm so sorry, Mar."

"Parents die, right? But she wasn't just a parent. I don't have anyone else."

Mari never talked like that, and cautious, I did not say, *You have me.* But my heart said it, and I knew she saw my face saying it. She shifted on the bed, her damp shoulder coming audibly unstuck from mine.

"But then the band started to take off," she said, her voice constrained, "and you know I never came out to her and people were calling me queer in print and I'm this big crazy dyke up onstage and—I don't know, that would've been hard, right? Anyway, you move on, yeah? You find something new, you move on."

"Not always," I said.

She laughed, more relaxed. "Fair," she said. "Anyway, where's that snakebite scar you were bragging about?"

"Right here." I tugged down the blanket to show her the shiny raised mark just above my knee.

She poked the scar. "I still don't believe you, that could be anything. Anyway, my turn to fuck you now." She fumbled under the bed, pulled out a large shoebox, and dug into it for a harness, lube, and purple dildo. "We call this guy the purple prince," she said, kneeling on the bed to buckle it around her hips.

"'We'?"

"Me." She was fiddling with the strap and didn't look up.

"Was this you and Amanda's dildo?"

"It's *my* dildo."

"OK." I knew I couldn't push it. Mari was harnessed now, on her knees above me with the purple prince jutting stiffly out. She stroked it, running her thumb over the tip, back and forth.

"How about you turn over," she said, and my brain scattered.

WE FUCKED UNTIL we were liquid and lost, then finally, birdsong coming through the grayish windows, I big-spooned her and tugged the blanket up around our shoulders. My knees bumped the sticky backs of her knees, my thighs brushed her butt. She fell asleep abruptly, the way she always had, dropping into sleep between two words or still holding up a book. And the way I always had, I lay awake, foggy with exhaustion but her presence like headlights slicing through.

When we woke up in the early afternoon, I was scared to look at her—would she have second thoughts, would she pull away? But she kissed me and snuggled close. Beavis had come into the bed at some point, and he cuddled against my other side, sandwiching me between her warm breasts and his soft back. When I got up to pee, my skin was fuzzy with orange cat hair.

Mari made eggs, and we sat at her kitchen island drinking coffee. In high school, everything had always been so covert and quick. We'd fuck in our bedrooms, separated by thin walls from our parents, and then we'd pull on pajamas and brush our teeth and wash our hands and faces and emerge looking respectable, answer questions about school. It felt strange to be half dressed in the kitchen, kissing Mari's shoulder as I poured myself a glass of orange juice—like different people in a very different kind of relationship.

But we didn't discuss that at all. We talked about the band, the kind of daydreaming we hadn't allowed ourselves since 2002. Lucia Brahe's manager had told Mari after the show that we could "probably" join the European tour next year, but we'd need to put out another EP first; we talked about which cities we'd want to see, about her record label, how it was good but maybe not quite right for us. We talked about what we could do if we started making a little more money, the investments in gear, a better practice space. Mari told me, with rare shyness, that there were other songs in her notebooks upstairs, not just "Tiny Animals," that she'd written for my vocal range. "You wrote them for me?" I asked, needing to hear her say it, and she nodded. I licked her face, not knowing how else to communicate such violent euphoria.

At one point, I said, "Are we going to tell everyone?"

"That you're staying in the band? I was thinking I might tell Amanda first, get her used to the idea, then enlist Freddie's help to calm her down."

"That's not what I meant."

"Oh, you mean tell everyone that we fucked?" She laughed. "James. Listen to me. This is happening, whatever this is, between you and me. It's real. But we definitely cannot tell anyone in the band."

"They might guess."

"How would they guess? It's not like it changes anything."

I stared into my coffee—how could she say that? The air was new, my skin was new, my body felt newly proportioned. But she was already running upstairs for her notebooks, and Beavis was nudging my leg for a head rub, and I put the worry aside for another day.

I TOOK THE Metro home that evening and spent much of the walk from Silver Spring station trying to force my face into a normal expression. My lips made a rictus smile, I kept giggling uncontrollably. I was gelatinous from sex, and although I'd showered and brushed my teeth with her toothbrush, I was sure I could smell Mari's cunt on my breath when I huffed into my cupped hand. I dropped my keys at the front door and laughed so hard my muscles got squiggly and I nearly couldn't bend to pick them up.

"Hi?" I yelled as I came in—hopefully no one was there and I could go be weird alone in my room. But Sally and my father were both on the living room couch. She sat beside him with her arms stretched across his lap; he was rubbing something into her wrists, giving off a sharp astringent smell.

As I came in, she was wincing with pain. Once she saw me, she blinked and put on a smile. "Welcome home, rock star," she said. "That show was amazing. How are you feeling?"

"Oh, pretty good," I said. "Sorry I didn't let you guys know where I was. We hung out after the show and it got late, so I stayed at a friend's house."

"That's fine," my father said. I could see Sally's pressure on his hand. "You're an adult." Sally smiled more genuinely—her sweet, exhausted smile—and guilt stabbed me through.

PART THREE

14

ON THE MORNING of September 11, 2001, I was sitting in twelfth grade English class when a girl opened the door and said, trembly but proud, aware of stepping into history, "Someone just flew a plane into the Pentagon!" The teacher, cut off in the middle of a lecture on *Romeo and Juliet*, said, "Hold on—hold on, everyone." Then one girl cried, "My *mom* works there," and commotion took root. I stuck my books in my backpack and walked straight out.

The hallway was in chaos. Kids ran, spilling papers, or clumped together and cried. Kids surged around the two lobby pay phones like ants on a crumb. But the science wing where Mari had first-period biology was calm, isolated from the information. I opened the door to Mari's classroom and forty eyes behind plastic safety goggles blinked at me. "Someone flew a plane into the Pentagon," I said. "Mari?"

She set down her goggles and threw her notebook into her bag, as the teacher called, "Mariam? Mariam?" I grabbed her hand, and we ran out together.

I'd felt dramatic with purpose, but once we pushed out through the lobby doors into stark-hot sun, I lost it. My skin prickled with sweat. Sirens droned, vibrating down the back of my neck. "What are we doing?" I asked Mari.

Mari was smiling—I remember that. Her teeth were little points, and her eyes shone eager. "We could spend the whole day practicing," she said. "My mom's at work until six."

"What are you talking about?" I said. "We can't practice today. Let's go to my mom's, she'll be freaking out."

"Why ask if you don't want my answer?" Mari said. I shoved her shoulder with mine, she smirked and dug hard back at me, and we started walking home.

It was a long walk, about three miles through the quasi-suburban neighborhoods of Upper Northwest DC. Restaurants and cafés were open; people milled around outside as if enjoying the unseasonable warmth. But when you got closer, you'd see their stunned expressions or notice someone crying openly in the street. Sirens whined without pause, and occasionally a fighter jet or military helicopter roared above in the direction of Northern Virginia. *Where someone had just flown an actual plane into an actual building,* I reminded myself. *Where actual people were right this moment screaming and dying.* Mari and I held hands the whole way, something we had never done in public. No one seemed to notice.

My mom wasn't home, just Millie slapping her paws against mouse squeaks behind the baseboards and the answering machine blinking: "Jamie, if you get this—just, please, if you get this, call me?" my mother's voice said. "Michael had to pick up his kids at school and I'm holding the fort down here. I love you so much. Please call me."

I called Michael's store just as Mari came out from the kitchen with two tubs of my mom's plain yogurt, spoons stuck in.

"Michael's Frames and Oddities, Eileen speaking," said my mother.

“Why are you still there?” I asked. Mari lay down across the couch, wedged her booted toes under my thighs, and shoveled yogurt into her mouth.

“Jamie! Oh my gosh. Michael told me to stay.” She’d be fretting on her stool behind the counter, I knew, eyes shooting back and forth between the shop’s door and her own agitated hands. “He didn’t want anyone to show up to an empty store.”

“Mom! No one’s coming in today. Put a note on the door and lock up.”

My mother said, “But you’re OK? You’re fine?”

“I’m fine, don’t worry about me,” I said. Mari’s chin was smeared with yogurt—I reached over to wipe it off with my sweatshirt sleeve.

“Are you *laughing*? What are you laughing about? Did you call your dad? Call him, Jamie!”

“Sure, sure,” I said, both of us aware I would not. “I’ll see you soon.”

Mari called Yevgenia’s hospital and left a message in Georgian on the nurses’ line. I always felt distant from Mari when she spoke her crackly, *chhh*-y language: like I didn’t really know her, just a part, and not the most essential part either. “Your mom’s going to be home soon, huh?” she said when she hung up. “Want to get out of here?”

We walked down into Rock Creek Park and followed the path where it verged away from the road, into the isolated stretch behind the zoo parking lots. There, we stepped off into a strip of sparse woods, pushing through low brush until we reached the rocky shore of the shallow, broad creek. Mari lit a cigarette and leaned against a tree while I crouched near the sewage-scented water. As I watched a family of ducks paddle against the current, I felt a teeth-rattling whoosh and looked up to see a fighter jet pounding over the city. “It’s like a movie, it doesn’t feel real,” I said.

“It’s real,” Mari said. She dragged on her Marlboro, then pulled it out between thumb and forefinger—she always smoked like a grown man, even when she was seventeen. "You've just never experienced this kind of reality before."

Mari had moved on from her cousin's hand-me-downs, and now we shopped together at the Value Village near my dad's house. That day, she had on frayed black Levi's, an oversized green sweater with sleeves unraveling over her raw knuckles, and—our best prize that summer, something I'd seen first but let Mari take, not without regrets—a faded Wrangler jean jacket. I stood up and wiped my hands on my corduroys. Pushing Mari back against a tree, I reached my hands around inside her jacket and kissed her. Her lips were soft and smoky, the cold sharp tip of her nose pressed my cheek.

"Youff neffer experienced thees kind off re-ull-ity beffore," I whispered, in a camped-up imitation of her accent, her hard-earned Soviet world-weariness.

"Shut up," Mari said, and she disengaged to flick her cigarette butt into the creek, where it fizzed out. Then she flat-palmed between my legs, pressing the seam of my pants hard up into me. I shivered; I bit her lips, kissed down to her collarbone, grabbed up under the sweater at her loose breasts.

"Is it fucked up," I whispered, "that we're doing this right now?"

"Probably." Grasping my shoulders, she spun us so that my back was against the tree, then knelt, crunching sticks. For a moment, she looked up at me, black eyes anime-girl huge. She unzipped my corduroys and tugged them down my thighs. Hooking her thumb around my underpants crotch, she bent close to lick me with a wide, warm tongue. The pleasure was so intense I didn't experience it as pleasure but as shock—my spine and shoulders contracted electrically, my legs nearly buckled. Mari placed a steadying hand on my belly, then sucked two fingers of her other hand and thrust them inside me. Her cold skinny fingers, her hot breath and tongue.

When she'd finished, Mari zipped up my corduroys and stood, leaning her body into my limp one, both of us braced against the tree. The ducks had barely moved in all this time, like they were on a duck treadmill. Lips brushing my cheek, Mari sang: "*You fall in love, zing boom . . .* " It was the Björk song, except Mari sang it an octave down, growling the whole chorus into my ear as I rested against the tree, sun on my hair.

As we walked out of the park, I put my arm around her hips and she dug her head into my neck. No one stared; no one even seemed to see us. At the bottom of the hill leading up to my mother's building, I stopped and swung Mari close. We stood for a long time on the curb, holding each other. We were in public, we were queer and in love, we were barely a few hundred yards away from our mothers' houses—mothers we still shielded from full knowledge of us. Every time I looked up, I saw strangers pushing by. But their heads remained bowed. They dignified us with privacy. The sun was warm, I could feel the after-mark of Mari's hands all over my body. Her hair kept getting stuck on my wet lips.

That day in memory looks literally dark, black-framed, like a funeral invitation. But the way I felt on the sidewalk holding Mari—it was nothing I'd felt before. Nothing I've felt since.

Monday morning, I woke up chilled by the certainty that everything with Mari after the concert had been a dream. It couldn't be real that we'd played an incredible show, fucked for hours, then cuddled and drank coffee. It couldn't be real that we'd discussed repeating that cycle on a regular basis into the foreseeable future! I went into the bathroom and checked my shoulder—she'd scratched me—and the marks were still there. Apparently it was real. But I still felt frightened to text her: what if she'd changed her mind? There had to be a boot-drop coming; it was not in the order of things for the universe to align itself so neatly with my most secret desires.

So instead of texting her, I spent about an hour doing *Bugle* work, then took a walk around my father's neighborhood, loud music on headphones so I felt like the protagonist of a '90s rom-com. The mulberry trees were fruiting and sidewalks were guanoed with squashed black berries, a small child in a Spider-Man costume yelled, "You're dead, you're dead!" at me, and the sun baked all thoughts out of my skull like alcohol from a cake. When I came back, I felt nothing but gratitude to be in air-conditioning. She had not texted yet, and I told myself, oh well, a fun one-off, best for the band that we stay friends, Sleater-Kinney, etc., etc.

But then my phone vibrated, and it was Mari, and she was home in bed and the text was a photo of her tits. I gaped, delirious: how was this my life? I had to reply, and so I sent some nonsensical words and spent twenty minutes in the bathroom trying out lighting and angles for a return photo. We didn't get to sext in high school, we deserve to sext, Mari wrote, and I could think of no coherent response.

Tuesday morning, she took a lunchtime selfie in the coffee shop bathroom mirror—boot propped on the sink, T-shirt tugged up over her black sports bra—and Sally was at prenatal yoga, so I posed shirtless on the blue velvet couch, and again, things unraveled. Mari had written everyone suggesting a week off after the show, so we didn't have practice that night. She and I texted through the evening until I fell asleep, clasping my phone like it was her hand.

On Wednesday, I took the train to Baltimore for the *Bugle* story meeting, where Nora gave me a hug, Jeremy congratulated me on the show, and I did not mention the abortion to anyone. Nora's story published online that afternoon. After a middling review of Lucia Brahe, she wrote, "Opening for Brahe was beloved DC indie band Les Somnambules. Les Soms, as fans call them, have been playing around DC and Baltimore for about two years. Tonight they performed with a new lead singer, keyboardist Mariam Dvali's former bandmate Jamie Cain from early '00s experimental punk duo the

Maidenheads. (Disclosure: Cain is an editor at *The Bugle.*) Dvali and Cain's reunion felt like a breakthrough moment for the band, which has long seemed poised for greatness: Cain's ethereal, electric voice gives Dvali's often ruminative music a new depth and emotional range." Mari posted the article on the band's social media accounts, and I got emails from a few old DC friends: "You're back!" "Are you in town???" I didn't reply. Mari and I texted all day, friendly flirty check-ins, and when I messaged her from the train going back to DC, she wrote, Come over tonight?

When I walked up to Mari's porch that evening, my mouth already forming a hungry smile, she was on the seersucker couch with her dirty bare feet tucked up beside her. She was smoking a cigarette and wore an incongruous dress: short, white, sequined, at least two sizes too large. Over the past three days, estrangement from her body had put me in a desperate place, and now it was an effort to sit beside her on the couch and kiss the corner of her mouth, as opposed to tearing off the dress and burrowing inside her like the fox devouring the Spartan boy's stomach.

"Missed you," I said.

"I missed *you*," she said, and I could see it was true.

I scooched nearer. "What's this dress?" I said, stroking a messy lock of hair behind her ear. I hadn't ever seen her in a dress, apart from our prom dresses, and this one had the same effect, emphasizing her surly boyishness.

"It's my mother's," she said, stubbing out her cigarette into the crowded shell ashtray, which she'd balanced on the couch arm. "This one I wear when I get upset, it was her happy dress."

"Aw, Mar—you're upset?"

She swiveled to face me, crossing her legs on the couch. Her eyes were very serious. "I had a hard conversation with Amanda today. I told her you'd had the abortion and that I wanted you to stay in the band, and she threatened to quit."

"Right, OK," I said, shrugging. It was almost a surprise to be reminded that Amanda was still in the band; I was so ready for her not to be.

Mari hardened her eyebrows. "Amanda cannot quit right now, you realize that, right?" she said. "Not before the EP, not if we're going to do it this fall so we can get on the tour. It'd take ages to find another guitarist and teach them all the songs."

"It's not really up to us, Mari," I said. "If she's going to leave, she's going to leave."

"Well, I convinced her to stay," Mari said. "But you may not love how I did it." I looked up, and she went on. "It seems like after I kissed you onstage, which, yeah, not my most thought-out decision—after that, she thought I'd been lying about you and me not fucking. So I told her we weren't, like we'd agreed. And then, because I was trying to make sure she didn't ask more questions, I told her I thought you might not even be into girls anymore and that I'd seen you with Peter after the show."

I backed away on the couch. "Mari."

"Listen, I was on the spot and this is what I came up with, but it's not the worst. And it's partially true, right? You said you do like boys, so it's not a complete lie. You won't have to pretend anything to her, except obviously that we're not fucking, but we'd already decided on that one."

Initially, I felt furious, but quickly it muddled into self-doubt. It had always confused me that anyone could look at me—boy's jeans, large clumsy hands, dyke slouch—and see a straight girl. But of course they could and had for years, and at times, I'd allowed them to, desired them to. Mari was only taking advantage of a situation that I'd frequently taken advantage of myself. "What did she say?" I asked.

Mari glanced up. "James," she said, "you know that's not what *I* think, obviously not!"

"Sure, but—what did she say?"

"Not much," Mari said. "We were on the phone. She got quiet."

"Do you think she believed you?"

"Amanda is a bit of a gold-star lesbian type. She might not think too hard about it. And that would be good—yeah?"

The dress's sequins were the sort that change color to the touch, flickering from silver to translucent white and back again like a fish swerving in and out of light. I reached out and swept my palm across Mari's belly, drawing a silver stripe. "I can understand why you might think that's good," I said slowly. "I'm just not sure you're thinking about how it might feel to me."

"Actually," Mari said, "I've thought about that quite a bit—it's something you require everyone around you to think about constantly."

"Wait—that's not fair . . ."

"No?" she said. "Let's remember why we're here in the first place. We could've signed with a label ten years ago if you hadn't freaked out about something that you had no business freaking out about. I'm just picking up the pieces, I've been *trying* to pick up the pieces for a fucking decade."

The words hit hard: it was 2002 again, Mari was coolly dumping me over the phone. I snatched my hand back from her stomach and lodged it between my thighs. "I'm so, so sorry," I said.

"I'm sorry too," she said, more gently. "I don't want to be a bitch, but just—I've been working toward this for so long. *We've* been working toward this for so long. And it won't happen if we lose Amanda right now. Do you understand?"

She was looking at me so hopefully, with such need. I knew what she was asking was risky and unkind, not just toward me but Amanda too. Although I was hoping Amanda would leave the band of her own accord, I didn't want to wound her deliberately, and I didn't want to lie to her. But I'd hurt Mari so much before, and I felt like I owed her this. And although I knew it wasn't a generous impulse, I didn't hate feeling like we had a secret together. I loved that old thrill of a shared scheme, like lying to our parents about what we did on our sleepovers, sneaking out the back staircase of Yevgenia's apartment to shows or to the one gay bar near Logan Circle that didn't card. Mari was doing this for me, in a sense—for us. To allow us to be together, keep making music together.

"I can't lie," I said. "But I don't have to volunteer information. Just until after the EP, though, right?"

"Just until after the EP," Mari said, speaking fast in a whoosh of relief. "It's maybe not the worst thing, anyway, to keep things between us quiet at first? And then we can tell everyone, and if Amanda wants to leave, we can cross that bridge when we come to it." She stroked my palm with a thumb. "I know this sucks for you. Honestly, I panicked in the moment—Amanda can be intense when she's jealous. Did I tell you she threw a chair at me once?"

I couldn't quite relax my fingers in hers. "You did cheat on her a bunch, though, right? I'm not saying it's OK to throw a chair, but . . ."

"Actually, the cheating happened years ago," Mari said. "But the chair—that was in February."

"Oh."

"It's important for me that you understand something," she said. "I am not the same person that I was when I was with Amanda. She may never see that, but I need you to."

"OK," I said. Her grip on my hand was inexorable; the edge of her thumbnail seemed to be scraping shadows across my vision. "Then tell me what happened, what changed."

"Amanda and I got together four years ago, right before Yevgenia died," Mari said, looking down at our joined hands. "And yeah, I cheated on her a bunch. But that was the worst period of my life. I did a lot of stupid shit, hurt a lot of people."

"What other stupid shit did you do?"

"Nothing I haven't stopped doing. I really need you to know that. OK?"

She sneaked a glance at me, eyebrows drawn, seeming so anxious over my opinion of her, and without thinking, I said, "I love you, Mari."

"Oh my lord," she said, laughing. "You are too much, James. But you know I love you too, always have."

I felt stupidly happy, holding her hand on the smelly couch, and couldn't respond. Mari went on, "There's something I've been wanting to ask you. You wrote those things about us in the *Bugle*, right? 'Kate Bush and Björk's musical love child'?"

"Maybe," I said.

She placed my fingers back on her stomach. "Do you know what I did after I read that? I fucked myself for days thinking about you. I fucked myself in the bathroom at work, I fucked myself in Earl's bathroom during practice."

"Mari . . ." I couldn't keep pace with her swings, they made me crazy, but my hand was on her hip and I couldn't stop myself from raking a silvery finger-trail down toward her thigh.

"I've never wanted anyone like I want you," she whispered. "It's out of control for me, I've wanted you so bad since you came back." She pushed up close against me on the couch, then swung a leg across my lap, dress hiking up as she straddled me. Underneath, she had on a pair of gray boxer briefs, hems torn. I ran a finger along their raveled edge, and I pushed my hands higher, drawing the skirt up her thighs.

There was nothing in my head now but the necessity of being against her. Pressing her close with a hand at her back, I ground my other knuckles into the damp groin of her underpants. She bucked against my hand, her inhale edged with a soft shriek, and I heard the echo in mine.

"Oh, I also told Amanda," she said, lungs tight, "that we wouldn't perform at the *Jennifer's Not There* opening in September. She was so hung up on that, and it doesn't seem like a big deal anyway, that space is small, and they weren't going to pay us much. You don't care about that, do you?"

"No, no, that's fine," I said. I did care, perhaps a lot, but I figured I could examine that later. I tugged helplessly at her boxers; she lifted her haunches to slip them down her thighs, then fumbled behind me to switch off the porch light. It was only 9:30, and the street was well lit, cars going by and families out walking. I could hear nearby voices, people on porches down the row of townhouses, the smell of barbecue and cigarettes. "Do you want to go inside?" I whispered, but Mari shook her head, eyes closed, as I thumbed her slippery vulva, flicked her clit. I swiveled my hand to reach my fingers up inside her, my wrist cramped in the too-short space between us, and she drove her body against mine, making me shiver, lose my rhythm.

I heard kids shouting, someone singing. "We should go in," I said.

"I'm so close," she whispered. She was fucking my hand now in short sharp motions; I wasn't adding much but resistance, my fingers and thumb rigid against her. "You're so good, I'm so close, just—"

"Mari."

"Just one minute, just . . ." Her muscles clamped my fingers, she let out a soft woof.

When she eased back down next to me, I saw the triumph in her eyes, a look of battles won. "You like that, huh," she said. "Making me come."

It was hard to express how much I liked it, how each time it felt like healing, safety. I'd loved it when she fucked me too, but it didn't compare to her sweaty face gleaming with satisfaction, the sense that I'd reached up into her and hit the self-destruct button. "I like it, yeah."

"You can do it again upstairs if you wanna."

"That would probably be a little more comfortable than this couch," I said.

"Maybe," she said, and arched into me like a hungry cat. But I got her on her feet and steered her upstairs and into bed, where I fucked her again and again and again until she was limp and wordless, all mine. Right before she fell asleep, she whispered to me, "I don't ever want this to stop, I just want you to fuck me every minute of the rest of my life," and I was glowing, all light and heat.

SATURDAY MORNING WAS our first practice after the Brahe show. On Friday night, Mari texted: Stop by tomorrow before practice? So first thing, I drove over in my dad's Subaru, winking at the sagged porch couch as I rang her doorbell. Mari pulled me into the living room and kissed me, her hair freshly washed, smelling like lemon soap.

"I want to just quickly," she said as I nibbled her jaw, "strategize for today's practice."

"Strategize," I said, laughing at her.

"We have to be careful. Are you good with that?"

"I'm good, Mari," I said. "You're the one panicking." Because she was—I could feel the tension in her back and shoulders.

"I'm not *panicking*, I'm just taking things seriously."

"Do you want to stop doing this?" I asked, pausing with my lips right by hers.

"That's not really an option anymore, huh."

"Nope," I said, and licked her earlobe, cocky now after days of sexting.

She bit my lower lip, then pulled back. "We really have to be careful," she said. "We'll need to show up at practice separately. And we have to make sure we act normal."

"What would that even look like for you, Mari?" I said. She

laughed and punched me, and with a glorious sense of permission, I backed her down onto the couch, sending Beavis scrambling. We sank into the gap between the leather cushions, getting partially stuck and needing to dislodge ourselves, her body rearing into mine, fighting to get close. I felt a violent intensity I hadn't felt in a long time, had been afraid to let myself feel. I held Mari down with my forearm across her chest, stifling her breaths, and ripped at her jeans as she shifted around on the cushions to help me. Her anxiety still felt like a bubble between us, and when I fucked her, I beat into her hard, still holding her down—trying to release it, break it up, like it was a muscle knot I could relax through impact. "Hit me," she whispered, nodding to double the consent, and I did. I slapped her legs and ass and back, I tore at her hair, I pulled her into me like a snake attacking its own tail.

After she came I collapsed, legs sprawled off the couch. "Are you OK?" I whispered, urgent, terrified. "I didn't hurt you?"

"James, I'm fine, I'm great. But hey—we really have to leave for practice, and maybe you should wash your face?"

SHE WANTED A head start on her bike, so I waited outside her house in my dad's car, listening to NPR and replaying the morning—had I misread her signs, had I screwed everything up? By the time I got to practice, I was twitching with the need to be reassured. I tried to shake it off as I walked down into Earl's basement.

Everyone else was already there. Mari was flipping through a music notebook, looking so placid I wondered again if the whole last week had been my fevered invention. Amanda was in the corner, humming as she replaced a broken string on her guitar, also looking surprisingly relaxed. Andrew was Windexing a drumhead and didn't look up at me, but Freddie gave me a slow stare.

"You OK?" she asked quietly. "You look down."

"Tired," I said.

Mari glared at me, no hint of playfulness at all. "You're late," she said.

"Traffic," I said—a ridiculous excuse, given that everyone knew my father's house was a ten-minute drive from Earl's, and it was Saturday morning.

"Leave earlier next time," she said, and turned away. I felt an internal crumple, like she'd kicked out one of my chair legs. "Anyway, dudes," she went on, "I'm so happy about the show and I hope you all are too. Amazing reviews in the *City Paper* and the *Bugle*, and we may get a mention in the *Post* as well. I talked to Lucia's manager and she seemed interested in talking more about the Europe tour next summer, but she definitely thought we should get a second EP going. So—a lot of stuff to think about, and a lot to work on! And, because I didn't do this very well last time, I want to have a group conversation about Jamie staying in the band permanently. How is everyone feeling about that?"

Amanda said, right away, "I think it's good. The show went well, it makes sense we'd record the EP together."

I looked at her in surprise; she smiled back, appearing sincere. Whatever Mari said had clearly been reassuring. Freddie and Andrew seemed relieved, both nodding. Freddie said, "I agree. Jamie, you killed 'Tiny Animals,' I had shivers. We couldn't get that sound without you."

Mari nodded approval, and I said, "Thanks, all—pleasure to be here." For the rest of practice we were all very polite, complimenting each other unnecessarily. My voice was clumsy, but everyone was kind about it, even Amanda, who said, "It's always rough the first time back after a show, huh?" When we took a break halfway through, Mari went out and bought Starbucks for everyone, passing out cups from the cardboard drink-holder like she was our intern. After we finished, she scuttled off in her black hoodie. She had given me no sign that things were OK with us, no wink or secret hand-press or anything else. Andrew and Amanda walked toward the Metro together, but Freddie hung back with me. When we came out of Earl's house into the swampy heat, she said, "Jamie, did you drive today? Any chance I could get a ride?"

Her face, as always, was kind and open. "Sure," I said.

Freddie climbed into the passenger's seat and set her violin case carefully between her bare calves. As I drove down Georgia Ave through Takoma and into Brightwood, she rambled about Liya, how well she was doing in pre-K, how she loved comic books and Taylor Swift. "After a certain point, you can't really make them do anything," she said. "You just have to model good behavior and hope for the best." Still discombobulated from the morning, I kept my hands glued to the wheel, my eyes on the road.

"Mari told me you had the abortion," Freddie said into a pause.

Although I'd been nervous to have this conversation, it was a relief compared to the other things I'd been worried she might say. "I'm sorry, I should've told you sooner," I said. "I was scared."

"Scared? Why?"

"Scared that you'd think it was selfish or something. Because you're a mom. And scared about the Three Exes thing, about Amanda."

Freddie joined her hands in her lap. "I would never judge anyone for getting an abortion," she said. "It's not selfish to recognize you don't want to be a parent right now; in fact, it's the opposite. And Amanda—that's Mari's fuckup, not yours. But I think it's going to be OK. I talked to Amanda last week. She was hurt after the show, for obvious reasons, but she and Mari talked and they're in a good place—at least for now, until Mari does something stupid again."

"Mari's dealing with a lot," I said, not meaning for it to come out so defensive. "She's doing her best."

We pulled up in front of Freddie and Dani's house. "I know," Freddie said. She laughed, atypically curt. "And her best is sometimes terrible. Jamie, I've been friends with Mari for a long time, and I assume she's mostly going to act in her own self-interest. That doesn't mean I think she's a bad person! I just know what to expect, and then I don't get disappointed. I know your history with her is more complicated, but I recommend detachment for you as well. See you Tuesday, anyway?"

"Sure," I said. I knew she was right, but I would never risk detaching from Mari; our attachment still felt so knife-edge. Freddie gave me a kind, impatient look, then kissed my cheek before climbing out, violin slung across her back. I watched her walk up to her tanstone row house, past a sun-faded plastic tricycle and an Obama-Biden sign in the small front yard. The porch was hung with fairy lights and a big Pride flag, as well as what looked like old Halloween decorations, stickers of skeletons and ghosts on the front door. Dani and Liya ran outside to meet Freddie, already laughing at something before she was on the porch; I watched until they'd all gone inside. Later I texted Mari, All good? and she wrote back, Better than good, James, way better.

AFTER THAT, AND through the stupefying heat of July and August, we picked up our old practice schedule again. We discussed a song list for the EP, researched recording studios, argued about titles. In between, we kept up our energetic politeness, and Mari made her Saturday morning coffee run a routine. I didn't talk about being queer in front of Amanda, didn't say the word, and because I'd done this at work for so long, it didn't feel too strange. What was strange was doing it with Mari right there, or after we finished a good run-through of a song and looked right at each other, as we always did.

She was my twin, she was inside of me, I couldn't divorce my body from hers. And I didn't have to call that queerness, I didn't have to call it anything at all, but I knew that every time I sang, I was calling it something. My voice sounded different to me in those practices, as if my mouth had been newly shaped by Mari's mouth, Mari's body. I sang like I was crying out for something lost, or like I was the lost thing, crying out for someone to find me. Afterward, emotionally spent, I would go home and make tea and lie in the bathtub with the lights out, my back scraping on the sandpapery sea-creature-shaped adhesives Sally had stuck on to catch the baby's slippery feet. I stroked my hips, belly, thighs, with appreciation: my body had a new function now, to collaborate with Mari, and I didn't feel the Franken-feeling anymore. When I looked down at my fishy, wrinkly limbs, I saw only a finely tuned instrument, a powerful and precise tool.

My time with Mari developed its own routines, its own unspoken rules. Two or three times a week, I'd go over, before practice or after her Sunday shift, when she'd be sweaty and silent, and I'd fuck her bullishly, elbowing her down on the bed until she woke up out of it and grabbed my hair and slapped me as if I stood in for all the customers she'd wanted to hit that day. Sex with Mari now felt less anarchic than in high school. We had skills, we knew how to ask for what we wanted, and Mari wanted to be fucked a lot, and hard; she wanted to be surprised, she wanted to be dominated, and sometimes she wanted to be hurt. I asked her why—I wanted to understand because it felt so scary after what had happened before. But she didn't really have an answer. "You seem really into it and that's incredibly hot to me," she said. I told myself I could take that as a sign of trust, and stopped asking.

In any case, I couldn't leave her alone. When she got up to pee, my hands would tremble, lonely for her; I'd knead one with the other to soothe it quiet. I'd trail her through the house—into the kitchen, out to the back patio—because it felt so bad to have a closed door or a staircase between us. I wanted to be braided into her all day long, and anytime I couldn't be, my skin seemed to harden slightly, like uncovered clay.

We didn't talk about our relationship at all. I assumed she felt the same way I did: obsessed, reawakened, although perhaps in a Mari way, quieter and more internal. We didn't say *I love you* again after the conversation on the porch, although I thought it all the time. We didn't talk about the effect of being together on the music, although I could tell we both felt excited by the way we sounded—the sound felt like a validation of the fucking to me, and I thought for her too.

Instead we talked about everything else. Some of it was heavy: we caught up on the past ten years, she told me about Yevgenia's final months, I told her about the year after college. Mostly, though, as we always had, we talked about music. She had gotten really into K-pop and texted me YouTube videos with excited emojis; I was digging back into '80s and '90s DC girl bands, correcting the gaps in my teenage music education, and sent her Fire Party, Chalk Circle, Autoclave, all the people who'd been on the scene a generation before us, who could've been our big sisters if we'd only known to reach out. Mari always resisted the idea of us being a DC band—she kept a skepticism about all things American—but I was growing to love the idea. DC's musical history was mostly Black, and I couldn't lay claim to that, but I still felt humbled to live in the city that had birthed not just hardcore but so much go-go, soul, jazz. I wished Mari could've understood that my love for DC music was not far removed from my love for her—that for me, Mari was DC and DC was Mari, and identifying myself as "from DC" just meant identifying myself as hers. I knew she would've hated that, though, and so I never said it—just texted her the Blackbyrds song "Rock Creek Park" when she told me she was fantasizing about fucking in a forest, and then hummed the riff for her when we did actually sneak out one afternoon to fuck in Rock Creek Park, not far from where we'd stood on September 11, birdsong in my ears, trees soft and blurred around me, reeling in the history and present and future of my love.

15

ONE WEDNESDAY IN mid-August, I took the 8:30 a.m. MARC train to Baltimore, as I always did for the story meeting. On the way, for the first time since before the pregnancy, I started bleeding. It had been so long since I'd had my period that I didn't have tampons in my bag, didn't own any except the unopened box in my old apartment, so I stopped at a pharmacy by the *Bugle* offices. In line for the cash register, dreaming up funny menstruation-related texts to send Mari, I turned and saw Jeremy, holding a bright green energy drink and a plastic container of sliced honeydew, his habitual breakfast. He smiled, looked down at my box of super-absorbency pads, back up at my torso.

"Are you OK?" he said, after we'd both paid and were walking out through the automatic doors. "You're not—nothing's happened to the pregnancy?"

I had not told Jeremy about the abortion, and I was pretty sure I shouldn't have to. I'd googled "can your employer ask about your abortion," and according to various sketchy legal-advice websites, he could not. I had assumed he'd already figured it out, but was waiting for me to say something, either out of delicacy or in some twisted power play. But now he looked genuinely concerned.

"I'm not pregnant anymore," I said.

"Oh no," he said. "Miscarriage? I'm so sorry, my wife had two, it was a real struggle. There's such a stigma."

It would've been best to lie, but I couldn't, somehow. "Actually, I had an abortion."

The *Bugle* had no HR department, no required trainings on harassment and discrimination. Jeremy took a long swig from his energy drink, looking perplexed, as if he himself were trying to recall what was allowed. "Well," he went on finally, "I'm glad you're taking care of yourself. Hope you're feeling OK!"

He said nothing else as we walked upstairs together, nothing after the story meeting, nothing that afternoon as we went over plans for the next issue. But when I passed his office on my way out, he called me in.

"So—we'll see you in the office tomorrow, right?" he said. He was standing by his desk with his hands clasped in front of him. I realized I'd walked into a scene he had spent the day rehearsing and consulting lawyers about.

"Um," I said, "is there any way I could keep working remotely?"

"Our agreement," Jeremy said, "as I understood it, was that you were working remotely during your pregnancy to be close to family. But since your pregnancy is over, that arrangement is over as well. Right?"

"I thought I'd been doing a good job from DC," I said, embarrassed by how plaintive I sounded. "I've been faster—my section's been done hours earlier than it used to be."

"It's not about efficiency," he said. "It's about team cohesion. Face-to-face time is so important for brainstorming, the editing process, collegiality, everything. And if I let you work remotely, I'd have to let everyone do it."

"Would you really, though?"

"Jamie," he said, "it was one thing when you were pregnant. But if it's just that you don't *feel* like coming in—that's a different matter. I couldn't justify that to your coworkers, let alone to WMP."

I was experiencing a full-body revulsion to the idea of moving away from Mari. "What if I can't come back?" I said.

Jeremy's expression was surprisingly gentle. "Then I'd be sorry to see you go," he said. "Why don't you take a couple of days to think on it and let me know by Friday? You can head back to DC while you're figuring it out, but I'll expect you here on Monday if you want to continue at the *Bugle*."

BACK AT MY father's house that evening, I was napping on the air mattress when Sally knocked on my bedroom door. "Sorry, can I come in?" she called. "Just doing some inventory. I might make another trip to Buy Buy Baby."

I blinked at her dozily as she knelt to rifle through the drawers of the baby's small yellow dresser. Sally didn't fit into her maternity clothes now—she'd outgrown the largest sizes and was just wearing a nursing bra under an unbuttoned shirt of my dad's. Her belly was tight and round, a dark brown line drawn down from her stretched-flat belly button. It was brutally hot out now, and she was perpetually sweaty, perpetually exhausted, slow to think, slow to talk. She had deactivated her Etsy account, she had dropped off Instagram entirely, she drifted through the house all day with an aimlessness that frightened me.

At the same time, she exuded a mysterious sexiness. When we went to the grocery store together, men stared with a mix of paternalism and lechery, like they wanted to carry her shopping basket home and then fuck her. Was it the extra weight, her heavy breasts and full, soft arms? Was it imagining another man's sperm wreaking all that gorgeous damage? It was confusing: pregnancy was caused by fucking but made fucking seem taboo. It turned your body into an unfuckable gated courtyard: there was a *baby* in there. Yet all anyone could think about (or was it just me?) when they looked at a pregnant woman was fucking.

My body was so discrete now, so private. I didn't have to absorb everyone's weird feelings about fecund femininity and the future of the species. I felt sorry for Sally, then annoyed at myself for feeling sorry: we had both made choices.

"Socks," she said. "Do babies even wear socks? They have those things on their onesies."

"What things?"

"At the ends of the legs. You know."

"Like little thingies for their feet?"

"Exactly," she said, smiling at me with gratitude. Sweat shone around her lips, as if she'd just taken a bite out of a ripe fruit. "I mostly just have hot-weather pajamas, but maybe I need more cold-weather pajamas? In what size, though."

"Do you want me to come to Buy Buy Baby with you?" I said.

"No, no," she said. She found a pair of fleece pajamas printed with pineapples, then sat back down on the ground with her legs stuck out and spread them across her knees. "I think *these* are winter weight? But will he be wearing six-month pajamas by the winter?"

"No fucking clue," I said, slightly too harsh. Sally glanced at me with a second's concern, and then we both laughed.

"Seriously, I'll come to Buy Buy Baby with you," I said, guilty again. "I should be more helpful, I know you need it right now. I'll move out soon too. I know everything will be easier once you have the room back."

"You know, you could stay after the baby comes," she said. "For a bit. He'll be in our room at first, I got a co-sleeper."

"Oh, you wouldn't want me—I'm terrible with babies."

"You sound like your dad," she said. "Of course we'd want you."

"Well, either way, I probably need to move out," I said. "Jeremy says I have to be full-time in the office by Monday or lose my job."

"I guess that's not *so* surprising," she said. "What are you going to do?"

"I'm not sure. My rent is paid through August, so I could just go back. But I don't want to be far from the band right now while we're getting ready to record the EP."

"Baltimore's not far."

I didn't want to live in Baltimore. I wanted to live no more than fifteen minutes away from Mari. I wanted to stop by her house on weeknights, wake up there on a Thursday and still get to work on time. I wanted to be convenient to Mari; I didn't want to find out what might happen if I became inconvenient.

"I guess also I want to be close to Mari," I admitted. It was the first time I had even hinted to anyone that Mari was more than a friend, and I felt nervous about it, like Mari would find out and get angry. "I want to look for jobs here, find an apartment here."

I thought Sally might act surprised, but she just ran a palm across the pajamas in her lap, smoothing them all the way down to their little attached socks. "You're putting a lot on hold for her, aren't you?" she said. "Your apartment, maybe now your job. Your life in Baltimore."

"I didn't really have a life in Baltimore, so it's not such a loss."

"Would you have a life if you moved here?" she asked. "A life outside of Mari?"

"I'd see you," I said, and added, knowing it would distract her, "I'd see Lingonberry."

Sally smiled. "That's not his name, your dad just made that up."

"Whatever his name, he's one lucky kid," I said to Sally, relieved we'd moved on from me and Mari. "You're going to be the best mother."

She nodded blankly, smoothed out the pajamas one more time into the flattened shape of a child.

I DIDN'T WANT to tell Mari about the Jeremy situation over text—it felt important to see her reaction in person—and we didn't have time alone on Wednesday or Thursday. But on Friday night, we went out together to a show at Comet Ping Pong in Northwest DC, not far from our old high school. Comet provided fancy pizza and Ping-Pong tables to neighborhood families in the early evening, but later on weekends folded up the tables and opened the back for local bands.

Mari knew the singer of a punk band called Tigress, had possibly—I didn't want to ask—dated her. As far as I could tell, they now had a frenemy relationship in which it would've been more shameful for Mari to miss their show (demonstrating deliberate avoidance) than to go. Mari and I met up on the platform at Fort Totten Metro station, then rode to Tenleytown together and walked from the station holding hands. A block from Comet, Mari let go. "Amanda knows Patty too," she said. "I don't think she's going, but just in case."

I didn't mind, I understood, but it made me hesitate to bring up the Jeremy conversation. We went in and pushed our way through the pizza tables into the back room—it was crowded for Comet, but I kept thinking about how much smaller it was than the Atrium, and feeling a competitiveness that I tried to chase away. We ordered beers and stood at the back waiting for the show to start. Mari was quiet, scanning the crowd—I wondered if she was worried about being seen with me.

"Are you OK?" I said. "You seem kind of nervous."

"We played here in March," she said. "They have way more people."

"Dude, we just played the Atrium! We had thousands of people there."

"For Lucia Brahe, though."

"For us too. And I bet if we played here now, we'd get a bigger crowd."

"Hmph," she said, and was quiet again for a moment. Then, "We should play here again in the winter. Just to see."

"Did you come out tonight just to measure dicks with Patty? Mari, it's *Tigress*. Everyone comes out for their shows." Tigress had been around for much longer than us, three women who'd come up in the DC hardcore scene and had ties to all the big '90s groups—had recorded with Ian MacKaye at Dischord Records, toured with members of Bikini Kill.

"I want everyone to come out for *our* shows," she said.

"They do! You're just insecure because it's Patty and you have some weird hang-up about her."

"Ridiculous, I don't have any weird hang-ups about anyone," Mari said, and I side-checked her. We were both laughing, arms brushing, when someone walked up and said hi to Mari—a drummer I semi-recognized from way back in the day. Mari's arm jerked back from mine. She chatted with the drummer for a minute, then introduced me: "This is Jamie Cain, I don't know if you—"

"Of course!" he said. "The Maidenheads! Wow, amazing to see you two together after all these years."

"Just Les Somnambules now," Mari said.

After he walked off, she said, "Good thing Amanda's not here, huh."

"Good thing."

"Don't be grouchy," she said. "I just mean, it's nice to be out alone with you."

The lights went down, and in the darkness, Mari relaxed. She passed me a pair of foam earplugs ("I knew you would forget") and twisted hers in, then leaned back against me. "You haven't told me how your day was," she said. "How's old Jeremy?" She had developed a forceful dislike for Jeremy after I told her about Bear—not just the attempted kiss, but what Jeremy said when I told him: "Bear's probably feeling just as awkward about it as you are, don't you think?"

Tigress walked out to cheers, Patty in cutoffs and Converse high-tops and a mesh T-shirt over a green sports bra. She was hot, completely different from me, ten years tougher, big and brash and bold. I involuntarily pictured her and Mari fucking, Patty pinning her like a lady wrestler.

"Actually," I said, "I think I'm going to quit the *Bugle*."

"What? Why would you do that?" Mari said.

Onstage, Patty roared, "WE ARE TIGRESS!!!" and the crowd lost it, stomping and shouting.

"Jeremy said I had to come back to the office full-time starting Monday. And I don't want to do that. I want to get a job here, move to DC."

Patty screamed, "WHAT'S UP, DC, WHAT'S UP," and whipped into their first track, a protest song about abortion rights, the type of song Mari usually found naive but which made me wince with emotion. The sound was so intense it seemed to clamp down around my ears and head and chest, brutal and cleansing.

Mari yelled, "You do? Really?"

"Yes!" I yelled back.

"You don't have to! We can make it work with you in Baltimore!"

"That's not what I want," I said, so quietly I could barely hear my own voice. "I want to be here all the time. With you."

Mari looked at me, then pulled me by the hand through the crowd and into the women's bathroom, which felt vibratingly still after the Tigress onslaught.

“Come here,” she said, and propelled me into a stall, locked the door behind us. She tugged out her earplugs, reached forward to tug out mine. “Now—what are you saying?”

“I know we could make it work with me in Baltimore,” I said, eyes lowered to Mari’s collarbone. “But I don’t want to. I want to focus on the band, not always be going back and forth. And I want to be near Sally to help with the baby, I want to be near my mom in case Michael dumps her and she ends up alone and depressed again. But—I also want to be close to you, Mari. I don’t want this to end.”

Mari looped her hands inside my hoodie’s kangaroo pocket. “I don’t either,” she said, and glanced up with a shy smile that undid my whole heart. “Just—”

“Don’t tell Amanda? Were you really going to say that?”

“*No.* Although that too. I meant, don’t do anything rash. You know? You have a good job there. You’re not far. We can figure it out.”

“I want to be here,” I said stubbornly, “with you,” and pressed my body into hers. I knew I would quit any job, break any lease, just to keep her close. Later that night, after Mari fell asleep on my shoulder in the cab and I tucked her into bed at home, I wrote Jeremy to put in my notice.

MARI HAD THAT Saturday off, so in the morning, we made our separate ways to practice, then made our separate ways back to her house, where we spent the afternoon and evening not doing much—just fucking, watching movies, eating takeout. It felt easy, safe; like a rhythm we could hold steady for a very long time.

Late that night, when we were watching TV on the couch, my father called. “We’re at George Washington Hospital,” he said. “Sally started labor a couple of hours ago.”

“Do you need me to do anything? Should I come?”

"No, no." He was too calm; it frightened me. "There's nothing you can do. I'll keep in touch."

After he hung up, Mari said, "Is it Sally? Is she OK?"

"I think?" I said. My dad's voice had sounded strained, like he was working to act normal in a hostage situation. "She's a little early, three weeks. But that's fine, right?"

"Three weeks is nothing," Mari said, with the confidence of a doctor's kid. We started the movie again, but five minutes later, she said, "Does this mean you'll have to move out?"

"I guess so." I'd been worrying about Sally, but of course there were other ramifications. I'd thought I'd have the room for at least another month. "Sally said I could stay a little longer, but I don't think she really wants me there. *I* wouldn't want me there."

"What are you going to do?"

"I can't go back to my mom's, Michael's basically living there now. So Baltimore, I guess? I can look for jobs here while I'm living there, it won't be too hard."

My cheek was resting on Mari's ribs. I couldn't see her face, but I felt her muscles tense as she lifted her head to look at me. "Would you want to stay here?" she said. "Just for a couple weeks, until you can find a job and an apartment?"

I sat up to see her expression: an open, soft smile. "Really? You'd be OK with that?"

"Sure," she said, reaching out to stroke my hair. "It'd be fun. And convenient for practices while we're about to record. We'd have to tell everyone that you're sleeping on the couch, that's all. But if it's only for a couple weeks, they might not even need to know."

"I'd like that," I said. We never discussed our future outside of music, but I had my private fantasies: Sunday walks to the farmers' market, picnics in Malcolm X Park, setting up a better practice space in Mari's basement, Mari writing new songs for us on Yevgenia's piano, camping and bike trips, holding hands at album release parties, and then someday, not to get ahead of myself, but someday maybe a puppy, even kids, running to meet me at the door like Dani and Liya with Freddie.

Mari would say she hated all that bougie shit, but I thought it was what she most needed. She was such a solitary person—even Yevgenia she'd kept at arm's length, frightened of losing her entirely. She owned this whole house, but she treated it like a campsite. With me, though, she could rest safely; she could have a real home, a family—and perhaps her inviting me to move in was a sign that she realized that as well.

When Mari got up to brush her teeth, I texted my father: Hope all's well. I'm going to move my stuff out and clean up, it'll be ready for the baby when you get back.

He wrote back: OK! Labor's going slow. All signs good so far. Are you going back to your mom's?

Going to stay with a friend. I'll be around, though. Can't wait to meet my lil bro.

I got up early the next morning, rode the Metro to Silver Spring, and let myself into the empty house. There were still two porcupine-boner plates on the table sticky with food, pots on the stove caked with hardened beans and rice: Sally must've gone into labor partway through dinner. I put everything in the sink to soak. Then I went to pack up my room, the baby's room, a place where I would always be a guest now. The makeshift half-life I'd built over the past three months fit into my one suitcase: my clothes hanging from the crib frame or jumbled on the changing table pad, leaking bottles of face wash and shampoo and conditioner, a few leftover Les Somnambules T-shirts from the merch table at the Lucia Brahe show. I deflated and packed away the air mattress, vacuumed the carpet, ran Lysol wipes over everything, swished the toilet with bowl cleaner. I straightened the stuffed animals on the shelves, dusted the abstract fish-shapes mobile over the crib, smoothed the baby blankets in the bureau. I thought about taking the cassette box in the closet, then decided to leave the tapes as a gift for the baby, who would maybe someday consider them valuable, if mysterious, relics. There was no other trace left of me except the strip of wallpaper in the closet and the stars on the ceiling. I looked around a final time, a hard ache in my throat; then I closed the door and went to clean up the kitchen.

AROUND THREE THAT afternoon, my father called again. "Rufus Thuong Cain," he said, "was born at eleven a.m. You have a brother!"

It had barely occurred to me until that moment that Sally's body was lodging a human—a *brother.* I took a cab from Mari's house to the GWU hospital and made my way into the maternity ward, past women in wheelchairs holding tiny clay-colored babies, a closed door behind which a woman screamed and screamed, a waiting room where a small girl in braids and a party dress sat next to an elderly couple, a bulletin board covered with photos of infants dressed like pumpkins or Yoda. A nurse led me into Sally's room, where she was asleep on the bed, IV drip in her arm.

My father shushed me from the armchair in the corner. On his lap was a mess of blankets, which I realized after a moment contained a miniature person. I'd never seen my father so exhausted or happy, and without warning, I was torn by hatred.

"Do you want to hold him?" he whispered. I sat next to him, and he lowered Rufus to rest in my lap.

Rufus was asleep, swaddled in a hospital blanket, white striped with blue and pink. He wore a little pink-and-blue beanie and a white ID bracelet. His hair, sticking out around the beanie, was black and thick; his scrunched face was raw-beef red. The arm with the bracelet was loose of the blankets and kept spasming out, and once, he slapped his own forehead so hard he blinked, revealing a slice of unseeing steel-gray eye. When I ran a finger down his cheek, it felt dry, scrapy.

This shrimp, apparently, would soon be occupying my room at my dad's house, staring at my glow-in-the-dark stars and Sally's parading elephants every night until they burned into his brain forever the way they already had mine. I'd call him on his birthday—this day, August 21—for the rest of our lives. We'd celebrate holidays together, know the private details of the other's medical history. Dad would probably come out to him at some point, and maybe I'd do for Rufus what my mom did for me, fill in the bits Dad didn't tell. He would love me, resent me, beg me to buy liquor for his underage friends. Rufus. I wasn't sure what to say.

"He's cute!" I told my dad.

"He's *beautiful*," my dad said, and I hated him again.

I lifted Rufus to give him back, and my dad circled his arms underneath mine so that Rufus's cradle was unbroken in the passage. "How did you come up with the name?" I asked, settling more relaxed into my chair once I was free of the baby.

"Sally loves Rufus Wainwright," he said, sounding embarrassed. "Anyway, at least it's not Lingonberry."

I asked about Sally's labor, and he said, "It was fine." We both looked at her, flattened and gray, and then looked away.

"I moved my things out," I said. "Sorry I didn't do it before."

"You know you could stay if you need to. Sally got a co-sleeper, he'll be in our room at the beginning."

"Actually, I moved in with Mari."

"Oh!" he said. "Are you sure?"

"Very sure," I said.

Rufus mewled softly, then escalated to a monotonous tinny cry. Without opening her eyes, Sally lifted her arms, and my father handed Rufus over and then turned respectfully away as she unsnapped her hospital gown.

"Finding the latch—it's been hard," my father whispered. Rufus rummaged into Sally's chest like a blind piglet. Sally squashed a floppy breast between her fingers and thumb, holding it like a hamburger, and hooked her other fingers under Rufus's chin to wrangle him closer. Rufus made a few sucking sounds, pecked his lips into all the wrong places, started howling again.

"Fuck, fuck fuck fuck," Sally said, then opened her eyes. "Jamie!"

"How's it going?"

"Been better! He's not eating anything. I don't know what's going to happen if I can't feed him."

My dad murmured, "It's going to be OK. They said they'd send in the lactation consultant."

"You don't know it's going to be OK, you don't know that." Her glare around the room was wild, searching.

The door opened, and Sally's parents came in—I recognized them from her photos. They were wearing matching navy blue raincoats and carrying a paper Whole Foods bag. They all spoke together in Vietnamese while my father sat holding his hands together in his lap, as if he were keeping Rufus's arm-cradle at the ready. Sally's mother smiled at me a few times, while Sally's father seemed more focused on ignoring my father.

"You can leave if you need to," my father whispered to me.

"I probably should get back, yeah . . ."

Sally's mother stopped and said, "You're Jamie? Pleasure to meet you." Sally said something in Vietnamese—I'd never heard her speak it before—and her mother laughed. Her father unpacked the groceries: sliced watermelon and pears and a box of crackers and a six-pack of the tangerine-flavored seltzer Sally loved. He didn't offer anything to my father, just laid it all out on the bed next to Sally.

"I need to go," I said to Sally, who had handed Rufus to her mother and was eating watermelon cubes. "I'll come back later."

She gave me an intense, frazzled look. "Come visit?" she said.

"Come soon?" She wasn't asking because she was worried about me, I saw. She was worried about something else: about the baby, about herself.

I didn't know what it was. But my curiosity was muffled by another feeling: the need to escape from this baby with all his chaotic urgencies, the way he'd already slashed through time, cutting me off from my father and Sally in their new, alien future. If I'd hadn't had the abortion, I might've preserved a meaningful role as the mother of Rufus's baby friend. But without that, I had no clear place in their family—perhaps I never really had.

"I will," I promised, feeling the insincerity. "Absolutely, I'll come right away." I fled the room, leaving Sally behind with her watermelon and her vengeful parents and my father, who was watching Rufus sleep in Sally's mother's arms. *Thank fucking god that's not me,* I told myself as I hurried down the hallway, rushing home to Mari as fast as possible.

16

THE MORNING AFTER Rufus was born, I woke up in Mari's bed with my roller suitcase in her downstairs hall closet, my toothbrush in her toothbrush cup, and my jeans and T-shirts folded in the new "Jamie drawer" in her bureau. It was Monday, the first day of my final week at the *Bugle*. I had two paychecks still coming. I had a small savings account, but it wouldn't support me for more than a month or two. I had no college debt, thanks to faculty-brat tuition at AU, but during the bad years after college, I'd accrued nearly $20,000 in credit card debt I was still paying off. September rent for the Baltimore apartment was due in a week; nonpayment would mean breaking the lease, so I'd lose my deposit.

But for at least another half hour, until Mari had to leave for work, we were under a heavy blanket together, in a cave of her smells, her hair prickling my shoulder, her breath on my lips. I wormed into her arms and, half awake, she opened them to me.

I dozed in the body-warmed sheets as Mari showered, dressed, kissed me goodbye. Once she was gone, I fetched coffee and toast from downstairs and brought my laptop back into bed, scooching to her side, where I could smell her shampoo on the pillow. Toast plate on my lap, I opened the media jobs listing site where I'd found the *Bugle* posting five years prior.

Jeremy had warned me I might have trouble finding something—the recession had permanently kicked out an entire rung of journalism jobs, he'd said—but I'd thought he was just trying to frighten me. Browsing the jobs page, however, I saw that I'd been wrong. In 2007, with almost no relevant experience, I'd applied for a bunch of entry-level positions—copyediting, fact-checking, assisting other editors—and gotten three interviews and an offer. Now I found a single opening in all of DC media, a video producer gig at the *Post* for which I was totally unqualified and which, in any case, paid less than I could earn babysitting. I looked on Craigslist and a few other sites: also nothing. I searched for copyediting jobs at nonprofits, research firms, consulting firms: nothing, or at least nothing that paid enough to cover DC rent. "All good!" I told Mari that night when she asked how the search was going.

Over the following week, in between finalizing my last *Bugle* issue, I called the manager at the coffee shop where I'd worked in high school and college, and he talked to me for an hour about the Denver airport, its underground bunkers, the shape of a sword in one of the murals ("A scimitar! Like the Muslims!"), and the likely involvement of the Illuminati, Barack Hussein Obama, and lizard people. I finally asked if there were any openings and he said, "Openings? Nah." Mari asked her boss, and he said the same, minus the Denver stuff. I kept checking the same job sites, and not only was there nothing I was qualified for, there was nothing at all. I looked at apartment listings, and everything was outside my budget. I was paying $700 a month for a one-bedroom in Baltimore, half of what I'd pay in DC for an apartment with similar square footage. But even DC studios and rooms in group houses were over $1,000 now. There was no way I'd be able to afford first and last month here before securing a job and getting paid, and it seemed like that could take a long time.

I had been nervous to call my mother after Rufus was born, I thought it likely she was having feelings I wouldn't enjoy witnessing. But she called on Thursday afternoon and said, "Your father said you're living with Mari."

I was lying across Mari's living room couch in a pair of her sweatpants, Beavis purring across my feet, a mug of wine balanced on my stomach. Afternoon light glowed warm in the yellow-painted room. I'd made a large pot of lentil soup for dinner, and the house smelled like garlic and ginger. "Not exactly *living with*," I said. "It's just while I'm looking for a job."

This was a mistake; immediately she asked, "And why do you need a job?"

"Well, actually, I quit the *Bugle* and I'm looking for jobs in DC."

"You quit the *Bugle* without lining up another job? *Jamie*."

"It was a bad job! Jeremy's a dick, I got sexually harassed. It was time to move on."

"Jamie! When you move on, you get another job first—you don't leap into space! And you're moving to *DC*? Is this because of Mari? Do you have an apartment, any job leads?"

Spoken aloud, these did sound like important questions. "It's for the band," I said, a reminder to myself as well as to her. "We're practicing a lot before we record the EP, and I didn't want to miss anything. I let Mari down last time—I can't do that now."

"I have to say it's very hard to watch you go through this again," she said.

"What do you mean?"

"You're sounding like you did in college. Like Mari's this perfect creature and you're terrible. Not to mention the poor life choices. Please tell me you're taking care of yourself?"

"I'm *taking care of myself*," I said, averting my eyes from the wine mug, as if that might prevent her from seeing it too. "Hey, Rufus is cute."

I could just about hear her frown, but she let herself be drawn away. "Does he look like Kenneth? You looked like Kenneth when you were born, or maybe Alfred Hitchcock."

"More Hitchcock."

"Do you think they'd want a lasagna? A pot of chili? I have some of the baby sweaters your grandma knitted you in the basement storage area."

"I don't think that's a good idea."

She let out an aggressive sigh. "Don't stay with Mari for too long—OK?" she said. "Just promise me that. And that you'll keep your Baltimore place for now, just in case."

"Sure, Mom," I said. But I had to admit she was right, at least about that one. After we got off the phone, I mailed off my September rent check.

That Friday was my last day at the *Bugle*, and I spent it helping Jeremy wind down my job, or jobs, since I'd been both calendar editor and copyeditor. Even at my tiny salary, there was no money to replace me, so Jeremy and the entertainment editor would split the calendar section, and they were giving up on copyediting. "We all know AP style, though." Jeremy shrugged. He had asked me to help them figure out how to jointly run the calendar, and although I thought this was a very bad idea, I wrote a memo divvying up my tasks.

Reading it before sending, I felt queasy. Leaping into space, my mother had called it, and I felt that in my stomach: the lift before the crash. But sometimes you had to leap, right? "Good luck," I typed at the end, and hit send.

• • •

SALLY CALLED THAT weekend, the first time I could remember her calling me. When I picked up, I heard Rufus crying so loudly I got scared—was this an emergency? But Sally just said, "How are you?" like no one was caterwauling in the background.

"I'm great. Um—you?"

"Great, just great. Just absolutely great."

"How's Rufus?" I asked. He was still screaming.

"He's great," she said. "Do you want to come over sometime?"

"Definitely," I said. I hadn't gone to my dad's house since they'd brought Rufus home a few days ago. It wasn't that I was so busy. I spent my mornings reading apartment and job listings and sending out applications. But there were only so many new listings each day, and then it would be the afternoon, and I'd have nothing to do. At one point, feeling ambitious, I'd decided to learn piano, so I was working through some old exercise books on Yevgenia's baby grand. Just as often, I lay across the leather sectional with Beavis on my stomach, his eyes partially closed as he rose and fell with my breath. I sat on the back patio and read Mari's novels, smoked Mari's weed. I took walks in her neighborhood, sat in her empty bathtub doing vocal exercises, drank her wine from her mugs.

I had wondered about Sally, but hadn't thought to call. I was sure she didn't actually want me there. She had her own baby now—she wouldn't want to see her husband's adult child, who, let's face it, was a bit of a mess. Besides, Rufus frightened me: so needy, so breakable. "I'll come over as soon as I can," I promised, believing that to be the easiest half-lie for both of us.

Over the next couple of weeks, I sent out dozens of résumés: to record stores, clothing stores, restaurants, coffee shops; to nonprofits, advocacy groups, trade magazines, the State Department; to the Smithsonian (to work as a security guard) and the Phillips Collection (another security guard job—this was apparently a growth industry, unlike everything I was qualified for). I applied to be a nanny, a personal assistant, a bra fitter, a dog-walker, a tree trimmer, a photo researcher on a book about whale extinction, a ghostwriter for the memoir of a disgraced former senator, a fact-checker on a book about Bolivian economics. I did not hear back about anything.

Mari was kind, but I felt disapproval lurking behind each "oh well." She had always made sensible money decisions. The house she bought back in 2002 with her *Jennifer* funds was now worth at least twice what she'd paid, and she'd paid off more than half her fifteen-year mortgage with the money she earned renting out the basement apartment. She'd always worked full-time—she'd been at the same coffee shop for years—and had savings built from Yevgenia's own cautious investments. They had, she'd often proudly reminded me, come to the US with nothing, and now she owned two-thirds of a house, plus a significant amount of expensive music gear. Meanwhile, I—a college-educated, middle-class, native-born American—had debt, very little savings, no job. She didn't need to say anything; I felt it in the way she offered to pay in restaurants now, left her card on the counter when she knew I was going out for groceries. She had made me a generous offer, and I was failing to keep my end of the bargain.

Working to demonstrate my value in nonmonetary ways, I cooked and cleaned and did laundry. I fixed the toilet, tore several yard-waste bags of ivy out of her front yard, and called pest control to eliminate a nest of rats in her back alley. On a rainy afternoon when her basement tenant, Geoff, called upstairs that his kitchen had flooded, I went downstairs and helped him mop out. I stocked Doritos, black tea, gummy bears. One night Mari came home around nine from a shift, fell on the couch, and pulled a blanket over her head. I brought out lasagna and gummy bears on a tray, then waited, feeling idiotic, for her to pull down the blanket and notice. Finally, she sat up. "Oh man, this looks amazing," she said, mussed head emerging from the blanket. "Smells so garlicky. And gummy bears! Damn, girl! You're spoiling me."

I set the tray on her lap and handed her a napkin. "How was your day?"

"I had to clean up puke in the bathroom again, so—not great. This time it was kid puke, though. Not as smelly. And the mom stuck a twenty in my back pocket too."

"Hot," I said.

"Moms are hot," she said, scooping up a handful of gummy bears. "All bleary and sex-starved and desperate. Like they'd just fuck you really fast and efficient and then run."

"That's hot to you?" I said.

"Weird, right?"

"Not so weird," I said, imagining briefly: kids, puppy, Mari mowing the lawn in cutoffs and a snap-back.

"Amanda was fucking a mom for a while," Mari said. Using her front teeth, she nipped the head off a red gummy bear. "Out in the suburbs, like *way* out. She would drive out 270 and tiptoe in after the kids were asleep."

"270! That's serious."

"I know, right? It ended badly. Like all of Amanda's things," she said, beheading an orange one—for reasons unknown, she had always done this, biting the heads off all the gummies before she'd eat their bodies. When she'd laid the headless corpse next to its red brother on the tray, she gave me a slightly embarrassed smile. "Listen," she said, "this meal looks delicious, but I actually need to go upstairs and hide for an hour, today was *intense*. That cool?"

I'd been at home alone that whole day, cleaning the house and preparing the meal. "Of course it's cool," I said. "Thanks for telling me."

Mari gave me another funny look, then took her tray upstairs. I heard her bedroom door shut, and then I heard music from inside, nothing I could make out.

Music played through the closed door for the next two hours while I cleaned up from dinner, then watched TV on the couch. Finally, I got under the couch blanket in my clothes, the leather cushions slipping apart beneath me so my arm lodged uncomfortably in the crack. Mari woke me around one a.m. "What are you doing?" she whispered in the dark. "Why didn't you come up?"

"I don't know. You were busy."

"You could've just knocked, you doof."

I could've; I was embarrassed that I hadn't. But the truth was I'd wanted Mari to realize I was asleep on the couch, feel sorry she'd left me alone, and rescue me from the slippery cushions. "I didn't know," I said, and let her lead me upstairs by the hand.

THE NEXT DAY was Saturday. Mari slept late while I drank coffee alone in the kitchen; then she wandered down, disheveled and leery in an old T-shirt and underpants. "Want to fuck?" she said, and we did. We fucked all the time now that we were living together, but somehow the job-search failures were seeping into that as well. I felt tentative, alert for signs that she was being kind, that her response was an effort to soothe. It was easier if I could have a drink first, but that morning, I was skinless, knocked off course by every ambiguous sound or movement.

When we finished, we lay in bed together. I dozed while Mari read, plastic tortoiseshell glasses slipping down her nose. Despite never having followed through on those UDC classes, or maybe exactly because she hadn't, Mari was a broad and compulsive reader. Her bedroom was stacked with library books and stuff picked up from free book drops, everything from sci-fi classics and folklore to lesbian romance novels with titles like *For Her Eyes Only* and *When a Duchess Meets a Duchess*. I'd only been guessing, in my *Bugle* preview, that Les Somnambules were named after the sleepwalking Robin Vote in *Nightwood*, but it had been a safe (and, I'd learned by now, correct) bet. Mari's ideas mostly came from books, and she kept a notebook by the bedside table where she wrote things down, usually in Georgian.

That morning, she was making notes with one of the tiny pencils she bought in bulk from a store that supplied mini-golf courses. When I stirred, she put the pencil down. "Hey," she said. "Hey, I wanted to ask about something."

"Hmm?"

"What's our plan for if you don't find a job right away?"

"I mean," I said, turning onto my back, "I just have to find a job. I'm trying really hard."

"I am not saying this is your fault at all. The economy is shit, DC rent is insane. But—maybe it'd help to talk through a backup plan?"

"I'll find something," I said.

"What if you don't?"

"I *will*."

"OK," she said. She knuckled her glasses up her nose, winced at me. "Because, you know, you can stay here a little longer. I'm not going to kick you out. But I think it'd be a bad idea for us to drift into permanently living together, right?"

"Of course!" I said, insincerely. "No, that'd be really bad."

"The band comes first—you know? We have to prioritize that, be careful about—" She made a swirling motion in the air between us.

"Right—of course."

"Good," Mari said. "I was thinking—I talked to Missy today, and she has an open weekend at her studio in late September. Maybe we treat that as sort of a deadline for you to find your own place? Maybe that would be helpful?"

"Sure," I said, feeling sludgy; late September was just a few weeks away. "Yeah, that would be helpful."

"Great," she said, nodding forcefully, and went back to her book.

Half an hour later, we left for practice, performing our usual dance of traveling separately: Mari biked while I took the Metro. This had felt increasingly ridiculous over the past few weeks and that day particularly so. I was wearing a pair of Mari's underpants, since mine were all in the laundry, and my skin smelled like her lemon soap. I could still taste her pussy at the back of my tongue, only partially obscured by the toothpaste we shared. When I came down into Earl's basement, Mari handed me a Starbucks cup, as if she hadn't already handed me two cups of coffee that morning. "How was your week?" she said, as if she hadn't been there the whole time, as if she weren't the singular force determining how my weeks went.

Defiance flared in me. Mari didn't get to set all the rules. "Crappy," I said.

"How so?" she asked warily.

"Dealing with some shit at work."

Mari's eyebrows gathered. "You're always dealing with some shit at work," she said. "Did you ever think the problem might be you, actually?" Her voice was sharp enough that Amanda and Freddie both looked over.

I felt slapped, but for so many reasons, I had to play it off. "Maybe I just have a bad boss."

"It's not always someone else's fault," she said, and turned back to the conversation she'd been having with Amanda. They were talking about Missy, the owner of the studio where Mari had booked us to record in September. Apparently Mari had done this unilaterally, and apparently Amanda was displeased.

"I didn't even think you liked Missy," Amanda was saying. "You said she made everything sound like Journey."

"Sure, but who doesn't love Journey?"

"Mari."

"OK, OK," she said. "I should've asked first. I haven't put down a deposit—if you don't want to record there, we don't have to."

"It's fine—just, when we talked after the Brahe show, you said you weren't going to do this anymore. And now you're doing it."

Freddie, who had been hovering anxiously, now cut in. "Guys. This is dumb. How about we put it to a vote?" So we voted. I was secretly rooting for Missy to lose, in part because I was upset with Mari, but also because it would postpone the date when I'd have to move out. But I couldn't say any of that aloud, couldn't even vote against Missy because Mari would know why. Everyone raised their hands for Missy except Amanda, who raised a finger and said, "It's not a no *exactly*, I just want to do more research."

"We could be researching forever," Mari said, laughing now because she'd won. "Let's just do this!"

We'd decided on four songs for the EP: "Forgotten," "Tiny Animals," and two other Les Somnambules songs, "Firebird" and "Above the Trees." We hadn't determined a sequence yet, but that day, Mari said, "I want to play through in order and see how it sounds—'Forgotten' first, yeah?"

Amanda sighed, she didn't even have to say anything. Mari spun around. "OK, no? Objections?"

I felt another surge of irritation. "Actually, I think we should start with 'Firebird,'" I said.

Amanda gave me a querying glance. "I agree," she said, sounding surprised. "'Firebird' sets the tone better, it's more like the other songs."

"'Forgotten' is a better song than 'Firebird,'" Mari said. "And no, 'Firebird' doesn't sound more like our other songs. Jamie barely sings on it."

"Jamie's voice isn't the only thing that determines our sound," Amanda said.

"But it's a big thing," said Mari.

"I think 'Firebird' is a better song than 'Forgotten,'" I said.

"You're wrong," Mari said, in a sort of horrified growl. The anger in her eyes didn't surprise me, but the pain did. I hadn't known I could hurt her, and the knowledge was enticing.

"'Forgotten' is old, too," I went on, making a show of carelessly pouring an extra half-and-half into my coffee. "Feels boring to start there. We should start with something people don't know as well."

"You didn't mind opening with 'Forgotten' at the Atrium," she said.

"Live shows are different," I said. "Makes sense to start with a familiar song, something up-tempo. For an EP, we should start with something new." I knew Mari was trapped. If she responded more angrily to me than to Amanda, she'd risk revealing too much. I could sense her frustration at the constraint, and it made me giddy.

"Jamie, can we talk upstairs?" Mari said, rage barely contained.

I followed her upstairs and into the pink bathroom, where she sat down on the fuzzy toilet seat and glowered at me. "What the fuck are you doing?" she said.

I balanced on the edge of the tub, knees tucked away from hers. "I'm not going to support every decision you make," I said, avoiding her eyes. "And I agree with Amanda, you can't keep making decisions without asking us."

"Sure, fine," she said. "But you don't think that 'Firebird' is a better song than 'Forgotten.' You're fucking with me, I don't like it."

"Actually, no. I do think it's a better song. Sure, I have personal attachments to 'Forgotten,' but just on the merits . . ."

"James! I wrote 'Forgotten' *for* you, about you, you cannot—"

She had never told me the song was about me. I relented for a moment, knowing what it cost Mari to admit that, but remembered her saying "It's not always someone else's fault" and hardened my resolve. "That doesn't mean I want it first," I said. "Anyway, aren't we trying not to let the relationship affect the band?"

"Yeah, but James—turns out you're actually incapable of doing that, which is how I know you're fucking with me. I need you to stop, especially in front of Amanda. She's already suspicious, and if we push her too much right now . . ."

"I'm not *incapable* of doing that," I said, my face going hot. "I'm doing that every day. I'm in the fucking *closet* right now because it's supposedly better for the band."

Mari stood up, stiff-shouldered. "Goddamnit," she said. "It's not even worth talking to you about this shit. You make everything about you."

She left the bathroom, and I followed. When we were downstairs, she said, her back to me, "We can start with 'Firebird' if that is the group's decision. Should we put it to a vote?"

"No need," Freddie said, without glancing up from her knitting. "Andrew and I both want to start with 'Firebird' as well."

"Fine," said Mari. She shot me a *you happy?* look. I saw Amanda notice it; her expression darkened. "So—what'll the second song be then?"

USUALLY I RODE the Metro back to Mari's from practice, arriving after she'd already biked home. That Saturday, I called a taxi I couldn't afford and was waiting on the porch couch when she rolled up and swung off the still-moving bike. She didn't look at me as she locked the bike to the porch railing and pulled off her helmet, shaking out her sweaty hair. I let her open the front door and I followed her in and pushed her onto the living room floor and held her down while she made impatient snorts and struggled to get away.

"Was this whole thing," she said in my ear, our heads dangerously close to the coffee table, Beavis yowling hungrily from the kitchen, "just some weird sex shit?"

"Do you not want to do this?" The panic breaking in again, the creeping humiliation, that she might not be enjoying it after all. I had ambushed her in this way to correct a power imbalance, but in the same moment, I was throwing myself at her feet, so desperate to be told that we were good, that I was good.

"No," she said, "no. It's fine. Just—not at practice, OK? That was too much."

But I had to stop, overwhelmed. "This is really hard," I said. I sat up against the edge of the couch, wrapping my arms around my knees. "I feel so messed up having to pretend we're not together."

"And so you throw tantrums?"

"That's not why I did that. You know what I mean."

She settled in next to me and took my hand. "James, I know," she said. "It's hard for me too. But you have to stay focused. If we can record this EP, it's the tour, it's getting signed, it's everything. Hotel rooms! Getting interviewed in obscure European music magazines!"

Mari knew me so well, knew how long I'd been imagining those interviews, dreaming of those hotel rooms. But in that moment the dreams felt pale and unreal. "I want that, yeah. You know I want that! I also want to be, like, girlfriends. I want both."

"Aren't we girlfriends?"

"Not if no one knows."

"I told my coworker yesterday," Mari said, tracing circles across my palm. "She was like, 'What are you up to this weekend,' and I said, 'Probably hanging out with my girlfriend.'"

"That's sweet," I said, picturing her saying it like that, casually, not having to think about it.

"It's going to be OK," she said. "Hey, we even have a deadline now—September! We are so close. Then we can tell everyone, and who knows, maybe the EP will sound so good that Amanda won't even care. You'll have a place of your own and a job, and we can be normal people who go on dates while also, you know, tearing it up onstage in Stockholm."

"I'd like that," I said. I couldn't help smiling, even though my insides still felt out of joint.

"Me too," she said. "But for now, I think you should finish fucking me, and then we should eat some ice cream." And we did, and afterward we lay holding each other for a long time, and everything felt very close to OK.

17

THAT THURSDAY, IT rained all day, a slow pour, and I barely left Mari's couch. There were no new jobs on any of the sites I regularly checked, no responses to any of the emails I'd sent over the past week. I watched a movie and let my legs go numb. In the afternoon, Sally texted, Everything OK over there? Since Rufus came home from the hospital, Sally had sent a few texts and photos of Rufus asleep or squalling in his bath. I'd responded only cursorily: I knew she didn't really want to talk to me, she was only being nice. This time, I didn't respond at all. I dragged Beavis onto my chest, trying to absorb his pea-brain calm, but it didn't work. I just felt jittery, and like I was failing on every front at once, in some global irreparable way.

By the time Mari got home that night, I was a little drunk. I had not intended to be, but I'd felt so sad, and a treat felt appropriate, so I took my mug into the living room to cuddle with Beavis, and I'd brought the bottle as well. I only wanted to be warm, and to stop feeling bad.

"You look hot," I said to Mari, "you're so hot in your dumb sweatshirt," but she laughed at me, then stomped upstairs to shower.

"Are you going to be OK at practice tonight?" she said when she came back down in a towel, wet hair spiraling out in all directions. "Do I need to make coffee?"

"I'm fine!" I told her. "Seriously, so fine."

She leaned over the couch, hair dripping on the leather cushions, to assess me: sweatpants orange with Beavis hair, wine mug, empty bottle on the floor. "You're drinking too much," she said.

"Ugh," I said, pulling up the blanket to hide my face, "*you're* drinking too much."

Her bare shoulders jerked up. "Want to order takeout?"

But I'd felt the splinter of her disapproval. "Actually," I said, "I thought I'd go to my dad's house before practice, see Rufus."

"You sure? You're not, maybe, in the best shape to see family."

"I'm *fine*," I said, and then texted Sally, What if I came over tonight? She wrote back immediately, Yes please.

I showered and changed into outside clothes, then rode the Metro to Silver Spring and walked from the station through a solid wall of rain, drenched and headachingly sober by the time I rang the bell at my father's house. When he opened the door, my father was wearing his fisherman sweater, sploshed with sticky-looking stains. His eyes looked bleary and hopeless; his shoulders were caved in.

"Oh no!" he said when he saw me. He ran to the bathroom for a towel, while I shivered and dripped onto the living room rug. The place was strewn with burp cloths, clothing in both infant and adult sizes, trays holding half-eaten dinners, diapers, dirty milk bottles. There was a fermented smell to the air, and it was at least ten degrees warmer than usual. Through the dining room, I could see dirty dishes and pans and glasses stacked in tipsy piles along the kitchen counters. I had never seen the house this upside down, not even in the months after my mom moved out.

"It's a bit of a mess, I was just about to start tidying up," my father said, returning with the towel. "Sally and Rufus are upstairs."

"I'll go on up then," I said, smiling to conceal my horror. I peeled off my drenched socks and draped them over the kitchen radiator, then walked upstairs on humid carpeting to my dad and Sally's bedroom. Their room was as much in shambles as downstairs: a pile of laundry in the corner, plates on the floor, bottles and diapers and mysterious baby apparatuses everywhere. Sally and Rufus were propped on pillows under the floral duvet. Sally wore a nursing bra and sweatpants, long hair loose around her face and shoulders. Rufus's sleeping body sprawled prone across her breasts like he'd fallen there. His fists were tucked under his chin, and a surprising amount of black hair thatched his softball-sized skull. At some point, they'd installed a TV at the foot of the bed, and it now played a cooking show, a sonorous English voice saying, "The currant flavor is not particularly present, and there's a rather dense quality to the . . ."

"Jamie, you're soaked," Sally said, turning very slowly to see me so the movement wouldn't disturb Rufus. "Is it raining outside?"

"Pouring," I said, surprised she hadn't noticed. But the room was a soundproof hotbox of baby stink: blinds closed, TV drowning out the steady roar of rain from the street. "Could I borrow some clothes?"

"Take whatever you want, I won't be wearing any of it soon," she said. I went to the closet and found the Juicy sweatsuit I'd worn at night when I first moved in, then changed with my back to her.

"I'm really sorry I didn't come sooner," I said when I was dressed.

"You're good, you're good," she said, and kicked laundry off the bed so I could sit. I leaned over to see Rufus's face: his lips were pouched out, and I could hear his soft rattling snores. "Right now he's sleeping six to eleven p.m., then he's awake for hours."

"So this is your naptime," I said. "Do you want me to come back later?"

"No, no. I can't ever sleep anyway. I just watch hours and hours of this," she said, nodding at the television.

I was so troubled by the house, by Sally's zombie stare; did people typically look like this after giving birth? It seemed cruel, that creating a new human would blast away everything recognizable from the old human. I asked, "Is everything OK?"

"Oh, it's *fine*," she said. She lifted herself up on an elbow, dislodging Rufus, who slumped sideways into her cleavage without waking up. "Like—so very fine. He's great. Just a great baby. I love the shit out of this little guy. Just love him. A lot."

"OK . . ."

"And yeah, he's not sleeping. Which is normal! They're not supposed to sleep! That's what they tell you! Don't have a baby if you want to sleep!"

"I mean I thought they were supposed to sleep, like, sometimes?"

She shook her head very hard, whipping the dirty hair. "No. Well, yes, sometimes. But you try taking a nap at six p.m. You try it! Six p.m., not a good time to take a fucking nap!"

"I'm so, so sorry," I said, and I meant it in a very broad way: sorry about my own crap ability to help her, sorry about my dad's crap abilities, sorry about biology, sorry about life.

"I think the baby might hate me too? He just seems mad all the time? I don't know, what happens if he really hates me and that's just it, like he hates me forever?"

"Rufus doesn't *hate* you."

"How do you know?" she said. "You don't, right? Babies can't talk. They could be thinking anything and you wouldn't fucking know!"

I was feeling a deep survivor's guilt, listening to her ramble, seeing her pale puffy cheeks and her hair, matte black with oil. I'd been meant to be Sally's pregnancy buddy, her mom buddy, and instead I was fucking around at Mari's while she went slowly insane. "Maybe you want to take a little break?" I said. "I could hold Rufus for a minute, if that's helpful?"

Her eyes were fear-furious. "You'd drop him."

"I won't! Really. I promise I won't. I'll sit right here on the bed."

Again she glared at me, and then down at Rufus's head. "Well, it's true I haven't had a shower in a bit," she admitted. "Or pooped. I've barely pooped since we got home."

"Please, please—go take a shower and poop," I said, and scrunched my body up near hers. She raised Rufus gingerly on her forearms and lifted him across to me; I nestled him close, glancing at Sally to make sure she saw how carefully I was holding him. Rufus sighed, poofed out his lips again, and wriggled up into my chest, still asleep. Watching us all the way, Sally slipped out of bed and into the bathroom.

Alone, I angled back against the pillows, stiff with anxiety: What if Sally was right and I did drop Rufus after all? What if he got SIDS while I was holding him—did that happen? What if he fell out of my arms, slipped-n-slid across the bed, and shattered on the floor? I tried to relax so my tension wouldn't somehow wake him up—could babies sense fear? I focused on the baking show, a competition to make a cake in the shape of a tiered garden. One of the bakers was a Bettie Page–ish femme with black hair and red lipstick, and I tried to get distracted by her—but not too distracted, not so distracted that I accidentally killed the baby.

My cell phone was in the back pocket of my jeans, and when I'd been holding Rufus for what felt like years, it vibrated. I snaked out a hand from under Rufus and dug between the mattress and my butt for the phone. It was a text from Mari: You coming? I'd lost track of time: it was almost eight o'clock, Mari would be walking up to Earl's house right now.

I started to type a message in reply, but just then Rufus shifted and whimpered, and I froze. I couldn't figure out a way to text without convulsing the muscles that were supporting him. I could hear Sally's shower going, and I didn't want to interrupt her—I was doing something generous, contrary to my usual habits, and I didn't want to stop. And it felt good, in a petty way, to have Mari chasing *me*. I let the phone drop, and it slipped down behind the mattress. I could hear it vibrating there, against the wood bed frame: first a series of text message blips, then the telegraph tat-tat-tat of my ringtone, then a long pause, then the ringtone again, then silence.

Meanwhile, I watched as the black-haired baker's cake got stuck to the pan and she cried, then put on a game face, said, "*Right*," and started mixing batter again. And I held Rufus. My fear of breaking him subsided. He was a warm liquid weight on my chest, not unlike Beavis but lighter: a human smaller than a cat. He smelled like fresh yogurt. Inside his head, his wee brain was clicking, sorting out big questions like the difference between light and dark, hot and cold, Sally's smell versus the smells of other humans. This is what it would've been like if I'd kept the baby, I thought, and searched myself for sadness, regret. But there was none. I looked at this actual baby, my Rufus baby, my *brother*, and just felt grateful he'd made it here, grateful we were here together.

"Hey there, Mr. Rufus," I whispered.

His eyelids fluttered, and I shut up. I leaned my head back against the pillows, watched the Bettie Page baker lose the contest catastrophically, let the heat of Rufus's peachy skin soothe my anxieties into a gentle hum.

After a while, the shower turned off and Sally came out from the bathroom, one towel wrapping her body and another turbaning her hair. When she saw that Rufus was still sleeping, she knocked some laundry off a chair, sat down with a large plastic comb, and began separating her hair into large, dripping sections.

"D'you poop?" I asked her.

"Sort of," she said, yanking the comb through tangles. "I tore through to my anus when I had Rufus and needed stitches and it's still healing. Plus hemorrhoids. So pooping has been a journey."

"Fuck," I said. "Does that always happen?"

"I don't know," she said. "No one even told me it was a possibility. I wasn't really thinking about the large-head, small-opening issue."

I stroked Rufus's stout square skull and winced, imagining it. "Not that it's not understandable, but you seem a little stressed," I said.

She swept back a section of hair. "I probably have some kind of postpartum depression type thing. But who doesn't, right?"

"Maybe you should talk to someone?"

"Who has time for that?" she said. "Anyway, I have a highly credentialed psychologist right here, what more could I need?" She waved a hand toward the stairs, and we both laughed knowingly. I remembered how surprised I'd been at first when Sally made fun of my dad. Now it was a comfort. It wasn't my fault, Sally's laugh told me, that my relationship with him was such a struggle. And yet Sally clearly loved my father, even seeing the same flaws I did.

Sally took her time getting dressed in sweatpants and a U Maryland T-shirt that soaked down the back from her hair, then went downstairs to make some tea. When she returned carrying the mug, she looked significantly calmer. "I can take him," she said, and sat next to me on the bed to scoop Rufus into her arms. After she'd securely cradled him, but while we were still elbow-to-elbow, I leaned over and hugged her.

"You're doing great," I said. "You're so good at this."

"Hah," she said, but I saw tears edging her eyes.

"And I'm here," I said. The affection I felt toward her and Rufus was making me hyper, overcaffeinated. "I'm in DC now, I don't have a job, so I can help out anytime you need me. Maybe I could come back tomorrow, take Rufus for a couple hours even. Just stick him in the stroller, walk him around town so you could take a nap, would that be good?"

"That would be amazing," she said. Her smile was wide and sleepy.

I told her I had to leave for practice but would come back the next day. Then I tiptoed out. My dad was snoring on the couch downstairs amid the piles of dirty plates and burp cloths. I unpeeled my wet socks from the radiator and put them on, then my wet shoes, and squished quietly out of the house. It wasn't until I was outside that I realized I'd left my phone upstairs. But I didn't want to bother Sally and Rufus by digging under her mattress, and I figured I'd be back tomorrow anyway. Instead I began the familiar walk through Silver Spring toward Earl's house.

It was still raining—less dramatic than before, but insistent. My wet socks chafed against my wet sneakers; I didn't even bother avoiding puddles. I walked past suburban yards that looked soaked and dejected, lawns beaten down to mud; past my old friend Richard's house, where we used to strap on his big brother's football helmets and ram each other until we got dizzy and fell down. The sky was dark, either because it was very late or because of the storm—I wasn't sure. It felt like I'd held Rufus for hours, but I had no idea how long it had actually been.

At Earl's, the lights were all on, and I pushed in. In the kitchen, I heard unfamiliar sounds: raised voices in the living room, a metallic white noise burr, and water running somewhere, too voluminous and unsteady to be a faucet. I went into the living room and saw Mari and Earl faced off, shouting at each other.

Mari was yelling, "You couldn't have gone down there at any point today? You couldn't have fucking checked on the instruments? Not once?"

"I told you," Earl yelled back, "I was *at work*."

I'd barely seen Earl talk before, let alone shout. He was much taller than Mari and threatening in his postal service uniform, like a police officer. I had an instinct to charge him, rescue Mari. "Mari?" I said. "What's going on?"

She spun around at me. "This fucking clown," she said, "let his basement flood and fucked up all of our gear."

"Um, you signed a liability waiver," Earl said.

"Fuck you, Earl!"

He threw up his hands in a gesture that looked childish on his large form, then stumped upstairs. I hadn't until then looked at the rest of the living room beyond Mari. Amanda, Andrew, and Freddie were all on a shabby pink print couch, legs crossed in parallel, looking very uncomfortable, clothes and hair wet. In a corner, our instruments and gear sat crammed together on towels like furniture abandoned on a curb. Freddie's violin, resting on the floor, wasn't the right color, and a string had snapped. Andrew's drumheads looked dark and blotchy. Someone had set up an industrial-sized oscillating fan in front of the instruments and turned it on high.

"What happened?" I asked. I was still enveloped by the buzzy calm I'd felt holding Rufus, and it was disorienting to walk into such an opposite space and mood.

Mari paced the room like she was stomping on Earl's head, or perhaps mine. "Why didn't you pick up your phone? I called you like ten times."

"I left my phone at my dad's house. Tell me what happened! Are you OK?"

"What the fuck kind of question is that?"

I could see in her white eyes, flared nostrils, the fear hidden beneath her rage. I went close and put my hands on her arms, halted her frantic pacing. "Mari," I said. I heard her exhale under the loud fan whirr. "Tell me what happened."

"I thought you weren't coming, I thought you'd decided you were done," she said quietly.

"Not at all. I was holding Rufus and the phone fell under the mattress and I forgot to get it. But I'm here, I'm not going anywhere."

Amanda was right there, but I put my arms around Mari, stroked her hair the way I'd stroked Rufus's, and she sagged into me. "Do you need to sit, can I get you water?" I whispered.

"I'm OK," she said. "It's just—James, he was at home all morning. He could've moved the gear at any point. And we've been on him for months about getting a sump pump, this happens every time it rains. Although this time it's way worse, because it came in through the window."

Earl's basement did flood all the time. But usually that just meant a few puddles on the sunken areas of the uneven cement floor. The damp air was bad for the instruments and probably our lungs, but at least nothing got wet because we always stored everything on higher ground. Also, Freddie didn't usually leave her violin overnight. But last practice, Dani had needed the car and Freddie didn't want to walk to the Metro carrying the large black case in the heat. She'd locked it in Earl's basement storage cabinet, where it should've been safe.

"Except that fucker Earl, of course, hasn't cleaned his gutters recently, and a jet of water started shooting down from one of them. Somehow it knocked open a basement window, probably because Earl never checks them, and now there's a waterfall through the window right behind the cabinet."

"Oh no," I said.

"When I came in," Mari said, "Freddie's violin case was a puddle. The drumheads were bowls of water. My keyboard was soaked, and it's not turning on. The amps aren't either. We just spent an hour bringing everything up and trying to dry it, but the keyboard and amps still won't turn on, and the drums are warped and they'll probably rust, and then Freddie's violin—you can see."

"Freddie, I'm so sorry," I said.

"It's OK," Freddie said from the couch, but her eyes were wet. Freddie had inherited her violin from a grandfather who bought it in Rome in the 1950s, when he was serving at the Ethiopian embassy there.

"It's not OK," Mari said. "Replacing everything is going to burn through all the money for recording the EP. And we can't afford to wait on that, we won't get on the tour next summer without it."

"That's not the most important thing, Mari," Freddie said, as if she'd been saying it already for the past hour.

Mari glared at her. "Not for you, maybe."

"Don't be nasty," Freddie said. "We all want this just as badly as you do. But we can save up money, do the EP in the winter."

"*No*, because Jamie will've moved back to Baltimore by then and we'll have to rewrite all the songs."

She wasn't looking at me when she said it, just spoke in a matter-of-fact way as if it were something we'd all agreed upon, a noncontroversial opinion. I laughed, confused. "I quit my job to move here, Mari. I'm not going back."

"Sure, but now you're just drinking on my couch all day. And you can't afford to stay if you don't find a job soon. You'll have an easier time finding work in Baltimore, it's cheaper, and you'll end up leaving because you never made a real plan to stay."

Her voice was angry, but in her eyes, I saw unshielded fear. "Mar," I said very softly, "I'm not leaving—OK? This isn't like last time. I'm going to find something." She turned away, shook her head.

Amanda said, "Hey, Mari?"

"What," Mari said.

"You and Jamie—you're together, aren't you."

Andrew hadn't spoken all night, I'd forgotten he was there, and now he said, "Ah, fuck," and stood up. "Guys," he said, "it's been fun. Call me when this has all settled down?" He went over to his drum set, ran a finger across the snare, then left without looking back.

Freddie said, "Amanda, for real, Andrew's right—this is not the time."

But Amanda leaned toward us and said, "Mari, you haven't answered my question. Are you guys together?"

"We're not together," Mari said. "I've told you a thousand times. Right, Jamie?"

"Jamie?" Amanda said, turning to me. She looked weary, almost bored: like she'd been hurt so many times by Mari that to be hurt again wasn't a new wound, just a blunted confirmation of the old one. "Mari told me you only date men now. Is that true?"

Mari's lips trembled, I could see the twitch at the corner of her eye. I loved her so hard in that instant, and I knew what she needed me to say. Our instruments were dripping muddy water in the corner; Mari's entire future was on the line. If Amanda had asked me the week before, I probably would've lied, or at least found a way to avoid answering. But I was also remembering Rufus's little head, how it felt to hold him, that elevated and pure warmth. My dad had lied to me about who he was, or at least allowed me to become confused, and I didn't want to lie about myself to Rufus, or lie about myself at all, now that Rufus was alive. And I was stung by Mari's lack of faith in me, in us. There didn't seem much point in keeping up the pretense if she was just assuming I would leave.

"No," I said. "It's not true."

I ventured a sideways glance at Mari, and her face looked cratered, like a bomb had gone off. "OK, fine, she's not straight, but we're not together," she said to Amanda.

"You are literally holding hands," Amanda pointed out, and Mari and I dropped each other's—I hadn't even realized. "Fuck, Mari. I don't even know why I let you do this to me. I'm done. Sorry, Freddie." And she left too.

Freddie had knelt by the pile of instruments to swaddle her violin in a dry towel. Over her shoulder, she said, "Mari, I'm not cleaning this one up for you."

"I'm not asking," Mari said, shaking her head. "I know. It's on me."

"Actually no, it's not 'on you,' because that would suggest that you might actually be capable of cleaning it up yourself. Which you aren't."

"I know." I'd never seen Mari looking so flat, and since nothing mattered anymore, I put my arm around her and kissed the hair above her ear. She flinched.

"I'd offer you guys a ride home," Freddie said, "but I really don't feel like it. Good night." She walked out with her violin cradled in her arms, and Mari and I were alone, standing over all the soaked and broken instruments. Her hair was wet, flat along the sides of her face; I could see a shiver starting to take hold in her shoulders.

"You didn't have to do that," she said, shaking her head.

"Why do you care so much what Amanda thinks, anyway?" I could feel loneliness and fear working through my body. "She's not your girlfriend anymore. Why are you protecting her?"

"It's not her I'm protecting," she said. She'd stepped away from me and was scratching the back of her neck. "Two of the amps are still downstairs. We need to get them up before we can leave."

When I saw Earl's basement that night, my heart contracted with grief. Water was still trickling in through the window at the back. The carpet was tufty like wet animal fur, and it smelled like sewage and rot. Dick-face Reagan had partially disintegrated, toppling over its knees the way it had when Andrew attacked it. Without speaking, Mari lifted Freddie's practice amp and I lifted Amanda's, and we carried them upstairs and set them on the towel in the living room. Somewhere in the house, Earl was playing the "Paint It Black" riff on his acoustic guitar; Mari said, glaring up at the ceiling, "He's got the tuning wrong, dumb fuck."

"You want to split a cab home?" I asked, thinking it would give us a chance to talk, break up our thick silence.

"I have my bike," Mari said, and walked out without looking back. I rode the Metro alone. The change to the Green Line at Fort Totten took twenty minutes, and I sat on a cold stone bench, shivering in my wet socks. A group of teenagers stood by the edge of the platform, laughing and tossing cigarette butts onto the tracks. I remembered doing the same with Mari years ago, and I felt homesick, or maybe timesick.

By the time I got back, Mari was already asleep. Yevgenia's sequined dress rested on the pillow by her cheek; on the bedside table was a bottle of Yevgenia's old chocolate liqueur. She didn't stir when I pulled off the damp-sticky sweatsuit and climbed into bed.

I WOKE LATE the next morning, reaching out in the dark shuttered room for my missing phone. Mari was already gone, along with Yevgenia's dress and the bottle. In the quiet house, I showered, half-heartedly applied for a couple jobs, napped with Beavis. By now, Beavis and I had achieved an understanding. I bought him the organic, enriched cat food with real fish and fed him four times a day, on time, instead of twice at random intervals the way Mari did. In return, he kneaded my feet through the couch blanket all afternoon, purring so loud it muffled the traffic sounds from outside. Occasionally a drop of wet mucus fell from his nose, spotting the blanket. Anxiety blared through my head, and I was craving the indulgent comfort of a wine mug, but I didn't want to chase Beavis away. Maybe I could get my own cat if I moved back to Baltimore, I thought, and then realized it was the first time all summer I'd imagined a future that didn't include Mari.

After four, Mari came home, looking like death. She was wearing her black work sweatshirt, and it was all bunched around her neck like she'd tried to turtle down into it. Her hair was flat with sweat, and her lips were cracked and beige.

"Are you OK?" I asked.

"Super fucking great," she said, speaking from deep inside, like it felt bad to move her mouth. She dropped her keys and phone on the table and lay down next to me, sticking a hand into Beavis's curled-up body like it was a hand muff. "I threw up in the employee bathroom," she said into a couch cushion. "Do we have Diet Cokes, because I would sell my tits for a Diet Coke."

"I will get you one, no tits required." I dislodged Beavis to go into the kitchen, then handed Mari the Coke and sat down just apart from her on the couch.

Raising herself on an elbow, Mari opened the can and tugged the tab back and forth like she was counting letters to see who she'd marry (I used to make a joke of it, ripping off the tab at *M*, while Mari groaned). Around *K*, she said, "Last night was pretty bad, huh."

"Yeah, it was," I said cautiously. "What are we going to do?"

She lifted her hands in a helpless half shrug. "Earl's homeowner's insurance, if he has it, might cover the instruments. But even if we get the money, we don't have a band. I've been texting everyone and no one's texting me back, not even Freddie. It's over, it's just fucking over."

As Beavis claw-massaged my feet that day, I'd fretted over my dependence on Mari, emotionally, artistically, financially. If she was angry at me, if she sent me away, I wouldn't have anything left but my sad apartment in Baltimore. And yes, perhaps it hadn't been the best decision to land in this precarious spot. But here I was, and I didn't know what to do but keep moving ahead.

I placed a hand on her tensed forearm. "It doesn't have to be over," I said, trying to sound staunch. "I'm still here. We can start over just the two of us—the Maidenheads again, but better. Find a few backing musicians, record the EP, get on the tour."

Mari ripped off the tab. "Why couldn't you've just told Amanda you were straight?"

"Mari, did you hear me? We don't need Amanda—you and I are enough."

She was suddenly so furious with me that she had to sit up, like she was lifted by fire. "*You're* not fucking enough! *You're* not fucking enough! If I can't ever count on you, if you're never going to stick up for me."

"What are you talking about?" I was shocked. "I'm here, I'm always going to be here. I love you, Mari."

"Oh, you *love me*. Oh, great, lucky me. A lot of help that's fucking been all summer."

I shook my head in bafflement. "Is this because I didn't lie to Amanda about being straight? Because it's fucked up to ask me to lie about that. You wouldn't lie about that."

"Of course I would've," she said. "In fact, I did, to Yevgenia, for many years. It was a kindness, it made both of our lives easier. And of course I would've done that to keep the band together. I would've done anything to keep the band together."

"But Mari, if the band is *us*, not them, we can keep it together without having to lie to anyone."

"Apparently not," she said, and laughed grimly.

"What do you mean?" But she didn't say anything, just shook her head, so I went on pleading my case: "We can still do the EP in September. We can find other musicians quickly. You know Amanda can't even do half the songs the way you need her to. We can do this, Mari."

"You're going to leave," she said. "There's no point."

"Mari, stop that. I quit my job, I had an abortion to be here. I'm not leaving."

She laughed again, this time more harshly. "Oh, come on, Jamie," she said. "Be honest with yourself, OK? You didn't *have an abortion to stay in the band*. You never actually wanted a baby. You were unhappy in Baltimore and wanted to blow up your life and thought, 'Ooh, maybe a baby will get me out of my stupid little rut.' And then I came along and offered you a more fun way to get out of the rut, so you took it. But you can't follow through, you never could. You were always going to get the abortion, you were always going to quit your job, and you were always going to quit the band."

I knew there was a cruel logic to some of this. But my most deeply rooted feeling was the desire to be where Mari was, and I couldn't let that part go. "I don't know how you could think that I'd leave," I said. "All I want is to stay here, play with you. I've said that a million times."

"Saying it means nothing," she said, waving a hand. "You don't do the hard things to make it happen."

"That's not fair," I said. "I've been working nonstop to find a job. And what did you want me to do? If I'd stayed at the *Bugle*, I wouldn't have been able to practice three times a week."

"We would've figured something out! I told you at the time not to quit—you didn't listen to me."

"You know it would've been hard."

"Hard?" she said, sputtering it out with fury. "No, Jamie, commuting to practice from Baltimore wouldn't have been *hard* and you know it. No. The actual reason you quit your job—against my advice!—was because you thought we had a relationship and you were scared to lose it. You put the relationship ahead of the band, and now we're all fucked because of it."

"Wait—what do you mean I *thought* we had a relationship?"

Her mouth curved; she shook her head. "OK, fine, if you want to do this. Jamie, the only reason I tried to fuck you that night, after the Atrium show, was because I wanted you to stay in the band—that was all! You got all starry-eyed about it, you quit your fucking *job* over it, but there was never anything there."

I just stared at her; I had no idea what to say. She looked like a child's drawing of herself, with huge heavy eyes, a line for a mouth, skin like tea-stained paper. "I'm not saying I didn't enjoy it," she went on. "You're hot, we've always fucked well! But I knew you had a foot out the door and I thought fucking you would keep you around. Backfired, though, you're too emotional."

"You did it to keep me around? That was it, there wasn't any other reason?" My voice had gotten very shy all of a sudden. I'd known it was possible we had different ideas about our future, but I had believed at least we were in tune on the present.

"Not really," Mari said, and I could feel a part of myself collapse. "I obviously care about you a lot," she went on, "but I also know you're a fucking child. You lie to yourself all the time about the most basic shit, about who you are, even. You run when things get difficult. So, yeah, I had to push you, I had to create incentives for you to stay."

"Incentives?"

"I know you, James," she said. Her smile was rueful, affectionate. "Sex is your currency. Like music, for me. So yes, incentives. But I never told you any different."

It was true she had never made promises, and yet—she'd told her coworker I was her girlfriend, she'd said the thing about going on dates. Even the fact that she'd asked me to lie about our relationship to Amanda implied that there was a relationship to be lied about. I watched Mari's agile skinny fingers, the fingers that had been inside me hundreds of times, stroking Beavis's shoulder blades. Our fox tattoo on her wrist.

"So all that was fake?" I said, hysteria squeezing my lungs. "Everything since the Lucia Brahe show, that's all been fake?"

"Not all of it," she said, shrugging.

"What parts were fake?" I said. "Tell me right now, what between us was fake and what was real?"

"It really doesn't matter," she said.

"It fucking matters. Mari—*what was fake?*" Images, sounds, moments were flashing through my head: Mari's rough-soft voice singing the Georgian lullaby on our first night together, Mari fucking my hand on her seersucker couch in Yevgenia's dress, Mari's hands in my pockets at the Tigress show, all the texting and fucking and crying and fucking.

"It won't make you feel any better to talk about it," she said. "You should just leave. You were always going to, anyway."

"What. Was. Fake!"

She stood up, dislodging Beavis, who yelped away across the wood floor, claws out. "We were never fake onstage. Apart from that, I don't even know. And it doesn't matter. The band is over, we're over, all thanks to you."

"Not thanks to me," I said, finally regaining my voice, even though I still felt her words impacting inside me like I'd swallowed a handful of cherry bombs. "Thanks to you. You're the one who fucked this up, Mari. You're terrible at relationships, you alienate everyone, you're cruel and selfish. If you're alone now, if you're alone for the rest of your life, it's your fault."

Mari stood above me, eyelid throbbing, shoulders shaking with rage. "Get the fuck out of my house, you fucking freeloader," she growl-yelled. She tromped into the kitchen, and I heard the fridge door open and slam shut. I stood up finally too, helplessly thinking about my new toothbrush, my clothes in the Jamie drawer, the suitcase I'd tucked into the downstairs closet so as not to oppress Mari with its presence. I knew I couldn't pack; I had to be gone faster than that. I ran up and got my shoulder bag, stuffed in my laptop and Sally's damp sweatsuit off the floor, crammed sweaty bare feet into sneakers still wet from last night.

When I got out to the front porch, I felt safer, but I was gasping for breath. Then Mari opened the door and called, "James?," an odd note in her voice. I couldn't look back, no matter what she might be thinking. I hurried away, stagger-running, wind in my ears. The shoulder bag was heavy to one side, and it dragged me down toward the sidewalk. I seemed to be limping. I imagined how I must look from where Mari stood, hair loose and legs uneven, comic and pathetic.

A few blocks away, out of her immediate reach, I slowed down. But even at a standstill, wind flooded my ears. My sneakers pinched my bare toes, my jeans felt twisted around my waist. I tugged everything back into place, smoothed my hair. I was trembling all over, but inside, I was dead and calm. When I touched my own hair, it felt like a doll's.

The farther I walked from Mari's house, the easier it got to breathe, so I just kept going. I walked past gingko trees and kids on bikes and dogs that tugged against their leashes to sniff my knees. I turned onto Georgia Avenue and passed Chinese takeout places with picture menus over the counter, a storefront daycare with handprints painted on the windows in the shape of a rainbow, barbecue restaurants and firehouses and Walmart, a psychic healer named Ms. Sandy, a thrift store with Gothic letters printed on the glass: "Be Your Best Self." The sun was harsh and scary. I saw my reflection in a blackened window, and I looked like a witch, eyes so red and skin so gray.

I couldn't call a cab, I couldn't call anyone, because my phone was still under Sally's mattress. So I kept walking. I had no direction, but I also knew I was walking home—to my father's house. It's about a four-mile walk from Petworth to Silver Spring, and it took hours, my feet on fire the entire way.

When I reached my father's street, I slowed my steps. I hadn't had a clear plan in coming here, and now I realized I couldn't go in. I'd told Sally I'd help today, I'd promised I would take Rufus out so she could poop, and instead, yet again, I'd let her down. I wandered past their house on the opposite sidewalk, and then I saw my father's

Subaru, parked on the street because he always let Sally take the driveway spot. The doors were unlocked.

It was nearly nine o'clock by now, according to the dashboard clock, but I would've believed four a.m. I hadn't eaten since lunch, and I'd missed dinner the night before. I unlatched Rufus's bulky car seat and stowed it in the trunk, where I found the thick wool blanket my father always kept there along with his other emergency supplies. In the back seat, I locked myself in and lay down sideways, knees tucked up, old crumbs pricking my elbows and shins. The blanket was large enough to cover my whole body, and I balled up my hoodie for a pillow.

It's a quiet street, and no one seemed to notice a person camped out in a car. I didn't hear any voices, just occasional cars passing, the electric hum of cicadas. I still had the feeling of not being exactly inside my body, and when I touched my face with my hands, I had to remind myself that it was my own touch. Every time I thought about Mari, my shoulders and mouth began to shiver uncontrollably, everything clenching like I was trying to shield a wound—sobbing without really crying. I fought to not think about her and failed, over and over again, for hours.

Very late at night, dreams painting my thoughts, I looked up through the window and saw a face there—a deer's face. She nuzzled the glass, then licked it, her thick gray tongue smearing through a fog of condensation. I watched her, transfixed, and then I finally fell asleep.

18

I WOKE UP blearily around six, body shocked with tightness and pain, homesick without knowing where home was. I knew I had to leave as soon as possible to avoid seeing my father or Sally. I folded the blanket and tried to relatch Rufus's car seat, but I couldn't figure out the buckles and got worried I'd do it wrong and injure him, so I left it lying sideways across the back. Tugging my shoulder strap over the less painful shoulder, limping from blisters, all muscles cramped from the night in the car, I rode the Metro to Union Station, where I bought coffee, a bagel, a train ticket to Baltimore. On Amtrak, among all the weekend-work commuters, I felt conspicuous in the jeans and T-shirt I'd worn for the past twenty-four hours. The absence of my phone nagged me like a phantom limb, but it felt impossible to return for it. The battery would've run out by now. Sally might not even know it was there, might still be waiting for me to call and set up a time to babysit Rufus.

It was very quiet in my Baltimore apartment, and it smelled foul. I'd left three apples in a bowl on the kitchen counter back in May, and they'd rotted into tiny brown fists. I threw out the whole mess, bowl and all, then took the trash to the dumpster downstairs. I was moving very tentatively now, because anytime my skin touched something, including my stiff, clammy clothes, it felt like scraping a laceration. Back upstairs, I stripped off my jeans and underwear, then found Peter's quilt crumpled in the laundry bin and wrapped myself in that.

I brushed my teeth with an old toothbrush—no toothpaste—and drank water from the tap. I found a forgotten box of stale cookies and ate five of them. I imagined the texts or calls I might've gotten over the past two days—or maybe I had none at all, just an empty screen. I climbed onto my mattress, tugging the blanket over my head, and fell back asleep. When I woke up late in the afternoon, I saw the Sansui in the corner and something skipped in my head. I picked it up, held it at chest height, then dropped it onto the wooden floor, where it jangled sadly, small parts skittering into the corners of the room.

Over the next twenty-four hours, I slept a lot, but I also couldn't sleep. As time passed without a phone, I felt increasingly disconnected, like I didn't exist, or existed only in my own head. No one knew where I was, so was I real? I didn't feel real. I ordered takeout on my laptop and wore Sally's sweatsuit downstairs to meet delivery workers. I drank through a couple of the bottles from the cardboard box in the kitchen—it felt like a past self had placed them there specifically for this purpose, and who was I to thwart the ambitions of my past selves? I found one of Mari's stupid mini-golf pencils in my sweatshirt pocket and tried to snap it in half, hated myself when I couldn't. I dreamed about Mari, tediously literal dreams of loss: she was drifting away in a sailboat and I couldn't swim; I went to her house and it was vacant, all the furniture gone; I watched her kiss someone else onstage while I stood in the audience.

In the weeks after we'd started having sex again, I used to lie in bed at my father's house with my eyes closed and trick myself into believing that Mari was beside me on the air mattress—that if I opened my eyes, I'd see her face. Now I tried that and it made me want to die. I would wake partway from a hazy dream, believing I was cupped around her, and then awake fully to her absence with a blaring sense of wrongness. The sensation was physical and intellectual. It ripped apart my stomach, but it also upset me on a logical level. It felt wrong, wrong, wrong that she wasn't there, a wrongness that dogged me like an unresolved chord.

I could tell myself that Mari had manipulated me, lied to me. But even so, I was experiencing a jarring disfigurement of my own self-perception. I'd believed she'd forgiven me for what happened in high school, I'd allowed myself to relax into believing I was a forgivable person, but apparently she hadn't and I wasn't. Then there was the gutting shame, that she'd only let me fuck her all those times because she wanted something out of me. *Apart from that, I don't even know*—the words echoed as if she'd just screamed them into my ear. In part, it was the old Josh sensation, the fear that I'd violated Mari, forced her into something. But the shame went even deeper than that, tangled among the bottommost roots of my queerness: the burning certainty that my desires were perverse, pathetic, broken. I was a fool, I was a sad freak. *You lie to yourself about who you are, even.*

I woke up on Monday afternoon with a feeling of intense panic, like my entire body was screaming out for something. The Franken-feeling seemed to have overnight rooted deep in my bones. Every time I looked down at myself, every time my arm brushed my thigh or my breasts chafed under my T-shirt, I felt like a tumbled pile of disembodied parts. There was something catastrophically wrong with me, I knew it and Mari knew it and now everyone would know it. I needed help, I needed to talk to someone, I was scared I might be dying. But I didn't know what I'd say—*my body's all wrong and I might be a monster?*—and in any case, I'd alienated everyone and didn't have a phone.

For days, I barely left my bed. The world reduced to minute observables. The sun coming through the window in the afternoon sometimes painted rainbows on the wall. My neighbor was going through a Mumford & Sons phase. Mice lived behind the baseboards. The neighbor had a boyfriend who came over at night; they put on network television news and fucked with a productive enthusiasm that sounded very heterosexual to me, like rutting farm animals. Other nights, the neighbor would cry, and I would usually be crying as well, and it felt comforting, like we were friends crying together. I tracked with experimental fascination the corn-chips-and-marijuana stench of my body, the quilt, the sheets. I was so drowned in Franken-feeling that I could barely feel it, or anything else.

When I'd been in Baltimore for about a week, I finally forced myself, through squinted eyes, to check my bank account on my laptop. I had about $2,000 in savings, with rent and a credit card debt payment due in the next two weeks. Living very cheaply—no more takeout—I could make it through another month. Or, if I found something part-time or freelance, I could hobble along at least into winter.

That afternoon, I showered, put on a clean pair of pants, and went to the grocery store. At home, I ate pasta standing at the kitchen counter and tried to give myself a pep talk. Being alive was a skin-crawling horror, yes. Still, I knew I wanted to see Rufus again, and I wanted to know whether Les Somnambules would end up on the Lucia Brahe tour without me. To live long enough for that, I would need money for rent and food. Sick about it, I emailed Jeremy and asked if we could meet for coffee.

The following Tuesday, I dug deep in my boxes and found a pencil skirt, rumpled rayon blouse, and low heels—business casual cosplay. Everything itched when I pulled it on; nothing fit right. The skirt hit above my knees instead of below, the blouse drooped loose over my breasts, the heels pinched. In the bathroom mirror, I was a horror-movie doll. But that was just me now, I told myself. I had to accept that feeling—it had outlasted Peter, it had outlasted Mari, it seemed an essential part of me.

I splurged on a cab because I didn't want to sweat through the blouse on the walk. But I misjudged the time and got there ten minutes late. Jeremy was waiting outside the Starbucks nearest the *Bugle* office, under the shade of the awning. As I ran up, now sweating from anxiety, I saw him check his watch.

"So sorry," I said a million times, and he laughed, grateful, like my lateness had relieved him of some guilt. Inside, he ordered for me—"Space for milk, right?" We found a table near the window, and Jeremy occupied himself correcting its wobble with a folded drink holder while I burned my lip on the coffee.

"So," he said, emerging from under the table, "how are you? Family good? DC treating you well?"

"Family is fine. My dad and stepmom had a baby, so I was helping with that."

"Oh, newborns are the best. Lucky you. And Les Somnambules? You guys playing Baltimore anytime soon?"

"No. I left the band."

"Oh no!" he said. He put his drink down hard, wobbling the table, then frowned at it. "What happened?"

"You know, creative differences," I said, with a deliberate shrug—I'd practiced this in the cab. "Actually, that's sort of what I wanted to talk to you about. I'm back in Baltimore and looking for work."

"Oh!" he said. I felt him evaluating me, noting the mark of failure on my face. "It is such a bad market for journalism jobs right now, isn't it."

"It doesn't have to be full-time. Just if you know of anyone who needs a freelance copyeditor or anything like that."

His smile was broad, satisfied. "I couldn't hire you back," he said—I mumbled, "No no no, of course"—"but if you want to do some copyediting for us on a contract basis, I could find room in the budget."

Jeremy named an hourly rate; it was absurdly low. I'd be doing my old job for half the salary, without health insurance. "Sure," I said. "I could do that."

"We could even let you use your office, if you wanted. Bear'd be happy to see you back, he keeps asking where you've gone off to."

"That's OK," I said. "I like working from home."

"It's going to be quiet," he said. "Nora's leaving the paper now too, did you know that?"

There would now be zero women on staff at the *Bugle*, and only one Black person, an intern on the music desk whom Nora had hired herself.

"She broke up with a girlfriend and is going through some kind of thing," Jeremy went on, circling a hand in the air. "Apparently she's moving in with her aunt in Ellicott City, applying for grad school."

"I didn't know she had a girlfriend," I said, rapidly revising everything I'd previously believed about Nora.

"Anyway, I'm glad you'll be back. Could you start very soon—maybe tomorrow afternoon, after we close this issue?"

Outside Starbucks, Jeremy and I traded awkward waves, and then he ran off toward the *Bugle* offices. I waited to let him go and caught a glimpse of myself in the Starbucks window, broken-faced in my poorly fitting costume. I was back where I'd been when I originally found the *Bugle* posting—fleeing DC, fleeing Mari, taking the first job that presented itself in a new city—except that now, I was earning even less money.

When I got home, I checked my cubby in the mailroom and found, in the white plastic crate someone had left to contain the piles of junk mail I'd received over the summer, a small cardboard box. Upstairs, I opened it with a kitchen knife: it was the black-and-white stuffed bear I'd ordered back in June for my theoretical baby. I took off the work clothes, got into bed, and rolled onto my stomach with the bear underneath me so it pressed into the soreness above my heart.

THE NEXT MORNING, I woke up around ten to the sound of the doorbell. I ignored it—probably some kid slapping all the buzzers—but five minutes later, there was a knock on my apartment door. I wrapped myself in the quilt and got up. Through the fish-eye, I saw a distorted pink-and-black shape that was, unmistakably, my mother.

"Hello?" I said, opening the door. We hadn't spoken since I'd left DC. She was wearing the nice version of her daily outfit, black slacks and a pink button-down shirt—my mother still dressed up to travel. The roller suitcase at her feet was *my* roller suitcase, the one I'd packed to move to my dad's, last seen in Mari's hall closet.

I couldn't figure out her expression—relief, fear, rage, pity—and then I realized: she had been expecting to find me dead. Inside, she glared vehemently around the bare space.

"There's nowhere to sit," I said. "I'm so, so sorry." I was crying now, wracked by humiliation.

She sniffed her way through the apartment, giving especially furious looks to the liquor box on the kitchen counter, the Sansui carcass in my bedroom. We sat down on the mattress, where she arranged a few pillows so we could lean against the wall together.

"It's OK," she said. "It's OK." Then she told me what had happened after I left. When she didn't hear from me for a week, she called my father. He hadn't heard from me either, but he was pretty sure I had been in their car. Rufus's car seat had been unfastened one night, and someone had clearly rummaged through the back seat and the trunk. At first, he thought they'd been robbed, but nothing was missing; meanwhile, Sally had found my phone behind their bed. Now frightened, my mother emailed Mari via the Les Somnambules website. Mari said she didn't know where I was, but I'd left my suitcase. So my mother went to Mari's house and picked it up.

"How was she?" I asked, despising myself.

"She was fine," said my mother. "It's a nice house."

"Is Dad angry? Is Sally angry?" I had assumed they all hated me so much they'd never speak to me again.

"Why would anyone be angry? We were just worried."

Again I felt ashamed—what was wrong with me, why hadn't I tried harder to get in touch? But I had felt unable to put my situation into words. Every version of it was humiliating.

My mother patted my hand and went on: after that, she'd called Peter to get my new Baltimore address.

"Oh no."

"You didn't leave us much choice," she said. "Anyway, I took the train up this morning, and here I am. Can you tell me what's going on?"

I imagined her waiting at my apartment door, unsure what she was about to find, and I leaned into her shoulder. "Nothing. I moved back to Baltimore and lost my phone and kind of forgot to tell anyone."

"No. You wouldn't do that if something weren't wrong, I kept telling your father that."

"I'm really OK."

"You don't seem OK. That box in the kitchen—"

"Seriously, drop it. I'm OK."

My mother reached sideways and stroked my arm. "I packed some of my clothes in the suitcase too," she said very gently. "I thought I might stay a few days. What do you think?"

"What about work?"

"Michael and I broke up," she said. I could see the effort it took to tell me. "He let me take some paid leave while I figure out what to do next."

"That was generous."

"Well, it was, given that I broke up with him."

"Really?"

"He was never going to move in with me," she said. "And he never would've let me move in with him."

"How are you doing?"

She was not well, I could see now. The lines in her face were deeper; her hair was flat in parts and frizzy in others. "I'm really OK," she said, a deadpan impression of me. "Seriously, drop it. I'm OK."

I wasn't sure I'd be able to handle someone perceiving me just then. But I couldn't send her away, not after she'd come prepared to find my days-old corpse. "Fine," I said. "You can stay."

Her smile broadened. She reached into the suitcase and handed me my phone. "You'll be wanting this," she said. It was heavy and cold. I shoved it under a pile of clothes by the bed without turning it on.

The next morning over breakfast, my mother said, "Your apartment is frightening," so we took the bus to IKEA. I'd always hated shopping with my mother—she was indecisive, spinning a choice out to its tiniest factors, then making a bad decision out of anxiety. It turned out that shopping for me was easier, though. She grabbed a cart and threw things into it: towels, utensils, napkins printed with sliced lemons.

"What are you going to do after you stop working for Michael?" I asked her. All around us, following the same arrows through theoretical living room arrangements, were college kids, young couples, pregnant women: people at a crossroads, people shopping for unfamiliar future families, unfamiliar future selves.

"I don't know that I'm going to stop working for him. I like the frame store."

"But it's just the two of you all day. What if he started dating someone else?"

She winced. "I wouldn't like that."

"You need a new job," I said.

"What do you think of this?" she said, pointing at a love seat. "It's only $59."

"You just spent my life savings on napkins."

She reached into her purse. "Know what," she said, "I still have the store expenses card. Let's let Michael buy this one, OK?"

"Um," I said. "Can you do that?"

"He's not going to *fire* me," she said. It was the happiest I'd seen her look, so I let Michael buy me the love seat.

Back at the apartment, we laid out our spoils, the apparatus of a life in crinkly blue bags. With everything spread across the living room floor, I felt claustrophobic. I'd gotten used to the empty rooms; I'd felt safe there. And I didn't like that Michael had bought me something. It was like he was here, looking creepily hot, chuckling about something unfunny.

"I'm going to pay you back for the love seat," I said. We were sitting on the floor next to the bags, drinking water out of new glasses.

"Don't be stupid," my mother said. "Michael owes me—owes us, after all this time."

"You always let men buy you stuff," I said. "It's not right."

"Jamie, not everyone is as tough as you," she said with some defensiveness, and I remembered Mari calling me a "fucking freeloader."

"God, I'm not at all tough," I said. "I'm a fucking disaster. I shouldn't ever tell anyone what to do."

My mother let out one of her exuberant, startling laughs. "I'm sure you'll still try, though," she said. She put her arms around me, and I fumbled to get my glass of water out of the way so she wouldn't spill it. I thought the motion would push her away—she was so easily spooked out of affection, so scared of doing the wrong thing in the wrong moment. But instead she held the hug for a long time, until finally, I rested my head on her soft chest and let the warmth of her body seep into mine.

MY MOTHER STAYED for a week, and by the time she left, I was living in an entirely different apartment. All day while I read *Bugle* proofs at the coffee shop down the street, she assembled IKEA furniture. She spackled the hole in the living room wall; she boxed up the mutilated Sansui and tucked it away in a closet. She painted the bathroom a pretty sea green, my bedroom lavender, the kitchen creamy yellow, the living room light blue. She found her old vaginal rose in my closet, bought it a nice frame, and hung it in the hallway. She tossed out Peter's liquor without asking me, and I pretended not to notice.

Every night, it was on the tip of my tongue to grumble. She never consulted me about anything, and I felt like a child, like the inhabitant of her Easter-egg-colored dollhouse. But secretly I loved it. At night, in my new lavender bedroom, she would take her clothes off with her back to me. I saw her soft bent shoulders dappled with white sun damage, the thick tan straps of her highly functional bra. She would pull the same old T-shirt over her head, the tight collar flattening her hair before it popped out into a conical frizz. The T-shirt said on the front, "Peterson Brewery: We Brew Good Beer, Period." It had belonged to Michael, and she said once, as she climbed into bed next to me, "It smells like him." But I only smelled detergent and her Nivea lotion. Her snores were high-pitched and whistling, like dolphin calls. She lay very still all night on the mattress beside me, then woke up early and blew her nose for ten minutes straight, a sound that had always been my alarm clock at home.

When she left the following Sunday, the apartment felt both full in a new way and empty in a new way. I moved from room to room touching all the things she'd bought and built me, alone again but with a new feeling of nestedness. I'd snuck a check for the love seat into her purse, but she never cashed it.

The afternoon she left, I finally plugged in my phone. It sat, buzzing malevolently, on the kitchen counter, and I ignored it for hours. Finally, I sidled up and peered at the screen. Over the past two weeks, I had received many texts and calls. Most of them were from my parents: Where are you? / Jamie please call us / We are so worried. Sally had also texted, starting the morning after the flood. Hi Jamie, the first text read, Just wanted to check to see if you're around today! No worries if not, we're all good! Then a pause for a couple of days, then a new string of texts: Seriously are you OK? / Just know we love you. I felt so wrenched by these, the narrative they told, that I put the phone down and pressed my fingers into my eyelids.

Peter had texted once to tell me to call my mother—hope you're OK, it ended. And Mari had texted six or seven times on the night of the flood: James I'm walking up to practice are you coming? / SOS JAMIE TEXT ME BACK RIGHT NOW / MOTHERFUCKER WHERE ARE YOU. Her final text, sent as I was walking over to Earl's, read: Please call. I need you. I'd been carrying a secret hope that she might've texted after the breakup to say she'd been wrong, things between us were never fake, she loved me, she wanted me back. But there was nothing else.

I knew I had repair to do, but I felt helpless when it came to my parents, exhausted when it came to Peter, overwhelmed by Mari. I reached out to Sally instead: Sally I'm so sorry I left without saying anything to you. Please forgive me.

She wrote back right away: Holy shit. Are you OK???

I'm fine. Mari and I broke up and tbh I kind of lost it and now I'm back in Baltimore. But I really fucked up not telling you guys, I'm so sorry. You OK? How's Rufus?

She replied with a photo: Rufus screaming, his red face distended around a wide open mouth. Fine lol, she wrote. You OK though? Really?

Sally I hate that you're asking that, you're the one who needs help right now and I ditched you. I'm really OK, can we talk about you for a change?

Her three dots flashed on and off for a moment, then: OK. Your mom came by to get your phone and she wanted to meet Rufus. We ended up spending a while together.

Oh nooooo Eileen!!!! Did she tell you she loved the new couch and wished that she'd replaced their old one years ago

Yep she said exactly that

did she tell you she wants to babysit Rufus

Hehe yes she is apparently coming over again tomorrow wtf have I done

Lollll

jk, she went on, i'm actually desperate, still haven't really pooped, not going to turn down help

I mean you even let ME hold him so you must be desperate

A pause with no dots at all, and then, Your dad does that too, she wrote. Makes a joke when he's actually sad.

I'm OK! Seriously! We're talking about you right now!

OK. Well—I got an appointment with a therapist. Apparently it's not actually normal to be so scared of harming your baby that you don't leave your room for weeks on end

Aw. Does knowing you have the appointment make you feel any less scared??

Not really. He's so vulnerable. I feel like I'm really bad at this, like I'm messing him up all the time already. Like even just me being scared is probably messing him up

You are the best mom in the world, seriously. You are not messing up.

Dots, then: How do you know?

Because I know you, I wrote. And you're the best.

The next weekend, I took the train back to DC to visit Sally and Rufus, sweatshirt hood pulled over my head, eyes lowered on the Metro so I wouldn't see Mari if she was there. Sally showered and pooped, and I held Rufus in my lap and watched the same baking show. My father dithered nearby making unhelpful offers of help until Sally finally told him to go take a nap. She had started drawing again, craning her arms around Rufus's sleeping head, and presented me proudly with a small portrait of a mother deer handing out lunch boxes to her fawns. When I got home, I hung it in the hallway next to my mother's rose.

I MARKED TIME that month by how often I cried, how often I was dragged down by thoughts of Mari: sometimes three times a day, sometimes fifteen times, never no times. I found a few things that caused me to cry less often and tried to do them regularly: visiting Rufus and Sally on the weekends, swimming laps at the YMCA, eating full meals, not drinking. Whereas for years I'd avoided music that reminded me of Mari, I found that now it helped to listen to Björk or Bruce Springsteen or Sleater-Kinney, almost like a vaccine shot building up my immunity. One Sunday morning, listening to *The Woods* on my headphones, I took a wander through my neighborhood and saw, clustered around the entrance to a large brick building, a group of women in orange vests printed with the word ESCORT, drinking coffee from takeout cups. Looking up at the building, I realized it was the Baltimore Planned Parenthood that I'd never called back in May. I walked by, but I couldn't stop thinking about the two kids praying outside the clinic in DC, how just those two relatively gentle protesters had ripped my nerves—and what if I'd been alone, what if there had been more of them or they'd been more aggressive? I turned back.

"Do you ever need more escorts?" I asked one of the women, a tattooed older punk with tired, kind eyes, who reminded me a little of Amanda. "Always," she said, and texted me her phone number. The next Sunday and every Sunday after that, I joined them in my sweat-stained orange vest at the legally mandated ten-foot line, offering a walk and a smile any time a scared kid rushed past the crowd of regular protesters. I didn't feel good after, exactly, but it seemed to help with the crying.

On a Thursday when I'd only cried twice, I was wrapped in my quilt reading through the *Bugle*'s calendar listings when I stopped on a movie title: *Jennifer's Not There*. I had forgotten that it was playing in September—and of course it was now September—at the AFI theater in Silver Spring, near my dad's house, this Saturday at 2:40 and 7:30 p.m.

I looked up the AFI website and saw a splashy banner advertising the movie. *"Jennifer's Not There,"* read the listing, "is an oddity, condemned on release for being problematic, and yet rising in reputation over the years as it's been embraced by a new generation of queer filmmakers. And yes, the characters are stereotypical; yes, the plot revisits (to avoid spoilers) some negative tropes. But there's a schlocky spunk to *Jennifer,* a quirky black humor that balances its problematic aspects. Not to mention some seriously hot leather dykes, an existential detective to rival Kyle MacLachlan's character in *Twin Peaks,* and a trippy chase scene running through the Baltimore Aquarium. On the film's tenth anniversary, you can decide for yourself. And keep your eyes peeled for the blink-and-you-miss-it cameo by early-'00s DC art-punk band the Maidenheads, then high school seniors at Douglass, in matching prom dresses."

I was annoyed at first—of *course* I couldn't escape Mari, not even in Baltimore—but that feeling was quickly replaced by a simple desire to go to the screening. I wouldn't see Mari, maybe not ever again. But I could see *Jennifer.*

I put off thinking about it for days, but on Saturday, I woke up determined to go. I rode Amtrak to DC that evening and walked up to the AFI at seven, amazed to see "JENNIFERS NOT THERE" scrolling around the LED marquee outside: Mari would've been so thrilled; she would've made me wait on the sidewalk while she took a video on her phone. I bought Twizzlers from the concession stand—Mari hated Twizzlers and once called them "puke ropes," which made us laugh tremendously when we were teenagers. Anytime I saw someone with short dark hair and a springy step, I started. But it wasn't likely I'd see her. She worked most Saturday afternoons through dinner. If she came, it would be at least eight, and later if she stopped home to shower.

I found a seat at the back of the theater but all the way to one side, so that just in case Mari did come, I'd see her before she saw me. A surprising number of people who weren't Mari filled the room, and then the lights went down, previews, fade to black. I had only seen the movie once, ten years ago with my mother, and I'd forgotten the opening-credits scene: Jennifer the pretty blond stewardess greeting a line of airline passengers, performing the safety demonstration as a nervous fast-paced song plays on the soundtrack. The plane takes off, then lands, and the passengers file out again. Jennifer strides through National Airport with her suitcase and hails a cab. As the driver pulls onto the GW Parkway, Jennifer shakes her hair out into a straggly pouf, draws on black lipstick, and laughs at her reflection in the rearview.

In the next scene, Jennifer is in a very '90s dance club, doing the '90s white-people dance under spinning red lights—hands over her head, gyrating and snapping, eyes closed. Then you watch a short-haired stocky person trail her home from the club, follow her upstairs and into her apartment, push her down on the bed, and cut her throat with a knife, bright red blood sloshing across the pink duvet. The camera zooms in on Jennifer's dead staring face, with its dramatic slice of black lipstick. After a neighbor discovers the body, Jennifer's kid sister hires a private detective. The detective, Huff McCallister, is rotund and frowsy in poorly fitted suits and a monocle. He drinks from a flask in his waistcoat, issues wistful sighs, and says things like, "Jennifer is no longer here, and yet she is *everywhere*."

Midway through the movie, Huff lumbers down a rainy street toward a bar under a vertical neon sign reading MUFF'S. Two women in chaps lean on bikes out front, shooting him the hairy eyeball. I slouched down in my seat, glancing at the people sitting near me as if I might be recognized, might be blamed for whatever was about to happen.

Huff enters Muff's. The bar is crowded, hazy with a bluish fog. The camera pans to the stage, to two children—so young!—in ripped-up dresses, holding oversized guitars. One kid, sturdy and olive-skinned in a pink dress, has short black hair and an elfin face. Green dress is gawkier with longer blond hair, a few strands shooting up with static.

When I'd watched this scene ten years before, eyes glazed over with self-disgust, I'd seen the kid in green as a monster: incoherent body, face a blank scream. I watched her now and was stunned instead by her handsomeness. She was nervous, sure. She fumbled with her guitar strap, with the torn hem of her dress. She was too skinny and her hair was a mess; she kept glancing at the camera through ragged self-cut bangs. But she was goofy-sweet, distracting the pink-dress kid with a shit-eating grin. She carried herself with stiff butch poise in her shoulders and hips. She was violently in love with the other kid—you could see it in the way she smiled down at her own clumsy hands on the guitar, so shy, so tender. And then she opened her mouth and a voice came out I couldn't believe.

"I combed my hair," the kid said, the recording of "Forgotten" dubbed over our lip synch, and already I was crying. The kid's voice was confident and muscular, edged with hysteria but calm at its core. It built in fury like a savage girl, like a keening boy, like no one thing but all things at once. I hadn't listened to the original recording of "Forgotten" in ten years. I hadn't ever understood how very good it was—how good *I* was.

As Mari's voice picks up the chorus, the camera cuts away, and Huff asks the beefy bartender if she knows any airline stewardesses. "We get a couple in here, yeah," the bartender says. "Forgotten" is still playing, but quieter. Huff glares across the bar one last time, tucks his monocle into his vest pocket, and leaves.

Shortly, I did too. I knew how the movie ended, and it was a long trip home. Plus, Mari clearly wasn't coming, and it was easier to admit now that I'd gone to *Jennifer* mostly because I was hoping I would see her. Instead I had seen myself, and that felt like enough.

19

I TURNED TWENTY-NINE in October and celebrated by going to IKEA alone and spending my birthday coupon on free meatballs. My parents called, Sally called, Peter texted, and Nora from the *Bugle* wrote to see if I'd want to get coffee. We met up the next day and talked for hours about why we hadn't come out to each other at the *Bugle*, about Jeremy and Bear, about all the music we couldn't listen to because of our exes (for obscure reasons, Nora couldn't hear "Moves Like Jagger" without crying, inconvenient in the year of our lord 2012). I also got coffee with a woman I met escorting: Nancy, older than me and with her shit together, a recently divorced femme lawyer who worked for a reproductive justice nonprofit and told me in the first few minutes of our hangout that she was "gay as in everyone but cis men." Afterward, I wondered, were we flirting? Did I want us to be?

Barack Obama was reelected, and I remembered four years ago celebrating in the streets with Peter, what babies we'd been. Maryland officially passed its gay marriage law the same night, and I thought about Mari and my stupid dreams. I hung out with Nancy a second time and wondered again if we were flirting, and also wondered if I'd ever again trust myself to know.

Mostly I copyedited for *The Bugle*, slept, occasionally talked to my mom or Sally ("Your dad says hi") on the phone. It was a listless, low-stakes existence, but I felt peace or at least a calmer version of the numbness. I'd always found copyediting the dullest part of my job, but now I discovered highs and lows beyond my previous imagination. How horrifying that an actual journalist, paid (to be fair, very little) to write, could mix up "your" and "you're"! Who were these buffoons with their comma splices, dangling modifiers, passive voice? I cackled as I corrected, slicing through error, inefficiency, obscurity. I wrote cutting margin notes: "YET ANOTHER RUN-ON!"

I was slipping into a new tenderness toward my body, but I still felt distant from it, awkward around it, like a roommate I'd lost the habit of speaking to. Over the past year, poor thing, it had worked so hard, played so many roles: a girl for Peter, a receptacle for a fetal human, a singer on a stage, a straight person for Amanda, plus whatever I'd been doing with Mari. Roles tangled you up with other bodies, roles cramped you, and I didn't want any of that. I wanted my body to announce what *it* wanted instead of always responding to other people's wants. And at least for now, my body wanted to be a small safe animal alone in my apartment with my quilt and pita chips.

My due date would've been in January, and as it got closer, I felt some wonderment at what my life might've been and what it was. I would've been huge just then, bent double with the weight—instead I was weightless, empty. Mari had been right about that: I would never have gone ahead with the pregnancy. But I wasn't sure she was right that I would've left her. I certainly hadn't wanted to. And yet Mari had believed so staunchly in my inevitable departure that she lied to make me stay—she thought manipulating me was the only way to keep me close, that on her own she wasn't enough. I thought about how a person might come to believe that people would only stay if you tricked them, and for the first time, instead of anger and pain, I felt just a quiet sadness.

In November, Nancy invited me to a Flock of Dimes show in Remington and I went, feeling like a sober person (which somehow I also was now) returning to a bar for the first time. She was wearing a tight silvery dress, dark curly hair tied messily back, and I remembered the Yevgenia dress that night with Mari when I'd fucked her on the porch, her body jerking against my hand. Right away, the old anxiety vortex swirled me down. I was a selfish cunt, a freeloader, dishonest, unreliable. I was just going to hurt Nancy, humiliate myself in front of this beautiful and highly functional person.

"What's up, you OK?" Nancy asked, leaning in to talk over the sound of the band. "You seem quiet tonight."

Her close-in face was so sweet, her eyes tender and curious. The rush to assess what she wanted and become that thing clicked in, flattening my own thoughts. I had to inhale hard to grow space for my body to speak for itself. "I really like you," I said, the words coming out unsteady. "I think I'm also feeling scared."

"To be clear," she said, ducking back, "you like me but don't want to date? Or what."

Still breathing through it, I said, "No, I like you *and* want to date. But I might need to take it really slow. What do you think about that?"

"I think we should go outside where I can hear you better," she said, and she pulled me by the hand through the crowd and out onto the sidewalk. There, she eased close to me. "I know you're hurting," she said, stroking the back of my neck with her thumb. "I'm hurting too. We can be close, we can explore, but we can go very slow. I couldn't manage anything more than that anyway."

"I'd like that," I said, and we stayed outside for a long time holding each other. I thought of Mari pressing me into the tree on September

11, but the memory didn't bore into me the way memories of her sometimes did. I just kept holding Nancy, my body softening against hers, dissolving into a new calm.

THE FOLLOWING WEEKEND I went to a punk show with Nora. As we waited for the band to come on she told me—hesitant, watching my face—that the real reason she left the *Bugle* was that Bear forcibly kissed her, at a concert he'd attended because he knew she was covering it. He'd followed her into the bathroom, he'd pushed her against a wall, he only let up when she poured her drink on him. Jeremy had said, "I *could* talk to him about it, but I think he's already learned his lesson, don't you?"

On Monday, after checking with Nora, I emailed Jeremy. I told him he had a sexual discrimination problem, that Bear had a pattern of harassment going back years and Jeremy was enabling it, and that I was quitting, this time permanently. He never replied, just stopped sending me checks, but I felt lighter than I had in ages. It didn't take long to find a new job at the coffee shop on my block where I'd gone to read *Bugle* proofs, Owl's Café—Mari right yet again, it was much easier to find work in Baltimore. My first day, I had to fill out a form for my name tag, engraved with my name and the coffee shop's logo, a cutesy owl like something Sally would draw. I'd felt distant from "Jamie" since I'd left DC, but "James" was too entangled with Mari. I hesitated, and then, remembering my gas station uniform shirt from middle school, wrote "JIM," which was what my new coworkers, mostly queer hipsters in their early twenties, started calling me. The name felt good, easy. It settled some abstract tension in my shoulders and neck. One night, Nancy came to an after-hours work party, heard people using Jim, and asked if I wanted her to call me Jim too. "That'd be great," I surprised myself by saying, and she took out her phone to change my contact name. By Sunday, all the other clinic escorts were calling me Jim as well. I realized, when I thought about it later that day, that I hadn't had the Franken-feeling in weeks. I hadn't cried, either.

For Thanksgiving, my entire family gathered at the house in Maryland: my mom, my dad, Sally, Rufus, and me. I spent days strategizing for this event with Nancy and my coworkers, gearing up for passive aggression from my mom, disengagement from my dad, a postpartum depression relapse from Sally. But in the end, it was fine. We ordered takeout so no one had to cook, then Rufus was so cute no one could be awkward, and by the time my mother and I were in the cab riding back to her place, she was contentedly telling me that *she* would've opened up the kitchen and living room years ago, only my father was too cheap.

Back in Baltimore, I was leaning over the counter on a quiet day at Owl's when I noticed a new flyer on the community bulletin board: "Looking for Vocal Instructor." A music school in my neighborhood needed someone to teach singing to kids: not choral or classical music, but rock songs for kids who wanted to be in bands. That afternoon, I called the number, and the next morning, before my shift, I went in for an interview.

"What's your background as a singer?" asked the school director, Bethann, probably ten years older than me in dark jeans and a flannel.

"I used to sing in a band," I said.

"Anyone I would've heard of?"

"The Maidenheads. Les Somnambules, for a bit."

"Les Soms!" she said. "They're broken up now, right? It's too bad, you guys were fantastic there for a bit. I saw you at Ottobar last year."

"I didn't sing in that show," I said. "I was only with them for a couple months."

Bethann looked disappointed, and I thought I wouldn't get hired. But she asked me to sing a few '90s standards—"Come As You Are,"

"Buddy Holly"—and then she asked how I'd teach a kid to sing them, and when I finished, she was smiling. "We'll be in touch soon," she said, and that night she called to say I'd gotten the job.

"Not to make you feel bad, but you were the only applicant," she said. "We need someone fast for the winter session. But I think you'll be great."

It was technically part-time, but I was still considered a salaried employee, so I'd get benefits as well. It paid better, broken out by hour, than any job I'd ever had. With that, plus a few weekly shifts at Owl's, I'd be able to earn significantly more than I'd made at the *Bugle*.

The first student on my first day was a nine-year-old kid named Winona, a quiet redhead wearing a sequined "Girl Power" T-shirt. "Ryder or Judd?" I asked her, and she stared at me in bewilderment, chewing on her lip. I was mortified, but had forty-five minutes to fill and couldn't just fall apart with embarrassment.

"I'm Jim," I went on, to steady myself. "What songs do you like to sing with your friends or when you're just hanging out?"

"We sing a lot of Taylor Swift?" she said, peering up shyly like I might not know the name. "And Adele. And sometimes with my mom we sing Beatles songs."

"Want to sing a Taylor Swift song with me?" I said, and she nodded. I put "Love Story" on my iPod speakers and sang along softly, trying to guide but not overwhelm her, like Mari guiding me through "Tiny Animals." Winona pitched her voice too high out of nerves, laboring to imitate Swift's overelaborate slides. I remembered Mari telling me in high school, "Sing it like it's you singing it, not Björk." When we finished, I said, "So what does this sound like if it's Winona singing it, not Taylor Swift?" She looked at me with wide, voracious eyes.

I had four more lessons that day, and three the following day, and I quickly developed a rhythm, backup plans for when things went quiet, tricks to make shy kids laugh. The students made it easy: they were earnest young music dorks with interesting haircuts who would listen to me sing a line of a Joan Jett song and moan, "Your voice is so *pretty*, how do you make it so *pretty*?" I introduced myself as Jim, but everyone started calling me Jimmy. "Jimmy, can I take your voice and put it in a box and bring it home with me?" a little boy asked me once. "Jimmy, if you went outside and sang on a street corner, you would get *so* many quarters," said a girl. I'd never had a job where I laughed so much, where I came home happy.

The other instructors were all in local bands, mostly dudes but gentle ones, grown-up versions of my middle school friends, some with kids of their own. They did karaoke every Thursday after work, and the first time I went, I picked "Hungry Heart." Mari would've done it all scowl and swagger, while my version was sweeter, more plaintive. But I could still hear her voice underlying mine as clearly as I heard the karaoke track, and I was aware I was singing it differently on purpose, so as not to echo her. For the first time in a while, though, glimpsing her fingerprints on my life didn't bother me. In the past, I'd reduced my life to just the surface imprinted by those fingers; I'd felt I wasn't much beyond that history of contact with Mari. Now I was growing aware of a solid bulk under the surface, something that endured regardless of outside influence. Everyone applauded when I finished. "Bro," said one of the guys, "that was fucking rad."

And I did sound fucking rad. I was singing all the time now, not just at school but to Rufus, on my bike ride to work, clearing up at Owl's, at karaoke on Thursdays, at shows with Nancy or Nora, during quiet moments at the clinic on Sunday mornings, at home along with the new record player I'd bought with my first paycheck from school. Music had always felt like something I could lose: by losing my voice, the way I had after high school, by losing Mari, or by failing as a musician. But I could never lose music, music was everywhere, and in fact, I was swimming in such an abundance of music that I lost all my fear, allowed myself to float.

IN JANUARY, AFTER a Christmas spent in Silver Spring with my now bizarrely functional extended family, I was stretched out on Michael's love seat one night drinking tea and watching a movie when my phone rang. It was Amanda.

I still hadn't talked to anyone from Les Somnambules since I'd left. At first, I'd tried to avoid hearing about them because I didn't like imagining them playing without me. But eventually I checked the band's social media accounts and found they'd all been inactive since the flood: no new posts, no upcoming show announcements, nothing about an EP or touring with Lucia Brahe or any of the things we'd been planning to do. I followed Freddie on Instagram, but she only posted cute photos of Liya, except for one post in November announcing that she and Dani were engaged (I'd written "Congrats you guys!" and she hit the like button on my comment; Amanda and Andrew also commented, but not Mari, who didn't do social media).

I figured it had to be a butt dial. Amanda had never called or texted me. I only had her number because of the band group text we'd all been on. "Hello?" I said, preparing to hear the static and beeps of the Georgetown University Hospital NICU.

"Jamie?" she said. She sounded nervous. "It's Amanda Schiff—you know, from the band. Is now an OK time?"

"Hey, Amanda, it's nice to hear your voice," I said, because it was. For so long, I'd felt only jealousy and mistrust toward Amanda. I'd wanted her out of the band so I could start fresh with Mari. But now I remembered the things I respected about her: she had strong principles, she was loyal, she fought for the things and people she loved. She was a talented guitarist who deserved a more generous band leader than Mari had been—deserved more generous bandmates than *I* had been.

"It's nice to hear *yours*," she said, and I could hear the smile. I'd surprised her into sincerity. "How've you been?"

"Pretty good, actually," I said. "You?"

"Everything's basically fine. Work is nuts, but that's always true. Hey, I called to ask you something. You can say no if you want to."

"No," I said, laughing, because I was sure it would be something bad. "I mean—kidding. What's going on?"

"OK, so I don't know how much you know about what happened after you left. But just from my perspective, I definitely never wanted to see Mari again, and I didn't, for a while. Then last month she called me, Freddie, and Andrew and asked us to come over. She said she needed to apologize. And—you may understand this, or maybe not—I went over. I felt like an idiot, a little. I've been through a lot of Mari apologies. But this time felt different."

"Really."

She laughed. "I knew you'd say that. I, actually—I've had this conversation with you in my head a lot. But yeah, it did feel different. Usually the apologies feel like a performance, right? She's *so* sorry, she'll *never* do it again. Or she's a total wreck and you're propping her up. One way or another, it's about her. This time, though, we did most of the talking. She said she knew she didn't deserve it, but she wanted to hear if there was anything at all she could do to keep the band together. So we talked to her for about two hours and she just listened."

I could easily imagine going back to Mari; I could not imagine her listening. "What did you say?" I asked.

"We started by saying we could never play with her again. That we felt lied to and betrayed and disrespected. We talked about you, how she'd brought you on without consulting us, how she'd lied about your relationship, asked you to lie to us. We said we had lost trust in her permanently, and that we didn't think we could work together anymore."

"Did she talk about me at all?"

"She did," Amanda said. "Some of it I can't really tell you, that's maybe a conversation for you two to have. But the most important thing was that she seemed to understand that she was fully at fault for everything. For what happened with you and what happened with the band. She seemed disgusted with herself. I haven't seen her that upset since Yevgenia died."

This all felt morbidly good to hear in the moment, but I could tell I'd be hurting over it later. I said, uncomfortable, "Well, I mean, it all happened a while ago now."

"Sure," Amanda said. She paused. "It's OK if you don't want to hear about this—or I can skip ahead?"

"You're fine," I said.

"The short version is that we ended up deciding to play together again, but with a new set of rules and boundaries. We have all recognized that Mari is a solo musician. She doesn't function well in a group, she's bad with democracy. So we're giving up on that. We're now officially her backing group, although we're keeping the name, and we let her make the creative decisions—we have a veto, but we're meant to exercise it cautiously. In return, though, we make one hundred percent of the management and logistical decisions: touring, recording, practice space, representation, everything else. And we all have the right to quit, no questions asked, under any circumstance. Finally, we made her start therapy."

"Oh, wow, yeah?"

"Her first appointment is next week," Amanda said. "Just hope it's not her last."

The image of Mari making these earnest improvements left me uneasy. It had taken serious effort to reach a point where I understood at least intellectually that she was dangerous for me. I didn't trust myself to make good decisions without that sense of threat. "So have you guys been practicing?" I asked.

"We're starting slowly," Amanda said. "We want to make sure it feels OK. But we are still planning to record the EP."

"Do you still have the Atrium money? How are you going to pay?"

"The Atrium money is long gone," Amanda said. "We talked to Missy, though, and she agreed to cut us a break, and Mari sold her piano to cover the rest."

"Yevgenia's piano?" I said. The white baby grand in all its Liberace glamour, finish so glossy you could see your face. Yevgenia had cleared out their bank account to buy it at a time when they didn't own a TV, a living room couch, clothes that weren't hand-me-downs. Mari composed all our early songs there, played it every Friday night as Yevgenia sang in her husky contralto.

"She sold it to a school near her house," Amanda said. "They said she can buy it back later, once she can afford to. But yeah. That was a rough one."

"When's the recording date?"

"Well, here's the thing. This weekend was the only slot Missy has free until next spring."

It was Tuesday. "Oh," I said.

"And—we don't have a lead singer, especially for 'Tiny Animals' and another couple of songs," Amanda said. "We can find a new one, or we can rewrite the songs to work for Mari and Freddie. But we can't do either of those things before Saturday." She was silent a moment. "You really don't have to. But I wanted to ask, just in case."

"Just to sing on the EP?" I said. "Not for good?"

Amanda sighed. "No one would expect you to come back to the band after what Mari did," she said. "Just for the EP, then we can find another singer in your range afterward. I know it's a huge favor, but we really need it."

I had to ask: "Does Mari want me to come back?"

"It's not fucking *up* to Mari," Amanda said, a brief rip of anger. "We don't want her screwups to capsize the band anymore. This is a business decision, not a creative one."

"But she knows you're asking me?"

"We informed her—yes," said Amanda. "She doesn't get to choose, though."

This could've meant a lot of things: maybe Mari didn't want me, maybe Amanda was just underlining her new dominancy. I didn't really want to know. "I'm not sure," I said. "I haven't practiced any of the songs in months."

"Mari doesn't have to be there, you know," Amanda said. "In case that would help. I checked already with Missy. We can record our tracks on Saturday and Sunday morning. You could come Sunday afternoon, do it alone."

I felt embarrassed, at first, that she'd think I would need this: it had been months since the breakup; surely I could coexist in the same space with Mari. But Amanda sounded respectful—she and I had been through the same war together. It was true I tightened up just talking about Mari. Her presence could absolutely affect how I sang. "Let me think about it overnight?" I said.

After I hung up with Amanda, I turned the movie back on but couldn't focus. I got up, paced the living room, looked out the window to where someone had just sloshed a bucket of water across the sidewalk outside the LOTTERY TICK store, washing cigarette butts and candy wrappers into the gutter. Placing a hand on the cold glass to anchor myself, I spoke the opening lines to "Forgotten." I felt self-conscious, silly, but I kept going. As the song built, I listened to my own voice in all its rich nerviness. It was so big, so independently alive. In the morning, I texted Amanda to let her know I was in.

For the rest of the week, alone in the apartment, I practiced with the rough recording they made for me—Mari emailed the file to Amanda, who forwarded it to me, a chain of events I spent days analyzing. I sang our songs in the tub, as I served espressos and wiped down tables at Owl's, in between students at the music school ("Jimmy, what's that song, I love it, can we sing it too?"), to Nora when we took a walk on Friday afternoon. Swimming at the YMCA, I worked on my breath control, diving deep and holding the bottom rung of the ladder in the dark blue. At night, I did the vocal exercises I assigned to my students: hummed through a straw, sirened up and down scales. I could feel my voice strengthening, and when I rested on Saturday—movies in bed, endless tea, not a single word spoken aloud—I could feel its strength continue to gather in the silence.

On Sunday, instead of walking four blocks to the clinic and donning my vest with Nancy, I rode the train to DC, then the Metro to the studio, which was near Earl's house. At the closest Starbucks, I ordered an herbal tea with honey, then sat at an outside table waiting for Amanda's "all clear" text. My hands shook, and I was sweating into my hoodie and puffer jacket. Nora had said, "It's OK if you change your mind, you know that, right? You don't owe Mari anything."

My phone went off, and it was Amanda texting to say they were done. I tossed out my cooled tea and ordered another, and then I carried it over to the studio, which was in a small building at the back of a hardware store parking lot. Missy opened the door—a trans woman in her forties, tall with long black hair, Motörhead T-shirt and full-sleeve tattoos on both arms. In a small front lounge, she offered a neatly arranged basket of snacks and several brands of bottled water. "Or more tea, whatever you want! I can run out and get you something. You let me know."

"I'm good, thanks," I said. "If I drink too much more tea, I'll just be peeing the whole time."

"Right on! Don't break that seal! Oh," she said, "I have something extra for you. From Mari."

Damnit. Missy handed me an envelope, which I opened to find a single piece of staff paper.

"Jamie," it read, in Mari's scratchy pencil-writing. "You're a brilliant singer—the best. And I am so, so sorry. Thank you for coming back, M." I folded it back into the envelope, then hung my coat and bag on the hooks behind the door, shuddered, ran a hand over my hair.

"All set?" Missy asked.

"All set," I said. She led me into the live room, where I could trace Mari's recent presence everywhere. A keyboard in the corner was draped with her maroon cloth cover. A black heap of cloth on the floor turned out to be, when I poked it with a toe, her sweatshirt. Missy led me to a mic stand facing the glass divider to the control room and adjusted everything for my standing height, clicking her tongue soothingly like she was fitting clothes on a child. She slipped headphones over my ears and said, "Where should we begin?"

"Can we start with 'Forgotten'?"

She nodded and stepped into the control room, where she slid on her headphones and spoke into mine, her voice disembodied although I could see her lips move through the glass: "I'll play you the tracks we already laid, OK?" I listened to Mari, Freddie, Amanda, and Andrew play "Forgotten" without me, Mari growling through the backup vocals.

"You set?" Missy asked after it was over.

Mari's voice echoed in my ears. "Guess so."

"We have plenty of time," Missy said. "Just so you know. If you don't get something on the first try, we can take a break and come back to it later." Through the glare that striped the window, I could see her gentle eyes. The soundlessness was comforting, like a swaddle. I told myself for the thousandth time that I was doing this for myself, not for Mari. Missy played a metronome track for a few bars, and then nodded for me to start, and in an instant my throat seized and I couldn't utter a sound.

"Fuck, hold on," I said, and Missy nodded.

"Take your time," she said.

I shook out my shoulders and rubbed my eyes. I stretched my jaw until it clicked. I tried humming; I did my vocal exercises. We started again, but again I sputtered. It was like stalling out on the diving board—the momentum of the sound gathered inside me, but my mouth refused to form words.

Missy said, "Want to try a different song?"

We tried two other songs, and both times the same thing happened. "I don't understand," I said, "just something's not working."

Missy's smile hovered between pity and impatience. "Let's take a break," she said. "I'll work on something else for a minute. Do whatever you need to do." I went to the bathroom, splashed water on my face, gave my reflection a harsh, commanding stare. But there was nothing to command. Something was missing, some essential force. I went into the lounge area and checked my phone. How's it going? Amanda had texted ten minutes earlier.

I gathered my breath and wrote back: I'm having trouble.

Immediately the phone rang. "What's happening?" Amanda said.

"I don't know," I said, aware of Missy through an open door in the control room, self-consciously humming to whatever her headphones were playing. "My voice isn't working, I keep trying, but it's not working."

"Mari wants to talk to you," Amanda said. "Is that OK?"

I knew I could say no; that Amanda, of all people, would understand. But I needed to know what Mari would say. "Sure," I said.

Then it was Mari's breath into the phone, her rough worried voice. "Jamie? How are you?"

"I'm OK," I said. "Mari, I've been trying, but I don't think I can do this. It's not on purpose."

"OK," she said. "That's OK."

I sighed shakily and heard her do the same. After a moment, she said, "Is there anything you want to talk about?"

I took the phone into the bathroom and sat down on the closed toilet lid. "How's Beavis?" I said.

"He keeps peeing on my side of the bed. I think he misses you."

"I miss him," I said.

"Hey," she said, "could I come over? Just for a bit, I won't stay. We're eating lunch a block away, I could be there in five."

"Sure." I waited in the lounge, feeling chastised by Missy's silence at her desk in the next room. A few minutes later, the outside door flew open and it was Mari in a swirl of cold air. She was wearing a white T-shirt and jeans, as if she'd run over so fast she'd forgotten a jacket. She had cut her hair very short, and it added a new starkness to her face. She looked strong, and frightened.

She came right in and stood a few feet away, no attempt at a hug, hands in her pockets. She and Missy nodded at each other, and then Missy turned back to her monitor.

"Want to go outside?" Mari asked me.

We sat down on opposite ends of a bench outside the studio, facing the hardware store's parking lot. Mari leaned forward with her elbows on her thighs, braced against the cold in her thin T-shirt. For a moment, we were quiet; then she said, "I wanted to talk to you anyway, I wanted to say I'm sorry for what I said. It wasn't true. You and I weren't all fake—you know that."

So much of my relationship with Mari had felt hyperreal, beyond real. But she'd said it was fake, and so I'd lost my confidence in reality. I'd told Nancy I couldn't handle anything serious, I'd avoided major decisions about my life or the future, because I was so sure I was capable of grievous error and couldn't be trusted.

"I lash out sometimes, I can be a real asshole," Mari went on. "I was freaking out about losing the band, and I said things I shouldn't have, things I didn't mean. I'm sorry."

She'd said it wasn't "all fake"—so some things could've been fake. I still felt the world shift closer to its accustomed axis.

"Thanks for saying that," I said.

She looked up, and I braced for the old flash between us, how it might twist my heart. But it was just Mari's sad, hunted eyes. "Thanks for coming back," she said. "I know I don't deserve that."

I shrugged, trying to keep it light. "I didn't come back for you—I came back for everyone else. And for me. Just to hear what the songs would sound like."

"I know," she said. Her hands were flat on her knees, and she splayed her fingers, then relaxed, like she was stretching to play. "I wanted to hear them too. But it's OK, it's OK! It's my fault."

"What are you going to do?" I asked, thinking about Yevgenia's piano.

"We'll figure it out, James. Don't worry about it. It was a bad idea to pull this all together so last minute anyway."

The rear door of the hardware store opened, and a teenage kid wearing the store's green logo T-shirt walked out, hugging a giant turquoise planter in the shape of a lion, so large it obscured most of his face from where we were sitting. A tiny woman followed him to her Lexus. "*Careful*," she snapped. "I'm burying my dog's ashes in that thing."

"Must've been a big dog," Mari said, and we both laughed, relieved to have something to focus on besides each other.

The hardware store clerk had loaded the Lexus now, and the tiny woman got in and drove away. Alone, the clerk spat and adjusted his balls through his uniform pants. Mari chuckled, then lit a cigarette, hunching her shoulders to shield her Bic. Curled into herself like that, she looked vulnerable, in need of protection. I wanted to give her something in exchange for her apology, and I said, "Some people are calling me Jim now."

"Oh yeah?" she said. "Is that what you want me to call you?"

I nodded, unable to speak, and she said, "Jim. I like it."

As she smiled at me, I could feel a new shimmer between us—not the old high-wire tension, something much more peaceful. "I went to the *Jennifer* screening," I said.

"Oh yeah? Was it as crappy as Amanda keeps saying?"

"It's pretty awful," I said. "*We* were good, though."

"Jim," Mari said, still smiling, "we were fucking brilliant."

"Mari—" I said, then stopped. Our eyes met again. I saw *Mari*, my/not-my Mari, all our timelines knotting: the hyperactive needy kid she'd been when we first met, the person who'd fucked me raw so many times, who'd healed me with her music, who had hurt me so badly, been so badly hurt by me. The person she was in this very instant, someone I didn't really know anymore, someone drifting away into a new life. A person I loved but couldn't touch.

A person who was family, just the same. A person who would always write the songs I most desperately wanted to sing. And perhaps she could just be that person, perhaps everything else didn't matter as much. Perhaps I could move forward more safely with her, now that I was finally learning to feel safe without her.

"What?" Mari said. She leaned back like she was bracing for a blow. Her fingers shivered around the cigarette.

I shrugged again, not wanting to give her any clues before I knew what I really wanted. "I'm going to head back in, give it another shot," I said.

She nodded, and I could tell she was also keeping some reaction under guard. I stood and walked away, back into the studio. She didn't follow, and when I glanced back with my hand on the doorknob, she was still on the bench, watching something in the parking lot, holding the cigarette at her knee. The sun hit her hair; it looked lighter, as if the haircut had made her younger. I closed the door, and her smoke swept inside with me. Missy turned in surprise, pushing back her headphones.

"Can we try 'Forgotten' again?" I said. Again, she led me into the live room and adjusted everything to fit.

"You'll be OK?" she said, and I nodded. Back in the control room, she gave me a thumbs-up through the glass and I raised a shaky one back. Insulated by the padded silence, alone but for Mari's lyrics in my heart, I opened my mouth to sing.

ACKNOWLEDGMENTS

I STARTED WRITING about the characters and locations in *The Maidenheads* in about 2016, which is to say, I owe thanks to a decade's worth of people for the fact that it's in your hands today. Principal among those is my bighearted, strong-minded agent, Julia Kardon, who found me in the slush pile and transformed my life. Hannah Popal, Ella Wang, Alex Reubert, and everyone else at HG Literary also fought for *The Maidenheads* from day one. Pilar Garcia-Brown is everything I dreamed of in an editor: warm and wise, with a sly wit and generous instincts. I feel grateful every day that I get to work with her and everyone else at Dutton, including Ella Kurki, Hannah Poole, Amanda Walker, Stephanie Cooper, Isabel DaSilva, Ryan Richardson, Maya Ziv, John Parsley, Meg Drislane, and Katrina Alonso. Mary Beth Constant did a beautiful copyedit of my book about a copyeditor. Jason Booher and Sophie Chu-O'Neil created this gorgeous and spunky cover. It was a longtime dream to have Farrah Skeiky, a legendary DC photographer and the person who would've photographed the characters in this book, take my author photo, and I feel very lucky she did.

At Bennington, Alice Mattison, Jill McCorkle, David Gates, and Claire Vaye Watkins read fetal versions of this book, while Megan Mayhew Bergman provided encouragement and goat visits. My grad school friends, including Amber Wheeler Bacon, Amelia Brown, Kate Martin-Rowe, and my beloved BBWU squad John West and JP Solheim, were a source of genius feedback, group-text commiseration, and karaoke fellowship.

Zach Carter, Dana Liebelson, and Julie Yoder gave thoughtful reads focused on music and the DC scene. Nini Arshakuni answered questions about Georgian culture and music. Bill Thomas explained film soundtrack contracts. Jordan Grobe at the 9:30 Club showed me around backstage and answered all my starstruck questions. I'm seriously indebted to the thorough, very helpful feedback of an anonymous authenticity reader who focused on my Black queer characters.

Many, many other people made me laugh, listened to me complain, focus-grouped cover options, made playlist suggestions, or in other myriad ways supported the writing of this book. Suzy Khimm, also a constant emotional support and writing buddy, let me steal the layout of her house. Jia-Lynn Yang bought me an actual rainbow balloon. Vanessa Dillen and Karen Racowsky provided an important music consult. Carrie Callahan walked me through a transformative early-stage rewrite. Rachael Shpak offered wise advice about portraying the intersections of trauma and sexuality. Jess Hall told me a story about "The Big Sky" that changed how I heard it forever. Miranda Shulman, my book twin, helped keep me sane in the final months. The members of my indispensable group chats (I love you Frenz, PMLB, and NBI!) let me get excited and propped me up. Mike Giordano helped chart a path through forests that often felt impenetrable. My neighbors and local queer and trans communities in DC and Maryland are a daily inspiration and comfort. Old friends from all over provided a sense of continuity and security during turbulent times. Even if you're not listed here, I still love you!

My officemates over the past decade—Roscoe, Sabrina, Tip, and Lucas—helped by being respectively the best dogs and the best cats ever.

Cinthia Quiñones kept my children feeling happy, safe, and loved while I wrote.

Leah Douglas opened their lion heart and deep wisdom on all topics musical, literary, and/or gay, making this book, and my life, immeasurably better.

My parents and my brother Bayne have always been my staunchest champions and my softest place to land. Nadia Haji Omar loaned her discerning gaze. My aunt Fiona modeled the creative life and encouraged mine. Bruce and Barbara provided love and support, and Katie, Matt, Mabel, and Lorelei have given me the gift of a loving and hilarious extended family.

To Adam: This book would not exist without you. Your stubborn belief in it through all the years when it seemed least believable gave me the courage I struggled to supply for myself. Thank you for introducing me to DC in the first place, for letting me rifle through your suburban Maryland adolescence for source material, and for only very gently correcting what I wrote about Fugazi. We built this dream together.

I've told my kids they can't read this book until they're at least ninety. But they are allowed to read this one part, so, Danny and Felix: You are the funniest, kindest, bravest, wisest, and most fiercely beloved kids in the world, and loving you is the best thing I've ever gotten to do. You make me feel like the luckiest human alive every single day.

Finally, I began and finished this book sitting a few miles away from a Trump White House. As I wrote these acknowledgements, federal agents in balaclavas ripped through the city I love, the imagined space of my fiction, the real space of my journalism, the birthplace of my children. The characters in *The Maidenheads*, were they real and living in DC today, would be facing a radically constricted autonomy compared to in 2012. If you enjoyed reading about them (and, hey, even if you didn't!), take some action now, however small, to support the rights of women and queer people to determine their own stories.